The Husband We Share

a novel by

London St. Charles

LS Charles Publishing Group
Chicago, Illinois

LS Charles Publishing Group
www.londonstcharles.com

Trade Paperback ISBN: 978-0-9993288-0-4
E-Book ISBN: 978-0-9993288-1-1

Cover designed by: J. L. Woodson www.woodsoncreativestudio.com
Interior design by: Lissa Woodson www.naleighnakai.com
Editorial Consultant: Naleighna Kai

Printed in the United States of America
October, 2017

Acknowledgements:

I give thanks to the Father above for giving me the gift to create, and the ability to use it.

Charles, my hubby: Thanks for not taking it personally the nights I chose the computer chair over the bed (role reversal lol). Thanks for encouraging me when things got sketchy. You told me to work on my book and don't worry about the rest. Because of you, I was able to do just that. Much love and respect to you, always, baby.

Sierra and Carrington, my daughters: You girls are the reasons I breathe and try to be the best me I can be. Thanks for bearing with mommy through the writing process. It hasn't always been easy. Thanks for understanding that this takes time, and my incessant focus has finally paid off. My goal is to make you ladies proud. Love, hugs, and kisses. P.S. Sierra, you finally get to read my story. The wait is over.

Marva, my mother: The woman who's responsible for the person I am. The one who knew I had the writing bug at the age of eight. Thanks for always being my number one fan and for supporting me in all things I do. You've listened to me rattle on about class and writing prompts, and listened to me read my stories and fed my energy. You've always been my biggest cheerleader. Thanks for breathing life into my dreams. No one compares to you (tear).

Lonnie, my big bro: You are the bomb.com and a bag of chips. When I first started writing this book, you were the one reading chapters and pushing me to hurry up and finish so that you could read the entire story. You were just as excited as I was when I would call or text you my daily and weekly word count. Every step of the way, you have been phenomenal.

Shanda, Sharon, Juma, Jackie, Joycelyne, Stacey, Mark, and Dee, my ride or dies: All of you have helped me along the way, from reading my manuscript, to talking out plots, research from my bestie who works with foster families, for not taking it personal when I'm unavailable to talk, for freeing up my evenings with my youngest so I could write uninterrupted, and for being spectacular friends. Thank you all.

Naleighna Kai, fellow author and editor extraordinaire: Who would've thought that a chance meeting in Walmart discussing whether to have milk with French toast would have turned into this? The man above sure has a sense of humor. He put me in your path for a reason, and I will be forever grateful. Your passion for writing is contagious. I have learned so much from you. Thanks for pushing me beyond what I could see. To J. L. (who was also in that Walmart), thank you for such an awesome cover. You are the absolute best.

Priscilla, Angela, Debra, and Michelle, my beta readers: You ladies rock! Thanks for taking the time to comb through my manuscript. Your critiques helped make my story better.

The most important people, my readers: I hope you enjoy the story and I look forward to your feedback.

One Love,
London St. Charles

Dedication:

Special thanks to the author,

Eric Jerome Dickey

After I finished reading *Cheaters*, I literally closed the book,
ran to the desktop, and wrote thirteen hours straight.
That story reignited my passion for writing.
Thank you!

Chapter One

Lauren Carter screamed and bolted upright in her bed, snatched from the reoccurring nightmare that had plagued her for years. She touched a finger to her right ear, expecting to feel a drop of blood, but found none. Damp tendrils of hair clung to her flushed face as she swiped a hand to move them to clear her vision.

"Help me please!"

That voice then, and now, still echoed in Lauren's mind along with the consequences of Lauren's mistake. Hours went by as Lauren was forced to listen to Shawn's shrieks of pain. Trapped on the other side of the door, Lauren was powerless to save the little girl who had come to depend on her for so much.

"You'd better stop screaming, or I'll kill you," a raspy voice had barked. *A voice belonging to a complete stranger; a man who'd managed to sneak in through the back door of the Community Center, then hide inside the building and lay in wait for the right time to…*

The twelve-year-old girl who cried out for Lauren's help had barely survived a horrific experience that would dismantle someone who didn't have the support it took to heal. Shawn had managed to piece her life back together. Unfortunately, Lauren still felt the aftereffects.

Disoriented from the recurring nightmare, a chill from the master bedroom rendered Lauren numb. A red lace gown clung to her petite frame, wet from the perspiration that peppered her golden skin. She wrapped trembling arms about her midriff, but they provided no comfort. Lauren had watched Shawn's ordeal in excruciating detail through the sliver pane of glass the steel door offered.

"Help me," the girl screamed, but the man wrapped his thick fingers around her throat and cutting off any further speech.

This time in her nightmare, tornado sirens had roared loud enough to shatter glass windows and pierce eardrums. A howling wind swept through the building as the steel bars finally receded, and the evil man disappeared, leaving a world of sadness and torment behind.

Lauren scanned the dark bedroom, panting as her heart hammered against her chest causing an ache that wouldn't subside anytime soon. The guilt threatened to swallow her whole. She had allowed fear of someone else to control her actions, making her less mindful of following proper procedures. Now, thirteen years later, she sat on her bed reliving an experience that had been all consuming to the point she had been forced to seek medical help.

Lauren lowered her head, then took several deep breaths, watching her chest slowly rise and fall in efforts to create a steady breathing pattern.

Though the siren in her dream had silenced when she opened her eyes, some type of siren was still going strong on this side of Lauren's waking nightmare.

"What is that noise?" she whispered, and her voice seemed to disappear into corners of the master bedroom.

She focused on the digital clock on the nightstand, then shifted from the warmth under the comforter, her heart hammering in her chest all over again. When she stepped a few feet, the chilling grip of the dream loosened, and the cause for the blaring sound became that much clearer in her mind. At nearly three in the morning someone's car alarm was wailing louder than a Jessye Norman opera performance.

Lauren shivered as another chill raced through her body the moment her feet absorbed the coolness of the mahogany floor. Snatching a red satin robe from its home on the arm of a pewter suede wingback chair, she wrapped it around her body before rushing down the winding staircase and straight to the living room window. By the time she peered out of the vertical blinds, a few answering chirps had caused the noise to come to a complete stop.

She let out a heavy sigh, realizing that sleep wouldn't revisit her so soon after such an adrenaline rush. Normally the pills would keep her in a restful state through the entire night—no matter what happened in this corner of the world.

So what's different this time?

Something was off, and her subconscious finally registered a particular issue with startling clarity. Xavier. Why didn't she wake him before venturing down to check things out for herself? Why hadn't he comforted her when she woke up shrieking from a horror that no longer existed?

The empty feel of the Tudor home they owned on the south side of Chicago, in the Beverly neighborhood, enveloped her like several layers of fog descending over Lake Michigan. Her husband's Cadillac Escalade wasn't in the driveway parked next to the White Lexus truck he'd bought her as a "just because" gift when she had been named as one of Chicago's Leading Hair Stylists in Essence Magazine.

She tried to shake off the feeling of melancholy which settled in as she made her way through the dark house, thinking that maybe she somehow misinterpreted things.

"Oh my Lord," she whispered as a shocking reality set in. "Maybe that alarm was from his truck, and the damn thieves got away with it."

That had to be the only explanation for him to be missing in action. Since more DEA agents had been sent to Chicago, undercover work by local police was at a minimum. Xavier would have told Lauren of any new assignments.

Lauren climbed the stairs to the upper level, ran the length of the hallway, passing a red bamboo floor vase and causing it to shake from her efforts.

"Xavier! Xavier, wake up," Lauren yelled, bursting into the master bedroom. She flipped the light switch and froze; placing her hands on hips that her husband said would cause a blind man to regain his sight and dance a grateful jig. Evidently, that blind man had a better chance of seeing them right now than her husband would.

"Where the hell is he?"

Lauren's gaze swept the area, taking in the king-sized black canopy poster bed with two sheer drapes cascading down evenly on both sides. Then her fingers tipped the dimmer. Her eyesight quickly adjusted to the bright light illuminating a room designed in shades of ruby red and Charleston gray—colors that spoke to a blend of the couple's taste.

Only Lauren's side of the bed showed signs of recent use. Xavier's was as silky smooth, just as it had been the morning before. Even the scent of Edge Shave gel was barely discernable.

She massaged her temples, allowing several scenarios to run through her mind. Her husband, a Narc with the Chicago Police Department, had been involved with the kind of cases that put him in the same vicinity with high-level drug dealers, managing confidential informants, and the type of surveillance that had made his career a sometimes-dangerous engagement. Nothing she was aware of would cause him to disappear without a word. And he certainly hadn't seemed worried about anything earlier that evening. Her body tingled with the sweet memories.

Xavier had touched, teased, and tongued every part of her soul along with every inch of her buttercream skin in the shower just hours ago. Her body had trembled and convulsed, as he drove her to the point that was completely out of control. He had perfected the craft of making Lauren experience the ultimate orgasmic euphoria. Their lovemaking now was as good as their wedding night had been a little over nine years ago. Only better. Coupled with the fact that he was also loving, caring, and an excellent provider, made her the happiest woman on the south side of Chicago, if not the world.

A smile crept across her face remembering that afterward, they had spooned and fell asleep in each other's arms. She ran her fingers through wavy shoulder-length hair, frowning as she tried to recall a fuzzier time, thinking; *I thought that's what happened?*

The smile disappeared the moment she tried putting the pieces together, and something didn't fit. Needless to say, no matter how much sleep was lacking and how much she needed to be on point to do an early morning favor for a last-minute client, she was too wired to put her head back on the pillow.

Lauren Carter wasn't sure if she should be pissed off at Xavier for being left alone, or concerned because he wasn't in the place he was supposed to be.

"Where the hell is my husband?"

Chapter Two

Fueled by anger, Lauren rocketed from the entryway of the master bedroom to the nightstand where her cell phone rested. She snatched the iPhone from the charging cradle so fast that tiny beads emptied from a little orange bottle of sleeping pills and tap-danced across the wooden floor.

"Damn it." She dropped to her knees scrambling to retrieve what had become a nightly crutch for the past thirteen years. Frustrated, she jabbed her finger into the home-button and snapped, "Call Xavier," engaging the phone's auto-dial feature.

Lauren continued the frantic search for the rest of those magic pills while the phone connected her to the only number she could use to reach him. A number that had been drilled into her since day one. And she heeded that directive. But finding him was only one part of her concern. Her dependency on Ambien happened gradually over the years, and Dr. Harden had been steadily trying to wean her off. Now she was taking more than the doctor prescribed.

Asking for another refill so soon would be completely suspect and out of the question.

Hi. You've reached Xavier Carter—

"Oh hell no." Lauren disconnected and dialed right back.

She spotted what she hoped was the last of the pills at the foot of the bed, blew on it, and dropped it in the cylindrical bottle, tightly fastened it, and gently placed it on the nightstand.

"Hi baby," Xavier answered on the second ring.

"Don't 'hi baby' me. Where the hell are you?" Lauren snapped. That abnormal chill hit her again, and she walked to the marble bureau to find something clean and much drier to wear.

"What's wrong?" he asked, concern etched in his tone. "I can hear it in your voice."

"What? You can hear that I'm pissed? Let's give this man a gold star," she snarled, maneuvering around the armoire to get into the master bathroom to wash off. "Where are you? Don't make me ask again."

"I'm in the Crown Vic," he replied smoothly. Almost *too smoothly*. "I know you can hear the police scanner."

"What's your point, Xavier?" she huffed, still not placated by the answer while placing her focus on the bathroom mirror. She needed to wash off not only the perspiration but the memories as well.

"I'm at work," he said in a calm voice that only served to piss her off even more. "I told you before we went to bed last night that I had to follow up on a lead."

"No, you didn't. I wouldn't have forgotten something like that."

"Baby, I *told* you," Xavier responded in that soothing manner reserved for times when she was making a big deal out of nothing. "Maybe your mind's fuzzy after our rendezvous between the sheets, or did you forget that too?"

Lauren sucked her teeth at his blatant attempt to sidetrack the issue. "Whatever. Like I said, you didn't tell me."

"For argument's sake, let's say I forgot and for that I'm sorry."

Xavier paused, waiting for Lauren to say something. When she didn't, he asked, "Now are you going to tell me what's wrong? It's not like you to wake up in the middle of the night."

She almost said, "How would you know?" as if her subconscious mind was planting the idea that this was not the first time.

Lauren snatched a face cloth from the gold bath ring, dampened it and dabbed her face, neck, and chest with cool water, then used another towel to pat herself dry. She wondered if she should mention the dream, but knowing that if she did, an ongoing argument would follow.

"I thought you took your meds?"

She opened her mouth to answer that he had been the one to bring water and the pills to her every night.

"Lauren, are you there?"

Her anger was quickly replaced with apprehension. Xavier had been adamant about Lauren seeking professional help for as long as she could remember. She wouldn't hear of it.

She already had a solution. Lauren figured if she could sleep soundly through the night, then that would make the dreams go away.

"I had another nightmare," she confessed, sliding her arms into a blue sleep shirt, then perching on the edge of the Jacuzzi. "I woke up, and you weren't here."

* * *

Xavier missed the overly confident woman he met in the barbershop. The Lauren who wasn't tainted by sins of something that had been out of her control. He wanted *her* back. Xavier closed his eyes while she unburdened her soul. He envisioned the "thick in all the right places" carefree woman he fell in love with. At that moment, the fragrance of her hair, coconut mixed, with vanilla wafted through his nostrils. He smiled behind closed lids, remembering how Lauren lit into him about something he believed to be fake.

"Your eyes are beautiful."

"Thank you."

"Are those contacts?"

"What did you just ask me?" she flipped, swinging the barber chair around. "My eyes are natural, brother. Do you need to take a closer look?"

He didn't know. They matched her strawberry blonde hair. He chuckled at the memory, but he definitely had wanted a closer look—— at all of her.

* * *

"Xavier, are you listening to me?"

"I'm sorry, babe," he said, and this time the regret in his tone was unmistakable. "You haven't had one of those dreams in a while."

She released a heavy sigh. "I don't know why this keeps haunting me after all this time. It's been thirteen years."

"Because you still blame yourself for what happened. You have to let yourself off the hook," Xavier urged. "It wasn't your fault."

Lauren traced the grout in the tile with a perfectly polished red toenail, "But I don't understand why the guilt is still there."

That evening thirteen years ago, she had been so worried about her boyfriend being upset that she neglected to follow procedure. The last thing she was required to do was make sure that all exit doors were locked and no one was hiding in the bathroom stalls or anywhere else. Teenagers would do that to have a place make out, but she never feared a stranger lurking. A man who'd been waiting for the perfect opportunity to prey on one of the teens who came to the place for a haven after school which provided tutoring, and counseling. How wrong she had been.

"You are not your mistakes bab—"

"Shawn's foster mother was never on time," she whispered leaning in to turn on the water, opting for a bath since that provided only temporary relief. "Not Ms. Ida, but the previous foster parent." Xavier had heard it all before.

Marcus, Lauren's boyfriend, had been thirty minutes late for work the day before. They'd fought the moment she slid into the passenger seat. He'd slapped her so hard that her jaw shifted and she saw stars.

Lauren caressed her left cheek at that ugly memory. Her cheekbone and lips suffered the consequences of that blow, leaving her with a crooked smile for a long while. She squeezed her eyes shut and swallowed hard, trying to wipe the visual of his cruelty from her. A man had never hit her before, not even her father who had found other ways to discipline her. Then Marcus stuck his index finger in her temple so hard that a headache sprang to life. He told her she'd better not *ever* have him waiting again or else he'd beat her ass, then leave her stranded.

She had just moved from New York and didn't know her way around Chicago. But that wasn't any excuse. As a New Yorker, she knew the ins and outs of public transportation. Chicago should be no different. She was so wrapped up in *him*, and his *ride*, and his *money*, and his *needs* that she couldn't think straight. Lauren's parents had her on such a short leash as a teenager; she couldn't do anything without one of them. The taste of freedom made Lauren lose her head—and her mind.

"I was so stupid back then," she admitted, meaning that day and those, which followed, as the abuse from Marcus became a recurring thing. All it took was that one time, and he felt entitled to hit her whenever he felt the urge—— which was too often for Lauren's taste.

"Stop saying that," he warned, and the scanner crackled in the background. "You were never stupid. I hate when you talk down about yourself."

She shifted on the edge of the tub, trying to hold back tears.

"We've all made bad choices when we were younger," Xavier said sincerely. "I know I've made quite a few."

Lauren wiped away the tears that fell but was unable to agree.

"Shawn doesn't blame you, and it's time for you to stop blaming yourself. She's like family."

She'd lost count the number of times Shawn had been to their home over the years. "You're right," Lauren responded, her gaze focused on the water filling the tub.

Lauren was quiet for a moment, picturing the vulnerable young girl Shawn was when she first came to the Thompson Center, instead of the fierce young woman she had become.

"But every time I have that dream, it takes me right back to that place and time."

"That's why you need to talk to somebody about it."

"Not this again," Lauren sighed, anger flaring. "I told you I'm good. I don't need to see a damn psychiatrist. I'm not crazy."

"Therapist, Lauren," he corrected.

"Whatever," she shot back. "Same thing."

Silence filled the air for a few moments.

"I can go with you if it'll make it easier."

She took a calming breath. "Hear me clearly, Xavier; I don't *want* or *need* to see a head doctor. You got it?"

"Says the woman who's been having nightmares for years," he countered. She had no comeback for that. "What happened to her affected you too."

Lauren stomped her foot so hard; she nearly slipped into the tub.

"So who do you think you are, Dr. Phil?"

This constant battle had her insides boiling like she'd ingested an entire bottle of Tabasco sauce. "I'm the one who left her alone after hours. I'm the one who didn't check the doors." She turned off the water, then stormed out of the bathroom, abandoning the whole idea of a bath. Why was he so ready to have the doctor certify her as crazy and put her on all kinds of heavier medication?

She pulled the duvet back on Xavier's side of the bed and laid down. "I don't need a head doctor telling me what I already know. All I need is sleep."

"Don't get an attitude with me, Lauren," he snapped. "All I'm saying is—"

"Nothing. I gotta get some sleep."

"Damn baby. It's like that?"

"Yep, it's *exactly* like that," she shot back, and Lauren disconnected the call.

Chapter Three

Xavier pulled the phone away from his ear and stared at it; unable to believe his wife had hung up on him. The series of beeps confirmed the abrupt disconnection of the call, so whether he couldn't believe it or not, the truth was——she had.

He flipped off the police scanner sitting on the bookcase, then shook his head. He returned the cell phone to the secret desk compartment in the study of the home he shared with Patricia, his wife of eighteen years and their fifteen-year-old son, Xavier Junior.

Xavier swept all concerns aside at the unexpected exchange, reclined in the leather office chair, folded his hands behind his head, then propped his feet on top of the smooth wooden surface of the desk before closing his eyes. Xavier's six-foot-five, dark chocolate, muscular frame contoured to the shape of the chair as the tension he didn't realize had coiled through him, finally eased.

With those pills securely in her system, he never worried about Lauren catching on that he rarely shared their bed overnight. He was there long before she closed her eyes, then left the moment that even breathing set in. Although the reason behind her Ambien habit was disturbing, it had worked in his favor for nine years. Usually, by the time she awakened from those nightmares, he was back in place on the other side of the bed.

What was so different about tonight?

He closed his eyes, envisioning what would happen if his worlds collided. Patricia would leave him and then he would rarely see his son. Lauren would pack up and go back to New York as she had threatened to do when she gave him that world-shattering ultimatum. The irreversible hurt and damage he would bring to the two women he loved would be unbearable.

Sometimes he wondered what he could have done differently, but none of the scenarios included having both women he loved so much. And he couldn't see that in his future. So the path he'd taken was one he had to live with. They did too. Although neither of them was aware, they shared a husband with another woman. He aimed to keep it that way forever.

The soft touch of silky hands and the scent of cherry blossoms stirred him from a nap of what seemed only minutes but might have been much longer. The feel and smell were both things he'd enjoyed since he first laid eyes on her during an Omega Psi Phi Step Show at Fisk University twenty years ago.

Xavier was in the middle of a routine with his line brothers when the chocolate beauty grabbed his attention. His eyes connected with hers the one-time Patricia glanced up from a book to sweep a loose strand of hair behind her ear. Her eyes smiled at him, causing Xavier to miss a step, and his brothers to give him a hard glare. Patricia grinned and returned to reading, unbothered by the controlled chaos of everything around her— student chatter, feet slamming against the bleachers, cheers of students encouraging the frat brothers. Xavier was intrigued. Women went out of their way to get— and keep— his attention, but not her.

After the show, he searched, but couldn't find her in the crowd. He waited outside of Jubilee Hall since that was the freshman residence hall for women. That had to be the only reason he had never seen her beautiful face before. He had no luck, so he headed back to Livingstone Hall.

Along the way to his dorm, the glowing lights from the library burned like the moon in the dark sky. On a Friday night, only someone who was serious about their studies would be there instead of partying with everyone else. Glancing down at his watch, he took off running. The library closed in fifteen minutes.

Patricia was packing up her things when he slid through the glass doors. He wiped the sweat from his hairline, took a deep breath, then approached the brown skinned beauty. Xavier had no idea then that she was the future Mrs. Carter, a woman who would capture his heart with beauty, class, and, brilliance. She didn't make things easy for him as other girls did, and he loved the challenge. Patricia was a lady in every sense. She even refused to sleep with him. Xavier had to choose her, and only her. And that worked for years, until… Lauren.

Xavier shifted his head on the headrest, nuzzled his nose on the back of Patricia's manicured hand and gently pressed his lips against the tip of her fingers.

"Hey, my beautiful Patty," he whispered, an endearment of sorts.

She tugged his earlobe slightly where he used to wear a princess-cut diamond earring that eventually became her engagement ring. One of Xavier's frat brothers worked for a carpenter. Xavier paid him to carve a replica of a ring Patricia always fawned over when they passed by Rogers & Hollands Jewelers in the mall. He set it with the diamond from his earring. A beautiful Indian Rosewood ring she loved and wore until this very day, even though Xavier upgraded her. "You spending the night down here?"

"Not at all. I received a work-related call and didn't want to disturb you, so I came down here."

Her thinly arched eyebrows drew in. "Really? Jason said he'd been ringing your phone non-stop for the past twenty minutes."

Jason was his partner and friend of fourteen years, and if he was going through all channels to get to Xavier, then something was definitely wrong—and his little lie wasn't going to cover him.

"He couldn't reach you," she added peering at him as she handed him the cordless phone. "That's what woke me up."

"Thank you, baby. I must have fallen asleep." Xavier swung his legs around to the side of the desk; the chair swiveled, landing him in an upright position. He covered the receiver and said, "I won't be long."

Patricia smiled as those wide shapely hips swayed slowly on the way out. "I sure hope not."

She pulled the door closed behind her, letting the unspoken seduction and expectation carry its weight.

* * *

Xavier went to the door, listening for Patricia to reach the top of the stairs, and the master bedroom door to shut.

"I *know* you know better than to call me at the crib," he growled into the receiver. "I'll call you right back on my cell."

Xavier disconnected the call, feeling almost as furious as Lauren had sounded earlier. He switched on his cell, and it immediately blew up with notices of recent calls and text messages from his partner. Jason picked up on half a ring, and Xavier said, "This better be good."

"Man, get your ass out here," Jason commanded, undeterred by Xavier's angry vibe. "Ain't nobody got time for your shenanigans. We got work to do."

Xavier tensed, pulling the phone away from his ear to check the time. "Wait … what?"

"Throw your drawers on— clean ones— and let's go. I'm outside."

Evidently, a night of passionate lovemaking and cuddling with the woman he'd been married to for eighteen years was not on the agenda. "Give me five minutes. I'll be right out."

"You got two."

Xavier ran upstairs into the master suite, pulled off his lounge pants and slipped into a pair of black jeans, a long sleeve black fitted shirt, and stepped into a pair of black steel toe work boots.

"Tonight's the night," he said staring at his beautiful wife whose radiant sable skin matched his own. Her expression transformed from joyful to one of disappointment, something he'd seen too much of lately.

While strapping on a bulletproof vest, Patricia finally eased off the bed, reached into the nightstand drawer and retrieved the undercover badge and ID holder. She paused for a moment, staring at his wedding band resting in the crystal dish inside the drawer. She still wasn't used to not seeing it on his finger. He'd explained that early on in their marriage that he couldn't wear it to work. Closing the drawer, she sauntered over to where he stood, went up on her tippy toes and slid the beaded silver chain over his head and tucked it in his shirt.

"You'd better come back to me, Detective Carter," she warned, smoothing his shirt over the badge.

"Always." His arms went around her thick waist, resting his fingertips on her ample bottom. Then he lowered to kiss her on the forehead. He lifted her chin so he could gaze into her deep-set cocoa eyes. "I will always come back to you. Believe that."

Xavier left her warmth, walked to the closet and extracted a black leather shoulder holster. Patricia adjusted the straps across his broad shoulders and chest. He slid the service weapon in the holder that rested along his torso, then she grabbed his waist-length black leather jacket and held it so he could slide his arms inside. This ritual was almost a seduction in itself if the reason hadn't been so deadly.

She playfully slapped his ass and gave him a frisky grin before turning to make her way back to their bed. She made the first few steps, he reached out to grab her hand and pulled her closer.

"I love you."

Xavier embraced her, enjoying the soft feel of her body against his. He kissed the tip of her nose, then her lips. "I'll see you later."

"I'll be waiting."

* * *

Xavier jogged down the curved staircase and was out the door. He hopped in an unmarked midnight blue Chevy Suburban parked in the driveway where Jason awaited.

"What's up, Jay?" They gave each other their customary fist bump.

"Hey. Did you kiss *my* wife and son goodbye?" Jason teased, a smirk on his thin lips.

"Whatever man," Xavier said, waving him off as he buckled up. "I told you about that shit."

"I'm just checking dude," he replied, laughing as he made a left turn out of the driveway. "I got to make sure my wife and kid are okay since fate's got you looking after them instead of me. What's up with that?"

"Keep cracking jokes man, and it's gonna be a 1-8-7 on an undercover cop," he warned. "For real, executed by yours truly."

Jason gave him the side eye. "Look who's Mr. Sensitive tonight. What's your problem?"

Xavier let out a long, slow breath. "Man, Lauren called me at the crack of dawn wanting to know where I was."

"Yikes."

"I thought Patty heard the phone ring, so I let the call go to voicemail, then I had to dash downstairs to my office before she called back."

Jason raised an eyebrow, before making a right turn onto the

Dan Ryan Expressway and flooring it. "I thought you said Lauren was a sound sleeper?"

"She usually is."

Jason took his focus off the road and put it on Xavier for a moment. "She's still taking those sleeping pills, right?"

"Yeah, man." Xavier grimaced at the memory of that heated conversation with Lauren. "Turns out she's still having crazy dreams about that incident from gazillion years ago," he said dryly. "If she'd get therapy like I told her, she wouldn't be having these problems. She thinks those sleeping pills are a cure, but they aren't."

"They must be doing something," Jason commented, checking the side mirror. "This is the first time you've said something like this has happened."

"True, but they can't replace speaking with someone who specializes in her kind of situations."

"Hold up," Jason said, taking another quick glance at Xavier. "Who is she getting the pills from then?"

"Her primary doctor." Xavier shrugged. "I don't know what story Lauren told her, but she's been filling them for years."

"Damn dude, is that legal?"

"Apparently so." Xavier adjusted the tuner on the police scanner to hear the call without static interference. "But in the meantime, she expects me to be her savior when her version of "therapy" falls through."

"Well, that's what you sign up for when you say I do..." Jason frowned. "And aw, that's right, you said that twice— so that's I do, and I do."

"Your ass is on a roll tonight, I see." Xavier pointed out. "Sandy must've broken you off a little something-something before you left home, huh?"

"Don't be mad at me, bruh," he said, popping his collar. "This sexy white chocolate has only one wife to please and not nearly the high blood pressure you signed up for." Jason winked one crystal-blue eye, flexing his boulder-sized biceps. "More wives..."

"Mo problems. Whatever dude."

"So what did you tell her?" Jason asked as he swiftly maneuvered into the local lanes and whizzed past the few cars.

Xavier shrugged, then put his focus on the traffic moving at a much slower pace than they were. "I told her I had to work."

"Well, for once you didn't lie," Jason teased. "It must be work trying to keep two women happy and clueless."

Lies. He'd been leading this double-life long enough to know they were necessary. The less his wives knew, the easier his life became.

Unfortunately, some of the new cases thrown their way were the high-profile types. The kind that the media sniffed around, vying to be first on the scene and the first to report.

Jason had requested a transfer from the Twenty-First District when his first partner, Scott, was killed in the middle of a drug bust. Though Sergeant Armstrong tried to deter Jason from leaving, his request was granted, but not before a new trainee was dropped in his lap. Though he wasn't happy about the situation, Jason took an eager young Detective Carter under his wing. He was impressed by Xavier's sharpness in the field and his quick ability to assess situations. After six months of training, Jason had bonded with Xavier so much so that he rescinded his request to transfer.

Xavier's street savvy coupled with Jason's experience rocketed the duo to the head of their unit. Fourteen years later, they were still dismantling cases that no one else could, drawing the jealous ire of some officers who had been working similar cases with less than stellar results. Now they had to watch their backs because Xavier and Jason believed that two detectives in their unit might be dirty. That would cause a major scandal. And as one of the lead investigators on the cases that put kingpins and distributors in prison, staying off the news was getting harder every day.

Chapter Four

Jason exited the Dan Ryan Expressway on 55th Street and made a sharp left turn. The busy intersection with Red Line train pedestrians racing to catch the connecting buses, strip mall traffic, and fast food joints was empty this time of night, except for a homeless panhandling man standing in the middle of the street. Thanks to his team's surveillance, the Drug Enforcement Agency had a warrant in place to execute a raid on an abandoned building on Fifty-sixth and Loomis. Hopefully, tonight, their efforts would pay off.

The Englewood area's poverty level had hit an all-time low, and only a small amount of businesses remained. The country's housing crisis caused too many foreclosures, leaving a slew of abandoned buildings and houses which were now infiltrated with drug dealers setting up shop or drug-addicted women and helpless children left to fend for themselves. No sooner had officers in the twenty-first unit wiped the area clear of some lower level dealers, then another crop popped up—creating a never-ending cycle of people who saw no way out, trying to cope in its wake and the police with a stream of arrests that filled Cook County Jail and neighboring prisons.

* * *

Six months ago while scoping out the Englewood area, Xavier witnessed a lone figure with clothes barely managing to stay on its lanky frame. The man climbed the stairs to the vacant building and made it to the door before they honed in on the fact that he shouldn't be there.

"Look, man," Jason mumbled, nodding toward that direction while finishing off his fries. "This sorry dude's so skinny he makes a skeleton look sexy."

Xavier tried to hold in a laugh, but choked on the Cocoa-Cola he was drinking from a Styrofoam cup. He covered his mouth as dark fizz oozed between his fingers and drizzled to his lap. "That's a good one, Jay."

Jason rifled through the glove compartment searching for napkins. "I hate those cluckers."

Xavier agreed. "Cluckers—" the name they gave crack heads served a singular purpose.

Jason inched the Crown Vic to a better vantage point. As though a sixth sense had kicked in, the hype looked over his shoulder; eyes widened to the size of Frisbees when he focused on the dark sedan. He ran off in the opposite direction at top speed.

They didn't bother to chase him down.

Xavier flanked Jason as he rubbed his sticky palms with hand sanitizer. They left the Crown Vic to get a better look at what that hype was aiming to get into.

A few months ago, the building had been a trap house overflowing with crack, cocaine, weed, and a flow of prostitutes that was like a Miss America Pagent. Since then, whoever had been supplying the dope in the area had been lying low. Unfortunately for the patrons who thought they were safe inside, that "clucker" had inadvertently tipped off Xavier and Jason that they were back in business.

Voices volleyed from behind the boarded up door. Xavier motioned for Jason to call for backup. With a quick flick of his wrist and a request spoken in a low tone into a device hidden in the arm cuff of his jacket, it didn't take long for fellow officers to arrive and swarm the building from all sides so that none of the remaining occupants could escape without capture.

The Lieutenant's firm voice boomed through the concealed earpieces. "Stand down. I repeat stand down."

"Copy," Xavier said into the receiver, and several other officers did the same, though the disappointed expressions signaled they didn't agree with that direct order. Officers and detectives trudged back to patrol cars and paddy wagons. Soon the area was quiet and normal again. Not a single one of the people inside were aware of how close they had come to spending a night in lockup.

At the end of the shift, the officers and detectives that had been on the scene filed into the lineup room for a debriefing with the Lieutenant of Detectives at the station.

"Thanks to Detective Carter and Detective Sharpe," the crisply dressed Lieutenant began, "we are now aware that the property at 5680 South Loomis has resumed its former business. We've had complaints from surrounding neighbors saying that they've witnessed increased traffic and have been complaining of lewd smells coming from that building. We received a tip from a CI that the dealer is receiving a shipment three days from now, instead of tonight. We haven't been able to find anything concrete, so we're going to do around-the-clock surveillance until we have hard enough evidence to hand out more than a nickel or dime bid."

Xavier and Jason had already sat on that property for over a month watching and biding their time. They learned the dealer's routine and knew that the man known on the street as Laz—government name Jeffrey Lucas, left the building on Wednesdays at one in the afternoon and returned about nine at night. Xavier glared at Detectives Simmons and Zamfoti and their team on the far side of the room. Those two had botched the case resulting in Jason and Xavier being made point team for any new engagements for that area. *Were they the dirty detectives?* Evidently, they were aiming to regain their status again. Not on his watch. Jason caught Xavier's eye and nodded. Apparently, he was thinking the same thing.

Soon, with several adjustments, the hypes in and around the building didn't pay them much attention. The officers who regularly wore department-issued blues now mirrored the hypes, all of it. Their clothes were scruffy and dirty; shoes were run down and torn, fingernails were embedded with dirt, and fingertips were burnt and brownish yellow. Xavier's lips were powdery white and severely crusted and chapped. Jason's skin was ghostly pale with deep red circles around his eyes, courtesy of the police department's makeup artist. While Jason rolled a fake blunt with the wannabe thugs and bought loose cigarettes from the neighborhood kid who more than likely, stole them from the corner liquor store; Xavier went dumpster diving in the trash cans behind the building "looking for food."

He discovered emptied cans of paint thinner, acetone, red stained towels and sheets, and empty bags of kitty litter. Since no one was renovating that property, every item was suspicious. Those products were used to make crystal meth, known on the street as *ice*.

The other red flag was when a *Beware of Dog* sign suddenly appeared on the back fence; a known deterrent used by drug dealers to keep folks away from the building. If they had been smart, they would've at least put a pit bull on the premises to make their lie somewhat real. Not real enough for seasoned officers to catch them in that lie, though.

* * *

"Kill the headlights," Xavier instructed Jason. They turned left on Loomis, creeping down the street, then parked the Suburban in the middle of the block. Xavier observed other plainclothes officers on the scene. Some resembled dope boys, and others were like hypes. A total of about twenty cops and detectives were scattered about the area in hopes that their latest efforts would cast a wide net and rake in a few low levels that would serve up their superiors to save their own skin.

Underneath their undercover outfits, Xavier and Jason were suited for war. Anything was possible when dealing with drug dealers who were unwilling to give up a prime spot or spend any time in jail. Young thugs wouldn't think twice about shooting a cop these days. Given what had happened in Iowa, Ohio, and Minnesota, where protests had ensued over unarmed Black men being shot by law enforcement—mistrust of police was at an all-time high.

Once upon a time, youngsters used to rap about being cop killers. Now they were and didn't have an ounce of remorse. A sad thing when the people who are supposed to serve and protect the citizens become targets themselves. Truthfully, if the arguments correct, others felt targeted by the police. When NWA and gangster rap came on the scene, children who weren't old enough to pee straight picked up the angry vibes and so did a generation of youngsters who now had no more respect for the police than they did their own parents.

The HAZMAT team was on site due to what Xavier found in the trash. Meth labs were toxic. Inhaling even a tiny bit of the substance could send anyone to the emergency room. The forensic team and a few K-9 dogs in tow meant they were prepared for any and everything.

Shadowy figures, thanks to the glare of streetlights shining on the broken mini-blinds, danced behind the scenes.

A team of detectives had situated at the back of the building, near the basement entrance, as well as in strategic places along the front. Officers posted at the beginning and end of the block and in the alley poised to stop anyone who tried to slip away.

Jason tapped the dashboard to get Xavier's attention. Booski, their confidential informant, wore a skullcap, black button down shirt, and sagging jeans. He walked toward the building, wearing an undetectable wire with a night-vision camera disguised as a button on the breast pocket of his shirt. Xavier signaled for the CI to approach by getting out of the truck and lighting a cigarette. Booski removed his hat and scratched his head, which was his response to receiving the signal. He made his way through the gangway, made a howling noise, then focused his bleary-eyed attention up to the second-floor window. If they didn't gain entry with the CI's help, tossing a flash-bang device inside would be a last resort since the place was a suspected meth lab. They didn't want to take a chance on an explosion.

A second later the lights flashed on and off, then Booski passed the unlatched gate and headed straight to the side entrance.

When the screen door opened, Booski slammed his hands in his pants pockets, then pulled out three crumpled up dollar bills and presented it to an armed man.

"Hey man," Booski croaked, aggressively scratching his sides, a sure sign of addiction. "All I got is three dollars. What can I get? I just need something man—anything!"

"Man, get the fuck outta here with that shit." The dealer barreled out of the door and pushed the informant to the ground, then turned to go back inside. That was all the leeway the police needed.

One detective rushed up from his hiding spot on the side, snatched the dealer from behind and hit him with a Billy club in the knee. Other detectives burst into the premises on his heels.

Xavier and Jason joined the rest of the detectives on the front porch and breached the door. The acrid smell hit them immediately, a sure sign that the information they'd been given was correct.

"Lights on," a raspy-voiced detective yelled.

When Xavier flipped the switch, an image of ten dealers lined up against the living room wall with their hands behind their backs getting handcuffed came into clear view. Xavier then entered the kitchen where two dealers were hog-tied on the floor along with their Booski. The CI would spend a night in jail like the others to ward off suspicion, but he would be placed in protective custody for his safety.

Three cluckers were stretched out in the basement suspended in a semi-conscious, paranoid state. Four women were servicing customers on the upper levels in various states of undress— Xavier shared a knowing glance with Jason. Another set of victims in this war on drugs.

* * *

"Good work fellas," their lieutenant acknowledged, adjusting his blue tie.

Xavier nodded, watching as the forensic team bagged evidence and dusted for fingerprints. All of the people they'd pulled from the building were going to be processed. Some questioned to see if they could be used in a bigger drug sting.

"Man lets get out of here," he turned and said to Jason.

"Sounds like a plan." Jason reached into his pocket to get the car keys. "The sooner we get to the station, the faster I can go home to my *one* and *only* lovely wife."

Xavier grimaced, pointing an index finger at his partner, "Don't you start that again."

They shared a laugh, which died the moment a series of shots rang out.

Total mayhem erupted.

Cops and detectives unlocked the safeties on their weapons.

Another gunshot.

A flurry of bodies rushed outside from houses that had been dark only moments before. The neighborhood came alive in a matter of seconds. Lights were on, windows opened, and people were pouring out onto the sidewalks and into the street.

"I saw him," a woman in an animal print bathrobe and fuzzy slippers shouted. She pointed to one of the detectives from their unit. "That cop shot that kid."

Chapter Five

Lauren's fingertips danced a fierce tango across the digital alarm clock, forcefully stabbing at the snooze button. In her efforts to silence the annoying alarm, it fell to the floor still singing its wake-up song. She moaned in agony as her body's defiant refusal to part ways with its second-favorite companion. She sighed, then managed to peel herself away from the silky pillows and sheets. She sat upright, stretched, and kicked the alarm clock across the floor.

A welcomed silence descended on the room.

Not even five minutes later, the backup alarm on the iPhone buzzed, and as much as she wanted to throw it across the room, that wasn't an option. She willed her exhausted body out of bed and into the bathroom to take a quick shower.

Thoughts of Xavier gracefully waltzed through her mind when

her gaze fell upon the black bathrobe hanging on the gold hook next to hers. She inhaled the woodsy fragrance of the Versace Eros cologne that lingered around the collar.

She pressed a few keys on the glass control panel, and steaming hot water streamed from the square showerhead. Lauren lifted her arms and pulled the overnight shirt over her head, shook out her hair, and stepped into the cascading water; letting it cover her as she attempted to push away the remnants of the nightmare that tried to inch its way into the corners of her mind.

Lauren closed her eyes, tilted her head and the stinging water massaged her scalp and found that the person who featured prominently came to mind.

* * *

Thirteen years ago, Lauren was eager to be on her own. She adored her parents, but they were overprotective and unaware that they dulled her shine by micromanaging every move she made, fearing the world would swallow her up. Lauren was an only child, her parent's miracle baby after so many failed attempts at having one. She made a bold move enrolling her last semester of cosmetology school in Chicago and didn't tell her parents until days before her departure. They were disappointed, but supportive and vowed to help her in any way they could.

Her dad was the Director at The Boys and Girls Club back home in Queens. Though he pulled some strings to get Lauren a job at the Thompson Community Center while she attended cosmetology school, she would have gotten the job on her own merits. She had been a volunteer at The Boys and Girls Club since she was fourteen. When she turned eighteen, she was hired on as full-time staff, which gave her eight years experience under her belt.

Shawn was one of the eight girls in the group that Lauren had the privilege to mentor. She was like a delicate butterfly, a unique beauty, who was extremely shy and kept to herself. Shawn was slender, and her skin was a special shade of porcelain. She had jet-black hair and sunken green eyes that had a story to tell if only someone would listen. Shawn's friend Candace was with another group of girls, but from what Lauren had seen, the two were as different as sugar and salt. Candace had an edge to her that made her hard and bitter, a reaction from being in the system for so long and at the hands of an abusive drug addict for a mother. Lauren understood that "edge" was only a front. When Candace thought no one was paying attention, her true personality made its presence known—and it was evident that she loved her friend.

Shawn, on the other hand, was still struggling to find herself. She never expressed her feelings in group sessions and kept everything bottled inside. Lauren took a particular interest in her and was determined to pull Shawn out of her shell so she could blossom into the lovely and confident young lady she was meant to be.

And then you failed her when she needed you most.

A horrible, fear-driven mistake on Lauren's part had crushed that butterfly and sent the wings floating into a dark oblivion and had taken Lauren along for the ride.

"No weapon formed against me shall prosper," she whispered under the spray immediately pushing that ugly thought away as quickly as it came. "Today will be a good day. Kick rocks, Lucifer."

* * *

Thirty minutes later, a more buoyant Lauren was parking a White Lexus truck in front of the salon, *Masterpieces By Lauren.* Shawn was already there waiting in her car. Lauren appreciated that the outside strip mall in Chicago Ridge where the shop was located stayed well lit like the Las Vegas Strip. Fluorescent lights underneath the white awning gleamed off the glass door and windows, which made her feel more secure when she came in before the sun rose or left after the sunset.

"Good morning," Lauren said, smiling as she handed Shawn a caramel latte from Ophelia's Café, a quaint little spot in Evergreen Park.

"Hey, girlie." She lifted the cup and inhaled. "Mmmm. Smells good. Thanks."

"You're welcome, lady." Lauren fumbled with the keys before opening the glass door to the salon. "Are you coming in or what?" she asked Shawn who was standing motionless in the doorway.

"I'm right behind you," she said, pointing across the street at the gas station. "Did you see that guy sitting at the bus stop?"

Lauren glanced in that direction. "No one's there."

"I know—but there was—a man just there," Shawn said, frowning as she closed the door. "I spotted him in the rearview mirror while I waited for you. He was there the whole time, staring at my car. Now all of a sudden he's disappeared since I'm not alone." Shawn locked the door and peered out again.

"It's probably nothing," Lauren reassured, as she flipped the light switch and pressed the code into the keypad to disarm the security system. The marble floors and full-length mirrors came to life as the recessed lighting illuminated all the areas that extended from the receptionist's desk and drying stations all the way to the stylist's lounge in the rear of the salon. The sofa and recliners in the client relaxation area carried the scent of rich leather and looked as if no one's hips had ever graced them at any time. "He's most likely on his way to work."

"I guess," Shawn shivered. "He gave me the creeps."

Lauren placed her cup of butter rum coffee on the vanity, retrieved a personalized stylist apron from a silver hook. "Make yourself comfortable while I set up shop."

"Cool," Shawn responded, swiveling in the stylist chair.

She gathered towels from the back that had the salon's name engraved in gold script on the lower right-hand corner, then brought them to her workstation situated near a plate glass window that overlooked a man-made pond along the side of the building.

Keys jingling in the door of the quiet salon made both of them snap to attention. Lauren's front desk assistant, Lynette, sauntered in two hours early.

"Good morning, divas," Lynette greeted in an exuberant tone, pink hair bouncing on her shoulders.

"Sweet Jesus. You scared the shit out of me," Lauren snapped, more harsh than intended. "What are you doing here so early?"

"Hey Lynette," Shawn said waving.

"Hi," she responded and locked the door, then sat her purse on the front desk. "I need to go over the inventory and purchase orders for the fundraiser."

The rigidness in Lauren's tone slacked. "That makes sense."

The Annual Halloween Fundraiser for the Thompson Center that Lauren sponsored every year was a few weeks away. The tickets had sold out during the first week of sales as she had projected, which further confirmed the business move she made last year. Instead of hosting the event at a different venue because it had outgrown the salon, Lauren had purchased the rental space next door. The wall had been knocked down and the area completely renovated. She had the forethought to have a shower installed in her office as some clients dressed for the event right after. Getting hair and makeup done at the salon.

"I was trying to get out of the way before clients came in," Lynette responded.

"It's all good," Lauren teased with a flourish of her hand. "It's too quiet in here. Turn the radio to V103."

Her favorite station that catered to people who loved R&B, Dusties and Old School music—something she shared in common with Xavier. "That's more like it." Lauren snapped her fingers. "Steve Harvey and Nephew Tommy will definitely have us cracking up and keep me on my toes."

"You couldn't be tired," Shawn said, a smile lifting the corners of her pink lips.

"Don't play with me," she replied. "The sun's not even up yet. I'm hardly functioning—that's what coffee's for."

"Well, you look like a million bucks, as always."

"Thanks. I think." Lauren swiveled the stylist chair and looked at Shawn like she had lost her mind.

"No seriously," Shawn countered, crossing one leg over the other. "Designer jeans, off the shoulder blouse, and new wavy hairdo looks spectacular on you. I'm jealous."

"Don't be," Lauren swung the chair back around, placed her hands in the crown of Shawn's head to start with a massage to stimulate the follicles. Shawn parted her lips to speak. "Enough about me." Lauren held up a hand to keep Shawn from saying another word. "You're looking like you're ready to conquer the world this morning in that power suit. Tell me about your interview today."

"It's with MedRx," she replied, eyes fluttering to close under Lauren's masterful touch, something that happened quite often.

Lauren had to keep conversation steady, or they'd fall asleep like Xavier once had when they first met. His fellow officers clowned him, calling him one of the seven dwarfs.

"I'm interviewing for a Pharmacy Technician position, and I'm super nervous."

"Why? Your education alone will speak volumes," Lauren reassured her. "Besides, you're going to be looking super cute and professional. You don't have anything to worry about."

Shawn's eyes opened, her gaze connected with Lauren's in the mirror. "I'm afraid the Pharmacy Manager won't like me."

"That's absurd. Why wouldn't he like you?"

"It's a she," Shawn corrected. "What if she doesn't approve of the way I look?"

Lauren dismissively waved her hand. "You look like a

businesswoman, and I'm going to do your hair in a neat, but chic updo that screams *hire me*. So be at ease, my friend. You've got this."

Shawn grimaced and looked away laying in the shampoo chair with her hair draping in the sink. She waited for the shampooing to end before she asked, "Have you been in touch with Mrs. Bradley?"

Mrs. Bradley was the teen liaison at the Thompson Community Center. She was the woman who had comforted Shawn, made sure she received counseling and kept Lauren abreast of the case involving the man who police had captured a week after he'd attacked Shawn. The cameras were functioning at the back entrance and caught the times he had slipped in and a full frontal image when he strutted away. Not ran. Strutted. The man was so unbothered by what he'd done; he felt no urgency; as though he relished the agony he had brought to a child whose innocence had been ripped away.

"I saw her last week," Lauren whispered. "Brings back bad memories, huh?"

Those words lingered for a while, then Shawn gave an anxious smile. "Thanks for always believing in me."

"Always have and always will."

The women shared a speaking glance before Lauren quickly put her attention to Shawn's hair, and making good on the promise that she'd do her part to help land her that job.

When Lauren was done perfecting the masterpiece she'd created with Shawn's silky hair, she spun the chair around. "Fifty should cover it."

"Half price?" Shawn said, beaming. "I love you so much. You always look out for me. Thank you."

"I love you too," Lauren said, returning the embrace before pulling away. "And I'll always be here for you no matter what." She cupped Shawn's face. "You don't wanna mess up that perfect hair and makeup before you get there."

"You're right. I'll call you later to let you know how it went."
She slipped her purse over her shoulder, waved to Lynette and was
out the door.

Lauren tried to hold back the moisture rushing to her eyes. A
single tear slipped down her cheek. A profound sense of relief
came over her the minute Shawn said those words. Shawn held
no grudge against her and had forgiven her. Now if only she could
forgive herself.

Chapter Six

Patricia Carter finished the consultation with a concerned mother about the type of medicine to give her three-year-old daughter to reduce a fever. A pair of high heels rapidly approached the window and paused in the space next to Patricia.

She turned to acknowledge the woman with, "I'll be right with you," and she froze. Her heart pounded, rushing a river of blood to her temples; her pupils bore into the green eyes of the young woman who stood nearly the same 5'3". Somehow, it felt as though she had seen a ghost in the image of a beautiful ivory skin woman with jet-black hair like hers, and piercing emerald eyes that were so familiar even though this was the first time the woman had ever been in her presence.

Patricia admired the professional black business suit and black heels the woman wore, which also were almost identical to her own.

"Good morning, welcome to MedRx. How may I be of assistance?"

"Good morning, I'm Shawn Johnston," she said, and her voice

was equal parts skittish and composed. "I have an interview scheduled with the Pharmacy Manager at nine."

Patricia extended a hand. "Nice to meet you, Ms. Johnston, I'm the person you're looking for."

The younger woman took Patricia's hand, showcasing a French manicure that also matched her own.

"Have a seat in the patient waiting area, and I'll be right with you."

"Thank you."

Patricia walked to the prescription filling station and paused, allowing her mind to travel back to the last time she had gazed into a pair of eyes identical to the woman who had perched on the edge of one of the aqua-colored cushioned chairs. Matthew O'Shaughnessy had been the love of her *life*. If not for her family's interference she would be on a much different path now. The love that she had experienced at such a tumultuous time in her life, still lingered despite the fact that she was happily married and had a teenage son.

"Is everything okay?" asked a petite Nigerian woman who wore exquisite African head wraps. Meilani was the Senior Pharmacy Technician, who had worked with Patricia for seven years, and though she was an excellent employee, Patricia didn't see her staying long. Her husband wanted Meilani to spend more time at home with the kids and to take care of their home, rather than working a nine to five.

Patricia's chest filled with air, then she slowly exhaled and replied, "Can you hold it down while I interview Ms. Johnston?"

"No problem," Meilani replied, but her gaze shifted to assess the newcomer in a matter of seconds. She moved away to take care of an elderly couple who were making their way up the incontinence aisle to the pick-up counter.

Patricia smoothed out the crisp white lab coat over the cream blouse and black flared-leg slacks. She ran a nervous hand through her short and sassy cropped hair, feeling more like the interviewee instead of the interviewer. What was it about *this* woman that brought on a sense of unease?

Shawn was already a top pick of all the resumes Patricia had received. She'd graduated from Holy Name Cathedral, then attended Chicago State University. In addition, she had certificates in Social Work, National Pharmacy Technician Certification Board, and CPR and First-Aid.

Her sixth sense was always on point, and it was killing her that she couldn't put her finger on why she felt an instant connection with this candidate.

Patricia cleared her throat, grabbed the manila folder tucked behind the computer, walked out of the pharmacy with a smile on her face, and took a seat next to the woman in the waiting area.

"This is impressive, Ms. Johnston," Patricia remarked as she thumbed through Shawn's resume, letters of recommendation, and references once again, giving her something else to focus on besides those piercing eyes. If she didn't know any better, she could almost swear she was being sized up as well.

"Thank you."

"Morning Patricia." The colorful tornado known as Javid twirled around the corner.

He was Patricia's part-time technician who'd been with her for two years. Life behind the counter of MedRx was always joyous when Javid was on the schedule.

"Good Morning."

"And who do we have here?" he asked with a hand on his hip, biting the tip of a pen.

"This is Shawn."

"Hello." Shawn waved taking in all of Javid's personality, which could be overpowering at first meet.

"Mmmmm, hey girl," Javid said giving Shawn a once-over before punching in the code on the keypad to enter the pharmacy. "Good luck," he said walking past the registers. "By the way, I love your shoes, girl."

"Thanks," Shawn said suppressing a grin.

He said something in Spanish, then disappeared to the back.

"It's okay," Patricia assured her. "Go on and laugh. That's our Javid. He keeps the flow around here cheerful."

Shawn remained poised, but the crinkle of her mouth lingered, making Shawn seem younger than her twenty-four years.

Patricia liked that she remained professional in the face of Javid's flamboyant ways. The north side brought on people of many cultures and orientations. She stacked Shawn's documents in a neat pile, slid them back in the folder, then placed it on an empty chair. She crossed her legs and placed her hands in her lap. "Tell me three interesting facts about yourself."

Shawn made direct eye contact as she responded, "I ranked number two in a class of three hundred twenty, I have a photographic memory, and I was a ward of the state."

Patricia nodded and managed to smile, but the hairs on the back of her neck stood at attention at those last words; almost as if they had been thrown out there to get a particular reaction. "Impressive. An academic scholar in the face of uncertainty," she replied slowly, still having a bit of a time trying to see what was so appealing about this specific candidate.

"Now give me three reasons why I should hire you."

Shawn shifted, as she answered, "I work hard, I'm cool under pressure, and I'm tenacious... I've had to fight for everything I have... The more someone said I couldn't do something, the more I was determined to get it done." She leveled a gaze at Patricia. "And I apply that same drive and determination to work and school.

"Point taken." Patricia nodded. "Your resume says you're attending Chicago State University for a Masters degree." Patricia paused as she put another thought behind what that could mean. "Then why are you applying for a pharmacy technician position?"

"I've always been interested in medicine. I may be working with children in the future who need medication for behavioral problems, and I would like to know first hand about how those drugs work and interact with a person's chemical imbalance."

"I see," she said, taking in the sincerity behind those words. The young woman was practical if anything and *incredibly* smart. "So you'll need to work part-time?"

"Yes ma'am," she replied, crossing one leg over the other. "Anytime before five o'clock works because I'll have evening classes."

"The commute will be brutal."

"Not when I'm traveling against rush hour times," she replied, a hint of a smile lifting her lips.

"Give me a copy of your schedule, and we'll go from there."

Patricia stood, and Shawn did the same. "It was nice meeting you, and I'll call you Monday morning to let you know of my decision. There are three more candidates that I was looking into, but I think I've already found what I'm looking for."

Shawn shook Patricia's hand, and her exuberance was on the eyes if not the eagerness of that final handshake. "Thank you for the opportunity. I promise you won't be disappointed."

Chapter Seven

Shawn burst through the door of the cozy two-bedroom apartment in Bronzeville that she shared with her best friend Candace, who had been like a sister since they first laid eyes on each other in foster care. "I met my biological mother today."

"Say what?" Candace darted out of her bedroom and into the quaint living room wearing spandex workout gear and her sandy-brown ponytail swinging.

"You heard me." Shawn slipped off her heels, laid the blazer across the back of the futon, and unclasped the top button of her white blouse. "And guess what? I think she's going to give me the job."

Candace dropped down on the futon and crossed her long skinny legs Indian style. "What was she like?"

"Not what I expected." Shawn took the space beside Candace, then wiggled and rubbed her aching toes. "I mean, she was nice, but I don't look anything like her. She's really pretty, but different than I visualized. She's not fat, but she's sort of built like Toni Braxton, but thicker and darker——much darker.

Candace chuckled. "Your daddy must've been extremely light-skinned or Caucasian because you can definitely pass for the other team."

"I know, right?" Shawn said, folding her arms. "If only finding him was as easy as it was for my mom."

"Don't sweat it. You'll be able to track him down too," Candace reassured her, as she loosened the band around her ponytail.

"My grandmother's neighbors have been living in the same home for over thirty years said he joined the army after high school." Shawn crossed her fingers. "I'm hoping Patricia will be able to help with that once I get to know her."

"I don't see why she wouldn't," Candace said, pulling out the band and shaking out her hair. "This feels so much better." She looked at her friend who was silent with her head hanging. "What's wrong?"

"I had the feeling when she first looked at me she recognized me or something, but she didn't say anything." Shawn shrugged. "That's just foolish thinking on my part, especially since she gave me up at birth." Shawn brushed a finger over the top of her nail, then locked gazes with her friend. "I don't know if she ever held me in her arms."

"You can't think like that," Candace admonished, rubbing a hand along Shawn's back. "At least you have the opportunity to meet your mom and maybe build a relationship with her."

How many people like them could say that? Candace certainly couldn't. Sometimes Candace mentioned the woman who had caused her to land in the hospital on several occasions before the Department of Children and Family Services stepped in. By then, Candace had become cold and numb, but she was the only one at Ms. Ida's who tried to befriend Shawn when she ended up being passed over by all the family she thought would love her forever. Grandma Marie died of a stroke, and no one else stepped in to claim her before DCFS swept her into the system.

"When the time is right, you can ask her why she gave you up. You don't have any tainted memories like I do." Candace glanced down at arms the color of ripe plums, noting the scars from cigarette burns that ran from her shoulder to elbow.

Shawn inched closer to Candace and wrapped her arms around her—sister—friend.

"I'm angry because I don't have any memories at all," Shawn said, sliding her head onto Candace's shoulder. "I know that sounds crazy. Even though your mom wasn't the best—"

"That's putting it too lightly. That bitch was a monster."

Well, monster was even putting it mildly. Unlike the loving home that Shawn had come from, Candace had pulled the cards of a drug-addicted woman with mental issues, and a father who she never knew. By age ten, she'd had a broken wrist, a fractured nose, and several broken ribs. Those were the least of the issues.

"But you *knew* her," Shawn countered. "My mom didn't even try to raise me. She took the easy way out."

"I know you don't believe that." Candace broke from her embrace, almost glaring at her. "With everything we've been through, you see there are many reasons women give their babies up for adoption. I could only wonder what my life might've been like had my mother done the same."

"Our paths wouldn't have crossed, and there'd be one less person who loves me."

"I believe we were supposed to find each other in this crazy world," Candace reasoned, putting a tighter grip on Shawn's hand.

"I agree."

Shawn should never have been in the foster care system. She'd had a happy childhood filled with love, laughter, birthday parties, and family trips to a different state every summer. Holidays were a blast with more family members than she could count. Then a car accident had taken both parents and landed her at the home of Grandma Marie, also a loving part of Shawn's family circle.

Grandma Marie fell ill one year after Shawn came to live with her. She had a stroke and never fully recovered. The tables turned to the point where Shawn was now caring for that wonderful old woman instead of the other way around. Thankfully, Shawn's aunts and uncles took turns sitting with and caring for Grandma Marie during the day while Shawn attended classes. As soon as she stepped a foot over the threshold, each one of them was out the door and back to their busy lives. The responsibility had been overwhelming, but after losing so many important people so early in life, Shawn did whatever it took because she didn't want to lose her grandmother, too.

Shawn didn't know at the time that the death of her grandmother would pale in comparison to losing every family member she'd come to love. The family had kept a secret that would shatter her world. None of the information was supposed to reach Shawn's ears until her eighteenth birthday. Unfortunately, due to her failing health, Grandma Marie had no choice but to go against her parent's wishes.

She read the series of letters left by the woman she knew as her mother. Evidently, life as she'd known it, had been one big fat lie, but the love and heartache she felt were very real. She forced herself to examine the other paperwork that Grandma Marie had kept hidden in a tan envelope that had been duck-taped behind the dresser's drawer mirror. She stared at a copy of an *original* birth certificate with her birth parents names. Folded along with it was the birth certificate with her adoptive parent's names.

Shawn wiped the tears streaking her face with the sleeve of a yellow sweatshirt that had been a present from her grandmother right before she'd started experiencing the health challenges that lead to that debilitating stroke. She continued to sift through the documents until she came upon a picture secured by a paperclip. The image was of her mom, a woman named Patricia, and Shawn as a newborn wearing a pink cap. On the back of the photo, someone had written: Special Delivery, December 29, 1992. Mercy Hospital. Birth Parents, Patricia Taylor and Matthew O'Shaughnessy of Chicago Illinois.

Am I part Irish? She wondered.

Shawn glanced at the life-altering papers and kicked them to the floor, getting a paper cut across the back of her ankle for the effort. She cried as a hole opened in her soul that could only be filled with one thing—knowing who was her real mother. When Shawn woke up two hours later, she was aware that her identity had been shattered. Everything she'd taken for granted—aunts and uncles, cousins—did they know? Only after reviewing the papers and photos once again, Shawn realized that she hadn't checked on Grandma Marie since venturing into the master bedroom a few hours before.

She rushed down the hallway, passing the bathroom and the glass étagère with family photographs on it, and zoned in on the family portrait taken when she was three-years-old, and another one when she was six. She picked it up, focusing on the features of both parents and the lack of any family resemblance. No wonder there were whispers of something she couldn't quite understand when she was growing up. Relatives didn't care for holding that secret, and would sometimes talk about it in a way that went over Shawn's head. Now it all made sense—the snide remarks about finding her under a tree or the stork dropping her off somewhere else first. Sometimes even meaner words that Shawn let roll off of her like oil because none of it pertained to her, though at times she had that sneaking suspicion that it did. Her eyes watered again, and she placed the frames face down.

She made it to Grandma Marie's bedroom and lingered around the entrance watching the old woman's sleeping form. Moments later, she whipped around to take refuge in her own space when Grandma Marie asked, "Are you alright, baby?"

Still too dazed to answer, Shawn rushed in, climbed in bed and couldn't keep the tears at bay. Grandma Marie patiently waited while Shawn went through all of the emotions one could feel upon learning that her entire world was nothing like she thought it had been.

Grandma Marie lived her final days comforting and reassuring

Shawn that her life had a purpose and that she *had* been loved, no matter what she might think right now. Shawn's parents had chosen her, and that made her special.

When Grandma Marie died, she was under the impression that Shawn would be taken in by Aunt Tracy or Uncle Lonnie and his wife or even cousin Lillian and her husband. The hymn-singing woman thought she could rest in eternal peace.

Unfortunately, Grandma Marie had more faith in her family than she should because not a single person showed any interest in her well-being.

* * *

"Those are the memories you need to hold on to—your parents, your grandmother," Candace said to Shawn, snatching her from thoughts of the past. "You know what *real* parental love feels like." Candace slid in front of Shawn, grabbing her shoulders. "We beat the odds, Sis. We're both high school graduates, you got your Undergraduate Degree, and now you're working on your Masters."

Candace was working full-time for the Chicago Transit Authority and had just finished truck-driving school. They had no student loans and still had that money in the bank from their time living with Ms. Ida. She was the best foster mother they could've asked for.

Ms. Ida was a stern, rare gem disguised as a sweet older woman with gray hair who loved God and cared for all living things that crossed her threshold.

"And we ain't got no babies running around here," she said, sounding like Ms. Ida. "So you can miss me with that nonsense." Candace shifted her weight to one side and waggled a finger at Shawn. "There'll be no pity parties around here. We have an abundance of positive things going for us."

Shawn sighed, picturing the images of the other girls from Ms. Ida's. Despite the love and stable home that Ms. Ida provided, many had not nearly gained the kind of success that Shawn and Candace had. "Okay. I hear you. That's why I need you around to keep my emotions in check."

"Damn straight." Candace winked, then began a series of simple stretches, ones she had taught Shawn while they were in high school when Candace went through a fitness craze. "Are you going to tell her who you are?"

Shawn left the futon and went to the refrigerator as she thought about Candace's question. She grabbed a leftover container of Chinese food and popped it in the microwave.

"I have to feel her out first." She dumped some shrimp fried rice in a bowl, stirred, and scooped a fork full in her mouth. "I want to see what kind of person she is."

Chapter Eight

Patricia took Lake Shore Drive home instead of the Dan Ryan to ensure that her evening commute was much calmer than the morning one. Besides, driving along the lakefront was more beautiful than seeing the buildings and homes that lined either side of the expressway. She passed sandy beaches, Millennium Park, Buckingham Fountain and the museum campus. She admired the serene view of Lake Michigan as the sun glistened on the rippled water while the bikers and joggers enjoyed the last hours of daylight and the lighter effects of the fall weather. Patricia slipped on a pair of Armani sunglasses, let the drop-top down on her black Mercedes Benz convertible, and took in the fresh air.

She turned up the radio and let Joe Soto tell her all about why Black women were losing their men to white women. Patricia wondered if white women felt the same way about losing their men to black women. She chuckled in retrospect. The first person Patricia had an emotional connection with was a White man. And if her parents hadn't sabotaged their relationship, she would probably still be with him today. No disrespect to Xavier, but first loves were hard to get over, especially when that love was unfairly snatched away.

Basking in the fading sunlight at memories of yesterday, just for a moment, Patricia was absorbed in Matthew's essence. The tender touch of his hand on her cheek had made goose bumps appear; the imperfect cleft in his chin that made him perfect in every way. The soul stare made her first kiss special at the age of fifteen. She knew her teenage sweetheart was her forever love. Until the day he wasn't.

Why did she have to get pregnant? Her eyes watered, but the wind whipped around her sunglasses and the moisture dissipated as quickly as it had come. Her parents were educators, and anything that stood in the way of Patricia finishing school was neutralized. She pleaded with her mom to keep that beautiful baby, but her dad's word was final and non-negotiable. Deep down, she understood the real reason she was forced to give the baby up for adoption. Although her parents would never admit it, they were embarrassed that their teenage daughter was in the family way without the "family" in place. No matter how much they said, her age and unfulfilled dreams played a factor.

They made her transfer schools until after the baby was born and kept Matthew at a distance. His parents were on board with hers, but for a different reason. They wanted to keep their Irish bloodline "pure," so the sooner the adoption happened, the better. His parents' preference was for Patricia to have an abortion, but Matthew threatened to emancipate himself if they ever brought it up again. Although Patricia and Matthew vowed always to love each other and never to let the obstacles their parents put before them to break them up, their relationship suffered from the stress, eventually tearing them apart.

The brash honking of a horn brought Patricia back to the married, one son, and full-time career reality. She glanced in the review mirror at a man who mouthed obscenities because she was driving ten miles per hour under the speed limit. She changed lanes, and he whizzed by, flipping her the bird.

She'd already put in a pizza order for dinner after she cleared

Navy Pier area, so it should be ready by the time she made it to Italian Fiesta.

Patricia dialed Junior, realizing she hadn't received a text from him when he arrived home which should've been forty-five minutes ago. "Hey, crazy boy. Did you finish your homework?"

"Everything is everything," he replied, his voice a smidgen deeper than it had been a few weeks ago. Patricia was losing her adorable little boy.

"Soooooo, is that a yes or no?"

"Of course, Moms. I'm on it."

"Did you empty the trash?" she asked, a little concerned about his relaxed manner that signaled that something was up. "I want my house the way I left it this morning."

"Okay," he said in a tone that gave her an indication that Brandon was hanging with him. These two could dirty every plate and cup in the kitchen and leave a mess more damaging than an F5 tornado.

"Alright then, I'll see you shortly."

"Yep."

Patricia ended the call. *Teenagers.*

Xavier worked second shift. She only had to worry about feeding Junior. After a long day, little things like smooth traffic, minus the rude guy, and not having to cook dinner made all the difference in the world.

Speaking of making a difference, Shawn Johnston would bring something extra to the pharmacy. Having another one that was as capable as Meilani would be awesome in giving her more time to spend with her family. Meilani's husband continued with his demands that she homeschool their three children, Patricia wasn't sure how long the young woman could hold out.

Patricia called Junior when she pulled in the semi-circular driveway to her home in Pill Hill. "I'm out front, come help me with the pizza and bags."

"You got pizza?" His voice raised an octave. The lanky teen was out the front door before he could think about hanging up the phone. He was still wearing a basketball practice jersey and shorts as though he didn't have time to change when he came in. Probably didn't if Brandon came home with him.

"Hey, Moms." He kissed her on the cheek and loaded plastic bags filled with pop on his arms, and paid close attention to those bright white flat boxes steaming with his favorite food.

Patricia slipped out of her black pumps and kicked the door closed with her foot the moment she crossed the threshold. She paused, staring at the empty glasses and potato chip bags on the cocktail table, but before she could say Junior's name, he appeared.

"I'm on it," he said, sprinting into the living room to clear his mess off the table.

She climbed the stairs and took a seat on an upholstered bench at the foot of the bed in the master bedroom and changed into navy blue sweatpants and one of Xavier's Chicago Police t-shirts. Patricia washed her hands in the pedestal sink, then glanced in the mirror and once again the image of that young woman came to mind. Shawn Johnston appeared to be a lovely girl who would fit in perfectly with the other technicians, Meilani and Javid, but there was still something about *her* that made Patricia uneasy. She wouldn't deny her employment for that reason alone, especially since all of her references checked out and she presented well. She brushed it aside and made her way downstairs to the kitchen.

When Patricia came back downstairs, Junior was already on his second plate of sausage and shrimp pizza.

Patricia whipped out her cell and tried to reach Xavier, but it went straight to voicemail. She glanced at her son, who was sprawled out on the leather couch in the family room with his gaze fixed on the antics of Wild 'N Out and asked, "Have you talked to your dad this evening?"

"Yeah, he called around six thirty to check on me," Junior said around a mouthful of food. "Sounded like he was under a waterfall somewhere."

"A what?"

When he shrugged, she waved her hand dismissing what he had to say with, "Never mind."

Junior put his focus back on his meal and the television show. *Teenagers.*

Xavier had called their son, but hadn't thought to pick up the phone and have a conversation with her? *Waterfall? What was that about?* She took in a few slices of pizza and savored an ice-cold glass of strawberry cream soda.

"How was school?"

"Cool. Ms. Delacruz gave us a Spanish project to work on for extra credit, and it's due in two weeks," he replied, trying to catch the stringy mozzarella cheese that was dangling with his mouth before it hit his shirt. "I already have an A in her class, but I'm gonna do it anyway."

"That's smart," Patricia remarked, beaming at the fact her son's work ethic was equal to the energy he put into sports. "You can never have too many points to bolster your GPA."

"Moms, I know that," he said, taking another bite.

Waterfall. None of Xavier's work took him to a place where a sound like that factored in. "How did practice go? Is Coach Kerr still crazy as ever?"

Junior gave his mom a serious side eye. "Yep, he's super cray cray. Got us running around like track stars instead of basketball players."

"Well, you know that's a part of keeping that endurance up. You guys can't win the championship if you can't hang with or be a step above the competition."

"Moms look," Junior said, sitting upright on the couch. "I know all that, but he's doing too much."

"Whatever," she said, waving him off. "Stop complaining." She whipped out her cell, squinting at the screen thoughtfully. "I'm going to call Coach Kerr and tell him to run you four times the norm tomorrow so you can work off those extra carbs you just inhaled."

Junior sat up and reached across her for the phone. "Moms, nooooo. Quit playing."

Patricia laughed, pulling the phone out of his reach. He sprawled over her planting kisses. "Boy get off of me, you know I'm just messing around."

"I'm a growing boy. So I get a free pass," he said, grabbing a slice of pizza from her plate.

Patricia gave her son a major side eye.

Junior was tall for fifteen, six-foot-two with long limbs. He was a perfect mix of his parents—dark complexion, with light brown eyes, and dimples like his dad, jet-black hair like hers, except his had a slight bit of curl, a little of Patricia's Indian heritage showing up two generations late.

She stood and stretched. "I'm calling it a night. Don't leave this mess in here. And make sure you wash the dishes."

"Hey, I cleaned up earlier."

"Yes and you can cleanup now."

"When you cook—I still have to cleanup," he protested.

"Well, that's only fair since I bought the groceries."

"I'll never win this one," Junior sighed.

"Not until you're grown and gone." She bent down and kissed him on the forehead. "Don't stay up too late."

"Okay. Good night." Junior grabbed the remote, changed the channel, and started in on yet another slice of pizza. If he weren't so active and worked out as much as he did, she'd probably have to roll him everywhere.

Patricia took a nice long, and steamy shower then grabbed a towel before drying off in front of a floor-length mirror and admired the forty-year-old body reflecting in the silver glass. No blemishes, no tummy pouch, and no saggy breasts. She was short and stacked, but tight despite the fact that she didn't have a consistent workout regimen. She reached for the Victoria's Secret, Love Spell Body Lotion that was infused with the sweet mixture of cherry blossom and peach fragrances that Xavier loved so much, then massaged it into her skin. She rifled through the top dresser drawer, pulling out one of her many negligees that were sure to turn Xavier on; slipped it over her ebony skin and wrapped a pretty red satin robe around her body and settled into bed.

Time ticked by in slow motion as she waited to hear something, anything from her husband. When it seemed that the waiting was in vain, she pulled out an Eric Jerome Dickey novel and took in a few chapters before her lids lost their battle to stay open and only one thought echoed as she fell off into a restless slumber.

Where was Xavier?

Chapter Nine

The director permitted Lauren to use the Thompson Community Center on Sunday afternoon. She met with current and former kids she mentored to go over the details for the upcoming Halloween Fashion Fundraiser.

"Thanks for coming in on your day off," Lauren said to Eddie, the maintenance guy. "I didn't mean to interrupt your workout." She glanced on the sly, admiring Eddie's robust muscles in fitted workout pants and shirt. A marked difference from the oversized work attire she was used to seeing him in.

"Anything for you, Lauren," he said unlocking the doors. "The kids look forward to it."

"And so do I," she replied in a flirty tone that's usually reserved for her husband.

While discussing the boy's wardrobes and colors, James Townsend popped up. He had known gang affiliations, but Lauren looked beyond that, even though she despised his father for molesting Shawn as a little girl.

James was an innocent child when the incident took place, but she couldn't say that now. He gravitated to the crooked path, which meant he needed the Thompson Center's guidance more than the average kid.

The older James got, the more he favored his father, which Lauren believed triggered her nightmares. But she couldn't allow her issues to influence his involvement with the facility. If his risky lifestyle brought harm into the Thompson Center, then that would be different. Lauren's goal was to bring out the best in him.

She used James' love of numbers to put him in the role of the math tutor. He was a smart kid underneath the hard exterior he portrayed, but it was hard to get that hood mentality to fold.

"I ain't wearing no blue and black, and none of my Lords will be wearing that either." James angled the brim of the baseball cap he wore to the left. "Red and black 'til the day I die."

"James, you know I don't tolerate that foolery up in here, so you'd better check yourself real fast."

Demetrius stood. "Yo dog, it's just for the fashion show. Ain't none of our homies gon' see us no how."

Lauren walked to the center of the room. "I would never put any of you in harm's way. Sometimes you have to step out of your comfort zone and experience something new and different."

"I know I betta not catch you wearing that shit," James threatened, scowling at Demetrius.

"And what the fuck you gone do if I do?" Demetrius said, walking toward James.

The other four boys in the room scooted their chairs back giving James and Demetrius room to go at it.

"Hey! We cussing now?" Lauren bellowed. "Sit down. Right now." She eyeballed both of them. "I'm not playin'. Sit down or get out." She whipped out her phone. "Y'all do know my husband's 5-0 or have y'all forgotten? Sit down." She dialed Xavier anyway, and it rang in her earpiece. He may need to de-escalate this situation once the boys left the Center. "This is not the place for that. This is everybody's temple."

"My bad for using the F-word, but he started it," Demetrius said, plopping in the chair.

"It doesn't matter," she replied, crossing her arms, looking from one to the other.

"Yeah. And I'ma end it if I see you wearing dem colors," James said, pointing his index finger with his thumb sticking up like a gun.

"Bye James," Lauren said, squaring off with the taller young man. "And I don't wanna see you back in here until you can show some respect to your peers and me, but most of all yourself."

"Whatever. I wouldn't be seen here or in that fashion show for all the kilos on the block," James shouted, barging out the door.

"Hi, you have reached Xavier Carter…"

* * *

Shawn looked down at the phone. "Candace, it's Patricia. What should I do?" she asked, driving home from Ms. Ida's Bakery in Hyde Park.

"Answer it," Candace replied. "But pull over first before you kill us."

"Okay." Maneuvering to the curb, she answered, "Hello."

"Hi, Ms. Johnston, this is Patricia from MedRx. I am calling to offer you the position if you're still interested."

Squeezing her eyes shut and digging her nails into the palm of her hand, she responded, "Yes. I would love the job."

"That's wonderful. I will see you first thing Monday morning at nine or a little earlier if you can manage so we can do the paperwork."

"I'll be there at eight," Shawn said, ending the call.

"You got it?" Candace asked.

"Yes," Shawn squealed.

"Maybe I should drive. You're gonna kill us on the way home, with your no driving self."

"Whatever."

* * *

"I'm Candace and this here ain't The Cosby's," a skinny girl said walking up to Shawn the first day she arrived at Ms. Ida's, the eighth foster care home that Shawn had landed in over a two-year period. "When I first came here, the girls thought I was the perfect candidate to be picked on. But I showed them who's boss," Candace said glancing at the other foster girls huddled near the television. They peered over their shoulders to check out what was going on and tried to listen in on the conversation. Only one of the girls sat at the end of the couch with her knees pulled to her chest and arms wrapped around her legs.

"What made them think they could come at you any kind of way?" Shawn asked frowning as she took in Candace's caramel skin that was several shades darker than her own, Candace's bony frame was barely holding up the jeans and t-shirt.

Candace rolled up her sleeves displaying an array of scars that marred the skin; some were red and blistered, others had crusty brown scabs that were round in diameter; all of which caused Shawn to gasp. "That's just the ones on my arms. You should see the rest of me. Mom was big on punishment. Short on patience."

"You didn't deserve that," Shawn whispered causing a neutral expression to fall over the other girl's face.

She scanned the new surroundings. It wasn't modern, but it was clean and had a sense of warmth, except for the scowl on a few of the older girl's faces. Brown leather couches faced each other with an Oriental rug in the center. Wood paneling surrounded the room with old artwork and a set of house rules and chores on a corkboard.

Candace cleared her throat and spoke loud enough for everyone to hear. "You don't have anything to worry about as long as I'm around. If one of these *wannabe* bad girls mess with you, just say Shadow."

"Shadow," Shawn repeated, looking at her new friend. "Who's that?"

"Ms. Ida's cat," Candace said with a smile. "Kitty litter mixed with cookies and cream ice cream can send a better message than giving them a beat down ever could."

"You didn't," Shawn whispered, trying to hold back a grin as the girls turned away and put their focus back on the television.

"Damn straight," she shot back, leaning against the wooden and glass china cabinet. "They held me down, and the big one over there cut off my ponytail and flushed it." She grinned when two of the girls glared at them. "After… Shadow, they didn't mess with me ever again. Probably lost a little weight, too."

This time Shawn busted out laughing. And from that day forward, Shawn and Candace were inseparable.

Ms. Ida's home proved to be better than Shawn expected, definitely a step up from the last ones she landed in. She found a best friend in Candace and everything else fell into place for the first couple of years. The information about her biological mother stayed in the recesses of her mind.

Then Ms. Ida fell on hard times, and their basic needs were barely being met. Ms. Ida was the best foster mother either of them had ever had, and they had to make sure the DCFS wouldn't take them from her. With the help of Ms. Ida's biological daughter Taletha, they found a way to make a change in their circumstances that altered the path of their lives.

Shawn tried to keep her focus on the road, but her mind wandered, worrying about how she would connect with Patricia Carter.

Chapter Ten

Patricia fumed, but she tried to push her anger to the background. She took a seat at the breakfast bar, already dressed for work while sipping a cup of morning java to calm the anger settling in when a car pulled up in the driveway.

She ignored the Good Morning America hosts sharing good-natured vibes and jibes as she glanced through the window half-expecting to see Xavier, but Brandon's Nissan Sentra had pulled out front instead.

Her husband had not made it home last night. Nor had he seen it necessary to place a call to at least let her know he was alright and that set her nerves on edge. Patricia resisted the urge to reach out to Jason because it was possible that they were in the middle of something important, but Xavier knew the rules. With the type of career he'd chosen, there were certain things put in place so she would not have sleepless nights or worry unnecessarily.

Evidently, he'd forgotten that critical part of things. What was going on with her husband?

"Junior, your ride's here."

Brandon had been friends with Junior since elementary school. Since the boys were so close, they attended the same karate classes, joined the same park district soccer team, and talked their parents into letting them attend the same high school, even though Junior was accepted into a magnet school on the west side. Brandon was more like a son to Patricia and brother to Junior, and his parents an English Professor and a Pediatrician. Brandon has been on the same track to college as Junior, as long as the young man didn't let his "little head" derail him. Thankfully, Junior wasn't thinking along those lines. He'd been interested in a girl or two, but nothing too serious it had Patricia worried she'd be a grandmother before he walked across the stage to get that diploma.

Junior ran down the stairs as though his boots were on fire.

"Morning, Moms." He bent down to kiss her on the cheek, smelling of Versace Eros, the same cologne her husband wore.

"Good morning, son, you've been hitting your father's stash."

"I thought I smelled coffee," Junior remarked with a perplexed expression.

Patricia lifted her cup, then took a sip. She placed her mug on the counter and wrapped her fingers around it allowing the heat to penetrate her skin. She tried to pretend to be interested in the segment on the screen, but felt Junior's stare, and turned to face him.

"What are you looking at?"

"Welcome back." He laughed. "You decided to stop being British and become an American like the rest of us."

"Be quiet, boy," she said, finding a smile from somewhere deep within. "Just because I'm drinking coffee one day out of the year doesn't mean I've given up my tea."

"So you're still hanging out with the Winston Churchill crew?" Junior joked.

"Absolutely," she shot back in a fake British accent.

They erupted in laughter. Junior slung his backpack over his right shoulder and grabbed a banana out of the crystal fruit bowl.

"See ya later, Mom."

She lifted her mug, stuck out her pinky finger and gave him a Princess Diana wave.

Laughing, Junior rushed toward the front door and was caught off guard when it opened to an impressive figure on the other side.

"Morning Pops."

Junior made a move to step around him, but Xavier pulled him into a tight embrace.

"What's with the mushy stuff?" Junior's words were muffled because his face was embedded in his father's neck. "You're smothering me."

Patricia rose, observing the awkward moment and walked over to them. Xavier was extremely affectionate with her but rarely hugged their son. They were men, and he said that men don't hug other men.

She corrected him on that when Junior was a little boy, telling him, "You need to show him some love, hug him every once in a while."

"That's what he has a momma for," Xavier protested. "My job is to teach him how to be a man."

"It wouldn't kill you to wrap your arms around him," she had said from the bedroom of the apartment they shared back then. "He needs to feel your love and acceptance."

"We speak our own language, Patty," Xavier countered. He knows I love him. I would lay down my life for this boy. Just because I don't show it the way, you think I should don't mean that I don't."

Well, now she had to figure out why she wasn't getting even the respect of a simple phone call. Affection was secondary to respect.

"What's going on, Xavier?"

She gauged his body language, and he seemed distressed. She touched the hands that held on to Junior like a papa bear shielding its cub from harm.

"Whatever it is, Junior will be alright," she said after a few moments had passed. Too long— since Junior gave her a pleading look and then a nod toward his watch. "Let him go, honey."

Patricia continued to comfort him with her soft voice while she alternated rubbing and patting his hand. Xavier slowly released his son. Tears glazed his tired eyes, and her heart broke.

Junior looked from his mother to his father, frowning.

She nudged him. "Go on to school, Brandon's waiting."

Patricia gave Xavier's hands a light squeeze, and he stepped out of the doorway.

"I love you, son," Xavier called after him.

"I love you too, Pops." Junior locked eyes with Patricia silently questioning his father's actions.

She'd find out soon enough.

Patricia closed the door behind their son and led Xavier to the kitchen. She pulled out the bar stool next to hers, and he absently took a seat, almost as if sitting required too much work. She poured him a cup of coffee—black with two sugars; while trying to hold her tongue. Would whatever was going on with him be something he was unable to talk about?

This quiet was unlike him, but he'd always been a little reserved, almost as if he was going through the motions of being married. Sometimes Patricia wondered what would have happened if she had listened to her sister's warning. Right before Patricia landed on Fisk campus, Latrice mentioned a guy who was sexy as hell but was the biggest man-whore on campus. She had warned Patricia more than once to steer clear of him. After so many others had also given her the same advice, Patricia had sworn off men— bad boys in particular.

That all changed the day, he ran into her at John Hope Library. The smooth basketball star approached her with a swagger, confidence, and charm like none other. Patricia was caught up from the moment he flashed that smile and said his name. But what made him seem more than just the sum of his parts—or one specific part, was his keen interest in her plans and the fact that he provided her with some thoughts on getting to her goals faster than she had anticipated. They talked a great deal about his family who had a long history in law enforcement, as well as how he was embracing the family career but wanted things to work differently for him.

The Xavier she talked with on a daily basis after that chance meeting was the exact opposite of the man Latrice and the dorm mates had told her about. Unlike the others who were singing the low down dirty blues, he was a gentleman and treated Patricia like she was the only woman on the planet. When she wasn't cramming for a test, and he wasn't working, or at basketball practice, Xavier wined and dined her, and he was inventive about doing so within a college budget. They drove around Nashville in his noisy Escort taking in the sites soaking up the town's history and nightlife.

Patricia knew she had fallen for him when she told Xavier about the change in plans where she would attend UIC College of Pharmacy back home in Chicago after undergrad, instead of Bill Gatton College of Pharmacy in Johnson City, Tennessee. When she mentioned it would require a lot of hard work and that dating anyone would be impossible; he didn't seem bothered.

"It's all good," Xavier had said. "While you'll be chasing your dream of becoming a pharmacist, I'll be chasing mine of becoming a *Chicago* cop." He shrugged and gave her that beautiful smile she'd come to love. "I'll be joining the Police Academy after graduation."

In other words, it wouldn't be a long distance relationship if she wanted to pursue something real. Patricia ignored all the naysayers who were waiting for her to have her heart broken as theirs had been. Women and men alike were eyeing their dating activities—the guys were waiting their turn with one of Xavier's leftovers. Easy pickings after Xavier had dogged them out and made them feel worthless. That would never be the case with Patricia Antoinette Taylor. He respected the fact that she didn't want to have sex until after marriage. What man as desirable as Xavier would choose to do that? He could have any girl he wanted, and he chose a brown-skinned girl from the south side.

Latrice and these others didn't know what they were talking about. At least she felt that way then, but lately, their marriage had seemed not quite as perfect as it had been—if perfect was even the right word to call it. Predictable? She had to wonder if he'd gotten into something that he couldn't talk about or if he'd embraced his former ways.

She wanted to rip into him, but she could see that something was amiss. She would hold her feelings at bay.

"Here you go." She placed the steaming cup in front of him and took a seat by his side.

"Thank you."

Patricia waited, turning down the volume on the television, letting the tension gradually ease, knowing that he would, as always, open up on his own. She found much comfort in the fact that they had always been able to communicate with little effort. Except for the past few days, when he seemed more guarded than usual.

He frowned, causing his forehead and nose to wrinkle. "Are you drinking ... *coffee*?"

She fluttered her eyelashes at him and said, "Yes."

"What brought that on?"

Oh, maybe because my husband doesn't know how to use a phone. "You sound like Junior," she teased. "I can mix it up now and then. Stop acting like y'all know me," Patricia said, giving him a "sister girl" head rock.

Xavier let out a hearty laugh, and she smiled at being able to pull one from him. She caressed his thigh, and in unison, they sipped their coffee then placed their mugs on the bar.

He leaned over and whispered in her ear, "Thank you for always taking care of Junior and me." He kissed her temple and slowly stroked her cheek, eliciting a shiver of pleasure.

Drawing away, he rested his elbows on the breakfast bar and folded his hands under his chin. "A little boy was shot and killed by one of our own last night. He couldn't have been no more than ten years old."

She gasped, taking in the implications of what that could mean for him and his unit. And why had this one affected him more than any others? "That's the fourth kid shot by law enforcement in the past two months."

Xavier nodded, his expression grave and worried.

"What the devil is going on in our city?" Patricia swiveled off the barstool. "What is this? The extinction of the black man." She didn't need to say anything behind that, though her thoughts panned to. It was bad enough with the gun violence and gang wars, but now the police were worse than the thugs. They were killing off our sons before they even reached puberty.

Chapter Eleven

Shawn leaned closer to the bathroom mirror, barely able to apply eyeliner and a touch of light pink lip-gloss, which made her lips shimmer. "I'm so nervous," she admitted to Candace as she pressed her lips together. She let the bristles tingle her scalp for the third time, and her silky strands fell graciously down her back to her shoulder blades.

"If you *brush your hair* one more time." Candace's warning words were muffled from talking around the toothbrush working steadily in her mouth. She gave Shawn the side eye, then spit the toothpaste out into the sink.

Shawn sighed and chuckled, then opened the wooden drawer under the sink and placed the brush inside. She swiftly angled, facing Candace who was wearing a yellow tank top and matching pajama pants that would soon be swapped out for the navy and powder blue CTA uniform she'd been wearing for five years. "I can't believe it's Monday already. Look at me. My hands are shaking," she said stretching her arms out, watching her fingers tremble involuntarily. She pulled them to her stomach and placed them there, along the maroon scrubs that the pharmacy shipped after she received the call from Patricia and accepted the position.

"My belly's doing flips," she whispered, bawling her fingers into a fist.

Candace rinsed her mouth, dabbed at the wet skin with a washcloth then turned to Shawn, grabbing her hands in her own.

"You've been waiting your whole life for this," she said, and her voice held none of its earlier sarcasm. "You're supposed to be nervous. It's okay."

Shawn embraced the one person she knew understood her plight, especially when their lives had started on such a rocky plain.

* * *

The first time Shawn had set foot in Ms. Ida's foster home, Candace Livingston gave her the lay of the land, not the matronly woman who would control Shawn's life for the next six years. Shawn promised to try her hardest to follow the rules. She didn't want to keep being bounced around as so many other children had. The tales that some of the children told were horrific, at least she'd never had anyone molest her, and she'd managed to keep all of her things, especially from moving around so much when many others had their things stolen. The women in these places had been indifferent and overwhelmed, letting the kids fend for themselves. Some had taken it too far. Shawn had to take a broom to one of the boys who thought she was easy prey.

The girls in Ms. Ida's home weren't all that bad after Shawn got to know them. Like her, they were wary of the system and having to adjust to new people, new living spaces, and being at the mercy of other people deciding their fates.

Like her grandmother who crocheted hats and scarfs, Ms. Ida also had a hobby. In the evenings after dinner, Ms. Ida, a brown-skinned woman of ageless beauty would sit at the kitchen table for hours combing over old family baking recipes. That woman made the best tasting cakes, pies, cookies, and bread Shawn had ever put in her mouth. On the nights that Shawn didn't have kitchen duty, she would help Ms. Ida rewrite those recipes and file them away.

Shawn asked tons of questions and took a genuine interest in baking the desserts Ms. Ida made to send out to people who weren't feeling well. She, along with Candace, learned how to knead the dough, use a rolling pin, and were taught the difference between baking flour versus cake flour, and spices that brought out particular tastes to the product. All that went into creating the wonderful treats she and the other girls loved to eat fascinated her. Ms. Ida even let Shawn bake on her own on Sunday afternoons after they returned home from the church that everyone in the house attended. Ms. Ida said they all needed some faith to hold on to. Faith. Yes. That was something that Shawn held onto. Faith that she'd be reunited with her biological mother.

Gradually things changed when Ms. Ida was laid off from the bank, five years before she was set to retire from the place she'd worked as a commercial credit analyst. The refrigerator that once overflowed with an abundance of food was now a little short in that area. The heat had been shut off, but thankfully the electricity was still going strong. Bill collectors called on the regular. Shawn noticed the sparkle missing from Ms. Ida's eyes when she gathered the ingredients to bake, something the woman loved almost as much as the children in her care. She used to hum gospel hymns and taught Shawn different browning and creaming techniques. Now she sat quietly going through the motions aimlessly and forced a smile when she caught Shawn or any of the girls looking her way.

The money Ms. Ida did receive was used to keep the house from going into something called "foreclosure." Some was put aside for the girls to buy the things they wanted, but now that the older girls aged out and were placed into independent living facilities and no other children had been placed in Ms. Ida's home, the money was disappearing a lot faster than usual. Even the church Ms. Ida attended only helped with food, but none of that tithe money she'd paid in that helped other families during their time of need, was available when she needed it most. How was that for faith?

Ms. Ida had always seemed to have a bounce to her step when the girls were around, but Shawn watched her one evening when she thought everyone was asleep. Ms. Ida sat at the kitchen table with a rosary looped between her fingers. The woman cried and prayed for help. She didn't want to lose her girls, nor did she want to lose her house.

That evening Shawn woke up everyone and had them come to that back bedroom after Ms. Ida went to bed. The three remaining girls sat on the floor, huddled around the space heater wearing skullcaps with blankets wrapped around them. "We have to find a way to help Ms. Ida," Shawn said, scooting closer to the heater. "We can't keep living like this. They're going to take us from her the minute that social service lady comes to check out the house in a few weeks."

Taletha rubbed her hands together in front of the heater, her expression solemn and anxious. Though she was Ms. Ida's biological daughter, she treated Candace and Shawn as if they were blood sisters and not just girls passing through. "I heard mom on the phone making arrangements with the light company earlier today."

"That's not okay," Candace said, pulling her body into a tight ball. "What can we do?"

"What if we hosted a bake sale during lunch?" Shawn asked blowing warm air into her hands. "I bet we could make a lot of money."

"That's cool," Candace agreed. "I'll make flyers on the computer at school with the items and prices and post them around the lunchroom. And I'll ask the secretary to make an announcement over the PA after we say the Pledge of Allegiance."

"Yeah. And you and Candace can also bake while I'm at choir

practice with mom on Friday nights," Taletha said, tucking the blanket under her feet. "We should have more than what we need to get through the week—maybe more."

"Wait a minute," Candace said, scooting closer to the heater. "How are we gonna pull that off and the stove doesn't work?"

"What about Ms. Adams?" Shawn suggested. "She'll help us."

"I don't know Shawn," Taletha said. "Mama will kill us if she knew we told Ms. Adams her business."

"Then we'd be out in the cold, for real," Candace teased, but no one laughed.

"I already baked snacks for us for the week on Sundays before the gas was cut off. I'll do the same at Ms. Adams house, but I'll triple the amount and store the extras in my room. That way we won't be inconveniencing her too much. Don't worry. I'll ask her."

Ms. Adams was close to Ms. Ida, but not close enough where she knew what was going on in their home. She was also the neighborhood gossip, and the girls couldn't risk her blabbing their business and it getting back to Ms. Ida, so Shawn came up with a better idea.

"Let's tell Ms. Adams we're trying to raise money for a birthday gift for Ms. Ida," Shawn suggested. "Her birthday's next month."

"That'll work," Candace agreed.

"We can tell mom that we got the money from the allowance she made us save," Taletha said. "She's circled a baker's rack in a Fingerhut Magazine. Maybe we can get it for her after we get the gas back on. Mom would love that."

Ms. Adams allowed the girls to use her kitchen as needed and promised to keep their secret. She contributed by selling the baked treats at the post office where she worked, raking in as much as the girls in less time, and she gave all the funds to the young ladies. In no time, the girls had consistent money coming in, saving it up to set Ms. Ida's finances straight.

Shawn, who had also started the search for her father in any spare time, was having a hard time keeping up with demand.

Candace and Taletha had to help out on Sundays. Shawn told Ms. Ida that Ms. Adams was teaching them more about baking as an explanation to why they spent so much time next door. Ms. Ida was so happy the girls were enjoying her favorite pastime that she purchased another mixer, spatulas and mixing bowls with points she earned on her credit card. That was more of a blessing than she knew. When needed, Shawn used some of the money they made to buy extra ingredients, saran wrap, clear plastic storage bags, and ribbons.

The first order of business was for them to use everything they earned in a week to make the arrangements needed for the gas company. Ms. Ida had instilled in them that they should never open anyone else's mail, so they had to get "creative" in getting the information they needed. Since Shawn had the more mature voice, the girls agreed that while Ms. Ida was out searching for work, she would be the one to intercept the phone calls from the bill collectors. She found out how much was due, had *them* "verify" the account numbers, where to mail the payments, or where to make the payments in person. Unfortunately, of all the bills, the gas company was one that required a letter of authorization for anyone else to make the payments. They did what they had to do.

Ms. Ida knew something was up when People Gas rang the doorbell to turn the gas meter on.

"This must be some type of mistake," Ms. Ida said.

Shawn, Candace, and Taletha smiled at one another. She was killing it on the hot plate, but one of Ms. Ida's full meals and a warm house were long overdue.

"That's not possible," Ms. Ida refuted after listening to the customer service rep for a moment. "Paid in full? I haven't paid anything." She fell silent, listening again as the girls looked on.

"By who?" Ms. Ida asked, her voice cracking as she spoke. "I didn't give anyone access to my account," she paused, focusing her eyes on the girls at the kitchen table with million dollar grins on their faces. "Thank you," she said and quickly disconnected the call.

Ms. Ida couldn't speak for a long while as the man worked to get the meter on and then came in, to light the pilot on the furnace. Soon that forced air rattled through the vents, and about thirty minutes later, the winter chill had been swept away.

With tears running down her plump cheeks, she asked, "How?"

Shawn looked at her friends first, who nodded, then explained mostly everything.

Ms. Ida sobbed her relief, then pulled them into her fluffy body and held them in a tight embrace that seemed to go on forever.

"God sent me the perfect angels," she whispered.

"We didn't want to lose you, Ms. Ida," Shawn whispered back. "We've already lost so much. We can't lose you, too. No way. No how."

Ms. Ida kissed each of their foreheads before letting them go. She inhaled, and pulled off her glasses, tilted her head down, then placed her hands on her wide hips. "I understand why you did this, but don't y'all *ever* forge my signature on anything *ever* again. It worked out this time, but it might get you into trouble at some point. That's how my cousin ended up doing five years in Club Fed." Shifting her eyes to each girl, she said, "Got it?"

——"Yes ma'am."

Everyone's head turned toward the front of the house at the sound of the doorbell. "I got it," Taletha shouted, running to the front door. "Ma. It's for you."

"Who is it?"

"FedEx."

"I didn't order anything," Ms. Ida said walking to the living room.

Shawn nudged Candace as they followed.

"Delivery for Ida Henderson," the man in the black and purple uniform announced, extending the palm pilot. "Sign here, please."

The man met his co-worker at the truck, and they carried a huge box inside the house. "Have a good day, ma'am."

"Thank you," Ms. Ida said closing the door. She turned to her three little angels who looked like they got caught with their hands in the cookie jar.

"Happy early birthday," they sang, throwing their arms around Ms. Ida.

* * *

"Thanks for the words of encouragement," Shawn said, releasing Candace from the embrace.

"Now you'd better go before your butt's late for your first day."

"Okay, I'm leaving." Shawn eased by Candace and went into her bedroom, and turned the cord on the mini blinds to allow the sunshine to come through, casting a shadow on the taupe walls. She dropped a notepad and ballpoint pens in a brand new tote bag she'd purchased for her first day at work. On her way out of the bedroom, Shawn fetched her keys from the dresser and took a deep breath. She gazed at the old crinkled picture of both of her mothers holding her when she was a newborn that had been stuck in the crease of her full-length mirror. She raised her hand, stroked it gently with the tips of her fingers.

"Thank you for making this possible," she whispered, focusing on the woman who raised her. "I love you always."

Then her mind turned to the woman she would encounter at work today and wondered if she had done the right thing.

Chapter Twelve

Lauren was in trouble. Two months had elapsed since she received that early refill on her meds from Dr. Harden. She had been seeing a new physician since Dr. Harden abruptly cut her off. Unfortunately, this new dude was more of a stickler for the rules than her primary doctor. He never allowed early refills, so she'd been forced to adjust her frequency. Instead of a whole tablet, sometimes she'd cut one in half and take a teaspoonful of liquid Benadryl with it to achieve the same results—a dangerous combination.

The possibilities of not having any sleeping pills and the nightmares that were sure to follow consumed Lauren to the point that she could hardly focus on the event being held tonight.

The media crews arrived early and were setting up for the epic event, which had been advertised at zero cost to her on the local networks and radio stations. She was grateful for the connections she had made doing community service over the years. This was her time, and every year the donations increased, and all of the proceeds went directly to The Thompson Community Center.

Lauren paid the vendors, private security, and staff out of her business account. Last year they raised enough money to build a new gymnasium. This year they were hoping to purchase fifty new computers and twenty smart boards for the classrooms and offices. The *Chicago Tribune* ran an article labeling her "an ambassador for Chicago's youth."

Lauren disappeared into the back office, closed and locked the door to escape the music booming through the speakers while the hired crew rearranged the salon. They took out the stylists chairs, set up a platform stage, and other tasks she had slated for them. She had to make an urgent call before the place became chaotic. Lauren tapped her red bottom five-inch heels as she waited for the call to connect, then she grabbed a tissue and patted the dots of perspiration that peppered her forehead.

"Dr. Harden speaking," a high-pitched voice finally came through.

"Hi Dr. Harden, it's Lauren Carter," she said, gripping the phone, sending a silent prayer for mercy.

A brief pause, then, "Hello Mrs. Carter. It's been a while. How are you?"

"I'm doing alright. Getting ready for the fundraiser. I hope you can make it this year."

"I received my invite via courier," she replied. "Thank you, but I won't be able to attend, but I will make a donation, as always. What you're doing for our youth is wonderful, and you're making a difference in our community. These kids are blessed to have you looking out for them." There was a shuffle of papers and then, "I know you're not calling every single attendee to make sure they show up. Or am I just special?"

The typically outspoken, decisive, straight to the point Lauren was now fumbling over the words she needed to say. Finally, she managed. "I know you said that last time was the last time that you would refill my prescription, but I really need it. I don't have any left. If you can give me just one more month, I promise I'll get off them completely."

A weary sigh on the other end tumbled any hope of success. "Ms. Carter, we've had this same conversation every month. You need an early refill for some reason or another." She paused as though realizing frustration had tempered her tone. "Have you tried the alternatives that I suggested?"

"Yes," Lauren lied, grimacing as she did, but the thought of having those nightmares invade her memories tonight spurred her own. "I haven't had any for almost two months. I tried the melatonin, and it didn't do much for me, but I take a Benadryl tablet one to two times a week and drink warm herbal tea every night before I go to bed. That has helped a lot. In the beginning, I thought it wouldn't do much, but I'm happy that I listened to you." As she paced back and forth, her heels clattered rhythmically against the ceramic floor in smooth strides. Perspiration threatened to ruin her dress. She should have made the call before she came to the salon. "It's just that this is a big night for me with the gala and I'm so wound that none of the usual stuff is going to work, and I'll need a little extra help, that's all."

Lauren ran her fingers through the flawless style that Donny, her main stylist, had given her a little while earlier.

She flinched at the sound of a hard knock at the office door. Xavier shouted her name over the music, and she rushed to unlock the entry to her haven to let him in. She closed the door but placed an index finger to his full lips. He puckered his lips against her finger and winked.

"It doesn't have to be a full month's supply," she continued. "I just need a few tablets to get me through tonight and the next couple of nights until my schedule returns to normal. Please."

Lauren stared at Xavier who frowned at her pleading tone.

"I'll call you in *one dose* for tonight and one tomorrow evening around seven. It's time for your annual physical anyway. We'll do a full round of labs, schedule your mammogram and a visit with your gynecologist. I can give you a few samples, but this—is—it. I won't do another refill."

Lauren pumped her fist in the air, and her bangles jingled. She smiled so wide that her cheeks hurt. Thank God for 24-hour MedRx.

"Thank you so much," she said on a relieved note. "I'll be there first thing Monday morning."

Relieved, she tossed the phone on the padded mat that protected the smoky tempered glass on her desk, then scooted closer to Xavier. She stroked a manicured hand across his firm chest, paying extra attention to the nipples. His hand rested on the small of her back as he pulled her into him; their bodies molded together. His erection pressed against her middle, and she shivered from the jolt of exhilaration that shot from her head to her feet. He nibbled her earlobe and traced the side of her neck with a warm, teasing tongue. Closing her eyes, she tingled from the sensuality of her husband's touch and moaned.

Another knock on the door snapped her back to reality.

"Excuse me, Ms. Carter," a thick voice spoke loudly. "What do you want me to do with the extra chairs?"

She breathed heavily and reluctantly stepped away from Xavier while straightening her clothes.

"Just a second."

She glanced over her shoulder at Xavier before addressing the hardworking young man on the other side of the door. "Do I look okay?"

He nodded.

The latch clicked, and she twisted the knob, cracking it a little to find a tall and husky man on the other side. "Lynette can handle that. If you or anyone else in your crew have any other questions or concerns, you can take them up with her."

The young man nodded and quickly scurried away. She shut and locked the door, leaning her back against the cold steel, taking a deep breath. Xavier approached her with stealth moves more like a lion in heat stalking its queen.

Lauren sized Xavier up; his body was delectable in a powder-blue button-down shirt that showed off his muscles and black slacks that made his firm rear stand out like a sculpted work of art. As much as she wanted to devour and savor him, now wasn't the time. Lauren had a salon full of people and money to raise. He bent to kiss her, and she maneuvered her face, brushing against his skin, and kissed his cheek instead.

"So are you staying for the fashion show?" she asked, already knowing the answer would disappoint.

Her words made him tense; then his shoulders slumped in defeat. "You know I can't," he replied gazing into her eyes as he unbuttoned her blouse.

Lauren plucked his hand and tossed it aside before walking to her personal bathroom. "Why not?" She turned and narrowed her gaze on him. "And don't tell me that mumbo jumbo about not wanting to be seen on TV."

He sighed wearily and followed her. "It's not that I don't want to, you know I can't risk blowing my cover."

The same words he always came up with when she wanted to show off her husband to the world. "It would be nice to pose as a united front for a change. Everyone hears about how awesome and supportive you are, but it would be wonderful to put a face with the name." She sighed, turning on the water. "It would also help boost the morale of the Chicago Police Department, with all the corruption going on lately. Any and all positive publicity can contribute to regaining the trust of the people. And what better way to do so than being a part of a function that's giving back to the community. The *Black* community. This is a win for both of us."

Lauren showered, making sure she was garden fresh after having done so much work on getting everything in order, kicking herself because that's all she seemed to be doing for the last hour. First Dr. Harden, now her husband. He stood an inch behind Lauren and lifted the hair up off of her ears while she put on her dazzling earrings.

"Can't you stay in the background? Blend in with the spectators," she pleaded. "No one knows who you are. I just want you here with me."

"It is too risky, baby. All it takes is for *one* person with a camera phone to snap my pic and post it on social media." Xavier released the strands so they could reclaim their place at the tip of her earlobes. "I may be in the background, but someone might recognize my face, and it's all over from there." Then he grinned. "You know your fashion show is the talk of the town. The networks will be airing coverage for at least two weeks."

Lauren recognized the subtle move of trying to use praise to make her give up on the request. "This undercover detective stuff is ruining my life."

He chuckled, wrapped his arms around her waist, and rested his chin on her shoulder, then gazed into those amber eyes in the mirror. "You know you're sexy as ever when you can't get your way."

She smirked, still not feeling his profession, which was more of a nuisance than she cared to admit. "That's what they all say."

"What?" he remarked and raised an eyebrow.

Some employees had gotten a glimpse of him. Only Shawn or Chipmunk as he liked to call her, saw Xavier on the regular. He barely met Lauren's parents before they tied the knot in New York, then he had to rush back to Chicago for another one of those "assignments."

He stood to his full height and gaped at her. She winked at him while toweling her stomach dry.

Without warning, he tickled her, and she laughed.

"Don't be giving me a hard time," he teased while she squirmed trying to get away.

"Xavier stop," she squealed, but he wouldn't let up.

She was at his mercy. He had her boxed in between his massive form and the glass sink. She would probably have a better chance at breaking through the drywall than attempting to get around two hundred and sixty pounds of pure muscle. His body was sculpted like the Greek God Poseidon—solid, powerful, and strong, but his touch was soft and gentle—soothing and provided a world of comfort. Always.

"I submit." Lauren giggled. "I can't take it anymore." She tried to escape his chamber of torture by using laughter to distract him.

"You submit, huh?" he asked staring at her with a devilish twinkle in his eyes.

"Stop looking at me like that," she spouted through chuckles. "I have to get ready."

She bumped him with her rear end, and he turned her around, lifted her hourglass frame and placed her on top of the sink.

"What are you doing?" Lauren asked as she positioned her legs around his hips and pulled him closer.

"You told me to stop, so I stopped." Then he deeply kissed her.

Moisture flooded Lauren's honeypot, and it throbbed as she passionately canoodled with her husband like a teenage girl making out with her high school sweetheart. She moaned, and Xavier pulled away.

"Where are you going?" she asked in a breathy voice.

"You have to get ready," he taunted, pulling her legs from around his waist and repositioning himself in his trousers. "I'll let you get to it."

"You're so wrong for that." Lauren's chest had heaved with indignation before she hopped down from the sink. Thoroughly aroused, she pressed her thighs together, trying to contain the pulsing sensations and moisture between her legs. Now she'd have to take another shower. "I got you, boo. I gotcha," she warned, pointing the finger at him.

* * *

"Hurry up, Junior," Patricia shouted from her bedroom. "We're going to be late for the ceremony."

"I'm coming." Junior entered his parents' room. "I can't get this tie right. Where's Pops?"

"I don't know, but he'll be here soon." Patricia pulled out the vanity bench. "Sit." She stood behind Junior, lifted the white collar, then fixed his red and blue tie.

Junior folded the collar and mumbled, "Thanks" as he called his dad. "Pops. Where are you? The ceremony starts in thirty minutes. We're waiting on you."

"Let me talk to your father," Patricia said, grabbing for the phone.

"It's voicemail."

Patricia sighed, her disappointment evident. "Get your suit jacket and meet me in the car."

"He's gonna miss it." Junior shuffled out the room.

"I promise. He'll be there."

Patricia grabbed her purse and headed to the car. If he missed his son's induction into the National Honor Society, she would never forgive him. She had been trying to reach Xavier for over an hour. It was one thing when he was on duty and didn't answer, but he was off today. Patricia tried him one last time before Junior got in the car. The voicemail greeted her, again.

"Where the hell are you? Your son will be heartbroken if you don't show up. It's bad enough that he's going to be late because we stuck around waiting for you. That'll never happen again." Patricia unlocked the doors as Junior approached the car. "I don't know what you're doing, but I know you'd better be there."

* * *

Xavier settled on the plush zebra print sofa while Lauren disrobed and got into the shower. Once the water was running, he turned the phone on, and tons of message alerts from Patricia and Junior came through. He didn't bother to read them. Instead, Xavier flicked the ring button to silent to prevent Lauren from hearing. Then he texted Patricia to let her know he was running late and to go on without him. He would meet them at the school.

He whistled appreciatively as Lauren emerged from the bathroom, looking more like one of the premiere models that were going to rip the runway at the event this evening. She wore a sparkling bronze fitted long-sleeve dress with one shoulder exposed and a killer split on the right side showing off a tantalizing view of leg and thigh. Her makeup was "barely there" and flawless, and her hair styled in a chic bob sweeping over one eye.

"Baby you look stunning," Xavier whispered, giving her the kind of once-over that he did on their wedding night.

"Thanks." She pranced in front of him extending her right leg. Her dress fell to the side, exposing a nice length of her thigh.

He leaned over and kissed her upper leg right where the spilt began and normally the fun did, too.

"Uh uh uh," Lauren warned, waggling her finger. "You can look, but you can't touch."

"Damn, you're sexy."

"I know," she replied tossing her streaked strawberry blonde hair to the side and placing one hand on her hip. "And you're going to miss every bit of it."

"I'll see it later tonight," he whispered, with the wink of an eye.

"Maybe. And then again some other man with swagger and sex appeal might come and sweep me away."

"I'd like to see them try," he said, all lightness had left his tone, and his face became a hard mask.

"Well, you'd have to actually *be here* to witness it, so I'm not worried."

She swept out of the office, leaving a fiery Xavier behind.

Chapter Thirteen

One hour later the fashion show was going better than she had planned. All the months of planning and stressing out had paid off. The silent auction had raked in twenty grand on its own steam. Lauren walked from behind the black curtain after intermission, and the applause erupted. She waved, then walked to the podium to introduce the second round of female models.

"Weren't the junior models amazing?" she said, speaking into the microphone over the crowd's applause, absorbing the energy of the room. As the clapping simmered, Lauren continued. "These young people dedicated their time, after homework and extracurricular activities, and they practiced endlessly to give us their best. And didn't they shine as bright as the moon in the sky tonight."

A massive round of applause and whistles swept through the salon.

"If you thought that was spectacular, hold on to your seats as the Thompson Center's fashion elite teen female models dazzle you like never before."

Lauren stepped to the side, right as the lights dimmed and the spotlight beamed at the opening curtain. James Townsend walked in wearing an outfit that wasn't exactly right for the occasion. Not all of the kids could afford suits and ties, but this seemed different. She'd make that one of the things to address at the next board meeting. James was a *former* kid at the Thompson Center, given his last outburst, he hadn't stepped foot in the door since. She was surprised but happy he was there especially after their last encounter at the center. James whispered something to Lynette, who was stationed at the front of the salon. Lynette pointed toward the back.

James slithered through the crowd, making his way backstage. Lauren smiled at him as he passed by. He sort of smiled, but quickly averted his eyes, dipping behind the side curtain. A shiver of alarm went through Lauren. Lynette was right behind him, but she hadn't managed to maneuver through the crowd as effortlessly as James did. One guest after another stopped Lynette on her path to follow him.

Lauren leaned into the walkway as Lynette approached. "I'm glad James decided to come. Did he say why he changed his mind?"

"About what?" Lynette asked, eyebrows drawing in.

"About participating."

Lynette stepped back to allow the next model to slide past as she responded, "I thought he was already a part of the show. He just asked me if Demetrius was here, so I sent——"

"Oh no." Lauren covered her mouth, and a sinking feeling hit the pit of her stomach.

"Did I do something wrong?"

Applause rang out as a tall, but curvy girl walked the stage in a white pants suit with a lime cape blazer and blinged-out gold stilettos.

"No, but we need to get to the back quick." Lauren smiled and applauded, turning to duck behind the side curtain.

Lynette grabbed her arm, holding her in place. "Wait. Don't you have to introduce the next segment?"

"Shit!" Lauren stomped her heel into the floor. "Go get him, Lynette. Go get him *now*."

Lauren ascended the stairs on the raised platform stage, grabbing the microphone off the podium, saying, "Let's give another round of applause for the beautiful young ladies of the Thompson Community Center. Did they strut their stuff or what?" She smiled, sweeping a look across the full room, but anxiety was tap dancing in her mind. "Be on the lookout Tyra Banks, some of America's Next Top Models have just graced our stage." After the applause had died down, Lauren continued, "If you thought the girls were a treat, get ready to be even more dazzled by the debonair young men coming——"

A loud uproar backstage overtook anything Lauren said. Her head snapped toward the black curtain, which fell from the ceiling with the ease of a leaf gliding to the ground on a fall day. Gasps echoed from every corner where the spectators sat. The stage was flooded with kids running and screaming. Panic set in. Chaos was keeping it company.

"He's got a gun," a girl shouted, nearly tripping in high heels and getting caught in the form-fitting evening gown.

Chairs tumbled over as the spectators and models rushed to the exit, trapping security and keeping them from coming toward Lauren. Lauren pushed her way through everyone in an effort to get backstage but was tackled by Demetrius who ran into her with his arms flung open.

A hard click and a thunderous boom filled the room.

Demetrius gulped for breath. His handsome features formed an agonizing mask. He toppled Lauren to the ground with a hard thud. Her head smacked the aluminum floor, and a headache followed at a rhythmic throb. Slowly glancing to the side, her gaze landed on Shawn crouched behind a chair near the far left wall. Shawn's wide green eyes were laced with fear, a fear similar to the one that Lauren had seen before.

"Ms. Lauren," Shawn yelled, scanning the area before leaving that safe spot. She rushed to Lauren's side. "Somebody help me," she screamed, then pulled her phone out of the bustier, and it fell in a pool of blood, splattering some on Shawn's face and dress. With trembling hands, she scooped it up and dialed.

"I. I can't breathe," Lauren mumbled in uneven gasps.

Shawn dropped the phone, pushed Demetrius's body trying to free Lauren, to no avail. He was too heavy for Shawn to move without assistance. "Hellllp," she screamed.

Lynette came running from the back. "Dear God, Demetrius." She gasped at the gaping hole in his back and shuddered. "James did this?"

Shawn gaze darted from one area to the next. "Where is he?"

"He ran out the back way."

"Are you sure?"

"Yeah."

"Help me move him," Shawn commanded gesturing toward Demetrius.

Lynette went to the opposite side. "Push him up from your side, and I'll roll him over, okay."

After several attempts, Demetrius toppled over. Relief filled their faces at the small victory until a gurgling sound caught their attention. Shawn glanced down and froze at the sight of blood spouting out of Lauren like a geyser.

"Oh my God," Shawn shrieked. "She's been shot."

Chapter Fourteen

Xavier had peeled out of the fundraiser like he was O.J. Simpson on the 405, and headed straight to St. Francis High School. Junior was being inducted into The National Honor Society, and he couldn't be more pleased with his son's accomplishments. Junior reminded Xavier of himself at that age. He was every parent's dream child—a stellar student, an outstanding athlete, and an all-around good kid, who managed not to get caught up with gangs or drugs, or knock up some girl who didn't have the presence of mind to keep her legs closed.

He paused at the top of the stairs in the rear of the fully occupied auditorium and quickly scanned to find the other person who mattered. Patricia was two rows from center stage with an empty seat to her right. He silenced his phone knowing that Lauren wouldn't call him until later that evening. She was going to be plenty busy working her fundraiser collecting rich people's money.

"Hi honey," he whispered, pecking her on the cheek and taking his seat. "Did I miss anything?"

"Junior accepted his award already," she whispered back, but there was no mistaking her angry tone.

Fuck.

"I'm sorry," he mumbled. "I got caught in traffic."

Patricia eyeballed Xavier so hard he thought he would melt into the chair. She gave him a wry smile, then shifted in her seat and crossed one thick brown leg over the other opposite him and firmly clutched her purse as if he was going to make off with the darn thing. She didn't say another word, and he knew better than to try any further explanation.

He surveyed the stage and sought out Junior among the other inductees and quickly waved. Junior smiled and waved back with a lot more enthusiasm at his presence than his mother had.

Toward the end of the ceremony, Xavier's phone began vibrating like crazy, but he couldn't justify taking a call when he knew Patty was already livid. He glanced at it the first couple of times to make sure it wasn't the job. Unfortunately, it was worse. *So much for being busy*. The minute the applause died down, he slipped out into the hall and returned Lauren's call, but it went straight to voicemail. Three times.

After the program, the school served light refreshments in the newly remodeled cafeteria. Xavier pulled Junior to the side before he reached his mother and said, "I'm proud of you son." He gave Junior an affectionate slap on the back.

"Thanks, Pops."

"National Honor Society," Xavier said, reading Junior's framed certificate. "This is great. Another step in securing the university of *your* choice," Xavier nudged Junior. "Hopefully it's Fisk."

Junior sighed, "I don't know about that. Maybe Harvard or Yale."

"Those are excellent choices as well." Xavier raised an eyebrow, "But no HBCU's?"

"I didn't say that, Pops. We'll see." Junior squinted, staring at Xavier's neck. "I still have two years to figure it out."

"Why are you looking at me like that?" Xavier asked.

Junior pointed. "You got something pink on your collar." He took the certificate out of Xavier's hands. "I'm going to show this to Moms."

Xavier adjusted his collar. A creamy pink residue was on his fingertips. *Shit.* Xavier ducked into the men's room. Lauren's lipstick was all over the right side of his neck and collar. He wet a brown paper towel and scrubbed what he could away. He made the mark in the shirt worse than it was.

You have got to be kidding me.

The harder he wiped, the more it smeared. Xavier put on his leather coat and zipped it all the way up before leaving the bathroom.

Patricia was her usual jovial self, well, when talking and laughing with other parents. As soon as Xavier approached, she practically turned to ice. He didn't know if anyone else paid attention, but the disdain was evident.

Xavier mingled with some of the parents, finding that a few of them were curious about last week's shooting. Most of the questions he couldn't answer with the investigation still underway, but he understood their concerns, especially with the Black Lives Matter movement being misconstrued.

When the gathering dissipated to a point the place was nearly empty, Patricia finally had no choice but to leave. Xavier walked his family to the car, opening the door for her and she settled into the driver's seat—all without saying a word to him. Not even a polite, *thank you.*

He sighed, hopped in the truck to tail them home, then placed the phone on the dashboard. The Fashion Show should be in full swing by now, so he didn't understand the three missed calls from Lauren. He knew that she wanted him there, but he'd always made it clear that wasn't possible. Xavier didn't bother to check the messages or texts.

Unlike his tigress Lauren, Patty would never cause a scene in public, but the silent treatment was a sure sign of what awaited once they got home. He pulled into the driveway behind her and Junior and scurried to make it in time to open the door, but she had already gotten out of the car and left the door wide open. He gently closed it and fell in step with Junior.

Patricia was leaning against the red brick blocking the entry door to their home with her arms folded, her gaze hard and unyielding. She moved to the side when Xavier approached. She might be upset, but not enough to forget the family's safety protocol. When Xavier wasn't around, Junior did the honors of entering the house first as a safety precaution. He knew how to use a gun, and could quickly get to the one he had locked and stashed in the foyer, but Xavier hoped that was never the case. Certainly, he'd rather his family remained breathing and telling the story, rather than dead, buried and unable to tell no lies.

Junior headed straight to the fridge and grabbed the rectangular glass dish of lasagna, garlic bread, and the pitcher of fruit punch.

"My goodness boy," Xavier said from his spot near the counter. "Didn't you just eat?"

"That was rabbit food, Pops," Junior said pulling out the big serving spoon. "I'm about to eat some of the dinner Moms made earlier today."

Shoot, I missed dinner too.

"You better make sure I get some of that."

"Yours is in the microwave," he said, digging the large spoon into the gooey entrée. "Moms made you a plate before we left."

Damn. Xavier thought he would have time to address this wrong, but when he turned to speak to Patricia, she had already disappeared. Then the master bedroom door slammed.

Junior gave him a long look, lowered his gaze to Xavier's collar, stuffed his mouth and shook his head.

* * *

Patricia dropped down on the bed, listening to the rant on the other end of the line, and wished she had never made the call. She never took her sister for the jealous type but was beginning to wonder if this lingering mistrust of Xavier had anything to do with the fact that Xavier had proven Latrice wrong and had been an excellent husband and father. Even though she was upset, she still had to give him that.

Three years on campus and when it seemed that their relationship was going the distance, Latrice still had something to say. Her sister, a slim beauty with light-brown eyes, a lovely smile, and dimples deep enough to swim in, always had men fawning over her. Patricia couldn't understand why Latrice couldn't be happy for her. She had finally landed a man who had matured and appreciated the woman Patricia was becoming. Besides her high school sweetheart Matthew, Patricia hadn't been with anyone else. She wrapped herself and her feelings in a bubble and swore off men after the painful experience with Matthew and agonizing forced adoption of their daughter.

Latrice had been the one to encourage Patricia to "get back out there and start dating again." Evidently, Patricia didn't understand the rules that it had to be done Latrice's way. The moment Patricia landed one of the finest brothers on campus, her sister had major problems and wasn't quiet about them, either. She spewed her distaste for their relationship at every opportunity. Once, her words were so ugly that Patricia believed something else was going on and accused Latrice of wanting Xavier for herself.

"You must be nuts," Latrice yelled across the dorm room she shared with Patricia; another mistake that Patricia wasn't aware she had made until it was too late. Before the first semester was over, Latrice acted more like her mother instead of her fun older sister.

Latrice was a sophomore when Patricia arrived on campus, and Patricia was elated that the special housing request her parents made on her behalf was granted. Instead of Latrice moving to a different dorm her sophomore year, she stayed at Jubilee Hall with Patricia, and their parents only paid one residence hall fee.

"If he was the last man on earth and I had to sleep with him to survive, I'd kill my damn self first."

"Well, it must be something, Latrice, 'cause you acting like a scorned woman."

"Seriously?" Latrice closed the gap between them. "All I'm trying to do is protect you. Since when didn't my word matter? Can you tell me that, Li'l Sis?"

Patricia lounged on the twin bed and gazed over at her older sister. "You never have *anything* positive to say. We've been together for three whole years. I think I know the man I love better than you."

"See that's the problem," Latrice shot back. "You *think* you know when I *know* for a *fact* he ain't no good. I've been telling you that since day one, but you act like you don't understand English these days."

"For Christ's sake Latrice, I'm about to marry this man. How are you going to stand up for me and feel this way about him?"

Latrice grabbed her sister by the shoulders. "I can be there for you despite my feelings about him." She shook her head, exasperated by the exchange. "But I can't shake it——there's something not right about him," she said, waving her index finger in Patricia's face. "I had an entire school year with him before you came down here. I know what he did to other girls and me."

"To *you?*" Patricia stepped in her sister's face.

"Girl move," Latrice said, backing away.

"What did you mean by that?"

"Nothing." Latrice waved her off. "He messed over two of my friends last year, and he's already cheated on you."

"Let his past stay in the past," Patricia pleaded with her sister. "I forgave him for messing around with that girl a long time ago, and that's all that matters. I'm tired of fighting with you about this," Patricia sighed. "I love you both. I don't want to lose my best friend because of the man I love."

"As if you could." Latrice pulled Patricia into her arms. "Just so you know, I told him if he ever fucks you over like that again, there would be hell to pay."

Evidently, Xavier must have forgotten that little piece of advice. Fucking with her was one thing, neglecting their son was another.

Chapter Fifteen

After sharing a meal with Junior, Xavier slowly migrated to the upper floor of their tri-level home anticipating the fall-out that was about to ensue.

Patricia ended a call with someone he figured by the tone, must be Latrice's trifling ass. That was all he needed right now. Xavier watched as Patricia's black dress slithered down her body and gathered around her curvy hips, revealing the black corset that hugged her gorgeous full figure. She grabbed the sides and shimmied the dress down her smooth thighs and legs that glistened underneath a pair of sheer pantyhose. It pooled around her delicate ankles, and she stepped out of it one graceful foot at a time.

She reached behind her back to unsnap the undergarment and Xavier rushed over to help. The feel of her warm and silky skin ignited a fire in him from his fingertips to his erection in an instant. She always had that affect on him, from the moment he saw her on Fisk campus. No matter how much her sister had tried to come between them and the woman had tried some truly sneaky things. He was certain that his wife had given her sister and earful, and he knew that Latrice was only too ready to listen—and judge.

"I just want to know why?" she said, interrupting his thoughts.

Patricia placed the restricting body foundation on the bed and carefully rolled down her stockings. "I don't ask for much, Xavier. You come and go as you please. You're getting home later than usual so much that it has become *the norm* and I haven't said anything." She paused and faced him with an angry glare. "But when you start neglecting our son, that's where I draw the line."

Xavier absorbed Patricia's condemnation. He entered the walk-in closet, unzipped his jacket, snatched his shirt loose like he was part of the Magic Mike Male Revue with buttons popping and flying everywhere. He tucked it in his slacks and pulled his white undershirt down over his waist.

"I'll be right back."

"I'm talking to—"

Xavier walked swiftly out the room, then bolted down the stairs. That was a bold move, and he was going to pay for that when he returned, but he had to get rid of that shirt.

He stuffed it in the bottom of the kitchen trash, then exited the back door and put the bag in a neighbors garbage can two houses down.

"I'm sorry," Xavier professed when he reentered the bedroom. "I had to—"

"Really?" Patricia said, glaring at him. "I don't give a damn what you had to do. That was rude."

"You're right." Xavier took off the patent leather Gucci loafers and slid them in the closet on the shelf. He walked out fiddling with the gold clasp on his linked watchband, buying a little time. The phone vibrated in his pants pocket, but he refused to answer.

"I'm not neglecting you or Junior," he said standing in front of her, commanding her attention by coming in close. "And I know things have been hectic lately, but they'll calm down."

"This was a huge night, and you can't get a do-over," she fussed, taking off her diamond drop earrings and placing them in a white jewelry box on the nightstand. "You can't miss the important things for no reason at all." Their gazes connected in the mirror. "It wasn't like you had to work tonight, so where were you that you couldn't make it to your son's ceremony on time?"

Xavier wished he hadn't invaded her personal space with such a direct question thrown at him. He had no wiggle room to escape her questioning glare.

"Are you going to answer that?" She gestured to his pocket, frowning. "Is that the reason you're all over the place?"

"What?"

She reached for him, scowling with the effort.

"What are you doing?" he scolded, backing away from her.

"Is there something that you don't want me to see?" she said, grabbing at his pants pocket.

"I don't know what's gotten into you, but you need to stop this nonsense now," Xavier warned, moving out of her reach and onto his side of the bed. "I was late. I'm sorry. I don't know what else you want me to say."

"Your phone is *still* vibrating," Patricia spat. "Are you going to answer it or not?"

"They can wait," he shot back, grabbing the remote and turning on the television.

"Just like *we* could wait?"

Xavier didn't take the bait on that one. The room's temperature dropped a few degrees.

"You are *not* going to dismiss me like that." Both hands slid upward to rest on those curvy hips. "I have a reason to be upset, and you're not going to ignore me," she yelled, throwing the pillow at him.

"Patty, you'd better stop it," he said, quickly deflecting it from his face.

She dove across the bed and snatched the remote out of his hand. He jumped to his feet and stared at her nude body, now sprawled over the comforter.

"What's going on Patty? You're taking this too far." He leaned against the wall, bumping into the gold and bronze floor statue of Nefertiti, almost tipping it over.

"Your actions are taking me back to a not so great time in our relationship."

He froze, then flickered a look at her in time to see her eyes glaze over. She wiped her face with the back of a manicured hand. She still had a good grip on the remote control as she changed her position and knelt in the center of the bed.

"The last time you were lying about your whereabouts and not answering your phone you were sneaking around with another girl."

"Patty, that's not what this is." He took a deep breath. Guilt stabbed him in the gut because she was right and the hurt was evident in her stiff shoulders and the tears falling from her eyes. If he could do it over, he would choose her and only her.

That low period in their marriage where he was about to engage a lawyer to leave altogether had allowed Lauren to slide in. He loved them both, but living a lie, going between two houses was becoming harder to manage. No matter what Xavier did, someone would get hurt, and at this point, he didn't see any way out. The best thing he could do was to make each marriage the best that they could be.

"I'm not that stupid college boy anymore," he said, taking her hand in his. "I love you and only you." Truth. He loved Lauren in a totally different way.

Xavier lifted her trembling hands to his lips and lightly kissed them, trying to gauge her expression.

She pulled away from him. "Are you going to answer your phone?"

This time, Xavier hadn't felt or heard it vibrate. He reluctantly plucked the phone from his pants pocket and was relieved to see that it was Jason, this time. He answered, but didn't give Jason a chance to respond.

"We're in the middle of something important. I'll call you back," Xavier disconnected.

Jason called right back. This time Xavier ignored the call, Patty's frown deepened. A chime notification pinged, cutting through the silence in the room, alerting all who were listening that three texts had come through. It was their day off so he couldn't figure out why Jason would be blowing him up like that. Xavier knew he needed to get back to his partner as soon as possible, but right now he had to take care of home first.

"I told you it was nothing." He leaned in and kissed her, but she was less than receptive. "I would never do anything to hurt you or our son intentionally."

Xavier let those words linger for a few moments. Although he'd been unintentionally hurting her ever since the day he said "I do" to Lauren.

"My mind is strong, but my heart is fragile. The beast in me will hurt you if you hurt me," Patricia remarked with a near-deadly expression, despite the lone tear sliding down her cheek.

"You don't have to worry about that," he replied, staying near her for a few moments.

He recovered the pillow from the floor, shook it out, and placed it back on the bed.

"Is it safe to lay here?" he asked, lifting one eyebrow like her favorite actor, Dwayne "The Rock" Johnson, hoping the action would ease the tension.

She grimaced. "I'm serious Xavier. I can't … I *won't* go through that kind of hurt again."

"You won't ever have to," he reassured her as he laid down and held out his arm. Patricia eased her head on his bare chest, and he embraced her.

"I hear you loud and clear Patty." Xavier rubbed his hands over her shoulder, side, and back. "You're freezing."

She turned into him a little more, and he flipped her over, positioning Patricia on her back as he straddled her thighs.

"I'll keep you warm," he whispered pressing his body into hers, placing a passionate kiss on her full, inviting lips.

Patricia wiggled her face away from his; halting his movement "I'm serious, Xavier."

"I know. I heard you." He stared into her eyes, and after several minutes of silently searching, he whispered, "I'll be right back."

He left and ran down the stairs to his office. Xavier pulled out a box from the top shelf of the closet and opened it. He retrieved a black silk drawstring pouch. Clasping it in the palm of his hand, he murmured, "This'll work."

Holding the object behind his back, Xavier entered their bedroom. Patricia appeared tense, sitting on the bed sporting a frown with her arms crossed.

"I have something for you," he said softly, easing closer.

Patricia glared as if she was looking right through him.

Xavier took a seat opposite her so he could gauge Patricia's expression when she opened the gift. He extended his hand, letting it rest in her lap.

"What is this?" she asked, opening the silky pouch.

A gold sapphire and diamond bracelet slid into her hand.

"This... oh, my." She placed a hand over her heart. "Wow... Xavier." She gasped. When did—"

"Merry Christmas." He lifted the bracelet from her hands unfastening the safety clasp. "I know it's two months early," Xavier explained as he placed the beautiful piece of jewelry around her wrist. "But now felt like the right time." Stroking Patricia's cheek and examining her soulful brown eyes, he purred. "I love you."

Time stood still as she gazed at him. She gradually leaned forward to meet his lips in a sensual kiss.

Xavier's heart now pulsed with feverishness instead of anxiety. He successfully manipulated that situation in his favor. He hovered over Patricia, wrapping an arm around her lower back pulling that enticing body to him. Without parting their lips, Xavier eased Patricia backward until he was laying on top of her.

She wrapped her arms around him and anchored her leg across his firm buttocks, moving him against her. He balanced his full body weight on one elbow trying to unsnap his trousers, and his elbow pressed hard into the remote control causing the television volume to spike loudly.

He readjusted, and they both laughed while trying to reach for the control. The flashing emergency red and blue lights from the flat screen illuminated the bedroom causing him to pause and drawing Patty's attention to the screen.

"Behind me, you can see that it's chaos as an unidentified man shot and killed one, and wounded another during an Annual Halloween Fashion Show Fundraiser to help raise money for Chicago's youth. Xavier stumbled out of bed like an intoxicated man, losing his footing as he stared at the screen and listened to the on-scene reporter.

"One of the victims was Lauren Carter, the owner of *Masterpieces by Lauren* where the yearly event was held. Police are on the scene, still taking statements from the eyewitnesses."

"Dear God. That's the event Shawn invited me to," Patricia gasped, sitting up in bed.

The rest of the newscast made him unaware of the impact of Patricia's revelation. He couldn't breathe or process any information. His heart was beating as fast as his mind was racing. Xavier stood upright and placed his hands behind his head to let fresh air into his lungs. He inhaled five deep breaths and slowly exhaled each one before his breathing returned to normal.

He startled at Patricia's touch. "Are you alright?" she asked.

"I have to go," he said, absently shaking her off.

"Where?"

"To the investigation site." He snatched a navy t-shirt from the dresser and yanked it over his head.

"Why? This isn't drug-related," she protested, reaching for his arm.

"We don't know that." Then he froze. "Maybe that's why Jason's been calling me. I have to go."

"I'm coming with you."

"No, you're not."

Patricia snatched the phone from the night table and dialed a few times. "Shawn is not answering her phone."

Xavier stepped in his sneakers, tied them, then holstered his service weapon on his belt, before turning to look at Patricia.

"What?"

"One of my employees was there tonight, and she isn't answering her phone, I'm worried," Patricia said, climbing off the bed.

"What are you doing? You can't go to an active crime scene, Patty."

She leaned against the bed, "I feel like I have to do something."

He grabbed the phone from her hands and placed it on the nightstand, "I'll check on her."

Xavier kissed Patricia's cheek and ran down the stairs two at a time and was in his truck in the time it took for him to take the next breath. At the stoplight, he pounded the steering wheel with his fists. His thoughts panned to Lauren, praying that she was alright. Their last words.

If Lauren died …

Chapter Sixteen

Lauren laid on the salon floor. She struggled to keep her eyes open as she slipped in and out of consciousness, trying to figure out why she couldn't feel anything but pain. The intensity of the torment was equivalent to a four thousand pound elephant stomping on her arm and chest, crushing every nerve ending.

"I love you, Ms. Lauren," Shawn said, squeezing her hand. Lynette had also stayed by her side until the EMT arrived.

Lauren's eyes widened at the sound of Shawn's voice. She opened her mouth to speak, but Shawn said, "Shhhhh."

"They're here." Lynette hopped up, running toward the flashing red lights that flickered through the salon's window like a rotating disco ball.

Seconds later, two paramedics rushed over, sliding their hands into protective gloves with several police officers in tow. The blonde man flocked to Demetrius. He applied two fingers in the groove of the young man's neck to check for a pulse. He shook his head at the unspoken question in his partner's eyes.

A copper-skin man with glasses, dropped to his knees accessing the severity of Lauren's injuries. Her chest filled and caved in at uneven intervals and her eyes darted as he cut the top of her sequined gown then ripped it completely open. Nate pressed his hands firmly against the hole in her shoulder. "Justin, I need some gauze," he stated calmly scanning for a second injury. Justin tore open several packages of sterile gauze pads. On the count of three, Nate removed his hand, and they quickly packed the hole in her shoulder. He replaced one hand over the gauze, applying pressure on the wound.

"What's your name?" Nate asked fetching the stethoscope.

Shawn supplied, "Lauren. Her name is Lauren."

"Hi Lauren, we're gonna take good care of you," Nate assured as he felt her skin. He pressed two fingertips to her wrist. "She's going into shock," Nate said to Justin.

"I'll start an IV," Justin said gathering what he needed from the kit.

Lauren's head slumped to the side as the lights slowly went out.

* * *

"What's happening to her?" Shawn screamed.

Lynette wrapped her arms around Shawn for comfort. Justin measured and wrapped a c-collar around Lauren's neck. "Give me a hand," Justin said to the officers, angling a flat board at Lauren's side. "Nate needs to keep his hand on the wound. On the count of three, I need you to roll her body to her right side so I can slide the board underneath."

"Would somebody answer me?" Shawn yelled, pulling away from the comfort of Lynette's arms.

"We have to get her to the hospital. Now," Justin said adjusting the straps across Lauren to hold her steady. He covered her with a thin blanket to protect her body from the elements. "You can follow us. We're taking her to Christ Hospital."

Shawn stalked behind them but was halted by an officer.

"Can you tell me what happened?"

She relayed the events that had turned what should have been a night of glitz and glamor, into one that was something out of her nightmares.

"Can I go now? Please," Shawn pleaded when she was done.

"Ma'am, we have mor—"

"I can answer your questions if you like," Lynette said standing near Shawn and the officer. "I spoke with the shooter before the incident."

The officer nodded, pulling a business card from his pocket and handing it to Shawn. Before he could say anything, she bolted. The ambulance had already taken off. The sirens roared in the distance. She hopped in her car and dialed Mr. Xavier on her way to the hospital. For the umpteenth time, he didn't answer.

* * *

Sirens screamed in the background. Lauren's eyes popped open. She scanned the area, and from her limited view, a silver metal ceiling and two strange men were hovering over her. She panted, causing the oxygen mask that covered her nose and mouth to fog and a consistent beeping sound to pierce the air.

The gurney was hard and cold against her skin causing her to quiver. Lauren parted her lips to speak, but her mouth felt as though it had been stuffed with cotton. *Where is Xavier?* She was forced to suck her tongue, trying to produce some moisture; but even that effort was too much.

"Stay calm Lauren," one of the men said, pressing down on her left shoulder. "You've lost a lot of blood, and I need you to be still. Can you do that for me?"

Justin started the second IV, with minimal effort.

She made a futile attempt to adjust her position, trying to process her surroundings. How did he know her name? When did they meet? She couldn't remember. Why was she being bumped around like she was on a rollercoaster? This never happened in her dream. Once the siren blared, those angry mockingbirds swarmed. *Where are the mockingbirds?*

Her world faded to black…again.

* * *

The next time Lauren was aware of anything, the bumping had changed to a lift and then a smoother ride. A crisp wind swept across her face as she stared upward at the midnight sky. Somehow she was on a giant skateboard struggling to make it across the concrete path.

The view transformed from the starry night sky to white ceilings with glaring fluorescent lights. Her senses instantly registered the smell of weak bleach and hand sanitizer. That smell—the night Shawn had been rushed to the emergency room thirteen years ago. That sound—every time a nurse or doctor entered the room and press their palm against a gray pump, rubbing the alcohol smelling substance in their hands. She was in a hospital.

Still unable to put her words together, she listened as the man, who she now believed was the paramedic; tell someone her information.

"The patient's name is Lauren Carter, age thirty-five. She suffered a GSW in the left shoulder and lost quite a bit of blood. She went into shock and has been in and out of consciousness. Blood pressure eighty-seven over fifty, pulse one forty-five," the paramedic said, still applying pressure to her wound.

"On the count of three," a thin, dark-haired man with pasty skin said, standing at her side.

"What's on the count of three?" Lauren tried to ask, but her lips still couldn't move.

A rainbow of people covered in yellow gowns encircled her. The cold surface she laid on lifted, then landed just as quickly. Soon her back rested on a softer surface. Lauren felt better for a split second.

"Hi, Lauren," he said, sticking the black rubber tips of a stethoscope in his hairy ears. "I'm Dr. Scofield, the trauma medical director. I'm going to take excellent care of you," he assured placing a cold round device on her chest.

"On my count, okay," a softer, but firm woman's voice said nearby.

Lauren's eyes shifted to the mocha, curvy woman standing next to the paramedic. In one fluid motion, the woman replaced the paramedic's hands with her own.

"Hello Lauren, I'm trauma point, Nurse Jackie," she said leaning over Lauren's face. "Do you know where you are?"

Her lips moved, but no sound escaped, mostly because the only Nurse Jackie she knew was from a television show. A pill-popping nurse.

"You're in the hospital," Nurse Jackie informed her. "Everything's going to be alright. Dr. Scofield is the best."

Lauren's eyes darted, taking in the movement surrounding her. Radiologist, respiratory specialist, the primary RN, technicians, and residents were all in the room moving around in synchronized controlled chaos.

"Turn on the patient monitor," Nurse Jackie ordered to no one in particular. In a matter of seconds, the machine beeped as one of the residents hooked the device to Lauren.

Dr. Scofield turned to Nurse Jackie and said, "Her airways are intact. There's no fluid in her lungs. I don't see an exit wound. She needs an x-ray, but first, let's get this bleeding under control."

"Sure thing, Dr. Scofield." Nurse Jackie nodded, and the radiologist stood holding the square metal screen, awaiting his turn to get in there.

"I need gauze pads, stat," she ordered.

Residents scurried, gathering the supplies that were at arm's length. Nurse Jackie packed the wound as fast as she could.

Lauren winced.

"Hang with me, Lauren," Nurse Jackie offered a slight smile.

Tears slithered down Lauren's cheeks, gathering in her ears. She was scared and alone.

"Someone get me some bags of normal saline," Nurse Jackie demanded. "She's not clotting, Dr. Scofield."

He rushed over, peered down at Lauren. "You're in the right place."

The patient monitor changed from a series of steady beeps and pings to an irregular beep, then flatlines. Lauren was unconscious.

Dr. Scofield checked the time. Exactly four minutes in and they couldn't get the bleeding under control. He reached over and picked up a black phone that was connected directly to the operating room. "It's Scofield. We have a Level-One that needs to go," he said, then placed the phone on the cradle. He faced his team. "We're taking her straight to the operating room, OR5."

Chapter Seventeen

Shawn settled into the waiting family area, feeling out of place in a crimson-stained dress and high heels while large families, couples, and even parents with small children overwhelmed the space in casual clothing. She placed a call to Lauren's mother and was able to connect with her in New York within the first five minutes. Shawn now was especially agitated that the person who Lauren needed the most, and who was the closest, was nowhere to be found after she'd spent two hours of trying to reach him.

She closed her eyes and prayed that Ms. Lauren would pull through. How on earth had James managed to get a gun, past security in the first place? And what on earth had possessed him to shoot Demetrius?

On her right, a raven-haired man looked down at her hands and grimaced. She followed his gaze, shifted, then rushed to the bathroom and washed out the dried blood as best she could.

"Ughhhhhhhhhhh," she yelled more in frustration at the situation, rather than her inability to remove the residue of Ms.

Lauren's blood on her hands. She returned to the family waiting room, where a familiar form was at the information desk.

"Candace?"

Her friend whipped around. "Shawn? What the fuck? Are you okay?" Candace rushed to Shawn, pulling her into an embrace that was as welcomed as her presence.

"I'm better now that you're here," Shawn whispered.

"Are you hurt?" she asked, sweeping a look over Shawn's clothing. "Why are you sitting out in the waiting room? Shouldn't somebody be taking care of you?" Candace snatched off a navy blue skullcap and a pair of leather gloves and stuffed them into the pocket of her CTA uniform coat. In one swoop she unzipped the dark blue sweater coat and turned to face the information desk clerk. "Excuse me?"

"This isn't my blood." Shawn pulled Candace away from the desk clerk. "I wasn't hurt. This is Ms. Lauren's blood. And the blood from the young man who saved her life."

"Girl, I was about to set it off up in here," Candace proclaimed, snapping her fingers, causing the clerk's lips to form a hard line.

"Sit your butt down, girl."

Candace followed Shawn to the spot she had just vacated.

"How did you know I was here?" Shawn asked, avoiding eye contact with the man who'd been staring her way.

"I turned on the radio on the way home from work and heard there'd been a shooting at Masterpieces. They said multiple people were shot and several injured. The only name they dropped was Lauren's and stated that she'd been transported to Christ Hospital, so here I am. I kept my fingers crossed that you weren't one of the people who..." Candace lowered her lids. "All I could think about was Taletha. I couldn't lose another sister."

Taletha had rebelled after graduating high school. She skipped out on the Air Force and hooked up with Ted, a low-life who helped fast-track the downward spiral she was headed in. She wouldn't listen to Ms. Ida or anyone else, and because she was of age, there wasn't anything that could be done to help. Taletha had to help herself. Unfortunately, she helped herself to a permanent spot six feet under. A man at the bus stop asked where she had bought her purse because he wanted to buy one for his teenage daughter. According to a witness, the man with Taletha, Ted, stabbed her repeatedly in the chest and neck, hitting the carotid artery, causing her to bleed out before help could arrive. Ms. Ida was never the same after losing one of her children.

Shawn laid her head on Candace's shoulder. "I'm glad you're here. My mind was getting the best of me just sitting here by myself."

"And why is that? Candace asked, leaning her head on top of Shawn's strewn curls. Where's her husband?"

Shawn shrugged. "I don't know where he is. I've been calling him for hours. I've spoken with aunts, uncles, and cousins, but they all live in New York. I called the precinct, and some rude man told me Xavier wasn't in. Before I could say it was an emergency, he switched me to Xavier's voicemail. *Asshole.* I finally broke down and called Lauren's mom," she said, picking at the sequin on the dress. "Someone had to tell her."

"Has anyone said how she's doing?" Candace asked, placing a hand on Shawn's arm.

"The doctor came out about an hour ago. She's still in surgery and needed a blood transfusion," Shawn said, gulping. "Candace... there was— so—much—blood. What if she doesn't make it?"

* * *

Shawn jumped to her feet when Mr. Xavier came rushing in the surgical waiting area. His movements were so spastic that the woman behind the information desk jumped, spilling her coffee. He wore wrinkled dress pants, a non-matching dark blue t-shirt, and gym shoes. Xavier's usually neat hair was unruly. His appearance

The Husband We Share 119

was completely different than the man she saw slipping out of the salon before the fundraiser began. If he wasn't with his wife, then why did he look so disheveled?

"Where the hell have you been?" Shawn screamed. "I've been calling you for over two hours."

"How is she, Chipmunk?" he asked, redirecting his steps to aim her way.

"She's in surgery."

"What happened?"

Candace stood. "What happened was that Shawn has been sitting here by herself for hours when you should've been here with your wife. What kind of husb——"

Shawn spun around, held up her hand. "Candace."

"I'm just saying," Candace shot back with an accusing glare at Xavier.

"Sit down. Please." Shawn tried to ignore the fact that all attention had shifted to them.

"Fine." Candace plopped down in the cushy chair.

Shawn smirked at Candace, silently scolding her behavior before turning to face Mr. Xavier who actually deserved it. "One of the rec kids shot Demetrius, and the bullet went through him and right into Ms. Lauren."

"How?" He shoved his hands in his coat pockets. They would've had to be extremely close together for that to happen."

"Seriously," Shawn said with sarcasm, angered that the only thing Xavier could think of was that his wife was too close to another man. "If you'd been there none of this would've happened. He was trying to protect her," she said, jabbing a finger in his face. "Something you should've been there to do."

Xavier opened his mouth to speak, but Shawn held her hand up in defiance. "I don't wanna hear it. Whatever you were doing wasn't *that* important."

He returned to pacing grooves in the carpet almost in the same manner she had before Candace arrived.

"I called Lauren's parents, and they're already on a flight. They should be here in a couple of hours."

"Thank you so much." Xavier hugged Shawn, who didn't miss Candace's death stare. "I don't know what we would've done without you."

"You're welcome," she said stiffly, picking up on a familiar fragrance of women's perfume. She didn't know what brand it was, but what she did know was that it couldn't have been from Ms. Lauren.

She eyed him carefully. "Your mother-in-law's has been trying to get a hold of you ever since I told her about the shooting. For some reason, she hasn't been able to reach you either.

"I was working." Xavier released Shawn and walked past the vending machine to the information desk. He approached the clerk to ask for an update on Lauren's surgery.

Shawn resisted the urge to say, *working, my ass*. She gathered her things. "Come on Candace, let's go." Then slipped into her coat. "I'll be back."

"You're about to go?" He had the nerve to sound surprised.

"I promised Ms. Lauren that I wouldn't leave, but now that you're here, I'm going home to change before I pick her parents up from Midway Airport. I'm sure your face is the first one she wants to see when she wakes up." She looked over her shoulder and added, "Since she certainly didn't see it anytime within the last few hours."

Chapter Eighteen

The moment the surgeon gave clearance; Xavier made a beeline to Lauren's room. Relief went through him when Dr. Lee said the surgery was a success and that she should be able to go home within 24-72 hours. He wanted to monitor her overnight and run more test to rule out any loss of brain function that might have occurred due to her losing consciousness or the impact of Lauren hitting her head when she fell to the floor.

Xavier settled into a spot by the bedside and waited for Lauren to awaken, thanking God that she survived. He held her hand focusing on her pale complexion, the tubes going into her nose, the thick white bandages and surgical tape wrapped around her collarbone, shoulder, and upper left arm. He had almost lost her.

Guilt set in and regret was not far behind. If Xavier had stayed at her event, then he would've been able to prevent this. But how he could have managed that tonight was beyond him. Never had conflicting engagements impacted his life in such a crucial way. He made sure of it. His wives schedules' were laid in better than a neurosurgeon's, six months out on the calendar on his phone. Junior's ceremony was a wild card—totally unpredictable.

"Baby, I'm sorry," he said, watching the machine beep every time it took Lauren's vitals. "I don't know what to do. I don't know how to fix it."

He closed his eyes and whispered, "I love you," then laid his head on her upper thigh, still holding her motionless hand as the tears came.

Years ago, being with another woman wasn't part of his plans. Patricia's focus on school had created a distance he thought would never cease. His insistence on counseling went ignored. Divorcing was best.

* * *

Xavier left the lawyer's office and went to his favorite spot. Smooth Cuts Barbershop was packed, filled with Chicago's Finest waiting for service. Fire Fighters received a fifteen percent discount on Tuesdays; Law enforcement received theirs on Wednesdays. Xavier made time in his schedule every two weeks to get a fresh fade. But he had to admit De'Andre, the owner, had a great marketing plan—plus enough muscle in the place just in case someone decided to get stupid.

While catching up with some of the more interesting cases with fellow officers and flipping through sports magazines, he looked up in time to witness a gorgeous woman walking with a purpose from the back room to the booth near the window. He glanced over the magazine to get a better view of the caramel beauty who was wearing large gold hoop earrings and a wrist full of gold bracelets. She wasn't one of the regular stylists. The sister stood out in skintight jeans and a fitted white crop top that said *Made to Perfection.*

He watched her interact with the barbers and clients and was taken with her bubbly personality as she bantered with them in a way that showed she was a lady, but could also hold her own. Her energy was magnetic, and her quick wit was refreshing. She wasn't arrogant like some of the other female stylists that had come and gone. The clients seemed to love her. Many of his fellow officers flocked to her waiting for a turn in her chair regardless of how long it took. In rare moments, both something vulnerable and edgy would creep into her speech.

Xavier tried to put the focus on the article, but the moment she finished prepping her station for the next client, Xavier sprang into action, approached her and asked, "Can you cut a 360 waves style?"

Before she could get an answer out, another officer taunted, "It's like that, huh?"

"*Exactly* like that," Xavier shot back.

"Man, you need to wait your turn," Officer Burch grumbled with a pointed look at the stylist, possibly wanting her to put him in check.

"Absolutely, Officer Carter," she replied, flickering a quick look at his left hand, missing his wedding ring.

While her statement caught Xavier by surprise, he was certain he had never told her his name.

She grinned at his confusion, pointed to his name badge and gave him a smile that showed off a set of whites that gleamed with movie star brightness.

"Have a seat." She swiveled the leather styling chair and held it in place for him. "I'm Lauren, and I'm at your service."

He chuckled, then shifted so that he could admire everything from her hourglass shape, streaked honey blonde and sandy brown hair, down to the black swanky ankle boots.

"Where are you from?"

"Why're you asking?"

"Your accent," Xavier settled in, ignoring the angry glare of Officer Burch. "I run into people from all over Chicago. You don't sound like any of them, and you don't roll like a south sider."

"Is that so," she said, grinning while balancing her weight on one leg and crossing her arms under her bosom, which made them perk out even more. "So what are you? FBI-in-training? You have the ability to *read* people?"

"Something like that," he said taking in her stance and trying not to be obvious that he was still scoping out the pleasant sight of her. Hips that welcomed the denim jeans she wore were calling to him. He hadn't made love to his wife in so long that the stove needed to be replaced. School, work, and Junior, all came first. His needs were on the backburner. "Becoming a detective's on my radar, so I'm practicing my technique on you."

"Humph." Lauren tossed her head, and the hair swayed with a grace that was sensual. "I'm from New York, and we don't have an accent. *Y'all* do." Everyone laughed. Well, almost everyone. Officer Burch was still giving them the evil eye.

"New York, huh?" Xavier said imaging how her glossy lips tasted.

"The Empire State, baby. You'd better know it," she quipped, then crooned, "Concrete jungle where dreams are made of there's nothing you can't do…"

"You sound better than Alicia Keys," he said of the impromptu rendition of Empire State.

"Heeeey, I could teach that old girl a thing or two."

"Is that right," he teased, eyeing her in the mirror. "Well, since you're new and all, let's see how well you do on making me look like a million bucks."

"That shouldn't be too hard," she shot back, and a slow, seductive smile lifted the corners of lips that were made for kissing as she draped the cape over him. "I mean, seeing what I have to work with."

Xavier leaned back in the chair, and her hands migrated slowly over his thick wavy hair, probably trying to get a feel for what she was getting into. He closed his eyes, allowing her to do the work—a massage that eased the tension of an upcoming assignment from his mind; the divorce that Patty knew nothing about, a delicate touch that brought on an erection that forced him to shift in his seat. Xavier tuned out the chatter from the married men sharing stories about things that were going wrong in their marriage. Something he could identify with.

Patty had become so focused on making it; that they never had a chance to enjoy what they'd worked so hard to achieve. At one point he'd even considered that maybe they'd married too young— that after they'd accomplished their personal goals would've set the stage for happily ever after. It wasn't that the marriage was as bad as the men spilling their guts in the salon—but it was missing that something which made coming home an enjoyable thing. The sex was good, Patty had always been superb in that department, but there was more to marriage than sex. In a haze of work and motherhood, there was nothing left over for her husband.

Xavier focused in on the gentlemen boasting about women they'd slept with; the droning voice of the newscaster speaking on the Black Lives Matter protest; and the sounds of the street hustler selling his latest wares. He pushed all thoughts of Patty and divorce to the background. Maybe because divorcing wasn't best because he didn't want to raise his son in a house divided. Once Junior turned eighteen, Xavier could see his way clear to leave. But he was not going to keep putting his physical needs to the side.

Instead, he put his attention on the vanilla scent of the woman whose breasts were pressed so close to his cheek that he fought the urge to pull her to him and nuzzle each one right out in the open. She smiled down at him as though reading his thoughts.

He was hooked from that moment on, New York accent and all.

Patricia was deep into her studies and seemed more focused and content with keeping him at arm's length. With extra schooling, working overtime, and a young son, he had never felt so alone, although he was married. How was that even possible? And it did not seem like it would change any time soon. Whenever there was a break, Patty would fill it with something else, despite his insistence that they spend some time together as a couple.

The fact that Lauren was pretty, easy to talk to, and made him laugh was the perfect trinity. Then, one year later, after they'd started with private dinners at her apartment that eventually led to earth-shattering love sessions, she gave him an ultimatum that he should have, but could not refuse.

* * *

Someone shook Xavier's shoulder, and he slowly lifted his head right into the sincere eyes of Lauren's mother.

"Hi, baby. Mom's here."

His in-laws were hovering over the hospital bed that held the wired-up form of his wife. Ms. Jackson bent down, sweeping her shiny copper hair to the side before kissing her sleeping daughter on the forehead, then heart-wrenching sobs wracked her body.

"Who would want to hurt my baby?" Ms. Jackson asked no one in particular, gripping the steel rail. "She's such a sweet and giving person."

"She wasn't the target," Xavier responded in a somber tone wondering if he should fill her in on the details. Then he decided against it since the woman was already distraught enough. All he knew was the moment he left this place; he was going to put every effort into finding the shooter who had eluded capture.

"Honey, she's going to pull through this." Mr. Jackson's tall frame leaned in as he wrapped his arm around her tiny waist. "Our baby girl will be okay."

As though suddenly realizing Xavier was there, Mr. Jackson touched his shoulder. "Hey son, how are you holding up?"

Xavier shifted a gaze to his wife and responded, "I'm okay." Sounded more like he was trying to convince himself than anyone else. But from Mr. Jackson's sad expression, evidently, Xavier's poker face needed much work. This was his baby girl. The last of their line—and one of the reasons the older couple had been pushing for Lauren and Xavier to have children. Then they'd tapered down to practically begging for one child. Xavier had been careful not to plant a seed. She was on birth control, but he couldn't risk it not working. Lauren getting pregnant while popping these sleeping pills could have a detrimental effect on an unborn baby.

First, having her so out of it worked in his favor, since broaching that subject of divorcing Patty had never materialized. Xavier wanted his son to be raised in a two-parent home. He'd become comfortable with maintaining both households, but seeing the effect on her only giving half-effort to their marriage was impacting more than just himself, an overwhelming sadness filled him.

"You have to remain positive, son," Mr. Jackson said. "The nurse told us that the surgery was successful and there weren't any complications. So let's hold on to that good news, okay?"

Xavier caressed Lauren's hand. "You're right, dad. It just pains me to see her like this."

"We understand," Mr. Jackson said rubbing a weathered hand on Xavier's shoulder. Then remembering the one person who should be there, but wasn't he asked, "Where's Shawn?"

"I had to force her to go home," Ms. Jackson remarked while stroking a manicured hand across her daughter's hair, removing some of the tangled strands. "I told her that we'd call if Lauren's condition changed. Shawn had insisted on staying when she dropped us off because she didn't want to break her promise to Lauren." She stroked Lauren's swollen hand. "But I reassured her that Lauren would understand and that she would want her to take care of herself. She seemed so shaken."

Ms. Jackson paused, adjusting the thin white blanket over Lauren's body and fluffed the pillows for yet a third time. "The same goes for you too." She glanced over to Xavier, her expression more sympathetic as she gave him a once-over that seemed to pierce his soul. "You look a mess. Why don't you go home, get a few hours of sleep and come back refreshed? We'll be here."

"As if I could," he protested, holding his stance near the foot of the bed. "I'm not going anywhere."

The silver-haired surgeon and a spunky redhead nurse came in to manually check her vitals and IV fluids.

"Hi, Dr. Lee," Xavier stood and moved out of the way allowing the nurse to tend to Lauren. "How much longer until she wakes up?"

"The anesthesia has worn off," he said, glancing at his watch. "The pain medication she was given tends to make you sleepy. She may be out for a while. The best thing you can do for her is to let her rest. She has a long road ahead with getting her arm and shoulder function back to normal. That will require lots of physical therapy. But don't worry, we have an excellent rehabilitation facility right here at the hospital."

"That's good to know," Ms. Jackson replied, touching her husband's hand, causing his weathered fingers to curve around hers.

"Please forgive me," Xavier said to the doctor who was examining Lauren's surgical site. "These are Lauren's parents, Mr. and Ms. Jackson. They just flew in from New York."

"Nice to meet you," Dr. Lee said with a pleasant smile. "I hear The Big Apple is very festive this time of year."

"Yes, it is," Ms. Jackson, remarked, trying to form a smile. "And with Thanksgiving and Christmas around the corner Times Square will be overflowing with tourists."

"I can only imagine," the doctor replied, lifting Lauren's eyelids and checking her pupils with a small flashlight. "I did my residency at Albert Einstein College of Medicine." Clicking the button and placing the tiny light in the upper left breast pocket on his white lab coat, Dr. Lee said, "I'll be back to take another look soon." Then he left the room.

The nurse turned to the family and said, "I know you all just flew in to be by your daughter's side, but it's a little tight in here.

There's only supposed to be two people in here at a time, so—"

"I'll step out." Xavier slowly rose and stretched, trying to stifle a yawn. He looked into the weary eyes of his in-laws, realizing that if it were Junior lying unconscious in a hospital bed, no one would be able to pry him away from his only child's side. "I'll be in the waiting room. Call me as soon as she wakes up."

Xavier trudged aimlessly along the hospital corridor with guilt. *If he had stayed.* He desperately wanted feisty Lauren to come out of this swinging. His footsteps came to a halt right in front of the nurse's station when the possible reality that because of her injury Lauren may not be able to work as a stylist anymore entered his mind. *Damn.* When he met her, she was on her hustle, working two jobs and going to Cosmetology school. Every weekend she was on the hunt with a real estate agent scoping out commercial property to open a salon. She wasn't satisfied with working for somebody else. Lauren always wanted her own business.

Not being able to do what she loved would devastate her.

He turned on his heels to put some distance between the images of Lauren laying in that bed helpless and headed for the elevator. He pressed the button, then whipped out his phone to call Jason.

"Hey man. What are they saying? Did y'all catch the guy?"

"Sorry X, not yet. I've been asking questions, but you know how it is. Not our case or department, so everyone's tight-lipped." Jason cleared his throat then whispered. "How's Lauren?"

"What do you mean tight-lipped?" Xavier pressed the elevator button again. "I need *you* to find this guy."

"I'll do my best——"

"That's not good enough, Jay."

"Whoa," Jason snapped. "I can't risk my shield and neither can you. If it ever came out that Lauren's your wife and we— I put myself on this case——"

"Just do this one thing for me, Jay. Damn." He stepped forward as the steel doors opened, angered at all the pushback from his partner. "I bet if it were Patty you would do it." Xavier stepped inside.

"Well, um, Patty's *your wife*."

"You never liked Lauren anyway." The doors closed and Xavier pressed the button to exit on the ground floor. "I'll be in touch."

He leaned against the back of the square enclosure, shoved his hands in his pockets, and laid his head back onto the paneling. He was tired, physically and emotionally. And his partner was choosing to exercise his moral code.

The bell chimed, and the doors opened, causing a swift arctic wind to swoop around him, causing Xavier to shiver. He departed and made a sharp left toward the emergency room exit when a short distance away a woman's breathy voice said, "Hold the door."

Xavier quickly turned to stick his arm in the elevator doorway to keep it from closing. He came eye to eye with a familiar form that was dressed as a basketball mom, sporting a St. Francis High School baseball cap, black puffy vest jacket, gray long sleeve shirt, jogging pants and Puma sneakers.

His throat tightened as he tried to swallow the golf ball sized knot that dared to choke him as he croaked out, "Patty?"

Chapter Nineteen

Shawn was grateful that Ms. Jackson had sent her home. She took a shower and changed into pajamas, then climbed into bed. Just as Shawn drifted off, Lauren's assistant popped into her mind. She slid her hand under the pillow to retrieve her phone. Evidently, Lynette must have been thinking the same thing because Shawn's phone rang before she could unlock the security code.

"Sorry it's so late, but I wanted to know how Lauren's doing?"

"It's okay," Shawn said, rolling over to her right side. "I was just about to call you."

"I'm finally leaving the salon," Lynette sighed. "The police just finished up the first part of their investigation. And since I knew the boy, they asked me a bunch of questions. "Hold on a minute."

A mysterious voice came through the receiver. Shawn bolted upright, turned the television down to hear who was talking to Lynette at such a late hour.

"Thank you, officer," Lynette said, courteously. "I'll be fine from here."

Shawn let out the breath she was holding, relieved that it was a cop and not a stranger. She'd had enough tragedy for one night and couldn't stomach anymore.

"I'm back. How's Lauren?"

"Surgery went well. Mr. Xavier and Lauren's parents are with her."

"Praise God," Lynette rejoiced. "This could've been more tragic than it was."

"I know." Shawn paused, absorbing the meaning of those words. Demetrius was the only person James seemed to have his sites on.

"I guess the wacky cop was able to relay the message I left for Xavier at the precinct."

"What message?" Shawn asked.

"I spoke with Officer Wilkins, who was a complete jerk. I told him who I was and that I was trying to reach Detective Xavier Carter. He said that he wasn't on duty."

Shawn stiffened with anger. "The same thing happened when I called. I could've sworn he told Ms. Lauren that he had to work tonight."

"That's what I thought, too. So I asked if he could get an urgent message to him. He told me that if this was a personal matter that I needed to call his cell phone, then he hung up on me."

"What an asshole," Shawn croaked. "You could've been anyone."

"So I called back, and put on my highfalutin business voice and threatened to go over his head if he didn't take the message."

Shawn chuckled. "I bet he fell in line then."

"Only briefly." Lynette paused. "When I told him that Xavier's wife, Lauren, had been shot and he needed to get to Christ hospital right away. Do you know that man laughed at me? He said I had the wrong precinct and to get my facts straight before I go threatening him and cursed me."

Shawn replayed those last words. "You called the Twenty-First Precinct, right?"

"Yes," Lynette replied. "He said Detective Carter wasn't married to a woman named Lauren and hung up. *I know* I dialed the correct number. I keep a book of emergency numbers of all the stylists in my desk drawer. And as far as I'm aware, nothing has changed."

Clothing was a mess, couldn't be reached for hours. Wasn't married to a woman named Lauren. "That's weird."

"But check this out," Lynette said. "I have Lauren's phone. I locked it in the desk drawer once the fundraiser began. I called the precinct from the salon's phone and got Officer Jerk Off, then I dialed the precinct from Lauren's phone, just in case I made a mistake. It went straight to Xavier's voicemail."

"What's so weird about that?" Shawn asked.

"Shawn, you're not hearing me," Lynette said in a frustrated tone. "The voicemail was Xavier leaving a message like someone called his personal office line. I dialed the main precinct number— that should've gone to the switchboard."

She lifted onto her elbow. "Wait a minute."

"...like his work calls are being forwarded to his personal cell for some reason," Lynette continued.

"Soooo," Shawn crooned, sitting upright. "If I'm Ms. Lauren and I call my hubby at *work* where he's *"supposed"* to be, the calls go straight to *his* cell as long as I call from *my* cell phone. Never really calling the precinct at all," she said slowly, as Lynette's point kicked in.

* * *

"Xavier?" Patricia stepped back and eyeballed him from head to toe, clutching the oversized Michael Kors bag that rested in the groove of her elbow to her chest. "What in God's name are you doing here?"

He swiftly removed his arm allowing the steel elevator doors to close, then let out an exhausted breath. For a moment, Xavier's breathing stopped, causing him to ball his fist. The pressure of the squeezed hand muscles made his knuckles burn when the exposed flesh stretched across the open wound. Pain brought him back, and he inhaled. "I got into a scuffle at the investigation site. It's nothing major," he said, glancing at the damage sustained when hitting the steering wheel. "Lieutenant made me get checked out." He shrugged. "Company policy."

She examined his inflamed knuckles, gently rubbing her fingertips over the raised broken skin. He winced at the touch, pulling away.

"What are *you* doing here?" Xavier asked, praying her answer wasn't what he anticipated.

Before she could answer, the elevator chimed, and they had to move aside so the next round of people could exit.

Maybe this wasn't about him. "Is Junior okay?"

"Junior's fine—I'm just—well." Patricia caressed Xavier's cheek. "Why are your eyes puffy and red? Were you hurt anywhere else?"

Her response was vague, and considering his situation, he wasn't going to push. Xavier took Patricia's concern about his well-being at face value. As long as she wasn't asking questions about his wife upstairs, he could handle whatever else might come his way. Xavier's secret was still intact. "I'm drained," he confessed, anxious tension building. "It's been a long day."

"Then let's go home."

"I can't. I mean." He shook his head. He must have understood the *what the fuck do you mean you can't go home expression* on Patricia's face and quickly conceded. "Okay."

* * *

The Chicago hawk swirled around Xavier and Patricia and helped push their bodies across the deserted street to the parking lot. The morning chill was bitter and unforgiving.

What the hell is happening?

The world as he'd known it was about to implode and he had no defenses in place to maneuver. Nor did he have the energy to try. For a fleeting moment, a sense of relief went through him. No more lies. No more hiding. That would be a good thing.

Then his heart physically ached. He couldn't leave the hospital without knowing if Lauren was okay. How would that look to her parents? They had given him an out. He didn't know it then, but certainly, with the tide turning, he had no choice but to take it. Xavier would call Lauren's parents to let them know he took their advice.

No matter what happened tonight, he had to be back at that hospital first thing in the morning, maybe even the next few days. But the bigger problem was how was he going to explain his extended daily absences to Patty and Junior? And how would he explain his absence in the evenings to Lauren's parents? Although no one voiced it, his in-laws wouldn't be going back to New York anytime soon. And that posed another problem.

Lauren's father already wasn't thrilled with Xavier because of how they married. No giving his daughter away. No family and friends present. No church wedding. Lauren was Catholic, and that was unheard of. The Catholic Church, without *convalidation*, didn't recognize civil weddings and as far as Lauren's father was concerned, God didn't govern it. Mr. Jackson only spoke and interacted with Xavier once a year, when they visited for New Year. Truthfully, Xavier preferred it that way. The old man was shrewd, and he would've figured something out long before now.

Xavier hunched his shoulders trying to block whatever wind he could from venturing around his neck as he briskly opened the passenger side door for Patricia and jogged around to the driver's side and climbed in the truck.

"I just found out I have to go undercover," Xavier said in a sorrowful tone sticking the key in the ignition.

"What?" she asked, shifting in the seat to face him. "When?"

"Tomorrow morning," he whispered, saying a silent prayer that half-truth went over smoothly.

Indeed, he was going undercover, just not for Chicago PD. "I'm not sure how long, but I'll be in the field the entire weekend," Xavier said, cautiously glancing her way. "Maybe longer."

Patricia narrowed her eyes at him but didn't utter one word.

Xavier didn't know what to make of her silence.

As he drove the three rows over to her vehicle, he couldn't help but wonder, *how did she know he was at the hospital?*

Chapter Twenty

Two weeks after Lauren's accident, she was recovering well according to Dr. Lee. She owed a big part of that to Xavier, and to her parents who refused to leave town until she could handle her basic needs on her own. She had started therapy, and the sessions were grueling, but she pushed through the pain because she was ready to get back to her life.

Xavier catered to her every need. She was more like the lucky lady who had won a dashing male servant at a charity auction but was fortunate enough to have it last for weeks instead of the slated "one-day" experience. He was the gentleman caller who pampered her to no end—— changing her bandages, bathing her, washing her hair, rubbing her feet, and serving her meals. She loved the attention but recently suggested that Xavier resume his regular schedule. At first, all that attention was nice, but then it became suffocating. He was reluctant at first but eventually gave in. Lauren wanted to take care of herself now that she could and go back to work as soon as possible.

In the wake of the shooting, the salon was closed for remodeling.

Lynette handled the contractors in Lauren's absence. She forwarded invoices to the insurance company, and they paid the claims.

The Thompson Center offered Lauren temporary space for the stylists to work free of charge while she recovered. Though Lauren was grateful, she declined. She met with the stylists, and they all agreed the client's satisfaction was most important. The Thompson Center was inconvenient being forty minutes away and in the opposite direction of Masterpieces. She made an arrangement with a nearby salon allowing her stylists to rent workspace. They paid the normal booth rent that Lauren charged them, and she paid the balance. Lauren's clients were divided amongst Masterpieces stylists in her absence.

What she did crave was some alone time with her husband. His idea of "alone time" was centered around putting up the Christmas tree and lights, and other busy activities. Though Lauren enjoyed those things, she needed more. She yearned for his physical touch.

Unfortunately, he was scared to touch her in "that way." As much as she reassured him that they could make love without further hurting her shoulder, Xavier wouldn't budge. It didn't help that mom and dad were hovering all of the time. They meant well, but she was glad to kiss them goodbye right before heading to the airport with Xavier.

"Why don't you ride with us?" Xavier inquired. "Are you going to be okay here all by yourself?"

That's exactly what she wanted. The house to herself. A moment of quiet to be alone with her thoughts and feelings; to pass gas and not have to try and hold it in or say excuse me to anyone. She missed the solitude that was a regular part of her existence.

"Yes," she responded leaning against the doorjamb. "I'll be fine."

Plus, Lauren had other plans in mind. Soon as they pulled off, she ventured into the kitchen, grabbed the tiny remote from the top of the sound system next to the coffee maker and turned on V103. The mellow voice of Frankie Beverly and Maze sang from the speakers . . .

Happy feelin's in the aaaaaaiiiir, touching people everywheeeeeere.

Lauren swayed side to side with her good hand laying over her heart. Yes, she was due for some "happy feelings" of her own.

Lauren two-stepped over to the black granite island in the middle of the kitchen and grabbed the silver extender made with a long, strong metal arm, a claw grip, and suction cups, using it to retrieve a skillet hanging overhead. Though it wasn't easy at first, she learned how to maneuver using only the one arm.

By the time she finished, she had made pan-seared honey glazed salmon and a tossed salad for lunch. One of the many things she appreciated about her mom being there was that she diced and individually stored the veggies in freezer bags; which meant prep work for meals was a cinch. The biggest challenge was setting the dining room table. She had to make several trips carrying the crystal dishes they received as a wedding gift from her aunt back and forth from the kitchen, but she managed to get it done.

The phone chimed, startling Lauren. She received a text message from her dad that they were checked in and Xavier was on his way home. *Sweet.* That gave her about forty-five minutes to do what she needed to do. But before she could respond to her dad's message, the phone rang. She ignored Xavier's call, letting it go to voicemail. She knew being unable to reach her would drive him up the wall, guaranteeing he'd come straight home. And she'd have something waiting for him when he got there.

Lauren was in the market for getting her honeypot serviced, so she went upstairs to make sure it was extra sweet and inviting. Her pheromones would be clawing at Xavier from the driveway and luring him across the threshold into their bed.

When Xavier stuck his key in the door, she was sitting at the seven-piece beautifully designed cherry finished veneer dining table in their formal dining room, wearing a black lace see-through top and black thongs, with red heels.

"Lauren," he shouted, walking in.

She remained silent, waiting.

"Call Lauren," Xavier said, sounding out of breath.

Covering her mouth, Lauren stifled a laugh, listening to his cell repeat the command.

Xavier rounded the corner and froze.

"Hey, baby." She stood so he could appreciate the full view of her ensemble—or lack thereof. "Do you like what you see?" Lauren blew Xavier a kiss, as his mouth gaped open.

"Why didn't you answer the phone?" he fussed, tapping the button to disconnect the call.

"Really?" she asked, placing her hand on her bare hip.

He swallowed, "What's all this?"

"What does it look like?"

"It looks like trouble," Xavier snickered, walking toward her with a hard-on that was trying to break free from his jeans.

"How did you prepare all of this?" He looked astounded at the spread, then to her, and back to the table again.

"With much TLC," she responded, stroking the bulging growth south of his belt.

"Lauren," he moaned. "We can't."

"Why not?" she asked in a sultry voice, tugging his shirt out of his pants and stroking his chest as she slightly nipped his nipple and passed her warm tongue over his dark areola.

"Because..." His eyes rolled under the lids and then to the back of his head. "Because…" His head fell back, putting his Adam's apple on full display.

"I can't hear you," Lauren teased as she struggled to unbuckle his belt with one hand.

He let out a throaty moan and lowered his gaze to connect with hers.

"Touch me," she purred.

He didn't utter another word as he worked his fingers through the back of her hair angling her head at the perfect slant, engulfing her lips in a tantalizing kiss. Lauren's insides tingled, and an instant jolt to her core drenched her thong with nectar. Her backside leaned against the elegant cherry wood table as she finally loosened his belt.

The pants pooled around his ankles. He stepped back, bending to untie his shoes and free his legs. Lauren admired the sculpted body that she was eager to explore.

Xavier pushed the lunch delicacies toward the opposite end of the table, along with the floral centerpiece and his phone. He firmly placed his hands on her tiny waist and carefully lifted Lauren onto the dining table.

"I'll be right back."

Her gaze followed Xavier in his birthday suit as he trotted to the family room, and he reemerged with a lumbar pillow.

He pecked her softly on the lips and gingerly laid her down on her back, guiding her along the way. He placed the pillow on her side and made sure that her shoulder and arm were in a comfortable position.

"Is this okay?"

She nodded, blowing Xavier a kiss.

Xavier's hands methodically inched up her thighs until his fingertips reached her strappy thong. His fingers lingered and explored that sweet spot causing another wave of pleasure to erupt. She let out a breathy cry as he worked the thin piece of material over and down her hips. His touch sent an endless amount of heat throughout her entire body as he lowered his bottom onto the chair, then lifted her knees on his shoulders and further explored her secret garden with his tongue. Lauren's back arched in response to the immense enjoyment, and she was grateful for the support of the pillow. She was at her highest peak, about to climax a second time when Xavier's phone vibrated just above her head.

Lauren's eyes flew open, and the tidal wave of pleasure that throbbed in the pit of her stomach fell flat and quietly rolled away. She slowly lowered her back and lifted her head, watching as Xavier exuberantly pruned her patch. He never stopped, and she sighed in frustration. She closed her eyes and tried, unsuccessfully, to stay in the moment. Unfortunately, she couldn't tune out that annoying buzzing sound in her ear.

Panting, Lauren reached her good arm above her head; feeling for the culprit. *She grabbed* the phone, along with a hand full of lettuce and salad dressing.

The Caller ID said *XJr.*

Who's XJr? Trying to get her breathing in check, she answered, "Hello?"

A young male voice on the other end said, "Hello. Who is this? Where's my dad?"

"Your dad? Honey, you've got the wrong number."

Chapter Twenty-One

Xavier's erection went south for the winter with zero chance of returning in the spring when Lauren told his son that he had the wrong number. Though she wasn't aware of who was on the other end, he understood that Xavier Junior was sure enough to know it wasn't *his* mother. His heartbeat was erratic, but regardless of his heightened inner state, he had to maintain his composure. He duly served Lauren up praying she wouldn't pose any questions in the middle of reaching her climax. But the irritating buzzing sound vibrated a second time causing Lauren to sigh in exasperation.

"Who keeps calling?"

"Don't worry baby. I gotcha," Xavier said, as he stood, hoping that the nerves running haywire in his body weren't recognizable. He scooped the phone in his hand and turned it off before Junior called a third time, then slid it in his pocket. He silently scolded himself for leaving his cell out in the open in the first place——that was something he never did around Lauren because she tended to snoop through his phone when she thought he wasn't aware.

Xavier had a second phone line app installed on his cellular device strictly for Lauren and her parents. A unique ringtone notified him when an incoming call was from one of them. And Lauren was identified in his phone as Detective London, after the beautiful actress Lauren London. The unfortunate downside, which he was powerless to override, was when he put the phone on silent; there wasn't any way to detect who was calling or from which line.

He lowered his rear end on the cushioned seat and repositioned her legs on his shoulders, rechanneling all of his attention into pleasing Lauren and putting her into that sex sleep coma. Though his pulse was slamming into his temples from a headache that hit hard and fast, Xavier carefully parted the sea with his fingers then dove into Lauren's center with his tongue until her body tensed and her legs trembled. She let out a cry of ecstasy; one that Xavier was familiar with when he pleasured her that way. He eased her legs off of his shoulders, stood, and helped her sit upright on the dining room table.

"How about that lunch," she said with a girlish giggle while panting.

Xavier searched those hooded bedroom eyes for any signs of alarm or concern. When there was none, relief swam through him. "I thought I just had it," he winked and assisted Lauren to her feet.

"Nah, you cheated and had dessert first, but I'm perfectly okay with that."

"I just bet you are," he replied placing a quick peck on her lips.

Lauren slid off the table, slowly rotating her shoulder.

"Are you okay?"

"Yeah. It's just a little stiff," Lauren responded sliding past him on her way to the staircase.

"Where're you going?"

"I'm not about to sit on one of my chairs bare-assed and juicy. I'll be right back."

He chuckled and admired her luscious rear end elevate one stair at a time while she held onto the rail with her right hand. Soon as she was out of sight, he floundered, trying to retrieve the phone from the floor. He powered it on to see if Junior had left a message.

"Wipe down the table," she shouted from the top of the stairs.

"Okay."

With the phone cradled between his ear and shoulder, Xavier walked to the kitchen sink and turned on the sprayer to comply with his wife's demands.

"You have no messages."

"Shit," he grumbled, wiping the towel over the area where their sexy interlude took place. He was flying blind and had no idea what approach to take with his son when he got home.

He had adjusted the hand-knit lace runner down the center of the table and was sitting the lunch plates in their respective spots when Lauren came into the dining room humming and singing. She wore form-fitting leggings and a loose shirt that gave her injured shoulder room to breathe.

"I've got love—— on my mind. I've got love——on my mind." She shimmied then slid into a strut. "When I think of your tender kiss—ahhhh."

Lauren ran her fingers across the back of his head before taking a seat to his left.

He gave an unsteady smile as he stabbed the lettuce and tomatoes with his fork and took a bite.

"Mmmm…this is good."

"Thanks," she responded, avoiding the leafy option on her plate and going straight for the flaky salmon.

She rubbed her toes up the inside of his leg as she continued to hum and take in the meal. Evidently, Lauren was feeling some kind of way with all the smiles and extra flirtation, but the only thing on his mind was Junior and the potential storm that might be waiting for him when he got home to Patty.

"Hey," she said, tapping her foot against his knee, putting a tighter grip on the personalized crystal wine chalice.

"Yeah," he responded in a daze.

"Where did you just go?" she asked, extending the goblet

motioning Xavier to pour her a glass of red wine. "What are you thinking about?"

"Nothing," he answered. "I'm good. I'm here with you." Xavier stepped away from the table and returned, screwing the spiral metal rod into the cork, all the while he was inwardly grateful that she hadn't said anything else about the phone call, he angled the forest-green bottle and poured Lauren one-fourth of a glass of bubbly.

She closed her eyes and took a long sip of the intoxicating liquid, leaving only a small amount in the bottom of the glass.

"Dang, you'd better slow down, or else I'm gonna add alcoholic to your list of ailments," he teased.

"Ailments?" She cut her eyes at Xavier and kicked his ankle under the table. "That seems to be your favorite word to describe me nowadays."

"Lauren—"

"I haven't had a drink in almost a month," she snapped. "My shoulder feels better. Nor am I popping pain pills like candy anymore, so leave me alone." She held her glass out again. "Don't be trying to ruin my high. I had to wait too damn long to get it. And I ain't talking about the alcohol."

"You know you weren't in any shape to be doing the nasty," he joked, refilling the glass, relieved that she had shifted the conversation.

"Technically, I still haven't 'done the nasty,' but I'm not complaining at the moment."

"Mmmm hmmm," Xavier mumbled with a mouth filled with salmon and salad, enjoying the mixture of the sweet flavor of the tender fish and crunchy carrots and water chestnuts.

"I find it weird you haven't touched me in a month. And to top it off, that phone call almost blew my orgasm," Lauren said, cutting a small piece of salmon with a fork and placing it in her mouth.

He froze with the fork midway to his lips.

"Where's my dad?" she scoffed. "That boy was so far in left field that he was out of the ballpark."

Xavier's throat swelled as the food trying to pass through lodged in his windpipe. He coughed until he was able to regain the ability to take a breath. Lauren handed Xavier her glass, and he gulped down that drink as quick as he could. He hoped his choking fit would end the conversation, but he knew better. He watched Lauren who had a keen eye on him. Her probing eyes spoke a language of their own; his distraction hadn't worked at all.

"You okay?" Lauren asked with a raised brow, and there was a sharpness in her tone that matched the unyielding glare.

Xavier nodded, intent on cutting his food into smaller pieces to buy him some time.

"Are you gonna answer my question?" she asked, refilling her glass.

"You just had surgery," he responded, finally looking Lauren directly in the eyes. "You needed time to recover." Guilt set in. He should have been there that night. She had begged him to stay, and yet he left her there, vulnerable. "You were in so much pain. I didn't want to cause you anymore."

"But that's never stopped you before," Lauren countered. "When I'm sick, or my back hurts from standing all day at the salon, you're still trying to creep up on me."

"True." He paused, aiming for a comeback that would shut this entire line of conversation down. "But you've never been *shot* before, either."

A long silence ensued before Lauren asked, "Why was that 'wrong number' programmed in your phone as X-J-R?" Her left eyebrow winged upwards. "Exactly who is X-J-R, Xavier?"

"It's a CI."

"Come again?"

"A confidential informant."

Thankfully, his line of work afforded him the skills to tell a convincing lie on the spot. It had saved his life on more than one occasion when he was out there in the streets infiltrating several neighborhood gangs.

"I know what a CI is Xavier," she replied slowly, a sure sign she was pissed. "I wanna know why was he calling you dad. *And* if you heard me talking to him, then why didn't you take the phone?" She polished off her wine but kept her focus squarely on him. "Correct me if I'm wrong, but if your CI reaches out to you——shouldn't you get back to him ASAP?"

"Well——I was a little busy at that particular moment." He playfully nudged her thigh with his knee under the table. "And DAD is our code word."

"Sure." She pursed her lips. "I know there's more to this than what you're telling me, but it's all good."

"Come on, Patty," he teased. "You're gonna hold it against me for taking care of you first?"

Lauren jabbed the fork at his nose with uncanny precision, grazing it. "Who the fuck is Patty?"

"Stop playing." He pushed back from the table. "You just scratched my nose." He touched the tip to see if he was bleeding, but was horrified at his slip of the tongue.

"You just called me Patty," she fumed, pushing the plate to the center of the table.

"Lauren, you're trippin', I did no such thing." He waved her off. "I don't even know a Patty."

"Xavier, I know what I heard," she roared. "Lauren and Patty don't sound shit alike, so I'm going to ask you again. Who *is* Patty?"

"Babe, you just finished grilling me about a CI and asking me a bunch of silly questions. I don't know what I said."

She stood so fast the chair fell backward. A loud thump echoed throughout the house. "You can blame it on twenty questions or whatever, but you called me another woman's name clear as the day is long, and I wanna know who the hell she is," Lauren snapped.

"Alright Patti LaBelle," he chortled. "You're always in here singing."

She eyed him for a moment. "Ha ha hell. I don't see a damn thing funny," Lauren spat, and grabbed the plate and dumped the contents down the garbage disposal.

Xavier approached her from behind at the sink knowing he had blown it big time. He leaned his chin on her shoulder and sang, *"I've must have rehearsed my lines, a thousa——"*

"Get the fuck away from me Xavier," she growled, then nudged him out of the way, storming out of the kitchen.

"Lauren," he shouted, following her to the front room. "Where are you going?" He asked as she grabbed her purse and keys off the end table.

"Ask Patty," she said in a sarcastic tone then slammed the door.

What the fuck am I going to do now?

Xavier sunk into the sofa and grunted. He waited a few minutes before dialing Lauren's number. She didn't answer. After an hour of his phone calls and texts being ignored, he placed the phone face down on the couch and turned on ESPN.

What was he thinking calling Lauren, Patty?

The background noise of the television stirred Xavier. The last thing he remembered hearing was Charles Barkley and Shaquille O'Neal passionately discussing who they thought would make it to the NBA Playoffs. Now sappy instrumental music filled the air. He yawned and stretched, wiping the sleep from his eyes. Once he was able to focus, he zeroed in on the Lifetime Movie Network logo on the bottom right-hand corner of the flat screen.

"Lauren," he called out, noticing his phone was laying face up on the couch. That was proof she had medaled with it. Xavier made a habit of laying the phone face down.

He wasn't going to make an issue out of it. Lauren would check his phone whenever the chance presented itself. That's why he frequently changed the access code to his voicemail as a precaution and deleted any text messages that she could interpret were questionable.

Xavier had hidden everyone that was important to his other life contact information in a secret calculator application, and that too was password protected thanks to a great leap in technology. Even if Patricia called, he had all her numbers blocked so nothing would register when he was home with Lauren, but he would get notifications sent to his work email under an alias, alerting Xavier that Patricia had called.

He glanced around, but there weren't any signs of Lauren.

Thoughts of Junior filtered his mind. Xavier was concerned about Lauren, but he was worried about his son more. The explanation he gave her was plausible regardless of the fact it was an outright lie. When Lauren calmed down, she would accept his reasoning. Junior, on the other hand, wouldn't understand this situation and Xavier was afraid that he would tell Patricia.

Xavier walked into every room on the first floor to ensure he was alone before giving Junior a buzz. He called several times, but evidently, his son was avoiding him. Though it was a little earlier than normal, it was time for Xavier to go home to Patricia.

Chapter Twenty-Two

Thirty minutes later, Xavier parked in the cobblestone driveway of the home he shared with Patricia. He cautiously opened the door and scanned the area, trying to get a feel for what he was about to encounter. He closed the wooden oval entry door, causing the wind chimes to play a familiar tune.

"Junior," Patricia yelled down from the upper level.

"No honey, it's me."

She appeared at the top of the stairs in a purple robe wearing an overnight headscarf. "You're home early."

"I finished a few minutes before normal, so here I am."

"More like a few *hours* earlier," she said, stifling a yawn. "It's only five after ten,"

"Where's Junior?" he asked, sweeping a gaze across the foyer, family room, and kitchen, frowning when there didn't seem to be any sign of his son.

"He should be home soon. Coach took the team out for pizza after their win against Middleton. You missed one hell of a game tonight." Her lips pulled into a frown, "I thought you were coming, but I guess Junior wasn't able to reach you early enough."

"What do you mean?" he asked, climbing the staircase.

"Junior said he had called and left you a voicemail giving you the game time."

Without a doubt in his mind, Xavier realized that Junior knew something was going on. "Oh, yeah——the time completely got away from me. I'm going to have to make it up to him. How did he do?"

"My-my-my, he played his butt off, but he seemed distracted." She shrugged. "If that's the right word to use. I couldn't quite put my finger on it," Patricia tried to explain, then brightened with the rest of the news she had to share. "But he scored twelve points, had eight assists, two steals, and shot the winning three-pointer at the buzzer."

"That's my boy," Xavier pumped his fist in the air. "I'll definitely make it to the next game."

"There *is* no next game." She stared down at Xavier as he climbed the stairs. "This was for the championship title. Why do you think he was so adamant about you being there?"

Xavier felt like an ass for disappointing his son and his wife—*again.* He stood on the second stair from the top so that they were at eye level. He untied her robe and placed his hands on those thick sepia hips, admiring the silky bikini-cut panties that rested on her hips.

"I *will* make it up to him. I promise."

Leaning in, he parted his lips and pressed them against hers, inhaling her sweet flowery scent. She grabbed his hand and violently snatched them away from her hips, and glowered at him. Xavier registered Patricia's look that was filled with disgust; he had to fight to keep his balance. A hard slap followed, which caused him to stumble backward down two steps. *Dammit, Junior told her*, he thought as he held onto the rail to steady himself.

She yanked her robe closed and growled, "You smell like pussy."

He watched her dash across the carpet, down the hallway into the bedroom and slammed the door. He closed his eyes replaying what had just happened. He massaged his temples so hard that they hurt when he realized that he hadn't brushed his teeth or showered after his episode with Lauren.

Xavier plopped on the stairs trying to figure out why his world was unraveling all at once. He willed himself to his feet and went to Patty. He attempted to open their bedroom door, but it was locked.

"Patty, please let me in," Xavier pleaded.

She didn't budge.

"Honey, would you please unlock the door?"

Silence.

"Patty, come on. It's not what you think. I would never do anything to hurt you or jeopardize our marriage." He leaned his face against the wooden door. "Patty, please let me in. I love you."

She didn't respond.

Xavier sat outside the door for ten minutes hoping she would unlock it thinking he had gone downstairs. He peeled himself off the floor and went down to the kitchen. He grabbed a cold bottle of Miller Genuine Draft, leaned against the kitchen island and took several long gulps. *"Lauren's scent..."*

Xavier pounded the counter with his fist and let the pain whip through him. Everything was coming at him all at once. How had things been so perfect and know he couldn't seem to deal with one aspect of his life without another needing his attention.

The wind chimes tingled a familiar song causing Xavier to perk up.

There was a thump, and Xavier assumed it was Junior dropping his gym bag in the foyer as always.

"Hey Moms, let me tell you what——" Junior froze mid-step into the kitchen. He locked gazes with Xavier for a split second, then quickly turned to walk away.

"Hello, son. How was your game?" Xavier ventured. "Mom told

me you brought down the house tonight." Xavier turned up the bottle and drank the last of the beer.

"Well if Moms told you, then why are you asking me?" Junior huffed.

"Is there a problem?" Xavier stepped on the lever and tossed the empty bottle into the recycle bin. "Do you have a reason for all this attitude you're slanging my way?"

"Nope. None at all," he mumbled, but his angry expression said enough.

"I'm sorry I missed your game," Xavier said, moving a little closer to him. "Your mother told me you tried to call me, but I never received one from you or got a message."

Junior sucked his teeth at the blatant lie. "Well, I guess I dialed the wrong number then."

"I reckon you did," Xavier said never breaking eye contact with him.

"Is there anything else?" Junior asked, turning to give him an icy glare.

"Yeah. Have a good night."

Junior scratched his head, put his back to Xavier, and jogged upstairs.

* * *

"It's not what you think?"

Patricia slammed and locked the bedroom door. She couldn't stop the tears from flowing. How dare he tell her that. She knew what a woman smelled like. He reeked of sex.

She went into the master bathroom and turned the faucet on full blast. She didn't want Xavier to hear her cry. The more he called her name, the more the tears fell at a rapid pace. She sat on the cold bathroom floor with her head on the lid of the toilet. *"How could he do this to me… to our family?"* Patricia flushed with heat as the contents of her stomach roiled with her emotional turmoil.

She managed to pull herself up off the floor and willed her body to the sink. Patricia cupped water from the faucet in her trembling hands and put her face in the cooling liquid. Her eyes burned as the cold water made contact with them and she squeezed them shut. Patricia patted her face with a plush hand towel, then turned the water off. She stared at herself in the mirror. Her face was puffy, her eyes were sunken, and the rims were red. Her heart physically hurt from pain and she just wanted it—and him—to go away. Patricia held onto the frame of the bathroom door for support for a few moments, then slowly walked into the bedroom.

Xavier's shadow wasn't underneath the door anymore, so he must have gone downstairs or in the guest room. Either way, she wasn't going to unlock the door anytime soon. She needed to be alone with her feelings—and doubts.

She knelt along the side of the bed, put her hands together, and bowed her head to ask God for guidance. A loud car engine roaring in the driveway interrupted her conversation with the Lord, startling her. The glow from headlights made her quickly get off of her knees and run to the window. She thought Xavier had left, but it was Coach dropping off Junior. She was glad that he was home, but she couldn't allow her son to see her in such a state. She laid down and buried her face in the pillow, and cried herself to sleep.

* * *

Xavier let out a long, slow breath, grabbed another beer from the refrigerator, went into the study, closed the door, and slumped into his office chair and dialed Jason.

"Hey X, what's up?"

"I fucked up man, and I need your help to get me out of this one."

"You know your timing sucks," Jason grumbled. "Hold on."

He listened as Jason told his wife to pause the movie and that he'd be right back. She giggled and said something, but Jason must have covered the receiver because her words were muffled.

Xavier envied the easiness of Jason's marriage. If only he would have stayed true to his vows—— *to be committed to one woman and only one woman till death do them part*, he wouldn't be in the predicament he was in now. And his son was now caught up in this mess.

"What the fuck did you do this time?" Jason demanded the minute he returned to the phone.

Xavier brushed off the fact that Jason was pissed off and ran the entire scenario down play by play—from Junior calling and Lauren answering, to him calling Lauren by the wrong name, Patricia being ticked that she smelled another woman on him, to the confrontation with Junior a few moments ago.

"I get all that, but what do you need from me?" Jason snapped.

Xavier almost said, "A miracle," but came up with "your help, man. I'm desperate."

"You know, the only reason I'm going to help you is that Patricia and Junior don't deserve this."

"What about me? What about Lauren?"

"Really X?" Jason replied, and his sarcasm wasn't hard to miss. "She doesn't deserve it either, but that was a problem *you* created. Patricia and my Godson are victims in all of this. My loyalties are to *their* happiness, and if that means helping you keep this hidden, so they don't get hurt, then that's what I'll do."

Chagrined, Xavier slumped further down in the chair. "Thanks, man."

"Don't thank me, but do realize that you keep hitting these snags. Give me a couple of hours. Sandy and I are in the middle of a movie. I'll get back to you before the night's over."

Xavier went into the guest bathroom to shower, sitting the phone on the windowsill. He never slipped up like that. Carelessness wasn't a trait Xavier possessed. His world couldn't have survived this long if he had. Both women pissed with him at the same time because of his negligence, was something he had a hard time comprehending.

He returned to his office, leaned back in the chair, and watched Netflix on the desktop, trying to keep his thoughts occupied until he heard from Jason, eventually nodding off. Five hours later Xavier's phone rang.

"Hey man, what's the good word?" Xavier asked Jason, snapping out of his grogginess.

"Your ass is sleeping while I'm over here humping for you," Jason fussed. "The paperwork is ready. You can pick it up in the morning."

"Oh, no," he said, stretching a little. "I'll pick it up tonight."

"Hold up, playa. Do you realize it's after three in the morning?"

Xavier slid a glance at his watch. "Yeah man, just leave it in the mailbox."

Jason sighed, and there was a world of aw with just that sound. "You owe me big time for this one."

"I know, man. You're a lifesaver."

Xavier made it to Jason's spot in Hyde Park in under an hour. He retrieved the package from the mailbox and made it back home in record time. He went straight to the study and locked the door. Xavier dumped the contents of the manila envelope on the desk. Jason had attached a Post-It on the cover sheet that read, *"You're such a dick."*

He chuckled as he crumbled the small yellow square and shot it into the wastebasket.

Jason had drafted an official-looking Confidential Undercover Operation Sting document. It showed all the officers involved, dates, places, and names of the potential targets. If Xavier didn't know any better, he would assume this was a legitimate operation.

Xavier carefully read through the document, amazed at, and thankful for, Jason's craftiness. He had weaved a story that put Xavier in a compromising situation with a female assassin who was tied to the Mexican Drug Cartel. She stripped him of his service weapon and held him at gunpoint. She and another hitman forced him to perform sexual acts and recorded the encounter. He had to oblige so he wouldn't blow his cover. He made sure it was understood that Xavier's life was at risk and that he didn't have any choice.

He nodded and the corners of his lips curved upward. Xavier placed the contents back in the envelope, went upstairs, and checked the knob. It was still locked, so he slid it under their bedroom door. Xavier trudged toward the guest room to get some rest. Today was going to present a whole new set of challenges.

Chapter Twenty-Three

The alarm was ungodly loud when it sounded off at five thirty. Patricia felt as though someone had socked her in both eyes because they were extremely weighted and she could barely open them. She reached over to hit the snooze button, accidentally knocking the television remote to the floor. The back cover came off and the batteries scattered across the carpet.

When she rolled out of bed and bent down to pick up one of the batteries, she saw an envelope on the carpet near the door. She snatched it up and took it in the bathroom with her. As she sat down to have that first thing in the morning pee, she tore open the envelope. The cover page was written in large bold print, which she recognized as Xavier's penmanship.

PLEASE READ. THIS WILL EXPLAIN EVERYTHING.

She huffed, then flipped through the pages. The white and blue Chicago Flag with four six-pointed red stars were situated at the top of each page, and she figured it was some type of police report.

* * *

Twenty minutes later, Patricia drew her hands to her chest and the papers scattered across the ceramic tiled floor. She wasn't sure how to feel, but the tears came anyway. *Xavier almost lost his life.*

She closed her eyes trying to suppress the tears as she thought about the ramifications.

My husband could've been killed.

She fell to her knees, scurried to gather the pages of the report, and returned them to the envelope.

After she had regained her composure, Patricia glanced at her swollen eyes and stressed filled face in the mirror. Her reflection confirmed that she wasn't going to work today. Patricia washed her hands and splashed some water on her face and hurried out of the bathroom to catch Xavier before he left for the day. But first, she needed to make sure Junior was squared away. He was leaving for Disney World with Brandon's family for Christmas break that morning.

Patricia threw on a pair of black yoga pants and a lavender sweatshirt and quickly traveled down the stairs in her bare feet. Junior gathered his bag in the foyer, and she halted. She wanted to avoid him seeing her this way. As soon as she veered to go back upstairs to put some makeup on the bags under her eyes, Junior said, "Hey, Moms."

"Good morn—"

"Can I open it now?" he asked, holding a red envelope in his hand with white snowflakes. "Or do I have to wait until Christmas morning?"

She laughed.

"Moms, pleeeease," he begged. "It's Christmas Eve."

Patricia made him sweat a little longer before she nodded. "You can open it."

There wasn't anything like watching the joy on your child's face on Christmas morning. Although the older Junior got, the reactions had changed, but it was happy nonetheless. This was the closest she was going to get to that, and it had been that way for a couple of years. She'd rather let Junior travel and enjoy that, experience than being selfish. She trusted Brandon's parents. They took care of Junior like he was their own.

This was the first year Patricia didn't bother to put up a tree or any decorations. She was flying solo. Xavier had to work, Junior wouldn't be home, and Latrice was spending the holiday at their parents' home.

That's a threshold Patricia refused to cross and hadn't in the past fifteen years. She wouldn't give her mother the opportunity to lie again about the adoption arrangement she made with Nurse Dominique regarding her daughter.

Junior grinned, holding up a GameStop gift card and five hundred dollars. "Thanks, Moms."

"Merry Christmas, baby." Patricia pulled up the collar of the robe, covering her cheeks, trying to hide her puffy face. "Is your dad still here?"

"Yeah," Junior mumbled as his happy facial expression changed. "He's in his office."

"Okay thanks," she said, mentally noting the difference in his demeanor. Patricia took in Junior's wardrobe. He wore a pair of dark denim jeans with a plaid button down shirt and wheat-colored Timberland boots. "Did you pack everything you need?"

"Yes."

"Where's your boarding pass and State ID?" she asked. "I know you don't need your ID to board since you're under eighteen, but I'd prefer you have it. Things happen and—"

"I have everything Moms. It's right here," Junior said, pulling the wallet out of the front pocket of his pants. "Stop worrying. I'm good," he laughed. "You do this every year."

She was happy that Junior listened. Xavier taught him always to keep his wallet in the front pocket when he traveled or was in a large crowd of people. He was less likely to be pick-pocketed. Interacting with her son made Patricia feel more like herself than she had all morning. "It's my job to worry. Have a good trip baby," she said, smiling. "I'll see you next week."

"Are you okay?" he asked, squinting. "You don't look like yourself."

"I'm fine, Junior," she said clearing her throat. Her son was more observant than she hoped this morning.

"Moms, are you sure?" Junior asked, again. "You sound weird, and you're not even dressed for work."

Patricia stared down at him from the top of the staircase and smirked. "Now you know I wasn't going to let you leave the state and not be here to see you off."

And that was the truth. Patricia had switched shifts with Aaron, the evening pharmacist so she could be home when Junior left, but after what just happened, she would take the entire day.

His phone chirped, and his attention shifted to the mobile device in his hand. "Brandon's mom is out front," he announced, dropping the overnight sack before running up the stairs two at a time and flung his long arms around her. "I'll see ya later." He gave her a quick peck on the cheek, raced down the stairs, and slung his backpack and duffle bag over his shoulder.

"Love you," she shouted, "Have a good time and call me when you land."

"Okay, bye."

The door slammed behind him, and Patricia let out a sigh of relief as she descended the stairs.

Junior had never seen her distraught before, and she planned on keeping it that way. They were far from being the perfect family, but she always made sure to protect him from any dissension. Growing up, she'd never been privy to their parents' disagreements. Her mom always told her that even though they were a family, she and her sister were not a part of their marriage. Patricia didn't understand what that meant when she was younger, but once she got married and had Junior, it had a whole new meaning.

Patricia hesitated when she saw the light from Xavier's office through the half-opened door. She slightly nudged, and it swung open. He was standing with his back facing her, rifling the contents of a duffle bag, so she softly rapped on the door.

Xavier gave her a shy smile and said, "Good morning."

"May I come in?"

She didn't wait for a response as she approached him with the report in her hand.

"Baby, I am soooooooo sorry." Once again she was crying. "I feel so foolish. I know you would never do anything to hurt me."

His eyes watered, and he opened his arms and stepped toward her. She cleared the distance between them, and held onto her husband and laid her head on his broad chest. She found comfort in feeling his heart pulse along the side of her face.

"I love you, Patty," he expressed, kissing the top of her head. "I apologize for what happened, but I didn't have any choice, baby. Please forgive me."

Patricia's heart ached for an entirely different reason than it did last night. The realization that she almost lost him was unbearable, and she sobbed harder. He was the second man that she had ever loved and she couldn't imagine losing him to these streets.

"I don't want to get that infamous knock on the door by officers telling me that something has happened to you," she said between sniffles.

Xavier kissed her forehead and gently wiped her tears with the tip of his thumb. "I'm not going anywhere Patty," he reassured, securely holding her in his arms for a long while.

She backed away and grabbed some Kleenex out of a leather facial tissue holder on his desk. "I'm okay."

"You sure?"

"Yes—no," she responded, dabbing her eyes. "I would never ask you to quit the police force, but can't you do something else? This has gotten way too dangerous."

"Patty. You know I'm—"

"Just stop, Xavier." She raised a hand. "There're other things you can do as a detective." She removed his gym bag from the chair and sat. She toyed with his phone, sliding it back and forth on the desk when a call from Detective London came in. "You have a call."

"Who is it?"

"Detective London." Patricia huffed, glaring at the phone. "He sure does call a lot. More than Jason ever calls—and *he's your partner.*"

"Let me get that," Xavier said, rushing to take the phone from her hand. "He's a new detective I'm training, and *man* does he ask a lot of questions." He hit the decline button instead of the answer key. "Shucks. I missed the call." Xavier sighed, sliding the phone to the floor. "I'll call him back later."

She frowned for a moment, then shook off whatever she was going to say and asked, "Do you have time for breakfast?"

"Sure, I can skip the gym this morning." He squinted and glanced down at her. "Wait, you're not going in today?"

She shook her head. "I didn't rest well last night, and people will notice."

"Tell you what," Xavier said, grabbing the armrest to steady her. "Go freshen up and I'll cook us breakfast."

Her lips split into a broad grin that could light up the sky on the gloomiest day. She couldn't remember the last time they shared a morning meal together. Xavier was always gone by four am. He kept a strict routine, early morning workouts, then straight to work. She rose from the seat and pecked Xavier's cheek.

The unmistakable aroma of waffles and bacon wafted through the house and hit her when she emerged from the bedroom. Xavier was sitting at the breakfast bar sipping coffee.

Patricia inhaled, leaning over the island as she said, "Everything looks and smells divine."

"I didn't know if you wanted tea or coffee, so I made both."

"I'm going to get my Winston Churchill on this morning." She stood poised, holding her tea mug with her pinky finger extended.

"Where do you come up with this stuff?" he snickered.

"You can credit your son for that one."

As they discussed work, a possible cruise, and reminisced about earlier days, Patricia enjoyed the quality time they shared this morning even though it didn't start out that way. She hadn't lost sight that the only reason they shared that time was because of the incident the previous night. Then she rolled everything over in her mind.

She glared at Xavier. Something about that explanation didn't sit well with Patricia. He had gone out of his way and broke his routine to make sure she was okay. Xavier never did that. Regardless of the circumstances, parent-teacher conference or an early morning basketball game, he kept his schedule. The scrumptious breakfast turned sour in her stomach.

"Play hooky with me today?" she asked, in an even tone. "Junior's gone. And I need to talk to you," she said, folding her hands on the table.

Xavier sipped his coffee. "Sounds nice, but—"

"No buts." She cupped his hand. "Say yes."

"I'm sorry, but I can't Patty. I have to get this report back before someone realizes it's gone." He brushed his fingers across her hand. "I can't make any promises, but I'll talk to lieutenant. Maybe he can assign me to—I don't know. Something less risky." And as if on cue, his phone rang. "I have to take this," he said, rising, then leaning across the table planting a kiss on her forehead.

"Is it Officer London calling again to corroborate your story?" she asked, sliding out the chair.

"What? Don't be silly," he replied walking to his office and closing the door.

Doubt crept in. He was acting... off.

Patricia gathered the dishes, rinsed them, and arranged them in the dishwasher. She didn't know why she said that. An invisible line had been drawn, and she was stuck in the middle. She was grateful for Xavier's life being spared and hurt because he was forced to share the one part of himself that he only shared with her, with another woman. Suppose it happened again and again.

"I'll see you later, beautiful," he said entering the kitchen, disrupting her thoughts. Xavier slid his hands on Patricia's hips, but she swatted them away.

"Don't—"

"Patty." He reached for her hand, but she recoiled at his touch.

"What just happened?" Xavier asked. "Everything was just fine. We—"

"This job. *Your* job. I can't handle this anymore."

"Patty—"

"No." She shoved her hand in his face, halting any further speech. "You slept with somebody else. How—Am I—Suppose to…" She walked over to the sink and wrung out the dishrag that was sitting in soapy water.

"Patty," he called, walking behind her.

"Just give me a minute," she shouted, slinging the dishrag onto the counter. "I forgive you, but this ain't cool, Xavier." She scrubbed the countertop. "You could've found another way out of that."

"Patty, if there was another way, don't you think I would've done it."

"I don't know what to believe." She turned on the water to rinse out the dishrag. "You just happened to have a copy of the report with you," she said giving him the side eye. "How convenient?"

"No. I drove to the station to get it. You refused to listen—"

"What if that trick gave you a sexually transmitted disease?" she barked, punching Xavier on the chest. "Now *my* life is at risk. I'm too old to be up in the clinic," Patricia yelled, flinging the dishrag in the sink causing water to splash everywhere. "What's to keep it from happening again?"

"It won't," he promised, wiping the splattered water off his face and arms.

"That's all you've got to say?" Patricia fumed.

"The case is closed." He stepped toward her with his hands in front of him. "I'll get tested, so you won't have to. I'm sorry, Patty." He caressed her shoulders. "I'll see you tonight."

Patricia finished up in the kitchen and headed upstairs to the bedroom to begin plans to take full advantage of her impromptu day off. She would pamper all the worries away with a trip to the spa, but first, she would run to Walgreens to buy a Self STD Test Kit. She couldn't wait on Xavier and refused to purchase one from another MedRx. Someone might recognize her, and that was the last thing Patricia needed.

Pulling the nightstand drawer open to retrieve a pair of gold hoops, she glanced at a tiny box in the back. Inside were engraved platinum cufflinks she bought Xavier as a Christmas present. She had the mind to return them.

Closing the drawer, she reached for the television remote to check the weather. The back cover and one of the batteries were still missing. Patricia grabbed her phone from the nightstand, then slithered down from the bed to look underneath. She tapped the glass screen until the bright illuminating flashlight turned on. Adjusting her body, she laid flat on the carpet to shine the beaming light under the bed. With her face to the floor, she found that the battery had rolled across to Xavier's side. She crawled to that side, reached under the bed and chipped a fingernail on her middle finger on something metal.

"Ouch" She yanked her hand back and shook it. She squeezed the nail bed, and it flushed pink, drawing blood to the tip of her finger.

This time, she focused the flashlight and gazing before she thrust her hand under the bed. She saw the battery and the culprit that ruined her perfect manicure. Patricia placed the battery on the bed, then carefully pulled out a steel gray metal toolbox she had never seen before. *Why would a toolbox be under the bed? Why not put it in the basement or the garage?* She tried to open it. After tugging on it a few more times without getting it to budge. She put it back in its original spot, then straightened the golden dust ruffle.

What skeletons are Xavier hiding in his secret case?

If his secrets were as life-altering as hers, it was a must that she find out what was in that toolbox.

Chapter Twenty-Four

"Merry Christmas, baby." Xavier lightly nudged Lauren's hip. "Wake up."

"Hmmm." She moaned, turning over in the bed.

Xavier was still on shaky ground with Lauren since his slip of the tongue, but she was coming around. Today's efforts should help with that.

He never spent Christmas mornings with her. It would be hard to explain to Patricia why he wasn't available to open presents with his son, but with Junior out of town, he was able to maneuver differently. His alibi of working Christmas day was usually reserved for Lauren, although he hadn't worked that holiday for over twelve years.

Xavier held a red rectangular box with a large silver bow over her head. He shook it causing the contents to make a scratching sound.

"Rise and shine, sleepyhead," he teased.

Lauren rolled over, pushed herself upright, then stretched, swiping the gift to the side. "Merry Christmas," she said in the middle of a yawn. "I thought you had to work."

"I switched shifts with Officer Felix." He lied effortlessly with a straight face. Officer Felix was just as fictitious as his marriage to Lauren. "He agreed to work my day shift if I covered his evening one," Xavier explained handing Lauren the red box. "This way I could spend the day with you."

The corners of Lauren's lips turned upward as she tugged the end of the bow.

"I have to clock in by seven," Xavier said, knowing he was going home to spend the evening with Patty. He waited to see the expression on her face at that news, but she was focused on opening the present.

Lauren placed the lid on the bed and unfolded the top piece of bright tissue paper. "Wait a minute." She stopped. "Go get your gift from under the tree. We can open them together."

"Will do." He leaned in and planted a kiss on her lips.

This was going better than he had expected.

Xavier retrieved an envelope with his name on it and a medium sized green box from the living room, then returned upstairs.

"Open the big one first," Lauren instructed.

"I thought we were doing this together?" he asked.

"We are." Lauren shifted on the bed, caressing his thigh. "You've already given me the best gift by being here."

His chest swelled realizing what he'd been missing all these years. He tore the box open and inside there were random items, sunscreen, snorkeling mask, and fins. Xavier paused when he pulled out a pair of red Speedos. "Lauren... what the... really?" he chuckled, examining the skimpy swimwear. "You know I prefer trunks."

Giggling, she said, "Open the envelope."

"You're aware it's December, right?" he teased, thrown off by the gifts. "Did you luck up on an early summer sale somewhere?" he said making fun of her, breaking the seal with his index finger.

"You're such the comedian this morning."

Xavier pointed to Lauren's lap. "Look at yours, too."

He pulled out a seven-day Norwegian Cruise Line brochure to Hawaii and two airline tickets.

Oh shit.

His predicament wouldn't allow him to get excited inwardly. There's no way he could disappear for seven days during July. The fact that he'd been pulling off going to New York at the end of the year was still shocking, but this. No way.

"Wow, baby," he whispered, his mind running in circles. "This is awesome, thank you."

"You're welcome," she said removing the tissue paper. "I can't wait for us to lay on the sandy beach and wiggle our toes in the clear ocean water. July is seven months away." Lauren slowly lifted a bronze sequin dress identical to the one she wore the night she'd been shot. "That gives you plenty of time to—"

"I did good, didn't I?" asked Xavier, proud of himself, totally misreading the shock in Lauren's eyes.

"Why would you buy this?"

The tone of her voice wasn't what he expected.

"I knew how much you loved that gown. And—"

"Why would I want a reminder of the worst day of my life, Xavier?" She balled the dress and threw it into the box. "I'm sure your heart was in the right place, but you missed the mark on this one."

* * *

Several hours later, Xavier was in the truck listening to music, heading "to work." Many scenarios ran through his brain, but none were going to grant the desired outcome. The Hawaii trip wasn't going to happen. Somehow he had to wiggle his way out of that and relay it to Lauren in a way that wouldn't cast blame on him.

The ringing phone halted his thoughts. He glanced at the Caller ID and tapped the green spot on the screen to answer.

"Merry Christmas, man. Was Mrs. Claus good to you?"

"Always," Jason responded. "Where are you?" he asked in a quiet tone.

"Five minutes away from the crib," he replied, turning the volume up to better hear Jason through the hands-free Bluetooth speakers. "Why are you whispering?"

"Because Patty's here."

Xavier damn near rear-ended the car in front of him. "What?"

"Yeah. She said you had to work." Jason paused. "So imagine how that looks when Sandy invited her to dinner with our family and friends, and I'm here, instead of at work with you. What the fuck are you doing, man?"

Silence.

"I can't believe you left her alone on Christmas."

Xavier ignored the condemnation in his tone. "I'll just come over there."

"That's not an option, dude," Jason said flatly. "I covered for you."

Loud talking, laughter, and music shot through the truck speakers all at once, forcing Xavier to turn the volume down.

"I'll be out in a minute," Jason shouted. "Close the door."

After a few seconds, the background noise ceased.

"Sounds like party central over there," Xavier commented pulling into the driveway. "Why can't I come by?"

"I didn't know what the hell you were doing or for how long. I told Patty you had to work a double— forced overtime."

"Damn, Jay." Xavier sighed in an exasperated tone. "What am I suppose to do with the rest of my day?"

"I guess whatever you were doing before you decided to come home to your *wife*."

"Jay, man, I gotta go." Xavier disconnected the call.

Xavier put the gear in park and turned off the engine. The homes on the block were sparkling with red, white, and multicolored lights with Rudolph and frosty the snowman glowing on the snow-covered lawns. His house was cold and dark without any decorations and the absence of his family. At that moment, he had an inkling of what Lauren and Patricia felt and it wasn't a good feeling. And to know he was the cause of that ache made him nauseated.

Turning on the end table lamp, he knocked over a small silver box. It flew open once it hit the floor. Picking up the lid, Xavier saw his name written in calligraphy. Two small silver pieces laid not too far away. He picked them up and held them under the light. The letters XCS were engraved in the jewelry.

Thanks, Patty.

He stood in the middle of the floor holding the cufflinks. The quiet was deafening. He couldn't go back to Lauren anytime soon, and he wasn't allowed to go to Jason's to be with Patty. He was alone and lonely, and it was his fault.

"Merry Christmas to me," he whispered as he reflected on his actions.

Chapter Twenty-Five

December twenty-ninth had always been bittersweet for Patricia. Today wasn't any different. Xavier had already left for the gym, Junior was in Florida and hadn't sent one of his standard two-word texts to say he was okay. Now she was left with her own secrets and thoughts and a sense of foreboding that signaled her life was about to change in a major way.

She pulled back the gold drapes and opened the blinds in the bedroom to allow the picturesque scene of snow-covered trees, full pallets of snow on the rooftops with icicles dangling, and the spotless baby blue sky to help brighten her mood.

Just as she turned to walk away, a quick movement caught her attention. She pulled the thick velvet robe she wore closed and peered out of the cold window. A little girl in pink moon boots and a snowsuit was trying to keep up with a shaggy tailed dog, who was tracking through the snow like an Alaskan Husky. Patricia inadvertently smiled, imagining that was her little girl laughing and having fun enjoying the simple pleasures of life that were free. After standing, almost in a trance for a few minutes, the glass began to fog from her breath, and that snapped Patricia back to the present.

She walked to her nightstand and extracted a small key from an old makeup bag. She knelt on the plush carpet and pulled back an eight by eight-inch square piece of rug under the bed that she sliced with a box cutter years ago. She felt around in the grooves of the wood before lifting three panels and retrieving a shoe box buried underneath. Brushing the dust away, Patricia opened the box, removed a small metal safe and sat it between her thighs.

Her fingers trembled as she unlocked it and gently touched a photo of a handsome teenage boy with tan spiked hair, and green eyes, wearing blue jeans and a tan Members Only jacket and diamond studs in both ears. She kissed the snapshot and smiled. At the moment, it seemed that she had it all. She loved Xavier, but it was hard to truly love him when there was a small sliver of something in her heart and mind that longed for Matthew O'Shaughnessy. Xavier was so secretive at times that it seemed like every thought was measured or every action was planned. At times, Patricia was wary of him. He explained his way out of a lot of things, but sometimes she wondered if she was missing something. That last issue with him having to "sleep" with that woman still didn't sit well. More so because he had failed to do something so basic as clean himself before he got home, then coming up with that explanation.

"Matthew," she spoke his name just above a whisper as if someone would overhear. A smile turned up the corners of her lips as she continued rifling through her hidden treasure box. She read the love letters, poems, and keepsake tokens. She held a movie stub from their first date twenty-six years ago that had started to fade. A slow tear fell from her eye when she held the discolored purple and white plastic pregnancy test stick in her hand that confirmed she and Matthew were going to be parents.

Patricia wiped her face with the sleeve of the robe so the memories she held wouldn't be ruined. A drop of moisture would surely do that if her tears hit the old pictures and letters. These were the only mementos she possessed of her first love and their baby girl.

She reached between the mattress and the box spring and pulled out a medium-sized lavender envelope she stashed there last night. Inside it was a beautiful birthday card from a mother to a daughter wishing her all the best on her twenty-fifth birthday and all the joys life had to offer.

Patricia closed her eyes, angled her head toward heaven and took several cleansing breaths. She then bowed her head and placed a hand over her heart, silently praying that God would continue to watch over her daughter, wherever she might be.

She moved everything to the side and crossed her legs, then picked up a tulle see-thru fuchsia pink bag filled with a single photo and numerous birthday cards from years past. She added this year's card to the collection and carefully removed the photograph.

"Happy twenty-fifth birthday, baby. Mommy loves you so much."

Patricia smiled and caressed the photograph of her child, Nurse Dominique, who would become her baby's mother, and herself. She lifted a small pink flower brooch. Nurse Dominique had given it to her the day Shawn was born. Patricia brought it to her lips.

She rocked back and forth letting the agony of loss flow out of her. This time she allowed herself to feel every gut-wrenching emotion that had been buried deep inside. Loss and sadness for the daughter she never knew and desperately wished she could have raised. A part of her was out in this world, and she had no way of knowing if that girl child was alright. The horror stories of young girls being abused, molested, and sold to the sex-trade played out in the news. She watched the news, read the papers, all the while hoping and praying that it wasn't her child.

Guilt, for not being strong enough to stand up to her parents and tell them she wanted to keep her baby racked her. Heartache, for a relationship, snatched away. Matthew was her everything, and they never recovered after they were badgered into doing something they didn't want. And lastly, deceit, because her husband had no idea that she had born a child before Junior and she never felt compelled to tell him.

While completely wallowing in nostalgia, the house phone rang. Patricia wasn't in the mood to speak with anyone. She ignored it, and the person clicked off before the voicemail kicked in. They called back another series of times until finally at the end of the recorded greeting she heard a familiar voice. "Patricia, it's me, pick-up the phone. I know you're there. Pick-up the phone. I'm gonna keep calling until you do."

The machine cuts off, and the phone rang again.

Patricia wiped her face, then gathered her keepsakes, with the exception of the pink brooch, and put them in the metal safe. She kissed the photo of her baby, Nurse Dominique, and herself and placed it underneath the contents of the safe.

"Pick-up the phone Li'l Sis. Don't make me come over there," Latrice warned, through the answering machine.

Patricia peeled herself off the floor and walked to the window. The little girl and her dog were long gone, but winter wonderland remained. She closed and locked the safe, then put it back in the shoebox.

"Hellooooooo—" Latrice yelled.

Then Patricia heard the machine cut off. Two seconds later the phone rang again.

She sighed then walked over to the bed, plopped down, and picked up the phone. Her sister *would* keep calling until she did.

"Stop stalking me."

"It's about time you answered," Latrice said in a concerned tone. "Are you okay?"

"Yeah, I guess."

"How old is my niece today?"

"Twenty-five. Can you believe it?"

"Wow, Li'l Sis. How old does that make *you?*" Latrice laughed.

"Old enough, but I'll always be *younger* than *you*, smarty."

She curled fetal position, nuzzled her head in the soft pillow and cradled the phone to her ear. "I often wonder how she and Junior would've gotten along being ten years apart. Would he look up to her? Would he be protective of her? Would she pick on him the way you picked on me?"

"Humph. I did no such thing," Latrice defended, and Patricia could practically see her lips in a pout.

"You keep lying to yourself 'cause I know the truth."

Latrice chuckled. "Well, I didn't do anything to you that you didn't deserve."

"Whatever." Patricia rolled over on her back, crossed her ankles in response.

"That's what I'm talking about," Latrice laughed along with her.

"What?"

"You're laughing. My job here is done. I love you, Li'l Sis, and if you need to talk, you know where to find me. I love you."

"I love you too, and thanks."

She smiled and returned the phone to the base.

No matter how much of a funk Patricia fell into, her sister was the antidote. It felt good to know she had one person that knew her secret and would allow her to fall apart and plunge into her feelings, whatever they may be, and it was okay.

Patricia's spirit had been lifted, and for a moment she felt at peace. She walked over and knelt on the carpet. She closed the old shoebox and placed it beneath the floorboards under the bed. As she patted and smoothed out the patch of carpet, she noticed that mysterious toolbox was missing. He must have come back to retrieve it at some point. Now her curiosity was running wild.

What is Xavier hiding?

* * *

The following day at work Patricia was her usual jovial self, multitasking to the max talking with customers, filling new prescription orders, and giving vaccinations when Shawn came in at eleven.

"Good morning everyone."

There was a collective good morning from Patricia and her coworkers, spicy Javid, and Afro-centric Meilani.

"Where do you need me?" Shawn asked Patricia, who had a handful of documents.

"Grab some labels from the stockroom and fill the printer please."

"That's pretty," Shawn said, pointing to the pink flower brooch on Patricia's lab coat. "Is it new?"

"No. I've had it for a long time," Patricia replied. "Twenty-five years."

"I've never seen you wear it before."

The corners of Patricia's lips curved upward. "It was a gift from a special friend."

Shawn disappeared into the back and Patricia went to the consultation window to help a customer who had questions about acid reflux medication. When she returned to her computer, Shawn was loading the printer with blank prescription labels.

"Thanks for letting me work early yesterday."

"You're welcome." Patricia smiled, taking in the pinkish hue that filled Shawn's cheeks.

Javid came strolling over with four prescription bottles that had been dropped off by Mr. Dunkin for a refill. "Yeah, we had a ball last night," he boasted while scanning the barcodes into the computer system.

"Where did you guys go?" Patricia inquired, reading the prescription notes on the computer.

"Cesar's Killer Margaritas to celebrate Shawn's birthday," Javid announced. His olive skin flushing with the memories of what must've been a fantastic time.

"How nice," Patricia grinned. "When was your birthday?"

"Yesterday."

Patricia slid a glance to Shawn. "Happy belated birthday. Why didn't you say anything?" she asked, gliding and clicking the mouse. "Y'all didn't want this old chick to tag along?"

"It wasn't anything like that——"

Patricia cut Shawn off. "I'm just teasing."

"Shawn said she didn't want to do much, but I told her no way, you only turn twenty-five once." Javid snapped his fingers. "So I called her other BFF Candace, and we put the plan into motion."

"Javid, you're so over the top." Shawn rolled her eyes and snickered as she closed the lid to the printer and hit the reset key.

"Anyway, you had a blast." Javid countered.

"I sure did," Shawn smirked at him and winked her eye. "Twenty-five never felt so good."

Twenty-five. Born on December twenty-ninth.

A sharp pain hit right above Patricia's navel; then it ruptured throughout her abdomen. She placed her hand protectively over her midsection and stared at Shawn. *Really* stared at Shawn. She took in the ivory complexion, dark hair and its silky texture, and these granny-smith apple green eyes. A stark resemblance and clarity made her heart race and pound against her chest. Perspiration dotted around Patricia's hairline. "Happy twenty-fifth birthday."

Her world faded to black.

Chapter Twenty-Six

Shawn dropped to her knees and lifted Patricia's head onto her lap. "Somebody help me," she screamed, fanning a hand over Patricia's clammy face.

"What happened?" Javid asked, kneeling as he tapped Patricia's cheek.

"I don't know," Shawn wailed. "She was talking … and then she wasn't."

She grabbed Patricia's shoulders and shook her. "Wake up. Oh my God, pleeease wake up."

This couldn't be happening. Shawn hadn't had the chance to tell Patricia she was her daughter. She'd lost so many people that she loved, and even Ms. Ida was a little distant after Taletha's death.

Shawn laid Patricia's head gently on the mat, jumped to her feet, snatched the phone from the cradle and pressed the intercom button.

"We need a manager in the pharmacy. Now." She dropped the receiver on the counter and ran to the back of the pharmacy, flung open the overhead white cabinet, and grabbed the ceramic mortar bowl that was used to crush tablets to make compound prescriptions.

With trembling hands, Shawn filled the bowl with cold tap water and ran to the front. Did Patricia have a medical condition she hadn't told anyone about?

"Move out the way, Javid," Shawn ordered but didn't wait for him to comply. She poured the cool water over Patricia's face. Shawn stared as a, now soaked Javid continued to tap Patricia's wet cheek. Nothing.

"Meilani, call 911," Shawn screamed.

The curvy woman rushed off in the direction of the phone at the pick-up counter. Shawn ran to the sink and refilled the bowl with water. She heard Meilani pressing keys on the phone over the intercom system.

"I can't get an outside line. There's no dial tone," Meilani yelled in frustration.

"Shit."

Shawn always thought the "no cell phone" policy at work was stupid. In the past, she would keep the phone on silent in the breast pocket of her scrubs, but while one of the suits from the corporate office was there, the screen had lit up and shown through the pocket, and that was the end of that.

She dropped the mortar bowl in the sink and balled her hands into tight fists. Water cascaded in the air like a fountain and flew in all directions. Shawn ran to the pick-up window where Meilani had been working, and customers stood frozen, staring. "Don't just stand there. Somebody dial 911," she ordered.

A shaky voice shouted, "I already have."

Thank God.

Shawn turned to go back to attend to Patricia.

"How much longer is it going to be?" another woman asked. "I have to get to work."

Halted for a moment by the audacity of the familiar woman's voice, Shawn whipped around. "Ms. Moran, it'll be however long it needs to be," Shawn snapped, burning a hole through the ignorant woman who lacked compassion.

The surrounding customers also glared at Ms. Moran. She huffed but averted her eyes.

The store manager, Mr. Slocum, had finally made his way to the pharmacy. He was gasping for air as he rounded the corner. Premature gray hair, pear-shaped body, and large plastic eyeglass frames made him look like a man in his mid-sixties rather than a prime forty-three.

"Sorry for the inconvenience folks, but the pharmacy is closed until further notice," Mr. Slocum announced as he lowered the security shutters with the touch of a button, drowning out angry grunts and profanities. "There's a twenty-four-hour MedRx less than a mile away on Sheffield." The silver metal hit the counter and separated the customers from the dealings within.

"My apologies for taking so long," he said, waddling past the registers. "A customer held me up with a complaint, but I could hear the chaos going on back here over the store's intercom system."

"Patricia fainted, and we can't wake her up," Shawn explained with a trembling voice. "We couldn't get an outside line, but one of the customers dialed 911."

Mr. Slocum walked his pudgy form over to each phone station and checked the lines. The phone at the pharmacist's station where Patricia's limp body lay unresponsive was on the counter. He pressed the red highlighted intercom button and then placed the phone on the base. He pressed line one, and Shawn had never been so happy to hear a dial tone in her life.

"Hold on Patricia. Help is on the way," Shawn reassured.

Javid was still tending to Patricia, keeping a steady stream of talk while tapping her cheek, shaking her shoulders, and checking her pulse. Shawn was thankful that Javid was calm. She didn't know he had it in him; since he'd always been the liveliest of the crew.

Shawn knelt along the side of Patricia, leaned over her chest and put her ear to Patricia's nose. She could feel tiny whispers of breath on her skin. Then she knelt and whispered so only Patricia would hear, "Mom, I need you."

"Here," Meilani said, shoving the first aid kit in Shawn's direction.

Shawn rummaged through the Band-Aids, gauze, antiseptic wipes, and other paraphernalia when she stumbled upon a box of smelling salts. Hopefulness filled her heart as she tore open the box then cracked the small white suppository looking packet in half and waved it under Patricia's nose. The gasp that escaped Patricia's mouth was the most heavenly sound on earth.

Chapter Twenty-Seven

Patricia jerked when her nostrils were infused with a strong pungent ammonia odor that hit her central nervous system with a vengeance. She moved her head from side to side to avoid inhaling it again. When she opened her eyes, the focus was hazy. Someone was beating an ugly rhythm inside her head.

A woman was crying nearby, and Patricia slowly turned her head, and her gaze landed on a sobbing Shawn. She reached for the younger woman's hand, though she was confused and everything was a blur, comforting her seemed like the natural thing to do.

"Welcome back," Shawn said, smiling as tears trickled down her pale cheeks.

"What happened?"

"You blacked out."

"I what?" Patricia asked, still unable to see clearly.

"You fainted," Javid interjected, placing a cold compress on her forehead.

"Don't you remember?" Shawn asked, affectionately rubbing her hand.

"I don't remember anything," Patricia said trying to prop up on her elbows.

"I don't think it's a good idea for you to sit up so fast," Shawn spoke in a voice filled with concern.

"I feel fine; I just have a slight headache. Help me up please?" Patricia grabbed the ice pack and held out her arms. Both Javid and Shawn assisted Patricia to her feet. Meilani fetched a chair from the patient waiting area. A bone-chilling shiver ravaged Patricia's body, and she wrapped her arms across her breast. "Why am I wet?"

"I threw water on you," Shawn admitted in a shaky voice. "I was trying to wake you up."

She held her arms even tighter, trying to ward off the cold. Patricia glanced upward, finally acknowledging her. "Thanks for your efforts."

The silence of the insanely busy pharmacy eluded her until now. "Why are the shutters closed?" she asked, scanning the threesome.

"Mr. Slocum thought it was best," Shawn responded, holding Patricia's arm as she reached for the armrest. "You needed some privacy."

Patricia positioned her body on the edge of the seat and lowered her head in between her knees to gain a sense of balance.

"Are you alright?" Javid asked, squatting in front of her.

Before she could answer, Meilani touched the back of her hand to Patricia's neck. "You don't have a fever."

Shawn rubbed her upper back and whispered, "Thank you, Jesus."

"I'm okay, guys," she said, trying to reassure them. Patricia planted her feet and slowly rose to her full height. She inched a few steps, then braced with her palms on the counter for additional support.

There was a rap on the pharmacy door. "EMT, did someone call for a paramedic?"

Javid jogged over to the locked door to let them in. Everyone stood back, but close enough to observe the paramedics in action.

They checked her blood pressure and pulse; then asked her a series of questions. After their assessment, it was concluded that stress, a drop in blood pressure, and dehydration were the cause of the fainting spell.

"This has never happened before," Patricia said. "Do I need to be worried?"

"No, but I do recommend following up with your doctor to rule out a more serious underlying problem, especially since this was your first episode," the paramedic suggested as he repacked the tactical medical kit bag. "You need to take it easy the rest of the day. No sudden movements, and if you feel like you're going to pass out; sit down and drop your head between your knees until it passes."

Patricia tried to remember what she was doing right before she passed out, but all thoughts swirled into a ball of confusion. She took the paramedic's advice and planned to go home for the rest of the day.

"I'll drive you home," Shawn volunteered.

"Thanks, but I feel well enough to drive myself."

"But you still have a headache."

"It's not as bad as it was," she replied. "I'm just a little lightheaded that's all."

"You can rest your head for a little bit in the back before I drive. Either way, I'm not taking no for an answer." Shawn walked over and took Patricia's purse and keys from the storage drawer. "Call your husband, tell him what happened, and to meet you at home."

Patricia was surprised how adamant Shawn was about not allowing her to leave on her own. She didn't have the energy to go back and forth. Patricia allowed Shawn to usher her out of the pharmacy.

* * *

Shawn pulled in the plowed circular driveway of Patricia's gorgeous home and took in the beauty. The immaculate curbside appeal of the majestic home belonged on the front cover of a Better Homes and Gardens Magazine.

"Thanks for your help today," Patricia said before getting out of the car. "I can be stubborn at times." She raised a finger to her lips. "But don't tell anyone I admitted that." She winked, then grinned at Shawn who laughed. "In all seriousness. I'm glad I listened to you. I feel much better."

"You're welcome." Shawn glanced around, her heart pounding fast from anxiety. "Is your husband here?"

"Not yet," Patricia frowned, staring at the empty spot in the driveway.

"I can stay with you until he gets here," Shawn said, praying that Patricia invited her inside.

"I'm alright," Patricia reassured. "I don't want to hold you up any longer."

Shawn's palms tingled, and her throat tightened as the reality of seeing the inside of Patricia's home became more tangible. Maybe Patricia had a picture of her dad on display or something else that would offer more information about his whereabouts. She didn't know when that opportunity might present itself again.

The google search on ancestry.com U.S. Military Collection served to be a useful tool in locating her father. Matthew had been stationed at Fort Bliss in El Paso Texas for basic training and the early part of his military career. He fought in the Bosnian War in 1994 and the Kosovo War in 1998. According to the records, Matthew had retired and was residing in Illinois.

"May I use your bathroom before I go?"

"Sure," Patricia said, extracting the keys from her purse.

"Thanks," Shawn said as a chill shot through her body from the hair follicles to her pink toenails.

Shawn took in a long, slow breath as she entered the foyer of her mother's home. She inhaled the fresh scent of cherry blossom that wafted through the air. The gold drapery, the hues of Sedona and cream walls, and African artwork in the living room made Patricia's home warm and inviting. Shawn thought about Junior. *Why did he have the chance to grow up with her and I didn't? What makes him so special?*

"You have a beautiful home."

"Thank you," Patricia said kicking off the black pumps and dropping her purse on the couch. "The bathroom's down the hall, second door on your left."

"Thanks." She traveled down the hallway, slowing at the first closed door on the left. Peering over her shoulder, she glanced to see if Patricia was watching. Instead, she was met with Val Warner's voice coming from the front of the house. Shawn sighed in relief and prayed that Windy City Live would keep Patricia entertained long enough for Shawn to feed her curiosity. She eased the door open, landing in someone's home office. She closed and locked the door, quickly scanning the room to find anything she could about her mother or possible father. The sun offered a little light through the partially opened wooden blinds, but it would have to do. The room smelled woodsy unlike the rest of the home. Right away Shawn knew she was in Patricia's husband's office. The desk was tidy with a computer and keyboard and didn't give away any information. She tried to open the drawer, but it was locked. *Damn.* She turned to leave, stepping on something crunchy. Shawn pulled out her cell and turned on the flashlight. It was a crumpled piece of yellow paper on the floor next to the wire wastepaper basket. Shawn bent to pick it up when a deep, taut voice asked in the distance.

"Is everything okay?"

Shawn froze, dropping the phone. Fear coursed through her body, causing Shawn's bladder muscles to betray her. She squeezed her thighs together and stood as still as possible. "No. No. No," she whispered, willing the urine to retreat. She listened. The television was no longer playing. Patricia's response wasn't loud enough to reach, but Shawn could only focus on getting out of that room before she was busted. She grabbed the phone from the floor, shoving it in her bra, then tiptoed to the door.

"Would you like something to drink?" Patricia asked.

She shivered, backing against the wall at the sound of Patricia's voice getting closer. Something fell on Shawn's head, piercing her scalp. She had caught the frame before it crashed to the floor, resisting the urge to cry out in pain. Patricia's footsteps halted, right outside the room. Beads of water gathered at Shawn's hairline, and her armpits were sticky like muddy puddles.

"I have coffee, iced-tea, pop, or would you like a beer?" Patricia asked.

"Tea would be nice," the man's voice answered.

I'm never going to get out of here.

"Tea it is," Patricia replied.

As the footsteps moved further away, Shawn tried her hardest to replace the frame on the wall in the dim light. A round blue seal outlined in yellow in the bottom left-hand corner was the only thing that stood out. She couldn't make out any words, and at this point, she wasn't trying to. All curiosity was gone, and she wanted to get the hell out of there unscathed. She succeeded on the sixth attempt.

She stood with her hand on the knob. As soon as Patricia walked back to the front of the house, Shawn gently turned the lock, praying that it didn't make a loud click. Cracking the door, she listened for the chance to escape. Shawn eased her way out and darted into the bathroom. She cleaned herself up with paper towels and headed to the living room.

"I was concerned when I saw a strange car in your driveway," the seasoned, white-haired man said, sitting in the living room with Patricia.

Relief coursed through Shawn.

"Hi." She waved with a cautious smile.

"Hello dear," he replied.

"Frank, this is Shawn," Patricia said, with a gesture of the hand. "She works with me at MedRx. Shawn, this is my neighbor, Frank."

"Nice to meet you, Mr. Frank," she said, fishing the car keys out of her pocket. "I'll see you at work tomorrow. Goodbye."

* * *

Patricia undressed, walking into the bathroom to turn on the water so she could wash away today's troubles and embrace the revelations.

She adjusted the water as hot as she could tolerate and allowed the cascading pellets to massage her body as she sat on the shower bench and meditated.

After Patricia dressed, she perched on the loveseat and touch-dialed Latrice who answered on the first ring.

"Why are you calling me in the middle of the day?"

"Can't you ever say hello first before you start acting crazy?"

Latrice chuckled. "No, not really. What's going on Li'l Sis?"

"I had a fainting episode at work today."

"You fainted," Latrice repeated. "Are you okay? What happened? Where's Xavier?"

"I'm fine. I blacked out while working and I'm not sure why" Patricia said wiggling her French-pedicured toes in the soft carpet. "They told me my pressure was low and I was probably dehydrated. My staff took excellent care of me. I'm going to pull the video footage tomorrow to see exactly what happened.

"And where's your husband?" Latrice asked.

"Down killer," Patricia warned. "Xavier's on his way home."

"He should already be there." The sarcasm and anger in her voice were unmistakable.

But she had a point. Where was Xavier? "Latrice, not today."

She switched off the lights in her bedroom and held the railing at the top of the stairs taking her time as she passed the champagne and gold mosaic artwork on the wall, taking small steady steps as she traveled down the stairs into the living room. As far back as Patricia could remember, Latrice couldn't stand Xavier. Something happened between them before Patricia met him, and neither her sister nor Xavier would fill her in.

"I'm just saying it seems like whenever you need him the most, he's *never* around. He's probably laid up with some trick."

Gliding an ebony hand along the dark maple crown molding that encompassed the fireplace, she lifted their ten-year anniversary photo and smiled. "You don't know what you're talking about."

"Like hell, I don't."

"You never liked him."

"That we can agree on, Li'l Sis."

Latrice's quick tongue was like venom, and her dislike of Xavier was embedded in her soul.

Patricia blocked out the nonsense spewing from Latrice's mouth and focused on the anniversary photo. She felt an inner desire burning as she reflected back on their first encounter as she confessed, "You know he was my first."

"Your first. Really? Are you rewriting history?" Latrice questioned in a sharp tone.

"Well … born again virgin," Patricia said in a low tone, trying not to let her mind wander to the most painful time in her history.

Latrice remained silent. She always had an arsenal of verbal weapons to hurl at Xavier. This time, she uncharacteristically kept her lips buttoned and listened.

"He never pressured me to have sex," she whispered, taking in the sharp lines of his chiseled features, pointed chin, and smoldering eyes. "Even before he knew I was a virgin. I think he loved me more because of it."

Patricia placed the framed photo back on the mantel and curled up on the brown chenille sofa adorned with cream, orange, and tan accent pillows. She didn't have to repeat the rest. Xavier supported her dream of becoming a pharmacist, pushed her to complete her internships when it seemed impossible after she gave birth to Junior during her final leg of pharmacy school; or that he held the family down by working two jobs, postponing his Police Academy

Training to keep them afloat. Latrice had heard it all many times before.

"This man is my rock."

Patricia pulled a throw blanket over her body and tucked it under her chin. She stared at the maple bookcase that housed tons of Criminal Justice and Pharmacy Law books, reminding her of their accomplishments, the things that helped in reaching their respective goals.

The roar of an engine outside the oversized picture window caught Patricia's attention, making her breath quicken.

"I'll talk to you later, Xavier's home."

"It's about damn time."

"You're such a killjoy——damn," Patricia remarked, annoyed.

* * *

Xavier came busting in the door, eyes wild and scared.

"Slow down, I'm alright," she said, holding her hands up to halt his movements.

He rushed over, lowered onto the leather ottoman, and placed a hand on her knee. "What happened?"

"I honestly don't know. One minute I was working and the next I was staring at the ceiling and everyone was hovering over me."

"Why didn't you call me sooner?" he asked, his gaze focused on the brooch attached to her lab coat.

"There wasn't need too," she said, warmed by his concern, but taken aback by his interest in the brooch.

Xavier had asked Patricia in the past where the pin came from and why she always wore it in family pictures. She lied and said that it belonged to her grandmother who was deceased. It made Patricia feel close to her. Xavier didn't verbally dispute the claim, but he always had a questioning expression when she wore it.

"My staff took care of me. And Shawn brought me home. I'll actually need a ride to work in the morning since my car is still at the job."

He stood, looked down at her, then paced the floor.

She watched him for a few seconds before she asked, "Why are you walking a roadmap in my good carpet?"

Xavier didn't respond. He shuffled over to the mantel and picked up Junior's baby photo. Their six-month-old son had on a blue and white sailor suit romper with a matching hat and red necktie.

"The last time you had unexplained fainting spells you were pregnant with Junior."

She threw her head back and laughed, "Baby, the harbor is closed. You can dock, but there'll be no vessels coming out."

"How can you be so sure?"

She rose from the couch and folded the throw blanket. "Because I had my tubes tied after Junior. Remember?" She lifted the ottoman lid and placed the blanket neatly inside.

Xavier was happy about the birth of his son but was so overwhelmed with going to school full time and pulling two part-time jobs in preparation for their new addition that when Patricia mentioned tubal ligation, he didn't give it a second thought.

The truth was Patricia had an abnormally shaped uterus. When she became pregnant at fifteen, the labor and delivery of that first child had damaged her birth canal. The doctor told her she was lucky that her daughter didn't suffer from Bell's Palsy, brain damage, or had any broken bones. When she became pregnant with Junior ten years later, the complications further damaged her uterus. She thought maybe it would be different since she was older and her pelvic muscles were fully developed, but that wasn't the case. Junior suffered from Subconjunctival Hemorrhage, which was bleeding that occurred when small blood vessels in the eyes broke. It didn't cause permanent eye damage, but she vowed never to bring another child into the world and put their life at risk.

He stared at Junior's picture. "Sometimes I wish we had a little girl. She would look just like you——dark skin with big beautiful brown eyes and two long pigtails."

"Yeah, that would've been nice," she mumbled, fighting back the tears. The guilt of keeping that secret all this time overshadowed any memories that she had of Matthew, her child and what her parents had done. If only Xavier knew that *she* did, in fact, have a daughter. Would he still feel the same?

Chapter Twenty-Eight

Lauren inhaled the peppery scent of the magenta oriental lilies on Dr. Harden's desk in a consultation suite while waiting to discuss her lab results.

When she went for her post-op appointment one week after the surgery, she also visited with Dr. Harden whose practice was in the same building. She was more than happy to see Lauren on *this* side of the dirt.

"How are you feeling?" Dr. Harden asked, sitting across from her wearing a red-ribbed turtleneck with gray slacks and black leather boots.

"Much better considering where I was when I saw you four weeks ago," she replied, adjusting the blue and white arm sling.

"I'm glad to hear it."

Lauren grinned. "And I'm back at work."

"Oh wow," Dr. Harden remarked.

"Well, I'm getting the salon back in order. There was a lot of damage, but that nine-letter word called 'insurance' is a blessing from above. My out-of-pocket cost was minimal."

"That's great."

"I thought I was going to be nervous entering the place, but everything was okay."

Lauren sat, then shifted in the oversized leather chair and crossed one leg over the other. "What's so urgent that you insisted on seeing me in person? You typically send my lab results through the mail."

"That's true, I have some news for you, but I wanted to ask you a couple of questions first," Dr. Harden said, clicking the mouse and sliding it across the mouse pad. "Here we go," she mumbled, adjusting her reading glasses and focusing on whatever was on the computer screen. "Are you still taking Zolpidem Tartrate?"

"What????"

"Are you still taking the Ambien?"

"Awww … no, I haven't had any Ambien in months." Lauren fingered the hem of her indigo sweater. "Right before my accident I asked you for some, but never had the chance to come in, except for when you sent me to get my blood work done. You said that you wanted the results before prescribing anymore."

"I remember that—" Dr. Harden removed her glasses—— "but your test results say something entirely different."

Lauren leaned forward and raked the sand in the Zen and rock garden on the oval coffee table, making four perfect rows of squiggly lines.

"You can be honest with me," Dr. Harden hedged. "Are you getting the pills from another doctor?"

"No … I haven't had any." Lauren leaned back in the soft leather. "Truthfully, I thought that's why I was coming in."

Dr. Harden's amber eyes narrowed to slits. "Is it a doctor in *this* practice?"

Lauren closed her eyes against the intensity of the interrogation, and couldn't wrap her lips around the truth. Lauren had been doing just that, but she refused to admit it to Dr. Harden. Lynette had recommended Dr. Thai who had been her physician at Northwestern Hospital for years.

"Listen, Mrs. Carter; blood work doesn't lie. It also showed in your urine sample, and the only way that's possible is if you've been taking it regularly because it wouldn't stay in your system for extended periods of time."

Lauren uncrossed her leg, shifted on her hip and folded her hands. "Maybe your lab technician got the blood samples mixed up," she countered with a straight face.

"I know how this works. You're not the first patient I've had who has become addicted to this medication. I'm familiar with all the 'lingo' that comes along with repeatedly getting early refills. And I've been documenting your frequency." She stood and opened the top drawer of the steel gray metal file cabinet and pulled out a file folder with Lauren's full name on it. "Now, I'm going to ask you again, who have you been getting the Ambien from for the past three months?"

Silence.

Dr. Harden came around from the desk and sat in the matching oversized seat facing Lauren. "Sleeping pills are narcotics, and if not taken correctly they can have adverse effects. This is especially important because your blood test also shows that your HCG levels are extremely high." She paused and grabbed Lauren's hand. "You're pregnant."

"Excuse me——what?" she gasped. "I'm pregnant."

"Yes."

Lauren froze at that revelation. "I'm going to be someone's mother," she murmured. A small smile crept upon her lips. And warmth rushed to her cheeks.

"Congratulations," Dr. Harden said, nodding, but her facial expression was anything but elated.

Still smiling, Lauren's hand wandered to her belly. "Thanks."

"In regards to the Ambien," Dr. Harden continued, "It's a

pregnancy category class C drug. It's only recommended for use during pregnancy when the benefit outweighs the risk. Some doctors allow it, but I do not."

Lauren met her eyes, now feeling like a fool for even trying to lie. She may have been harming her unborn son or daughter.

Dr. Harden cleared her throat, "Did you *understand* what I just said, Mrs. Carter? *No more Ambien.*"

* * *

Lauren could hardly contain her excitement as the elevator descended to the ground level of the indoor parking garage. Soon as she made it to the car, she dug her phone out of her purse. Xavier should have been her first call, but her fingers automatically dialed her mother. She didn't even give her mom a chance to say hello.

"Guess who's going to be a grandma?" she teased.

Her mother squealed before calling the Lord's name, then she yelled, "Rodney, come here, quick."

Lauren placed a comforting hand on her belly smiling; listening to the commotion on the other end of the phone.

"Tell your father what you just said to me. I'm going to put you on the speaker."

"Hey, Pudding Pie. What has your mom all excited and yelling like a mad woman?"

Lauren laughed. "I told mom that you're going to be grandparents."

"Dear God," he yelled, and she could imagine the look on her dad's face. "Awwww Pudding Pie that's fantastic news."

"Thanks, daddy."

"How far along are you?" her mother inquired.

Lauren rubbed her belly again, grinning. "Nine weeks according to my HCG levels, but I'm scheduled to have an ultrasound in two weeks to find out for sure," she said practically unable to control her excitement. "The doctor wanted to schedule it for next week, but there's no way I'm going to miss coming home to see you and dad. And it'll be our ten year anniversary."

"Oh, this is the best news I've heard since that horrible accident. I am so happy for you and Xavier. Is he excited?" Mom asked.

"I haven't told him yet."

"What?" her parents chorused in unison.

"I just left my appointment," she said, suddenly defensive. "I'm sitting in the parking garage of the doctor's office."

"Chile, get off this phone and call your husband——right now," her mother ordered.

"Bye Ma, bye Daddy."

"Bye Pudding Pie, I love you," Dad said in a soft tone.

"I love you too."

Midway to disconnecting the call, her mother said, "Lauren, wait."

"Yes, ma'am?"

"Thanks for calling me first," she whispered in a conspiratorial tone.

"Ma, you're a mess," Lauren said with a hearty chuckle. "Love you. Bye."

Lauren was a daddy's girl, but she had a bond with her mother like none other. She was her best friend and confidant, and she trusted no one the way she trusted her mother. She inserted the key in the ignition and dialed Xavier.

"Hey baby," he answered on the third ring.

"Hey, you." Her voice was light and airy, the same way she felt inside. "We're going out tonight. My treat. And I'm not taking no for an answer. So clear your schedule."

There was a long pause, and she thought he was going to say he was busy.

"What's the occasion?"

"Just be ready by seven."

"Why are you being secretive?"

"Just make sure you're home on time," she warned. "It's worth the suspense." She disconnected the call before he could say otherwise.

Chapter Twenty-Nine

Xavier thought he'd been discreet when he glanced down at his watch, but Jason, asked, "You got someplace to be that's more important than *this* moment?"

His lips were moving, and the sound was barely discernible. They were at the funeral of Elijah Patrick, the ten-year-old boy who had been shot on Loomis after the raid.

Speaking in the same fashion as Jason, Xavier responded, in a whisper. "Not at this moment, but soon."

Outside of St. Dorothy's Church, the people of the community chanted Black Lives Matter. This was one of those times that Xavier wished he could be out there with his people instead of standing with the boys in blue. No matter how the media or the department tried to spin the story, he knew there was no reason for that young boy to be shot and left for dead in the middle of the street. None at all.

Xavier had gotten a chance to know Elijah while working undercover. He watched him come and go on his bike at all hours of the day and night. His proper diction and preppy dress told Xavier that Elijah didn't grow up in the hood. Xavier befriended the youngster, schooling him on how to survive in the neighborhood he now called home.

Elijah wasn't a bad kid; he was simply a victim of his circumstances. His mother worked two jobs, second and third shift so she could be home to send him off to school with a hot breakfast and a prayer. She cooked meals in bulk and froze them in servings so he would have food throughout the week. His father had been killed during his second deployment in the War in Afghanistan. That's when Elijah's world drastically changed. Forced to move out of their suburban home in Orland Park because she could no longer afford the mortgage on her income alone, she did the best that she could in a neighborhood rife with poverty, drugs, and gang violence.

It made Xavier's stomach turn that out of all the officers that were outside during the tragic incident no one saw or knew anything.

"You know they're classifying this as an accident," Jason said, sliding into the driver's seat of the Suburban.

"That's what they would like for us to believe." Xavier huffed, slamming the door on the passenger's side.

"I would've given anything to have been out there first." Jason commented, "I'd blow the whistle on all of them bastards."

"And your white ass would be out of a job. They aren't going to protect you like the others." Xavier cut his eyes in Jason's direction and looked him up and down. "You're a black man trapped in a white person's body. You're like Eminem. The White community don't claim him either."

Jason cut the wheel to pull out of the parking space when Xavier tapped his shoulder. "Hold up. Did you see the three dudes at the back of the church?"

"From the raid?" His brow furrowed. "Yeah, I peeped that. They made bail real quick."

"Too damn quick," Xavier mused. "And they may have made us too, so watch your back."

* * *

Xavier hopped in his truck when they arrived at the station. His clouded breath fogged the frosty windows until the truck warmed up.

He grabbed his phone to call Lauren when a text message from Patricia came through.

Just checking on you. I know today was a rough day, how are you? How was the funeral?

He sighed, leaning back against the headrest. Elijah's murder brought back the feelings he experienced when his father was killed.

* * *

Xavier's dad had bought him a car as a graduation gift the end of his senior year of high school. He had to maintain a 3.5 GPA or better to receive it. Xavier graduated with a 4.0 GPA and a handful of scholarships.

He ran home that last day of school, one week before graduation with his final grades in hand. Xavier was so excited that he didn't focus on the crowd of people, yellow tape, or the six squad cars sitting in front of his house until an officer stopped him from entering his home.

"Who are you?" the aggressive cop asked blocking the way.

"I live here," Xavier said, trying to get around him.

"You didn't answer the question."

"Dad," he yelled. "What happened? Mom," he screamed out. "Are my parents okay?" he asked the officer, trying to get around him. Xavier almost bypassed him, but the cop regained control, holding Xavier in place.

People outside shouted and screamed that Xavier lived there. Eventually, a few officers from inside the house came out see what the commotion was about. "Let him go. That's Officer Carter's son," several officers shouted at the same time.

Xavier snatched away, then skipped the stairs, two at a time calling for his dad. He entered the living room, and the adrenaline came crashing down the moment he'd seen his mother's face. The paper slipped from his hand to the floor.

"Where's dad?" he asked.

His mother patted the space next to her on the couch.

"I don't wanna sit down. Where's my dad?" He scanned the living room, taking in several pairs of eyes on him. Most of the people there were in blue police uniforms.

A tall female cop approached him. She rubbed his shoulder. "Xavier," she said softly as she nudged him in the direction of his mother. "Let's have a seat," she suggested, wiping tears from her eyes.

He faced his dad's partner of twenty-six years, Officer Reed. She was distraught and sad. The strong, kick-ass woman he knew was only a shell of herself. The ghostly complexion of her dark-skin and red rims under her eyes said more than he was prepared to know.

Xavier's dad had been murdered in front of their home. Someone tried to steal his car and rob him according to Ms. Toliver, the little old lady who lived across the street that always sat in her window.

He had gotten out of his car, and two men approached him from behind. One man put a black plastic bag over his head and tried to smother him while the other man struggled to get the car keys out of his hand. Xavier's dad fought like hell and flipped the guy over his shoulder that was strangling him.

The other man got knocked down in the process. In the midst of his dad pulling the plastic bag from over his face, one of the guys let off a round of shots, and a bullet hit his father in the chest. The perpetrator was still trying to wrestle the keys from his hand when Xavier's dad shot him in the head at point-blank range. The other suspect ran off.

The cops and ambulance were already on the way, thanks to Ms. Toliver, but it was too late. Xavier's father was already gone. The EMT had to pry his fingers from around the keys. Those were the keys to Xavier's Ford Escort.

Xavier blamed himself for a long time because his dad died fulfilling a promise he made to him. His mother immediately sought counseling for Xavier, but it wasn't until his second year at Fisk when he met Patricia that he learned to open up and the healing process began.

She was the first person he told about his dad and how he died. She hung in there through his mood swings and attitudes. Patricia had talked him out of some really dark places when the longing for his dad had become unbearable.

* * *

He replied to Patricia's text before pulling off, thanking her for checking on him and informing her that he'd be home in a few hours.

During the drive, Xavier couldn't get the image of Elijah's mother out of his head. She was so overcome with grief that he felt it deep in his soul. He pictured Junior lying in that casket and his eyes watered. Xavier made sure that his family would be provided for if the streets ever claimed his life. He couldn't imagine Patricia reduced to struggling to care for herself and Junior. Although Patricia made a six-figure salary, it was his job as the head of his household to make sure he provided stability even after he was gone. Earlier in the week, he had increased his life insurance policy to half a million dollars. Two hundred fifty thousand would go to Patricia. And a second insurance policy from a different company for the same amount would go to Lauren.

Maybe it was time to end things and put his energy into raising Junior and strengthening his relationship with Patricia. Lauren would be hurt, but his son was much more important.

Xavier texted Lauren feeling a hint of sadness overcome him with what he planned to say. He put his phone on vibrate and dropped it in the cup holder.

* * *

He had been like Elijah. Xavier and his mom had to fend for themselves after his dad died, and it wasn't easy. His mom picked up a second job to maintain what little hold she had on their lives. Xavier felt as if he had lost two parents instead of one. Where he used to be her number one priority, he became her burden.

At least that's what he thought back then. The mother who was always present at his football games or chess matches didn't exist anymore. She always missed PTA meetings, and the only time he saw her was early morning when she came into his room to say goodbye before she left out for work. Xavier was depressed and had no one. He didn't think his mom noticed because she was always at work. He felt abandoned, and he never wanted to feel like that again.

Now as a grown man and father, he knew that his mom was only doing the best she could to make sure that they stayed afloat. She was forced to be a single mother and was trying to provide for Xavier as if his father was still there. He didn't want for anything tangible, but what he needed was out of reach. He didn't feel loved. Xavier still feared to be alone which was the main reason Lauren slid into his life.

He thought back to the day Lauren put that ultimatum on him.

"If you love me like you say you do, then why are you so hesitant to marry me? I don't understand. You treat me as if I'm your wife already. I don't know any man that would purchase commercial property as a gift to his girlfriend. You helped my dream of owning my salon come to fruition. That's husband type shit. And as much as I love you for it, I'm going to have to step away because I want more. I deserve more. I'm not telling you what to do; I'm just telling you what I'm *not* going to do."

He was compelled to marry her, but the truth was she was someone *else* that would be there for him. And the fact that he loved her was sweeter than honey.

* * *

Xavier pulled in front of the home he shared with Lauren, and she came out wearing fitted jeans and knee-high leather boots. He watched that saucy little strut all the way until she made it to the truck. Her hair bounced with every step. Xavier hopped out and opened the door on the passenger side. "Damn you're sexy." He kissed her on the cheek and opened the door.

"Sho' you right." Lauren blew him a kiss and climbed inside.

Xavier laughed and shook his head. "You're so vain."

"I prefer confident."

"Do I have a minute to change clothes?"

She gave him a quick once-over. "You're fine just the way you are."

"If you say so." Behind the wheel, he looked over to her. "Where to?"

"The location of our first date," she said with a wink of the eye.

"Giordano's on Randolph?" He asked, revving up the engine.

"That would be the one."

Forty-five minutes later they were being seated at a window

booth. The hostess brought two large glasses of water and handed them menus. Xavier ordered their usual appetizer, stuffed pizza with sausage, mushroom, and onion, and a pitcher of beer.

Xavier stared at Lauren, taking in her beauty and the immense glow about her.

She returned his gaze and grinned. "Can I help you with something?"

"Are you gonna make me ask or are you gonna tell me what's going on?"

Lauren smirked at him. "Whatever do you mean?"

"You're such a tease."

She parted her lips for a comeback, but the waitress showed up with a platter of Garlic Parmesan Fries and a pitcher of beer.

Dipping her fries in ranch sauce, Lauren said, "Remember how I was saying that I should make one of the guest bedrooms my office."

Around a mouth full of fries, Xavier responded, "yes."

"Well, how about we make it a nursery?" Lauren asked as the corners of her lips turned upward into a full smile.

"You're pregnant?" Xavier frowned. "We're having a baby?" *Shit.* He gulped down an enormous amount of beer. "I thought that was something you never wanted."

"Humph." Lauren's smile faded with her eyes locked on his. "Well, it wasn't like I planned it *or* that we did anything to prevent it."

"You're on the pill."

"I haven't taken birth control in almost three years," she said shifting in the seat. "We talked about this—"

"And you told me you didn't want any kids," he countered, trying to keep his panic at bay. "You wanted to focus on your 'business' and become the next Neal Far—somebody."

"It's Neal Farinah, Beyonce's stylist. And that's beside the point," she said with a dismissive wave of the hand. "That was so long ago. I'm thirty-five years old. It's past time to start a family." She slumped down in the seat. "I can't believe this is your response."

A baby? Any hope of ending things with Lauren went right out the window. There was no way he could abandon her while she was pregnant with his child or afterward. A new baby in the mix equaled complications that would be sure to put more strain on an already turbulent situation.

Xavier scooted out the booth and slipped into the booth next to her. He placed a hand on her belly. "I'm sorry, baby."

She put a hand over his and laid her head on his shoulder.

"How far along are we?"

"Look at you speaking in plurals." Lauren nudged him with her shoulder. "About nine weeks. Dr. Harden scheduled an ultrasound for me next Tuesday. I told her it would have to be after we got back from New York."

"Can you fly?"

"Sure, silly. I wouldn't miss celebrating our ten year anniversary in The Big Apple for anything."

"A decade later and a baby on the way. I can dig it," he said, and his enthusiasm wasn't hard to hear. "Let me know when that appointment is."

"Will do."

He was indeed happy about the baby. Xavier might finally get the daughter he always wanted.

"This is cause for a celebration," Xavier said, rubbing her belly. He grabbed his mug of foamy beer and lifted it. "To new beginnings."

Lauren lifted her glass of water and toasted with her husband.

"No more spirits for you for the next seven months huh," Xavier said, sipping the golden substance.

"I know. Maybe longer if I decide to breastfeed."

"Is that something you want to do?" he asked, placing the mug on the table.

"I don't know. Pediatricians say it's best for the baby." Lauren shifted in her seat. "What's going to suck is that I can't take anymore Ambien. I mean——I know I have to do what's best for the baby and I'm fine with that. But how the heck am I supposed to sleep?"

Xavier held his breath as what she said registered. His happy place crumbled one piece at a time. What was he going to do now? How was he going to slip out at night to go home to Patricia and Junior? He depended on Lauren's sleeping pills just as much as she did.

Chapter Thirty

"This is unexpected. Thank you, Patricia." Shawn gleamed as she received a placard and a fifty-dollar Amex Gift Card for being Technician of the Month.

"You earned it. You have exceeded our expectations, and you go above and beyond helping the customers. We here at MedRx wanted to show our appreciation, and I want to say thank you."

"Wow, thank you. I've only been here four months." Instinctively, Shawn embraced her, and she reciprocated.

Patricia smiled and placed her arm around the younger woman's shoulder as Shawn held the placard to pose for a photograph that would be published in the company newsletter.

Shawn's heart had thumped a little faster when Patricia embraced her. And rightly so. After all, this was her first time posing for a picture with her mother.

* * *

She didn't believe her day could get any sweeter, then Lauren walked into the pharmacy, ten minutes before her shift ended.

"What are you doing here?" Shawn asked.

"I came to check you out at your new gig," Lauren teased with a wink. "But I do have a prescription to pick up, though."

"One moment," Shawn said peering over Lauren's shoulder. "Ms. Smith, your order will be ready in ten minutes, and then the pharmacist will come out to check your blood pressure."

The elderly woman settled in a cushioned seat in the waiting area, nodded, and smiled.

Shawn put her focus back on Lauren. "Why come all the way up here? I know you passed at least a dozen MedRx's before you made it to the north side."

"My obstetrician's affiliated with Saint Joseph's, so this works out perfect. You'll be seeing me on the regular for the next eight months."

"Are you saying what I think you're saying?" Shawn reached over the counter and gave Lauren's belly a gentle squeeze.

Then Shawn lifted her hands to her mouth to muffle a squeal. "Congratulations."

"Um, excuse me," Javid interrupted, sliding near the register. "Who's your friend?"

"This is Ms. Lauren. She was the mentor I told you about. If you had come with me to the Fashion Show a few months back, you would've already met her." Shawn clamped down when she realized what she had just said.

Lauren met her stare and mouthed, "It's okay," and the corner of her lips curved into a slight smile.

He waved Shawn off. "Girl, you didn't lie, she is certainly a fashionista," Javid remarked, ogling Lauren's outfit. "Sexy golden belt spliced geometric design bodycon dress. I see you."

"Thank you," Lauren smiled. "I like him."

"Everyone does," Shawn said with a smirk.

"I'll take care of her," Javid announced, signing on to the register. He was the flamboyant evening technician that had clocked into work the second shift. "What's your last name, love?"

"Carter."

Patricia lifted one finger in their direction at the mention of her surname; she was on the phone with a doctor taking a new prescription order.

"I made Technician of the Month," Shawn told Lauren.

"What did I say to you?" Lauren gave Shawn the thumbs up sign. "Congratulations, Rockstar."

"Thanks," she replied, beaming. "I like it here."

Javid walked over with a small white bag with the instructions stapled to the top.

"I'll take it from here. Thanks, Javid." Shawn grabbed the prescription from his hands.

"Nice meeting you Lauren," Javid said with a circular snap of his fingers and an appreciative perusal. "Keep werking it, girl." He turned, disappearing into the back to start filling prescriptions.

Lauren looked at Shawn and smiled.

Shawn raised an eyebrow. "He thinks he's the next RuPaul honey."

"Well, if he can rattle off my ensemble like that, he just might be."

* * *

"Hello," Patricia said to Lauren as she placed the phone on the cradle then walked over to the counter. "Sorry for the delay. I was finishing up a call. How may I help you?"

"She doesn't need anything," Shawn said. "She's all set."

"I thought you called me over while I was on the phone."

"No," Shawn repeatedly tapped her finger on the counter. "Ohhhhhh, the customer's last name is Carter. Javid asked her name so he could find her script in the pick-up bins."

"Okay, now that makes sense," Patricia remarked. "Occupational hazard."

All three women laughed.

"My husband blessed me with this last name eighteen years ago," Patricia said, with a smile that expanded from Canada all the way down to Florida.

"Mine did too," Lauren chuckled, "Just not that long ago. Wow, eighteen years of marriage; what a blessing. Now that's longevity."

"But not long enough," Shawn spoke without thinking. She realized her slip of the tongue and tried to rectify her out of place response with, "I mean it should be an eternity."

No one commented. Shawn thought Patricia's husband might have been her biological father. Eighteen years of marriage did not add up to a twenty-five-year-old child. Evidently, she needed to start searching for her father.

"Do you have any questions about your medication, Mrs. Carter?" Patricia asked.

"No, my doctor thoroughly explained everything, but thanks."

"You have a good day," Patricia said, before heading back to the computer.

"Thank you, and you do the same." Lauren leaned in.over the counter. "I can't believe you were worried about your boss not liking you. She seems lovely."

I think so too. "I gotta go, girl," Shawn whispered. "I'm off in five minutes. Let me take care of the customer behind you before anyone else shows up.

Lauren put the prescription into her purse. "I'll talk to you later."

* * *

"Hi, Mr. Williams." Shawn greeted with a smile, hoping the transaction went smoothly so that she could go home on time. "You're picking up today?"

"I need you to fill my new prescription." He handed it to her along with his driver's license.

She glanced at it and said, "One moment please, I need the pharmacist to check to see if we have it in stock."

Shawn gave the hard copy to Patricia. After a few minutes of checking his profile, Patricia turned back to Shawn. "Let Mr. Williams know that it's too soon to fill. It'll go through on insurance tomorrow. I'll check the safe to make sure we have enough."

Before she could convey the message, Mr. Williams screamed. "I need it today."

"I can have it ready for you first thing in the morning. We open at seven," Shawn said, holding out the driver's license. "I'll keep the hard copy, that way you won't have to wait. It'll be ready when you come in."

"I can't wait 'til tomorrow, I barely made it in here today," Mr. Williams said, rubbing his wrinkly cheek. "I'm in so much pain."

"I'm sorry sir, but—"

"Listen to me, you little green eyed bitch. I need my medicine now!"

"Hey, that was uncalled for," Javid rushed to the counter and nudged Shawn to the side. "You can't talk to her like that. It's time for you to leave."

"I'm not going anywhere without my Oxy."

"Call security," Javid yelled over his shoulder,

The moment Shawn picked up the phone, Mr. Williams pulled a gun from his waistband that was concealed by his coat and pointed it at her.

Ms. Smith gasped. A startled Mr. Williams swung around and yelled, "Get out of here." He never took the gun off of Shawn. She balanced on the arms of the chair and pulled herself upright. Ms. Smith hobbled out of there, dropping her cane in the process.

Shawn prayed that she would call the police.

Mr. Williams put all of his attention back on Shawn. "You push one button on that phone, and I will shoot you. Put the phone down."

Her hands were shaking so bad that she dropped the receiver, but not before hitting the emergency call button on the side of the phone, which automatically alerted the front office. The handset bounced off the counter to the floor onto her foot. She wanted to scream but managed to keep it inside.

Javid raised his hands in surrender. "Mr. Williams, please put the gun down. I can—"

He struck Javid in the face with the pistol. "I'm not interested in what you have to say if you can't get my medication."

Shawn stared in horror at the bleeding laceration on Javid's swollen cheek. She fell to her knees. "Please, Mr. Williams you don't have to—"

"Shut up." He waved the gun in her direction. "Where's that Pharmacy lady?"

She glanced Patricia's way between the bays that held the pharmacy's drug inventory. Patricia held a finger to her mouth and pointed to her cell.

"I'm right here, Mr. Williams." Patricia placed the phone on the carpet and walked out with a white bottle in her hand.

Shawn flickered a gaze at the phone and found that the screen was still illuminated. *Thank goodness Patricia didn't follow the policy about no cell phones in the pharmacy.*

"I know you're in pain and don't mean us any harm," she said in soothing tones. "How about I give you some and I'll call the insurance company right now and get this straightened out."

"I just want my medicine. I can't take this anymore," Mr. Williams howled, knocking the handle of the gun on the counter.

"I understand. I'm going to do everything I can for you, but first put the gun down," Patricia stated calmly.

"Not until I get my Oxy," he growled.

Shawn glanced around. No other customers or staff had come back in the pharmacy area. She was a little relieved because that meant the store was on lockdown. The police would arrive soon.

"Mr. Williams," Shawn spoke cautiously. "If you allow me to get up I can call your insurance company while Patricia gets your prescription ready. Is that alright?" Her eyes locked with his. "We just want to help you."

Shawn slowly rose with her hands extended in the air. "I'll put the phone on hands-free so you can hear if you like. I promise I won't call security."

He didn't say anything. Shawn stood next to Patricia and reached across the counter to press the button on the phone while keeping a watchful eye on Mr. Williams. The loudness of the dial tone echoed throughout the empty pharmacy. His hand gradually fell to his side, and he slumped over the counter and leaned on the register in front of Javid.

A monotone voice resonated through the speaker as Shawn punched the buttons answering each question on Blue Cross Blue Shield's automated service until she could get through to a live person.

Patricia nodded, gazing at Shawn, and she felt a sense of tranquility overcome her. She took assurance in her mother's confidence that everything would be alright even though there wasn't any guarantee.

A throaty voice with a strong accent jarred Shawn from her fuzzy feelings. She answered the insurance representative when the police inched into the waiting area behind Mr. Williams. He was leaning over the pickup counter, totally unaware.

In one swift move, the officer knocked the gun out of his hand, then yanked his arms behind his back and slapped handcuffs on him. He winced as the cop shoved him in one of the seats in the patient waiting area.

Shawn forgot all about the man on the phone as she ran to Javid. "Are you okay?" She grabbed his shoulders and guided him to the back sink to clean and then bandage his face. Patricia joined them, grabbing cotton balls, antiseptic, and gauze from the first aid kit in the overhead cabinet.

"Thanks for standing up for me," Shawn said swabbing his cheek with a brown paper towel.

"You're welcome, honey," Javid said smiling through his pain. "You owe me for life now."

She frowned, and he added, "Like when Omar Epps pushed Sanaa Lathan down in Love and Basketball and scarred her face. I'm never gonna let you forget it."

Mr. Slocum entered with one of the cops trailing behind him. "Thank God that you're all okay. This is Officer Windham," he said, stepping aside to let the burly man past. "He would like an account of everything that took place. There are officers in the front office viewing the security footage, but as you know there isn't any audio; so be as forthcoming as you can, please."

* * *

"Patty," A man yelled, his voice filled with fear. "Patty, Where are you?"

"I'm back here," Patricia responded.

Shawn secured the bandage on Javid's face and was washing her hands when she heard the commotion at the pharmacist consultation window. She turned in time to witness a man jumping across the counter. He moved so fast that she didn't get a good look at him. Patricia ran toward the front, and Xavier met her halfway. He swooped her in his arms and twirled her around.

"Baby, I was so scared," Patricia confessed.

"I got you, baby. Always," he said as he palmed Patricia's wet cheeks in his hands and kissed her with a passion that Shawn could only imagine would happen to her one day. "I didn't know what to think when you called and didn't say anything. I thought you pocket dialed me at first. Then I heard someone say gun, and then someone screaming. I knew that you were in trouble. I dropped everything to get up here to you."

He fell to his knees and encircled his muscular arms around Patricia's waist resting his head on her stomach the way a small child would. She rubbed the back of his head as he held onto her like he would suffocate if she weren't a part of his world.

Javid stood behind Shawn and draped his arms around her shoulders as they watched, transfixed.

"I pray that I find a love like that in this lifetime," Shawn mumbled.

Javid lightly squeezed her shoulders. "You will."

Shawn had never met Patricia's husband before, but from what she could see, he was truly in love with his wife. She wondered, *what if he was her dad? Matthew O'Shaughnessy. They could've gotten married years later. How awesome would that be? Two people who loved each other with every fiber of their being could be capable of loving her the same as her adoptive parents, but even more, because their blood ran through her veins.*

"Shawn, I would like you to meet my husband." Patricia gestured with a wave of the hand.

The man stood and faced her.

Chapter Thirty-One

"This is my husband Xavier," Patricia said with her arm locked in his. "Xavier this is the young woman, Shawn I've been telling you about."

He extended his hand, giving her a speaking glare. "Nice to meet you, Shawn. I hear that you make my wife's day a little less stressful," he said with a million dollar grin.

Shawn nearly slipped onto the floor. She was too stunned to speak.

What the hell? Lauren's husband. And he's not my daddy. This clown was up in there acting like he hadn't known her since she was a little girl. Holy shit. Her head was spinning, and she felt like she was going to faint.

"Hi, what a pleasure to meet you." She shook his hand, resisting the urge to say "again."

Patricia rubbed Shawn's back and then touched her forehead with the back of her hand. "Your skin is pale, and you feel warm. I think you need to go home and get some rest. We've been through enough for one day."

She was right. Shawn was livid with confusion and anger, and her temperature was about to boil over, but it had nothing to do with today's madness.

"Xavier, would you walk her out, please?" Patricia asked. "Mr. Williams is still in the waiting area with the arresting officer, but I would feel more comfortable if you would escort Shawn to her car."

"Is that alright with you?" Patricia turned her attention to Shawn.

"Thanks. It's perfect," Shawn said through her teeth.

Shawn rushed to the locker room and gathered her coat and purse. Her mind was racing. Patricia didn't seem like the kind of woman who would play second fiddle or break up another woman's happy home, but Xavier and Lauren had been together for as far back as she could remember. Didn't Patricia say eighteen years? The only conclusion she could come up with was that he was playing them both dirty.

"I'm ready." Shawn emerged from the locker room and walked toward the exit forcing him to make strides to catch up with her.

As soon as they stepped outside, she whirled to him, folded her arms and snapped, "Does Ms. Lauren know about your second wife? Or is it the other way around?"

* * *

For a physically fit man, Xavier was every bit of weak. His palms were sweaty, and he forced himself to keep his lunch down in the pit of his stomach where it belonged. Xavier couldn't believe the Shawn that Patty boasted about was the same Shawn that was like a surrogate daughter to him and Lauren. He had managed to keep his lives separate for over ten years, and it all had come tumbling down in a matter of five minutes.

The crisp air whipped around them as they stood outside. People were walking their dogs, pushing strollers, sipping coffee, and talking on their phones. They were tripping over themselves, turning their heads to get a peek at the argument that was taking place outside of MedRx.

"I asked you a question," she barked. "Does Lauren know about Patricia?"

"No, she doesn't," he whispered. "And Patty doesn't know about her either. I'd like to keep it that way."

"You've got a lot of nerve," Shawn growled and turned to walk away. "How could you do that to her? To them?"

"Chipmunk, wait." He grabbed her arm.

"Don't Chipmunk me," she said, glaring at him. He quickly released his hold. "I knew something was off the day you came to the hospital all late. Your wife was shot. I smelled her perfume on your clothes. Now it all makes sense. *You were with Patricia.*"

Xavier shifted and opened his mouth to speak, but she cut him off.

"When did you have time to marry someone else and then have a kid?" She walked around in a complete circle. *Eighteen years. Ten years.* "Oh wait a minute—Lauren doesn't know about Junior, does she?" Her eyes widened at the weight behind those revealing words.

An elderly couple bundled in winter gear sitting at the bus stop with a well-used portable shopping cart filled with groceries, stared at them, along with the passing pedestrians.

"Listen Chip—Shawn," he said as he went to grab her again but pulled back when she jerked out of his reach.

"It's complicated. I know that sounds like an excuse, but it's not." He rubbed his hands together, cupped and raised them to his mouth and blew warm air inside. "Where did you park? We can walk and talk. It's cold out here."

She stormed off, and he followed her lead. He didn't know how she was going to respond to what he was about to say, but he had to put some kind of explanation on the table. "Patty was my college sweetheart, I've known her for over half of my life and many, many years before I knew Lauren." He could practically see the hamster wheel turning in her brain trying to put the timeline together. "We've been together for over twenty years."

Her surprised expression was expected. There was no way possible that she could understand the profound love that he had for both of the women who shared his last name.

Patricia was the love of his life; she had been there since the beginning. When Xavier had nothing, and when he was still hurting over his father's death, Patricia loved him when he was unlovable and trying to find himself. It was more than gratitude; Xavier was truly in love with her.

Lauren's fierceness and ambition were like a drug. She had a hold on him from the day they met at the barbershop. She pushed him forward in his career, and he became a detective a year sooner than his original goal. Her aura was addictive, and he loved the way she made him feel. In the beginning, he thought it was lust; something new after being with the same woman for many years, but when he thought he might lose her, his heart physically ached, and Xavier knew he loved her too.

"Wait, so; you're telling me that *Ms. Lauren* is your second wife?"

"Yes."

Shawn pressed the key fob to unlock the doors of a purple Chevy Cobalt. "This is unbelievable, Mr. Xavier. I thought you were one of the good guys."

He opened the driver's side door for her. "I am."

"Isn't this sweet," she taunted, giving him the evil eye. "A cheating gentleman."

"I'm still the same Xavier who's been there for you since you were a little girl, needing refuge from your foster care situations before you ended up with Ms. Ida or the father figure you used at your convenience to run off some stupid boy who tried to take it too far. So don't take that tone with me."

"You can't guilt trip me because *you* fucked up," Shawn shot back, sliding behind the steering wheel. "You know I love Ms. Lauren. You guys have been there for me during some of the roughest times in my life. How am I supposed to be anywhere near her knowing what I know and not say anything?"

Xavier sighed, wondering the same thing. "It's not your story to tell."

"And what about Patricia?" she snapped, green eyes flashing fire. "I see her every day. This is putting me in an ugly position."

"Please Chipmunk," he whispered. "I beg you. Let me handle my personal affairs; this doesn't concern you. Just know that I wouldn't do anything intentionally to hurt them."

"Right. Like you married two women by mistake," she said harshly before slamming the car door and driving off.

* * *

Xavier jogged the two blocks back from Shawn's parking space to MedRx. He prayed that she wouldn't feel compelled to tell Lauren what she learned today; no good would come from it.

Patricia was sitting in the patient lobby area talking with his partner when he returned. The shutters were drawn, and she had closed the pharmacy for the rest of the day.

"I sent Javid home. I offered to give him a ride, but his friend was on the way to pick him up. Is Shawn alright?"

"She's a little shaken up, but she's fine," he said, realizing she was more disturbed because of what she'd just found out, than what had happened earlier.

"That's to be expected. None of us are in any position to work the rest of the day. Jason stayed with me while the other officer took Mr. Williams to the station."

"Thanks, man, I got it from here," Xavier told Jason. "I'll catch you later. I'm riding home with Patty."

"Baby, you don't have to do that," Patricia said, digging the car keys out of her purse. "I'm fine. Go on back to work."

"Nonsense. You're my priority."

Jason gave Patricia a reassuring rub on the arm and nodded at Xavier, but there was a flash of something in his eyes.

"Thanks for everything," she said, giving Jason a shy smile as she adjusted the purse strap on her shoulder.

Xavier held her hand as they left MedRx. His thoughts were doing cartwheels and summersaults on the drive home. Patricia went on and on about Mr. Williams, but nothing registered.

He did not like the feeling that Shawn held his life in her hands. Xavier thought about coming clean and ending one part of his life. But who? Patricia would never understand. He would lose her and his son. And Lauren was pregnant with their first child. He would miss out on so much with this new baby.

Chapter Thirty-Two

Shawn drove to the coffee shop and waited over an hour for Candace because she was too hyped to go home. The Barista brought an apple fritter, and a large caramel-iced coffee loaded with tons of cream and sugar and placed it on the table. Shawn scanned the area, and an eerie feeling crept up her spine.

"Hey girl," Candace greeted and sat down. "What's up?"

Shawn let out a heavy sigh. "You wouldn't believe the day I had," she said glancing over her friend's shoulder.

"Who are you looking for?" Candace asked, scanning the area before her eyes landed back on Shawn.

"I think I'm being followed."

"You're so dramatic," Candace cackled.

"No. Seriously." She leaned in. "This isn't the first time I'd felt this way. It'll be when I go to lunch, or while I'm walking to the car after work," Shawn said sipping the iced-coffee.

"Maybe it's a crazy customer that's fallen in love with your charisma," Candace teased.

"That's possible, but I don't think that's the case."

"Where we come from you learn to trust your instincts. Be careful," Candace warned.

Shawn nodded. "Speaking of a crazy customer—"

"Hold up. Would this story be told better over drinks?" Candace asked, studying Shawn's face and lowering her eyes to the outfit that wasn't on quite right. "You look like shit."

"Gee. Thanks." Shawn grimaced.

"I'm just saying." Candace shrugged. "Drinks?"

"Absolutely."

"Okay——let's go." Candace grabbed the clear cup of iced coffee and tossed it in the trash.

"Damn Candace," Shawn snapped, "That cost six bucks."

"I'll buy the drinks."

"Damn straight." She grabbed her purse and followed Candace outside. They walked across the street to a dimly lit bar. It was still before rush hour, so the place wasn't overly crowded. They were able to get a corner table in the back, which gave them a bit of privacy.

Vodka and orange juice was Shawn's go-to drink when she wanted to unburden her soul. She ordered two for herself and asked for them to be brought out at the same time. She placed her elbows on the wooden round table and folded her hands under her chin.

"How about a customer held me at gunpoint today because his Oxycontin prescription was too early to fill."

"Whattttt!!!!!" Candace yelled, smacking her palm on the table.

The few patrons several booths away paused their conversations to look their way.

"Oh wait, it gets worst," Shawn said, then halted as the scantily dressed hostess sat their drinks on the table. "Thanks."

Candace pursed her lips. "How?"

Shawn sipped the orange drink. "At least I can sympathize with the customer a little bit even though I was scared out of my mind."

"Are you crazy?"

"Not at all. Mr. Williams is a cancer patient. I feel sorry for him," Shawn said lowering her lids. "He's deteriorating right before my eyes. He used to be so strong and handsome. Now he's frail with wrinkly hanging skin. He's a sweet man. The same thing happened last month. He's just suffering."

"A really sweet man who tried to kill you. Yeah. Okay. Continue." Candace's eyes narrowed as she took a sip of the vodka.

Shawn stared at her friend. Candace was a riot under normal circumstances, so she knew she was about to cut up in this bar over this next bit of foolery.

"Short version so I can get to the good part?"

Candace nodded.

"We made the best of a touchy situation while we waited for the police to arrive." Shawn folded her arms across her small chest. "In walks, the cops and one of them happen to be Patricia's husband.

Candace leaned forward, eyes wide with excitement. "Is he your dad?"

"That's what I was initially thinking, too." This time, she took a long gulp of her drink. "And the worst part is——I *know* this cat."

"Well, spit it out," Candace shouted. "Who the fuck is he?"

"Mr. Xavier." She let that hang for a minute.

"*Ms. Lauren's* husband," Candace yelled.

Shawn nodded.

"Excuse me." Candace stood, snapping her fingers in the air, signaling the hostess. "We're gonna need an entire bottle of Absolut."

Shawn ran her fingers through jet-black tresses that were a little tangled. "I was stunned. Patricia introduced us, and he acted like he didn't even know me——like he wasn't fazed at all."

"Trust me," she said with a laugh. "I betcha he was shitting his pants."

"I don't know Candace," she said, swirling the liquid in her glass.

"You could blow his shit up, and I'm shocked you didn't," Candace said tapping a fingernail on the table. "You work for his wife, and Ms. Lauren was your mentor. Oh, hell yeah. He was shitting hella bricks."

The hostess came with the second round of libations. Shawn sipped the drink, and paused, savoring the distinct taste of the clear liquid and orange juice.

"So this would make Mr. Xavier my step-dad?" Shawn said it more as a question than a statement.

"I guess so," Candace cosigned. "Well, at least you already have a relationship with him. You said he'd always been a cool guy."

"Yeah, but under different circumstances." She took a deep breath. "How can I do this? How can I pursue a relationship with my mother knowing that she's married to Ms. Lauren's husband? How can I not tell her what I know? Because I know she's clueless the way she goes on and on about Senior—"

"Wait … who is Senior?" Candace asked frowning and as confused as Shawn was earlier.

"Mr. Xavier. She never says his name. Come to think about it, when she refers to her son, she always calls him Junior." Shawn sighed. "Anyway… if I do tell her, she might not believe me and hate me for it. She'll probably accuse me of trying to break up her family. I'm going to lose her before we're even found."

Candace slid the small square napkin from under her drink and handed it to Shawn. "Don't cry we'll figure something out."

Shawn threw her head back, willing the tears to retreat to their home base. "How can I look Ms. Lauren in the eyes knowing that her husband is married to my mother? You know how good she's been to me." Against her wishes, the drops slithered down her cheeks. "If it wasn't for her, I might not be here. Ms. Lauren saved me."

She rubbed the inside of her wrist over the scars where she used to cut herself. The pain of that experience marred her soul, more than it did physically. "I can't betray her, Candace——I just can't. But I also don't want to hurt my mother." She sighed. "Where should my loyalties lie?"

"Your loyalty is what you feel and in your heart," Candace said in a low tone. "These are both spectacular women and Xavier is manipulating them. Maybe your purpose in all of this is to bring everything to light. What's the chance that you would be connected to all three of these people?"

The woman did have a point. Keeping the secret that the women shared a husband would only serve to benefit one person—Xavier Carter.

Not anymore. No matter how much he tried to pull the guilt card, hurting, two women she loved meant she shouldn't have any loyalty to him.

* * *

"Thanks for agreeing to come with me to find my dad," Shawn said, inserting the key into the apartment door. "It's a turn-around trip. We leave at eleven tonight, and we'll be back late tomorrow evening." Shawn extracted Candace's boarding pass out of her pocket.

"I can't believe you talked me into doing this," Candace replied closing the door behind them. "I'm giving up the first New Year's Day I've ever had off to go on a fishing expedition with you in Texas."

"I appreciate it." Shawn smiled. "I hope our return flight from El Paso isn't delayed. I can't miss Patricia's party."

"I don't see why it would be." Candace draped her scarf on the coat rack. "We'll be with the rest of those fools traveling home on New Year's Eve."

"Whatever." Shawn giggled.

"You'll be flying solo to Patricia's. I had to switch days and bribe the replacement with one hundred dollars for her to give up being off on New Year's Eve."

"Oooooo…that's tough," Shawn said, grabbing a pint of pralines and cream from the freezer. She sat at the kitchen table with her laptop open to the previous search. "I'll pay you back."

"It's cool. You bought the tickets." Candace took a spoon from the drawer. "If you find your dad, it'll be worth it."

Chapter Thirty-Three

Xavier gently shook Patricia's thigh. "Wake up. We're home."

"I didn't realize I fell asleep," she moaned.

As her eyes came into focus, she noticed that the blinds were half shut. She always opened them when she was gone so the plants could get maximum sunlight.

"My baby's home," Patricia said, pointing at the picture window.

"How did you know that?" Xavier asked.

"Because the blinds are closed. Junior always does that as if I'm not going to see the mess once I walk in the door."

But today, Patricia didn't care. She hadn't seen him since he left for Florida five days ago. The day's worries faded away knowing her son had made it home safely from his trip.

"Brandon's father dropped him off. He said he called, but couldn't get a hold of you."

Patricia touched Xavier's shoulder. "Junior doesn't need to know about what happened today. You know how that boy feels about me. I can't have him worrying every day that I'm at work."

"I won't say anything," Xavier promised.

He came around and opened the door for Patricia and reached for her hand.

"Thank you, baby," she said, firmly holding his hand as she slid out of the leather seat. She gave him a long look. Something was different about him, but she couldn't place it.

"You were pretty brave today, calling me like that."

"I remembered what you told me," she responded, squeezing his hand. "Stay calm and think your way out of a situation instead of reacting on impulse. I'm just glad that you were able to figure out what was going on." Patricia hooked her arm under Xavier's, and they traipsed along the walkway. The music thumped, and the bass rattled the windows the closer they made it to the house.

"Teenagers." Patricia huffed.

"Welcome back." Xavier let out a menacing laugh.

He unlocked and swung the door open, peering inside before allowing Patricia to enter. Besides the music greeting them with a vengeance, everything seemed to be in place. Patricia stepped over the threshold first, tripping over Junior's duffle bag.

"Junior," she screamed, bracing her fall on the wall in the foyer. Xavier tried to grab Patricia, but in his efforts, he tripped over her knocking them both to the floor.

They exchanged a knowing glance, followed by laughter.

"I'm too old to be taking nose dives to the floor. Sheesh," Patricia said, shifting to a sitting position.

"Are you okay?" Xavier asked, kicking Junior's bag across the floor.

She rolled her shoulder to loosen the tension in her body. "I'm good."

"Junior," Xavier's baritone voice shouted over the music. He rose to his feet and then helped Patricia stand.

"Are you sure you're alright?" he asked a second time.

Patricia nodded but kept her gaze on him far longer than warranted.

They stepped into the living room. Right away Patricia noticed that something was awry. She was used to seeing plates, half-empty cups, and soda cans on the table in the family room. Brandon was over their house on the regular, so it was a common sight.

Not this. A pair of women's flats were parked underneath the coffee table, and a purse was lying on the couch. Patricia turned to look at Xavier whose eyes were the size of saucers. She glanced upward, pointing toward the ceiling. Xavier nodded as they approached the stairs. He tapped her arm and pointed toward the sound system.

Patricia climbed two stairs so she could be level with Xavier. She leaned in and whispered, "Leave it on."

They quickly, but quietly, ascended the staircase until they made it outside of Junior's bedroom. The door was ajar, so Patricia peeked in. Her fifteen-year-old son was making out with a young lady that she'd never seen before. She slid her arm through the crack and flipped the light switch. A piercing scream rang out. Xavier reached over Patricia and tried to push the door open, but she held the doorknob and pulled it to her.

"Get dressed," Patricia ordered. "And make your way downstairs. You've got two minutes."

She closed the door.

"What are you doing?" Xavier asked, frowning.

"That's a young lady in there. She needs her privacy."

Exactly four minutes later, Junior and a girl whose hair was ruffled, clothes wrinkled, with hazel eyes and golden skin were doing the walk of shame down the stairs. Patricia stood with her arms folded, tapping her foot on the bottom step, trying to keep her anger in check.

"Have a seat," she commanded, walking into the family room. Xavier was already there sitting in the recliner.

"First off, what's your name?" Patricia asked.

"Zoe."

"Hello," Patricia said curtly. "I would say nice to meet you, but I'd be lying."

"Moms, let me explain," Junior pleaded, holding his hands out to keep her from saying more.

"I don't want to hear anything from you," Patricia snapped.

"This is Brandon's cousin."

"So that makes it okay?" she asked, scooting to the edge of the couch. "You know there's no company of the opposite sex when we aren't home."

"I know, but——"

"There are no buts."

Silence.

"I'm sorry," Junior said, dropping his head. "Nothing happened."

"What if your dad and I came home ten minutes later? Would you be able to say the same thing?"

Junior didn't utter a word. He twiddled his thumbs.

"Where do your parents think you are?"

Zoe lifted her head and mumbled, "Over Brandon's house."

"I see——and just how long has this been going on?" Patricia laced her hands.

Utter silence.

"Well, how 'bout I call your mother. Since I can't get answers out of one of you, I'm sure she can enlighten me."

"No. Please don't, Mrs. Carter," Zoe pleaded, and a few crocodile tears fell from her eyes.

"We've never done anything like this before Moms, I swear," Junior confessed. "I just wanted to spend some time with Zoe. I missed her. Haven't seen her in a long time."

The doorbell rang. Everyone's head snapped in the direction of the sound.

"I'll get it," Xavier volunteered, rising from the sofa.

"Hey Mr. Carter," Brandon cheerfully greeted, giving Xavier a fist bump.

"Come on in," Xavier said, following Brandon into the family room.

Brandon walked in and froze. His brown eyes scanned the room.

And he nearly tripped over his feet, stammering, "H-hi-hi, Mrs. Carter."

"Oh, so now I'm Mrs. Carter." Patricia got up, placing her hands on her hips.

"I—I—I mean——hey—hey ma," Brandon stuttered, flickering a wary gaze toward Zoe and Junior.

"Are you here to pick her up?" Patricia asked pointing to Zoe.

"Uhhhhhh," he looked at Junior.

Junior lowered his eyelids and nodded.

"Yes, ma'am."

"Bye, Zoe." Patricia waved the girl off.

Zoe slid her feet in her flats and grabbed her purse. "I'm sorry Mr. and Mrs. Carter."

She stood to leave and gave Junior a timid wave.

Junior resembled a wounded puppy with his head hung low. He watched her walk to the door through hooded eyes.

"I raised you better," Patricia snapped. "Go walk her out then bring your behind right back here."

"Yes, ma'am."

As soon as Junior crossed the threshold, Patricia glared at Xavier. "Why haven't you said anything?"

"You were handling it."

She crossed her arms. "Junior needs to know that you back me."

"I did, by making sure I didn't wring his neck."

The front door closed and the squeal of tires signaled that they were gone. Junior trudged back in and plopped down in his original spot on the sofa.

"I'm very disappointed in you," Patricia said in the calmest tone she could manage. "I have to be able to trust you, Junior." Patricia left her spot on the sofa to sit next to their son. "You're too young to make grown-up decisions. And that's exactly what sex is."

"Moms, *nothing happened.* I'm not lying. I didn't mean to disobey you." Junior hung his head low again. "I just wanted to see my girl."

"Upstairs in your room???" Patricia gave Junior the side eye. "That's a recipe for mischief. *Never* put yourself in a situation where things can get out of control." She glanced over at Xavier and widened her eyes, signaling him to chime in at any time.

"You know there are consequences for your actions," Xavier commented, finally saying something worthwhile. "You made a mistake, and now you have to be held accountable."

Junior mumbled, "Whatever," under his breath.

"What did you say?" Patricia asked, unable to believe her son was talking back.

"Nothing."

"Two weeks without your phone and no allowance," Xavier scolded. "You can't just do whatever you want and think there won't be any punishment."

"That's what you do," Junior spat, and there was anger in his tone.

"Junior," Patricia shouted, slapping his back.

"So you think it's okay to talk back to me, boy," Xavier barked, rising so he was eye level with his son. "I know you're not used to being punished, but you will not be disrespectful to me. *Ever*."

"You're such a hypocrite, Pops," Junior, shot back with an icy expression.

"What's gotten into you?" Patricia inquired, grabbing his arm. "You don't talk to your father that way."

"It's alright, Patty," Xavier said, narrowing the space between him and Junior. "Make it three weeks."

"I don't care," Junior bellowed, crossing his arms. "You're the biggest liar there is."

Xavier yanked Junior's arms loose and grabbed him by his shirt. He lifted Junior off his feet. "You betta watch it, boy."

"Or what?" Junior challenged him.

"Stop it right now. The both of you," Patricia commanded, but it fell on deaf ears. "Let him go, Xavier." She wedged her body between them, using all of her girl power to push them apart.

"Break this up I said." She turned and faced her son. "Junior, go to your room. Right now——Go!"

He stumbled backward falling on the couch. Patricia stood in front of him, while Xavier hovered like he was ready to attack.

"I don't know what the hell just happened here, but it stops now," Patricia demanded.

Junior stuck his hands in the pocket of his jeans. "Moms, I'm sorry."

"I'm not the one you should be apologizing to." When he didn't say anything, she pointed toward the stairs. "Get on out of here."

Patricia watched Junior until he was out of sight. She turned and eyeballed Xavier, giving him all of her attention. "What's going on between you two?" She couldn't believe what she had just witnessed. Her normally mild-mannered son had never been disrespectful to anyone. He wasn't a saint by any means, but the behavior she just witnessed, was not like him.

"Nothing. Junior's just smelling himself," Xavier said walking into the kitchen.

"He was out of line, but the way he performed … it seems much deeper than that," Patricia expressed following Xavier into the kitchen.

Junior called Xavier a liar. But why? What was that about? There had to be more to it than him being upset. And the way Xavier responded was completely out of character.

"Why would he say those things about you?" Patricia asked, arching an eyebrow.

Xavier leaned, resting his elbows on the island. "I don't know."

"I could see if he said you got on his nerves——but a *liar*. That's accusatory."

"He's pissed because he got caught with his girlfriend," he shot back, turning away to make it to the refrigerator. "Don't make more out of it than what it is, Patty."

"Maybe…" Since Xavier was too busy to do more than dole

out punishment, Patricia had already resigned herself to having a conversation with her son, first, about his behavior, and second, about the exchange with his dad and what it really meant.

* * *

Later that evening Patricia was in their bedroom packing Xavier's suitcase. He had a mandatory seminar and fieldwork that he attended in New York every year with Jason and the other detectives in their precinct. She hated it in the beginning, but now she had gotten used to bringing in the New Year without him. Though the timing this year sucked with the turmoil going on in their home.

As a way to make the blow less painful, she hosted a small get together with close friends and family on New Years Day. People used to ask where Xavier was, but now they were as accustomed to him not being there as Patricia was.

"You should talk to Junior before you go," Patricia suggested.

"I think it's best that we have a few days apart. It'll give us both time to cool down," Xavier said, folding his boarding pass and stuffing it in his wallet. "I won't leave without saying goodbye."

"Go 'head on then." Patricia lightly shoved him toward the door. "We have to get going if you don't want to miss your flight."

"I got an Uber."

Patricia's hands fell to her sides. "Uber? Since when? I always take you to the airport."

"With everything going on I thought it was best." He lifted the suitcase off the bed and placed it on the floor. "You stay here and look after Junior. The driver will be here in less than ten minutes."

Though Patricia appreciated his thoughtfulness, her spirit was crushed. She looked forward to those last few minutes in the car with him.

He sauntered over to her. "Don't be sad," Xavier whispered, lifting her chin.

Patricia went up on her tippy toes, closing her eyes awaiting the feel of his lips on hers. Not even a Nanosecond later a horn blew. Her eyes shot open with disappointment.

Xavier gave Patricia a quick peck on the lips. "Baby, I gotta go."

"That was the fastest ten minutes that I've ever seen," Patricia pouted.

"I'll text you when I land," he said, snatching the suitcase handle and wheeling it down the hall.

She was right behind him. "What about Junior?" she asked, knocking on his bedroom door as Xavier whizzed by.

"Tell Junior I love him, and we'll sort this out when I get back." Xavier paused at the top of the staircase to lift the luggage.

Patricia followed him, and he gave her one last hug before he walked out the door. "I'll see you in a few days."

She watched him load his bag in the trunk of a silver Impala and just like that he was gone. Patricia mumbled, "Happy New Year to you too" as she rested her head on the doorjamb. She closed the door, shut her eyes, inhaling until her chest expanded, then slowly exhaled.

She opened her eyes and took a step forward, then stilled her movements. Junior stood two feet in front of her like a statue—strong, tall, and unmoving. She hadn't heard him come down. Patricia gazed into her son's eyes and witnessed a mixture of anger and a hint of sadness that he was desperately trying to hide.

Motherly instinct was screaming on the inside. She could feel Junior's discomfort. Patricia took in his rigidness, glancing down at his hands which were balled into tight fists, and she reached for him. Junior took a step back, which made her freeze in place. She studied him a moment, and he returned her stare with a steady gaze.

Junior swallowed hard before uttering the words, "I hate him."

Chapter Thirty-Four

Lauren was at the salon with Lynette making sure everything was in order before she left for her trip. She was elated because the renovations were complete and she could finally get back to doing what she loved.

During her recovery, Lauren had been studying up on natural hair care. This would be an excellent time to expand the business. Many women adored their natural twists and curly Afros. She even made the decision to give it a go and chopped off her relaxed hair. Xavier thought she was going through a mid-life crisis, but she assured him that wasn't the case. The best way to learn was from first hand, so she dove right into the natural hair craze. She attended natural hair classes where she learned about healthy hair treatments that would add moisture and sheen to all curl patterns and textures.

She went over the itemized purchase order for the new products with Lynette. Lauren had complete faith that Lynette could get the job done, but the salon was her baby. And like a new baby, she wanted to know everything down to the minor details.

Lauren was finishing up when bright headlights bore down on them through the glass windows. Shielding her eyes with a clipboard, Lauren quickly rose to her feet. A shadowy figure appeared in the doorway. She trotted over to unlock the door for Xavier.

"What took you so long?" she asked, allowing him to brush past.

"I had some last minute stuff to take care of," he responded, taking in the new and improved salon.

Lauren gauged his expression. "It's nice, isn't it," she said, smiling. "I know I went a little overboard adding the mounted water fountain, but I couldn't resist."

She anticipated a larger clientele now that she embraced styling natural hair, and her goal was to ensure that everyone was happy. The soothing sound of water cascading down would create a calm, Zen atmosphere for those clients who had to wait for a short while.

"Nice," he said, leaning on the front desk. "How's it going, Lynette?"

"Everything's good, no complaints," Lynette responded, patting her twists.

"Don't work too hard while we're gone," Xavier teased.

"I can handle it." Lynette punched, fingers flying over the keyboard.

"Are you ready?" he asked Lauren. "Where are your suitcases?"

"In the back." She gestured over her shoulder.

Lauren stepped aside so Xavier could retrieve the bags from her office. She replenished the petty cash and went over the things she wanted Lynette to handle in her absence. The plan was to be open for business when she got back the following week.

* * *

Xavier opened the rear door behind the driver for Lauren to get in. He loaded the trunk and then joined her on the opposite side. "Did you get everything accomplished?" he asked, caressing her hand.

"Yes, I did." She tapped the tip of his nose with her finger. "I told you I wouldn't be long."

They arrived at Midway Airport two hours before their flight. They checked their luggage in with the curbside skycap and headed to security.

"I told you Uber would be much quicker. We didn't have to waste all of that time trying to find a short-term parking space." Lauren stepped forward at the TSA request and held her arms out. "And we saved some money."

The TSA worker waved her through the body scanner. She retrieved her belongings from the gray bin while Xavier was being screened.

"You were right," he agreed after the TSA worker waved him through.

"Come again," Lauren said smiling, placing her hand to her ear.

"Whatever." Xavier sucked his teeth while gathering his shoes and belt from the bin.

"I'm gonna have to write this down on a calendar." She nudged Xavier almost knocking him over while he was putting on his shoes.

"I can't believe we've been married for ten years," Lauren said, affectionately squeezing Xavier's hand.

"Me either," he agreed, smiling down at her.

The boarding area of gate B2 was practically deserted. The only thing missing was the tumbleweed twirling along the moving walkway.

"Take your pick." Xavier spread his arms wide at the various seats that were available.

Lauren sat across from the windows so she could stare at the moonlight. She loved the way the red lights flickered in the midnight sky when the planes were descending on the runway.

She turned to face Xavier. "I already told mom and dad about the baby."

"That's cool," he replied. "I know they're excited."

"Yep——their first grandbaby." Lauren rubbed her midsection. "Who knew this airport would be the common denominator in every new journey in our life." She smiled. "Think about it, Xavier … the salon, our marriage, and now a new baby."

"Look at you getting all mushy," he teased, stroking her cheek.

"Thanks for making sure we always spend our anniversary in New York. You just don't know how much that means to me."

"I do," he said with a kiss. "And you're welcome."

* * *

Shawn and Candace arrived in El Paso and went to Fort Bliss Military Base. Before 9/11, they would have been able to go on the grounds. Now, they were flagged at the perimeter and were met by armed soldiers who carried the kind of weapons that Shawn only saw in the movies. Luckily, with the documents she had in her possession, she was able to get to someone who could put her in touch with Matthew O'Shaughnessy.

After waiting for twenty minutes in the sweltering heat with a soldier standing on each side of their rental car, an oversized dusty green Unimog kicked up sand as it approached at a modest speed.

A man hopped out wearing a black uniform with gold buttons and a white button-down shirt and black necktie. On the sleeve, there were gold embroidered stripes shaped like an upside-down kite with a five-point star surrounded by two wings on each side. "I'm Command Sergeant Major Cullin," he said extending his hand.

"I'm Shawn Johnston." She smiled, shaking it, before letting her hand fall by her side. "Daughter of Command Sergeant Major Matthew O'Shaughnessy and this is my friend, Candace Livingston."

"Hello." Candace waved.

He nodded, then turned his focus back to Shawn and said, "State your business."

She swallowed, intimidated by the firmness in his tone. The armed soldiers did little to put her at ease. "I'm looking for my father," she stated, retrieving the documents and handing them to CSM Cullin. "I was adopted as an infant. The man I believe to be my father, Matthew O'Shaughnessy, signed the birth certificate—"

"Let me stop you right there," he said raising his hand, but Shawn ignored him.

"I've checked his old neighborhood and the people who remembered him said he enlisted after high school, but they didn't know his current whereabouts. I've been on ancestry.com and found nothing," she said, taking a breath before continuing. "Then I googled U.S. military records collection, and that pointed me to Fort Bliss." Shawn eyed CSM Cullin. "This is the last place he was stationed according to the online file."

"I'm sorry you had to come all this way," CSM Cullin expressed with sincerity. "CSM O'Shaughnessy hasn't lived on this base in years."

Shawn lowered her gaze; disappointment filtered her mind and body.

"Excuse me, sir," Candace interjected. "Do you know where we can find him?"

He didn't answer Candace's question. After looking over the documents for several minutes, he glanced at Shawn. "Ms. Johnston."

"Yes," she responded.

He eyed her long enough to make her uncomfortable.

"Yes," she huffed, exasperated by his presence.

"I know your father," he said pointing to Matthew's signature on the birth certificate. "I could identify that writing with my eyes closed."

Shawn's rigidness eased. The breath she wasn't aware she was holding came out at a steady rate, causing her chest to deflate.

"CSM O'Shaughnessy—Matthew and I served together." He handed her the documents. "You look just like him."

"That's what I was told," she mumbled, thinking back to when she met her grandmother.

"He comes back and teaches a basic training class every four months. If y—"

"I thought he was retired," Shawn said.

"He couldn't leave this if he tried," CSM Cullin snickered. "Officially, he's retired. He volunteers his time, and he's been doing it for so long that he has a permanent home on Fort Bragg Military Base in North Carolina. Let me give him a call."

"You have his number," Shawn squealed in excitement.

A broad smile splayed across CSM Cullin's weather-beaten face. "Yes, we're old friends."

"Thank you so much, sir."

Shawn rocked side to side, fidgeting with the zipper on her purse.

"How would he know who I am?" she asked Candace. "We never met."

Candace slid her hand in Shawn's. "We didn't come this far to go home without answers," she countered, offering Shawn a reassuring smile. "Breathe easy."

"I'm trying."

"Excuse me, Ms. Johnston," he said. "CSM O'Shaughnessy would like to speak with you."

* * *

"Good evening folks, welcome to Midway Airport in Chicago. The time is eight forty-three pm, and the temperature is twenty-two degrees. For your safety, please remain seated with your seatbelt fastened."

"I can't stop smiling." Shawn gleamed, pulling a wool hat over her head.

"From scorching hot to freezing cold in less than two hours." Candace shook her head, wrapping a scarf around her neck.

"Thank you for flying Southwest Airlines. We look forward to seeing you again. Have a safe and wonderful New Year, bundle up and enjoy the Windy City," the flight attendant announced over the microphone.

Soon as the seatbelt sign turned off, Shawn and Candace retrieved their carry-on luggage from the overhead compartment and disembarked from the plane.

"I can't believe he's sending for me next weekend," Shawn said as they approached the moving walkway. "Fort Bragg, North Carolina, here I come."

"Are you nervous?"

"Hell yeah," Shawn shouted, then laughed as her outburst caused travelers and airport staff to stare. "I have to find a way to get off work on Friday. I can't ask Javid because he'll want to know all the juice before he agrees. I'm not ready to share this with anyone yet."

"Tell Patricia it's for school," Candace suggested while adjusting the handle on her luggage. "Your field work for the internship is coming up soon, right?"

"Candace, you're a geniu—"

"Are you okay?" Candace asked, grabbing Shawn by the arm. She stumbled stepping onto the moving walkway.

"That bastard," Shawn muttered, struggling to regain her balance. She pointed to gate B2.

Candace gasped, "Is that—"

"Yep. Ms. Lauren and that no good, two-timing, Mr. Xavier."

* * *

"Xavier Carter? Man, I haven't seen you since college," said a short, slender man sitting across the aisle on the plane. He got up to give Xavier a friendly hug. "What's been going on?"

"Derek, my man." Xavier returned the greeting. "What's happening?" he said, glancing over his shoulder at Lauren who was in the window seat wearing headphones and had her eyes closed.

"Pardon me," a lady said, carrying an infant trying to get past them.

"My apologies," Xavier responded, both taking their seats.

"I'm traveling to spend the holiday with my brother and his family."

"That's cool," Xavier squinted, trying to remember the details of this man's life. "I thought your hometown was in Nashville."

"It is, but—"

"Would you like something to drink?" asked the flight attendant wearing a navy blue uniform with a yellow and red pendant designed with a pair of wings and a red heart in the middle.

"Miller Draft, please," Derek replied.

"I'll have the same." Xavier glanced over to see if Lauren wanted anything, but she was sleeping. "That's all."

The flight attendant smiled, then walked to the next set of seats.

"What were you saying?" Xavier asked Derek.

"My brother's wife's family lives in New York. We alternate locations every year."

"That's what's up." Xavier nodded, then the reality of what Derek was in college filtered his mind.

"How are Patricia and her crazy sister Latrice?"

"She's good," Xavier murmured.

"Man those were the good old days." Derek nodded with a devilish grin. "The fun we had at the after after *after* parties——oh yeah. I couldn't believe you were the first to settle down and get married, man." Derek chuckled. "All the crazy things we did, I'm surprised Patricia married you in the first place."

Xavier put his index finger to his lips to try and quiet Derek, but he was too caught up rambling down memory lane. He always talked too damn much.

"Did she ever find out you slept with her sister?"

Xavier shook his head. "It wasn't like that," he whispered. "What happened between Latrice and me was over with wayyyyyy before Patricia came to Fisk."

"You did that girl so wrong."

Xavier glanced over his shoulder. "And she still hates me to this day."

A piercing scream, followed by continuous cries halted their conversation. The lady with the infant apologized as she passed each set of chairs, making her way back to her seat. A series of grunts from unhappy passengers accompanied the woman along the way.

"Whoa." Lauren removed the headphones. "That baby drowned out my music," she said placing them on the tray. "Who's your friend?"

A cold chill ran down Xavier's spine. "This is Derek. We went to college together."

"Nice to meet you, Derek. I'm Lauren, his wife."

"Hi," Derek flinched, narrowed his beady-eyes on the beautiful woman. "I didn't know you got remarried."

Xavier closed his eyes tight.

"Remarried? What's he talking about Xavier?"

He faced Derek, practically growling as he said, "You got me mixed up with Xavier Johnson. He's on wife number three."

"My bad," Derek corrected. "We had three Xavier's in our graduating class. It's hard to keep up."

Lauren slipped her headphones back in place and turned her head toward the window.

Xavier mouthed a breathy, "Thank you."

Derek shrugged, gave him a fist bump, and whispered, "Playa playa."

Chapter Thirty-Five

I hate him.

Those three words were on a continuous loop in Patricia's head as she prepared for the New Years Day party being held at her home. She had never seen her son so upset, and he still wouldn't tell her why. The only thing Junior said when she asked what was wrong was that he didn't want to hurt her.

How could he hurt me?

Instinct told her to leave it alone at that time, but she surely was going to revisit the subject today.

Patricia spruced up the house for her guest. She made sure extra toiletries, paper towels, and soap dispensers were full. She wiped down the kitchen island and lined it with buffet tray stands and warmers. Then Patricia retrieved the champagne flutes from the dishwasher and arranged them on the counter on top of a beautiful lace tablecloth. She turned to get the coolers from the pantry when

Junior startled her.

"Morning Moms," he greeted wiping his puffy eyes, less cheerful than usual. "Do you need any help?"

"Boy," Patricia said catching her breath. "You're gonna have to stop doing that."

"I didn't mean to scare you."

She gave him a careful once-over. For some reason, he was uncomfortable in her presence. That was her baby, and she knew him better than he knew himself. That sparkle in his eye had lost its shimmer.

"I've got this," she said, pulling the coolers out of the pantry. "I need you to go downstairs and get the ice out of the freezer."

She was cleaning one of the coolers when he got back upstairs. Junior sat the bags of ice on one side of the dual sink, pulled the other cooler over, grabbed a soapy rag and wiped it down.

"So——how long have you and Zoe been dating?" Patricia asked, standing upright, stretching her back.

"About six months," he whispered.

"Wow." That was a long time for Patricia not to know anything about her. She couldn't believe that she had no inkling.

"Does she go to St. Francis?"

"Yeah," he replied, rinsing out the cooler. "Zoe's on the volleyball team."

"That's cool." Patricia rolled the other cooler to the sink. She stood next to Junior, placing a gentle hand on his back. "Why didn't you tell me about her?"

Junior tensed at her touch.

"I don't know."

"Come here son," she said, turning off the water. She took his hand and led him to the table. "You know you can tell me anything."

"I know," he replied, sitting down.

"Did you think I was going to be mad that you had a girlfriend?" she asked, lifting his chin.

He didn't say anything.

"Anyone important to you is important to me," Patricia said, searching his eyes. "I would love to get a chance to know Zoe. Why don't you invite her to the party? And her parents too."

A hesitant smile crept across Junior's face. "Thanks, Moms." He shifted in his seat, breaking eye contact. "I thought you were mad at me."

"I'm not." She cleared her throat. "I'm disappointed. That's a totally different thing. I just know what can happen when you get caught up in the moment," she said thinking about the daughter she was forced to give away as a teenager. She leaned in close, "You're not ready for a baby, and neither is she."

Patricia laced her fingers under the table, hoping that the answer to her next question was the one she wanted to hear. "Have you already had sex?"

"No," he responded, and his tone was forceful and sure.

She pulled his hands from his mouth and stared at him. "Junior…"

"No Moms, I promise. I haven't."

Patricia's gut told her he was telling the truth. She almost said make sure you talk to your father before you do since he was a man, but she stopped as another issue came to the forefront. "What's going on with you and your dad? And don't tell me it's nothing."

Junior pulled his hands away from hers, slouching in the chair. He dropped his chin to his chest and closed his eyes. He was doing that a lot lately.

"Why would you say you hate him?" She tapped the table to get him to look up. "That's a very harsh word and shouldn't be used lightly."

"Because he's a jerk," he mumbled under his breath.

Barely keeping her composure, she asked, "Why is he a jerk?"

She didn't like Junior's choice of words, but her goal was to get answers, so she rolled with however he needed to express himself.

The silence was deafening, so she asked again. "*Why* is your father a jerk? You told me last night that you didn't want to hurt me. Does his being a jerk have something to do with me?"

Junior's chest heaved. He didn't say a word. He sniffled, and that's when Patricia noticed the wet spots on his gray t-shirt. She scooted her chair closer to him. "Why are you crying?" She wrapped an arm around his shoulder. "You can talk to me, Junior."

"Moms, I'm sorry." Junior's voice was filled with such emotion that she feared that something was so wrong in his life that she wouldn't be able to help him.

"It's okay baby, whatever it is." Patricia comforted her son with words and a gentle stroke of her hand over his. "Why did you call your father a jerk? You can tell me, Junior. What did he do?" She wiped his tears with the back of her hand.

"He's been lying to you, Moms. He's been…"

Her heart jolted. "Lying to me about what?"

"Moms, I'm sorry." He sniffled. "I don't want to hurt you."

There that phrase goes again.

Although Patricia reassured him that he could never hurt her, she was afraid of what Junior was about to say.

"What is it, Junior?" Her voice quivered, and the thoughts running through her mind ranged from something else happening at his job to straight out infidelity.

"He's just a liar." Junior rose from the chair. He walked over to the sink, turned on the water and continued to rinse out the cooler.

"Junior," she pleaded, following him to the sink. "What aren't you telling me?"

"Moms——I can't." He closed his eyes tight and shook his head. "Pleaseeeee just leave it alone."

Junior's body shook, and Patricia hugged him from behind. "I love you Junior, and I see that you're hurting," she said, holding back tears. "I'm going to cancel the party so we ca——"

"Moms, no. I'm okay." Junior turned to face her, brushing away his tears with the back of his shaky hand. "Don't cancel the party."

Patricia cupped his cheeks in her palms, staring up at him. "You know you're more important to me than this party."

"I'm okay." He grabbed her hands, removing them from his

face. "I just don't want to talk about it right now."

Patricia could see that he wasn't okay. When did conversing with Junior become so strained? What was he afraid to tell her?

* * *

Plagued by unanswered questions, Patricia was determined to enjoy the party. The conversation she had earlier with Junior was still at the forefront of her mind.

She finished applying burnt orange lipstick and rubbed her lips together. She stood in front of the vanity mirror taking in the strapless off-white jumpsuit that hugged her womanly curves in all the right places. She complemented her ensemble with a gold belt and a single button orange blazer that flared over her hips. She stepped into matching suede heels that would probably be kicked under the cocktail table before the night was over.

A knock at her bedroom door caught her attention. "Come in."

"Moms you look pretty," Junior said, admiring her outfit.

"Thank you, baby," she replied, striking a pose. "What's up?"

"I just wanted to let you know that Brandon and Zoe were on their way. Her parents already had plans."

"Okay." She smiled, walking toward Junior. "I love you." She gently pecked his cheek, leaving orange residue behind, then wiping it off with her thumb.

"I love you too."

"Let's have fun tonight." She held out her fist.

They fist bumped, then blew it up.

The doorbell rang, and Junior shouted, "That's Auntie Latrice."

Patricia turned off the bedroom light and shut the door. Latrice was inside by the time Patricia made it down the stairs.

"Hey Li'l Sis," Latrice said, holding up two bottles of champagne. "You look fabulous, chick."

"Thank you." Patricia curtsied, then embraced her sister who wore a long sleeve black wrap dress with a deep neck plunge.

"You ain't short stopping yourself."

Patricia gave Latrice a playful side eye. "You know all my male friends are married, right?"

"What's your point?" Latrice handed the bottles to Patricia. "I do all of this for me. If one of them choose to look, that's on them."

Junior started cracking up. "Auntie, you're funny."

Latrice zeroed in on him. "Who's this little girl who has your nose wide open?"

"Moms," Junior yelled, his cheeks flushing red with embarrassment.

Patricia looked at him and shrugged, taking the bottles of wine into the kitchen.

"Oh no, nephew. Your business is *my* business."

"Her name is Zoe," he said with a big grin, showcasing his dimples.

"Is she coming tonight?"

"Yes, auntie." Junior sighed, placing his hands on her shoulders. "Please don't ask her a thousand questions."

"Good luck with that," Patricia shouted from the kitchen.

* * *

An hour later, the house was jumping with feel-good music, family, and friends. Everyone was full, tipsy and having a great time.

Patricia's employees were in attendance. And as usual, Javid was the life of the party, dancing like he was the main attraction. His French boyfriend, Evan looked like he wanted to melt into the sofa. Meilani was laid back in her fitted Kente dress with matching head garb. She and her husband, Adeyemi was enjoying themselves socializing with other guests. Shawn was there, and she came solo since her friend Candace had to work. Patricia was delighted that she was able to make it.

She was surprised to see Shawn hanging more with Junior and his friends than she was with people her own age. The laughter in their corner of the room was endless, and Patricia was overjoyed to see Junior acting more like his usual self.

Latrice was in her element, playing bartender—— mixing drinks, sticking toothpicks in cherries and oranges, then topping them off with cute umbrellas.

Patricia hung with Latrice behind the bar, sipping a fruity drink.

"Yoooo——nephew and crew," Latrice summoned over the loud music to the under twenty-one crowd to get virgin daiquiris made especially for them.

Patricia shook her head, laughing at her big sister's antics. Junior, Brandon, Zoe, and Shawn came rushing to the bar.

"Auntie, can I have just an incy-wincy squirt of alcohol?" Junior asked, holding his thumb and index fingers close together.

"If it were up to me," Latrice said, rolling her eyes. "I would let you have it, but *you know who* is watching."

"Yeah right." Patricia smirked, sipping her drink. "Gone head. I'ma have your butt arrested."

Junior and his friends cracked up.

"By who?" Latrice looked around. "I don't see any cops in here tonight."

"Speaking of cops. Where's Mr. Xavier?" Shawn intervened.

The laughter at the bar subsided as Patricia responded, "He's away on business." She glanced at Junior, at the same moment his jaw tightened at the mention of his father's name.

"Do you want one of these kiddie drinks or the real deal?" Patricia asked Shawn, swiftly changing the subject.

"The real deal works for me." Shawn grinned, pointing toward the bottles of liquor.

Patricia nudged Latrice who seemed to be frozen in place. "Make Shawn a mai tai."

Then Patricia turned back to Shawn. "And *you* make sure not to share it with Junior and his friends."

Giggling, Shawn said, "I won't."

Patricia glanced at Latrice who looked as if she had seen a ghost. "Earth to Latrice," Patricia snapped her fingers in her sister's face.

"Yeah. What?" Latrice responded, seeming confused.

"Never mind," Patricia said, pushing her to the side with her hip. "I'll do it."

Patricia filled a glass with ice cubes, then poured rum and amaretto in it. "I might have to cut you off if you zone out on me like that again." She poured equal parts of orange and pineapple juice in the glass until it was filled, then added a smidgen of grenadine for color.

"Here you go." Patricia stuck a toothpick through a cherry and lime, then wedged it alongside the glass.

"Thanks." Shawn smiled, taking a sip. "This is perfect."

Patricia turned to Latrice, placing her hands on her hips after Shawn walked away. "Where did you just go?"

"Shawn——" Latrice paused. "I'd be damned. She's the spitting image of Matthew."

Patricia's heart palpitated. "What did you just say?"

Latrice spoke slow and deliberate, "Straight hair, green eyes, light pink lips——damn near passing for a white girl." Latrice covered her mouth. "I don't know how you didn't see it, Li'l Sis." Latrice wrapped her arm around Patricia. "That girl could be your daughter."

Chapter Thirty-Six

Patricia placed her drink on the table, then slowly eased from behind the bar. Almost as if in a trance, she walked toward Shawn. Their first meeting was when Patricia interviewed her at MedRx. Patricia's sixth sense had kicked in that day, but she didn't know why. Now she did.

She stopped walking in the middle of the floor as a chill hit her core. She shuddered, looking down at her fingers.

Meilani tapped Patricia's shoulder. "Are you alright?"

Startled by her touch, she responded, "Yes," with a shaky voice, taking in several pairs of eyes glued to her.

"You sure?" Meilani asked, concerned. "You're staring off into space."

Latrice rushed to Patricia's side. "She's good," she said, wrapping an arm around Patricia's waist. "I think she had a little too much to drink."

Meilani chuckled. "I'm running a close second." She took a sip of her drink and rejoined her husband on the sofa.

"Come on, Li'l Sis, I got you."

A sense of calm accompanied Latrice's touch, which helped Patricia regain some semblance of inner peace. She took a single step, then stopped again. She closed her eyes and Shawn's voice echoed in her ear, *Mom I need you.* Her eyes flung open. "Latrice. That's my baby girl," she whispered, raising praying hands to her chin. "I remember."

"Remember what?" Latrice inquired, searching Patricia's watery eyes.

"When I fainted. It was because—"

"Moms," Junior hollered over the music. "Auntie Sandy is here."

Sandy was Jason's wife. They had become good friends thanks to their husband's occupation. She was a regular fixture at Patricia's parties.

"Are you straight?" Latrice asked, giving Patricia's waist a tight squeeze.

"Yeah." Patricia took a deep breath, staring at Shawn across the room. "This is the best New Year's Day ever. Not another one will ever compare."

"I can't believe she's been under your nose all this time." Latrice paused. "That's my niece," she said smiling, staring at Shawn. "I'll be right back. I'm going to get us some more drinks." They were going to need it.

* * *

Sandy approached Patricia after Junior took her coat. "Hey girl," Sandy pulled Patricia into a hug. "Good to see you."

"You look gorgeous as always," Patricia complimented, admiring Sandy's outfit of skinny jeans, a red satin Chinese wrap blouse that hugged her petite waist, and her jet black hair in a high silky ponytail, which made her almond-shaped eyes more prominent.

"Is everything okay?" Sandy asked in a thick accent. "Your eyes are so red."

"I just received some great news, and my emotions got the best of me," Patricia explained, looking over Sandy's shoulder at Shawn. "Everything is everything as Junior would say."

"That's good." Sandy smiled. "I brought kung pao chicken. Jason's getting it out of the car."

"You know you didn't have to bring anythi——" Patricia halted mid-sentence. "Wait. Jason's here?"

"Yeah. Junior is helping him get the food and drinks out of the trunk."

Patricia blinked and tilted her head while processing what Sandy had said. "Isn't he supposed to be in New York with Xavier?"

"Noooo," Sandy replied. "I don't know anything about New York."

Patricia threw daggers at Latrice behind the bar. Latrice crossed her arms, but she didn't say a word, which rarely happened. Junior walked in carrying cases of pop, and Jason followed with the aluminum tray.

"Hey, everyone," Jason shouted over the music, his exuberant tone not matching the expression on his face. "Happy New Year."

Patricia met him in the kitchen, opening the oven to place the tray inside.

"Hey Patty," Jason said, his voice a little shaky. He bent down kissing her on the cheek. "Everything looks fantastic."

"Thanks," she replied, folding her arms. "What are you doing here? I thought you were supposed to be in New York with Xavier?"

Jason opened his mouth then shut it just as quickly.

Latrice was leaning on the doorjamb, ear hustling, but Patricia didn't care.

"Why aren't you at the seminar?" Patricia asked, setting the oven to one hundred degrees to keep the food warm. "I thought it was mandatory for all detectives. Some mass crowd control training during New York's biggest tourist season or something like that."

Just then, Sandy walked into the kitchen. "Jason, would you like me to fix your plate?" she asked, turning on the faucet to wash her hands.

"Uh–uh–um—yes."

Sandy glanced over. "What is going on here?"

"That's what I would like to know," Patricia shot back.

Patricia grabbed her phone from the counter and called Xavier. The phone went straight to voicemail. "Xavier, this is Patty. Call me back."

She ignored the tense feelings surrounding everyone in the room. Her focus was on learning the truth.

"Jason, I know you're Xavier's partner, but I would also like to think that I'm your friend. You're Junior's godfather. I consider you and Sandy family. Please, tell me where my husband is."

Sandy stared at Jason. "Tell Patty where Xavier is."

Years ago, Xavier came up with a scheme to get out of town without suspicion from Patty, but he needed Jason to corroborate his story. While Xavier was in New York with Lauren, Jason worked overtime. The department always needed a stronger police presence on the streets over the New Year holiday. This guaranteed Jason wouldn't be available to attend Patricia's parties, and it kept him out of sight for days. And he didn't have to lie to Sandy about his whereabouts.

Regret was written all over Jason's face. His dashing blue eyes looked sad. "It's not my place to say, Patty. And I don't want to hurt you."

"Everyone seems to be so *concerned* about not *hurting me* that they don't realize *they are hurting me* by not telling me the truth," she shouted. "Junior." Patricia's head snapped to the family room. "Upstairs. Now."

All eyes were on them. Patricia's outburst caught everyone by surprise. In an attempt to lessen the tension, Latrice whipped out several decks of cards from the kitchen drawer. "Who's ready to get their ass kicked? 'Cause y'all know I'm the queen of Spades, Bid Whist, Pity-Pat, Go Fish or any other card game y'all can think of," she boasted, patting Patricia's back before she followed Junior up the stairs.

Patricia was grateful for her sister being there. Though she could be loud and overbearing at times, she always knew what to do in any given situation.

Soon as they walked into her bedroom, Patricia closed the door. "What's going on with your father? And you not telling me isn't an option."

Junior sat down on the side of Patricia's bed and placed his hands over his face. "Moms, please don't do this," he pleaded. "I can't."

"But you can. I need to know." She paced the floor, then stopped directly in front of him. "Spit it out, Junior."

With tears rolling down his chocolate face, Junior's tone was filled with regret as he said, "He's cheating on you."

Patricia had been sucker punched in the stomach. She wrapped her arms around her midriff and rocked back and forth, trying to snuff out the pain.

"I'm sorry," he mumbled, scratching his head.

"What makes you say that?"

"I found out the night I called Pops to tell him about the championship game," Junior said, picking the dirt from underneath his nails. "A woman answered his phone. She said I had the wrong number and when I called back it went straight to his voicemail."

Knowing her son was telling the truth, she still had to ask, "Are you sure you dialed the correct number?" Patricia was hoping, wishing for any sign of hope.

"I'm sure, Moms." Junior's knee bounced nervously. "I voice dialed him from Siri like I always do. I told Pops I called after I got home from my game, but he said he never received a call from me." Junior huffed. "Then he threatened me."

"What do you mean he threatened you?" Patricia asked, ready to pounce.

"He tried to scare me, in that cop voice. *Pops* told me that I dialed the wrong number. Like he wanted to convince me or something." Junior fidgeted with his fingers. "Then he stared me down like I was the bad guy. And he's been acting weird with me ever since. I *know* I dialed the right number. I bet that *woman* didn't even tell him I called. But it doesn't matter," he said struggling. "If you look at the phone bill, it'll show three calls from me the night of the championship game."

Xavier paid the cell phone bill. Patricia had sat it, along with the other bills he was responsible for on his desk two days ago. She was certain it was still there.

"Moms, did you hear me?" Junior asked, tapping her thigh.

"No—What did you say, honey?"

"The night of the National Honor Society ceremony pops had pink lipstick on the inside of his collar," Junior said shifting on the bed. "You never wear pink lipstick. You said it makes your lips look like." He paused. "A baboon's you know what."

Patricia gasped, drawing a hand to her opened mouth.

"Oh," he said, then looked away. "I heard you guys arguing that night."

"It wasn't about that," Patricia confessed. "It was because he missed your ceremony." She thought back to both nights. "That was weeks ago," she said, looking at Junior. "And you've been carrying this burden this whole time."

Patricia dropped to her knees with her arms still wrapped around her midriff, trying to keep the torment at bay.

"I'm sorry Moms," Junior cried. He fell to his knees, embracing his mother.

She held onto him, pushing the pain to the background. She would cry on her own time. Right now her son needed her more than she needed to give in to despair. "You didn't hurt me, Junior. You told me the truth, and I would rather know the truth than living happily behind a lie any day." Patricia kissed his cheek. "You did the right thing."

"Knock. Knock." Latrice cautiously entered the room. She observed her Li'l Sis and nephew huddled together on the floor. I'm sending folks home."

"No. Don't do that," Patricia said. "It's the holiday. Give me a few minutes, and I'll be down."

"It's okay. Most of the guests have already left. I'm sure they understand." Latrice glanced down at Junior, "I thought you might want to say goodbye to Zoe before she leaves."

"Nah, just tell her I'll see her later," Junior mumbled, pulling his shirt over his eyes to dry his tears.

"No," Patricia said. "Go in my bathroom, throw some water on your face, and walk Zoe to the car."

He opened his mouth to protest, but Patricia cut him off. "I'm fine. Just go, I need a few minutes to myself."

Junior complied. As soon as he left the room, Latrice rushed to her sister. "Are you alright?" she asked, helping Patricia to her feet.

Patricia was embarrassed and hurt, not just for herself, but for Junior. She wiped her eyes with the back of her hand and took a deep breath. "You were right about him," Patricia said, her voice barely above a whisper. "He's been cheating on me. Junior found out."

Latrice pulled Patricia into an embrace. "I never wanted to be," she admitted. "I'm just sorry that it came out like this."

Patricia stepped back from Latrice. She was hollow inside but was trying to put on a strong face. She flicked off her heels and took off the orange blazer. Her phone fell from the blazer pocket when she tossed it on the bed, landing at her feet. Patricia blankly stared at it.

Latrice followed her glance. "Do you want me to call that bastard?" she asked, her voice laced with venom.

"It wouldn't make a difference." Patricia shrugged. "Xavier is unreachable when he goes on those semin——" Patricia stopped mid-sentence as realization slammed into her. "That's probably a lie too." Patricia plopped down on the bed. "How gullible am I?"

"Not gullible, Li'l Sis——just blindly in love with the man you married." Latrice picked up the phone and placed it on the nightstand.

Patricia let that marinate for what seemed like an eternity but was only five minutes. Her thoughts and emotions were tossed in a mixer and got blended into something she couldn't describe. She glanced down at her wedding ring and smirked. A fire ignited from the pit of Patricia's stomach then burst into roaring flames. "How could he do this to me? To Junior?" Her gaze bore into Latrice's. "My twenties and thirties were wasted on a no good son of a bitch." She bit down on her bottom lip, breathing deeply through her nostrils. "How could all of this be a lie?" she questioned, looking about the room, taking in everything that represented her marriage.

"I don't know," Latrice replied. "But whatever you need, I'm here."

Patricia pursed her lips and nodded. The unity candle that sat on the dresser along with a bride and groom snow globe with their wedding date engraved on it. The African art that she had admired at the gallery. Xavier bought it for her as an anniversary gift. The old sentimental loveseat that they refused to get rid of since it was the first piece of furniture they purchased together as husband and wife. Junior was conceived on that very loveseat. Then her eyes landed on a framed photo of them holding Junior in the hospital, moments after she had given birth.

She turned to her sister. "Would you check on Junior for me, and my guests?" Patricia asked, reaching around to unzip her jumpsuit. "I'll be down in a minute."

"Okay." Latrice locked gazes with Patricia, giving her a reassuring smile before exiting the bedroom.

Soon as the door closed, Patricia let out a long sigh. She slipped into a pair of jogging pants and an oversized sweatshirt. When she entered the master bathroom, the cold marble under her bare feet made her shiver. But Patricia didn't mind; it was a far better feeling than the gut-wrenching pain that had set up shop in her heart. She stared at her reflection in the mirror and didn't recognize herself. The red-rimmed, puffy eyes weren't the culprits, but the woman who had allowed herself to be mistreated was. Patricia removed what was left of her makeup and washed her face.

She left the bathroom, stopping by the vanity to take off her jewelry. She set the diamond earrings and tennis bracelet in their respective places. She held out her left hand, thinking of the vows she took and everything that her wedding band should've represented. She closed her eyes and worked it half way off her finger. Clearing her throat, Patricia opened her eyes again, gauging her reflection in the mirror. She was hurt and pissed off at the same time, but she was still Xavier's wife. She couldn't bring herself to remove her wedding band, so she eased it back down, over her knuckle to its forever spot until she had the opportunity to confront him herself.

When Patricia emerged from the room, the silence choked her. She would have welcomed the lack of sound under normal circumstances, but this wasn't tranquil at all. The house was eerily quiet in comparison to what it had been an hour ago.

She descended the stairs and entered the clean kitchen. Latrice and Junior were sitting at the breakfast bar talking. "Who did this?" she asked scoping the area before opening the refrigerator. The food had been transferred to Tupperware bowls and stacked neatly on the shelves. Patricia's ear keened in on a slight humming and water spraying sound. The dishwasher was running a cycle.

Junior had just finished chugging down the last of his pop when he responded, "Shawn was in the kitchen when I came downstairs to say bye to Zoe."

Patricia and Latrice shared a knowing glance. Patricia was so distraught by Xavier's infidelity that she forgot about Latrice's revelation.

"She did all of this herself?" Patricia asked.

"Yeah," Junior replied, tossing the aluminum can in the recycle bin. "Shawn said she didn't want you to worry about cleaning up."

A lone tear slithered down Patricia's face. The infidelity issues swirling around her marriage paled in comparison to Shawn's simple act of kindness. The fact that it was *her daughter* looking out for her took Patricia's emotions over the edge.

* * *

Later that evening when Patricia was able to be alone with her thoughts, she pulled out the keepsake box and read every single one of the birthday cards she had purchased for her long-lost daughter. Being there in the pharmacy, in Patricia's life was something that had to be planned. Patricia vowed that her daughter would get to know her, and she prayed that Shawn would understand why she had given her up.

She lifted the old picture of Matthew and wondered what her life might have been like had they fought their parents and raised their baby. Then she scolded herself for being selfish. Shawn deserved a better life than they were able to offer at that time on their own. Then she thought about Junior. Had she not met Xavier, she wouldn't have that beautiful, but troubled, spirit who slept down the hall.

"Xavier." She huffed. "Damn you."

Staring at Matthew's photo, her stomach fluttered. Shawn's image clearly came into view. There wasn't any doubt in Patricia's mind that Shawn was her daughter. Even Shawn's bone structure matched her father's. Patricia laid on the bed, still holding Matthew's photo in her hand. She brought it to her lips, kissing it gently.

Patricia had lost a husband but gained a daughter. She pulled the covers over her body and cradled Matthew's picture to her chest—a bittersweet moment, but sweet nonetheless. Before dozing off to sleep, Patricia whispered, "My sweet love, we got our baby back."

Chapter Thirty-Seven

Sitting outside on the concrete steps of her apartment in Bronzeville, the scent of fresh flowers from Patricia's home still lingered on Shawn's clothing. She inhaled as the breeze coming off of Lake Michigan swirled about her.

Leaning her head on the banister, Shawn closed her eyes with the apartment keys clutched in her fist. She never lost sight that she was outdoors, but her memory served her best behind closed lids. The remembrance of the toasty flames from the fireplace and the crackling wood kept her warm. James Brown, The Whispers, and The Temptations filtered the room through the surround sound speakers while people danced and others congregated in small groups socializing. She was grateful that Mr. Xavier hadn't been there. Her interaction with him had left a sour taste in her mouth and also had her torn about how keeping the information to herself was hurting both women.

Shawn had all intentions of telling Patricia she was her daughter, but matters beyond her control prevented that from happening. She was still happy that she got a chance to meet and interact with her Aunt Latrice, her little brother, and his friends. Part of her was set to resent that Junior had spent all his life with the woman who had given birth to them both, but his silly charismatic charm won her over. Junior was your average fifteen-year-old boy who played the dozens with his homeboy and crushed hard on his girlfriend, who seemed sweet, if not a little clingy.

Glass breaking at her feet halted her happy thoughts and caused Shawn's eyes to fly open. She locked gazes with a man in a ski mask that only showed his eyes and lips. Her heart stopped. She was twelve years old again at the mercy of a predator. Her deep breaths beat like bass percussions in her eardrums.

Police sirens roared in the distance, too far away to help whatever was about to happen on her doorstep. The crime was rampant in Chicago, but she never thought it would come this close to home.

"Come on man. We didn't come here for this," a voice yelled from behind another black ski mask, pulling at the perpetrator's arm.

The man gave Shawn a wicked grin. "My daddy died in prison because of your lies," he growled. "I've been watching you." He backed down the cement steps and ran off with his buddy.

I knew I wasn't paranoid.

Shawn scrambled to her feet fiddling with the keys to unlock the door. Once inside the building, she bolted up the stairs to her apartment. Banging on the apartment door like a mad woman, she was shaking too bad to get the key in the lock.

"Who is it?" Candace hollered from the other side of the door.

"Let. Me. In," Shawn cried.

The latches clicked, and Shawn dashed inside, slamming the door behind her. She double bolted the locks, then slid to the floor. Tears flowed down her face as she thanked the man above for keeping her safe.

Candace stood over Shawn, in bra and panties and a metal baseball bat in her hand. "What's wrong?"

Shawn whispered, "He threatened me."

"Who?" Candace squatted in front of Shawn, lifting her chin.

"The son of that monster," Shawn wailed. "He knows where we live."

"Whose son?"

"The man who raped me."

Candace jumped up, snatching her long winter coat off the coat rack and jamming her feet in boots that sat by the front door. "Move out the way," she ordered, unlocking the front door with the bat in her hand. "I'm going to beat the crap out of that piece of shit."

"No," Shawn screamed, refusing to move. "He's gone."

"You need to call the police," Candace said, tossing the bat onto the futon. "I know he's not your favorite person, but maybe Mr. Xavier can help," she suggested, reaching down to help Shawn off the floor.

"That's not an option."

"Why not?"

"It's just not," Shawn snapped, plopping down on the futon. "I'll call Ms. Lauren in the morning. She'll know what to do."

Candace folded her arms. "What happened between you and Mr. Xavier tonight?"

Shawn filled Candace in on her evening at Patricia's home. "I feel sorry for Patricia. If you could've seen the look on her face when Xavier's partner walked in the door, you would've felt bad too. I didn't know what was going on at first, but I put two and two together, and it didn't equal four."

"That's messed up," Candace said, swiping loose strands of hair from her face. "Well, at least you didn't have to be the one to inform her."

"True, but now I don't know when I'll get a chance to tell Patricia I'm her daughter. I mean——how will I know when the time is right? It seems like her life is already complicated."

"It's not complicated," Candace snapped, her forehead furrowed. "Just tell her. I don't know why it's taken you this long. You've been working with her for the past four months. That's more than enough time to get to know someone."

"She's not just someone. She's..." Shawn crooked her fingers as quotes. " My mother. My *real* mother."

Candace cut her eyes and smirked, something that didn't look good on her friend. "Well, tell her then since you're so excited to have found your *real* mom," she said, mimicking Shawn's air quotations.

Shawn couldn't believe the attitude that was coming off of Candace. It's not like Candace's life was about to implode. Shawn had to face the possibility of being rejected. She didn't know what to expect from Patricia when she came to her in her most vulnerable state. Shawn had every right to wait as long as she saw fit, and it hurt her to know that Candace didn't understand.

"Remember when Ms. Ida told Taletha she was adopted?" Shawn asked, keeping a teary-eyed focus on Candace.

"That was different."

"No, it wasn't," she shot back. "Taletha felt rejected and betrayed, and she blamed us for not telling her."

"We didn't even know the truth," Candace countered, crossing her arms, looking every bit the defiant kid she used to be.

"But that didn't change the way she felt." Shawn leaned forward. "How could you forget? Taletha told us she felt worthless and unwanted. And she didn't trust us anymore. We lost our sister." Shawn rose from the futon and headed toward the bedroom. "I'm going to bed."

"Wait," Candace yelled, grabbing Shawn by the wrist. "I'm sorry."

"You, of all people, I expected to be happy for me," Shawn said, glaring at her best friend.

"I am." Candace sighed, "I just wish——"

"What?" Shawn yelled, snatching away. "We lost Taletha *and* the only mother we'd known who actually loved us. Losing Ms. Ida was as gut-wrenching as when my parents got killed, and Grandma Marie died. Did you ever stop to think that I'm struggling to tell Patricia because of that?" Shawn slipped down onto the floor. "Everyone I love dies."

Ms. Ida died in her sleep the night before Shawn went to tell her she located her biological mother. Was that an omen of things to come? Taletha met her end at the hands of Ted.

"I just wish it was me——okay," Candace admitted, wiping at the tears flowing down her cheeks. "I don't have anyone out there who gives a crap about me, except you. As much as I loved my mother, she never loved me the way I needed to be loved. She chose booze and dick over me," she whispered, and the pain was evident on her tear-streaked face. "And that same booze and dick sent her to an early grave." She stared down at her hands, grimacing. "I wish I had a second chance for my mother to get it right."

* * *

"Good morning handsome," Lauren cooed, kissing Xavier's neck.

They stayed in her childhood bedroom in Brooklyn, New York. Her parents wouldn't have it any other way. Hotels were for guests, not family, was her mother's favorite saying. The small bedroom with a whistling radiator and exposed brick walls made Lauren feel like a kid again. It was perfect.

He rubbed her belly. "Morning beautiful."

"We'd better get up before mom starts banging on the door. You know how she gets about cooking us breakfast when we're here."

"Lay with me five more minutes," Xavier pleaded, snuggling close.

Her lips brushed his nipple, causing him to shiver. "We can do a lot in five minutes."

"You promise," he teased, just as the phone rang.

"To be continued." Lauren rolled over, swiping her phone off the nightstand. "It's Shawn."

She touched the accept button. "Hey, Shawn. What's up?"

Xavier tensed.

Three minutes into the conversation, where Shawn explained an unsettling experience that happened the night before, Lauren bolted upright. "Are you alright?"

"It stunned me, but I'm okay now," Shawn responded, but her tone was still off. "The weird thing is the man's voice sounded familiar."

Lauren sighed, "That's because you know him. It's James."

"Wait a minute. The same James *who shot you?*" Shawn screeched. "I don't understand."

Lauren's gaze lowered to the ground. "James was a Thompson Center kid when his father assaulted you. He was like four or five years old then."

Xavier scooted behind Lauren, wrapping his arms around her waist.

The comfort in his arms gave Lauren more strength than he could ever know.

"James always got picked up before my shift started. I didn't know him or his folks. After his father had been arrested, Mr. Thurmond, the director at the time continued to let James come to the center. Mr. Thurmond didn't want to punish the kid because of the father, especially since he needed the center more than ever."

"So that man had been scoping me out for how long?" Shawn's voice quivered with emotion.

"Shawn. No. Don't think like that."

"You could've warned me," Shawn said, and the anger in her voice was undeniable. "I can't believe you *of all people*, kept this from me?"

"I didn't think— he was just a little boy."

"Well *that little boy* is a grown man, and he's stalking me,"

Shawn shouted. "What am I supposed to do? He knows where I live!"

Lauren stood, crossing her arms over her breasts and squeezing her eyes shut to ward off the pain that stabbed her. She had let Shawn down, again. "Did you call the police? We can get an order of protection," she suggested, turning to face her husband whose stony expression said he wasn't feeling any of the conversation. "I'm gonna put Xavier on. He can tell you how to go about it."

"I don't wanna talk to Mr. Xavier," Shawn roared, causing Lauren to flinch.

"He can help you."

No response.

"Hello? Shawn?" Lauren pulled the phone away from her ear, looked at it in disbelief. "She hung up on me."

* * *

After breakfast, Lauren excused herself under the pretense that she didn't feel well. She was having a hard time processing what Shawn had told her that morning.

"Dad, we're gonna pass on the game," Xavier said, but he didn't seem too upset about it. "I need to stay with Lauren. How much do I owe you for the tickets?"

"No, no," Lauren said before dad could answer. "Go to the game. I'm just tired. A few hours of sleep is all I need." She playfully shooed him toward the door. "Go have fun."

"Are you sure?" Xavier asked, and the concern laced in his voice was touching.

She wanted to be alone. Guilt was riding her, and she wasn't in the mood to attend the New York Knicks basketball game that afternoon with them.

"Yes. Go."

After Lauren had coaxed Xavier into spending the day with her parents, she disappeared into the bedroom. She dug in her purse, pulling out a bottle of prenatal pills. With thoughts of Shawn filtering her brain, she dumped the entire bottle on the bed until the two Ambien tablets she had stashed away fell out.

Once again, she failed Shawn by her inaction. She needed something to dull the ache. "God, please protect my baby," Lauren prayed, holding the little white tablet between her fingers. She lifted it to her mouth and closed her eyes. Lauren's free hand slid to her belly, and an automatic smile lifted the corners of her lips. "My baby." She stared at the tablet in her trembling hand. "I'm stronger than this. I could never do anything to hurt you." Lauren grabbed the second pill, ran to the bathroom and flushed them both.

Chapter Thirty-Eight

"What's all this?" Junior asked, waking his mom. Patricia stirred from a surprisingly restful slumber, rubbing her blurry eyes she responded, "Nothing." Alarmed, she pushed her body upward, resting her back against the headboard.

Then something slid down her chest, landing on her lap, and that's when she remembered she had slept with Matthew. Well, his picture. She had fallen asleep last night with a photo of Matthew on her chest and Shawn's birthday cards strewn across the bed.

Junior sifted through the birthday cards, and inwardly, panic set in. But if she made more of it than necessary, he would realize something was amiss. Holding out her hand, she demanded, "Give me those."

As thrilled as she was, thanks to powers beyond, to share the same breathing space with her daughter for months, she didn't know how to break it to Junior that he had a sister. She didn't want to say anything to anyone until she had a chance to speak with Shawn first.

"Why are you collecting little girl birthday cards?" Junior asked, handing her the glittery pink items with butterflies and princesses images on them. "So you're keeping secrets, too?"

"I promise to tell you when the time is right," Patricia replied, stacking the cards in a pile and sliding them under her pillow.

She extended her arms above her head and yawned. "Why are you waking me up so early on a Sunday morning?"

"It's after ten," Junior said, pouncing on the bed. "I was just checking on you. You never sleep past seven."

Her body and brain must have needed to decompress and reboot. She truly did have a restful night's sleep, absent of dreams, and the events of the evening before. This marriage wouldn't survive infidelity. There were some things she could forgive, but that wasn't one of them. She glanced at Junior sprawled out on his father's side of the bed and smiled. He was the best thing to come from this marriage, and for that, Patricia would always be grateful, but Xavier was going to be voted off the island for good.

"I needed the rest," she said, tickling his underarm.

"Moms," he chuckled, rolling about the bed. "Cut that out."

She found it funny how his voice cracked when he laughed. The last remnants of adolescence were slipping away. She loved watching his transformation but was missing her baby at the same time. Junior fell to the floor in the midst of his antics. He scrambled to his feet, ran toward the door, then leaned on the frame trying to catch his breath.

"You're too young to be winded," Patricia said with a laugh. "That's what you get for waking me up."

Patricia shifted on the bed, and Junior jumped back in, trying to tackle her. She rolled out of his way just in time. "Boy, ain't nobody thinking about you. I'm trying to get comfortable."

"Yeah——that's what you always say before you attack," he said with one foot out the door.

She pulled the covers back, and Junior bolted down the hallway. She chortled, making her way to the bathroom.

Patricia washed away her worries with a hot shower and vowed to have a good day in spite of everything. Crying wasn't going to solve a damn thing, but being decisive would. When she entered the bedroom, Matthew's picture was still on the floor. She hurried over, sliding her bare feet along the plush carpet, and scooped it up. She gave it a once-over and was happy that hadn't been damaged or that Junior hadn't questioned her further.

Reaching under the pillowcase, she collected each one of Shawn's birthday cards. She scanned the room, searching for the shoebox she kept all things about her first love and their child. She must have knocked it to the floor while sleeping. Tightening her robe, she went to Xavier's side of the bed. She bent down, and Xavier's gray metal toolbox was missing. She placed the picture and cards in the shoebox and sat it on the bed.

Anything that had to be locked away was a secret. Apparently, she wasn't alone in that department, but she'd be damned if Xavier was going to continue to make a fool out of her. She went downstairs into his office and closed the door. Patricia zeroed in on the closet. File boxes were stacked neatly in one corner, shoeboxes in the other, and miscellaneous boxes on the top shelf. No signs of that toolbox. Patricia pulled everything out, anyway. Once she checked the contents of the boxes, which were old police cases and photos, she felt around on the carpet to see if any pieces were loose or if the floor had more give than it should have. Then she checked under the couch and behind the metal file cabinet. Nothing. Everything else was open space.

Not bothering to put anything as she found it, Patricia left his office in shambles then entered the attached garage from the door opposite the kitchen. She sighed, staring at the disarray. The garage was used for storage, and the clutter was a bit overwhelming. Junior's bikes throughout the years hung from the walls, the lawnmower and snowblower took up a decent amount of space of their own, old lawn furniture, gardening tools, a refrigerator, a deep freezer, and tons of boxes and toolkits were all over.

She started in one corner and worked her way around. Three hours later, Patricia found the first toolbox that she couldn't open. "This has to be it," she mumbled.

Patricia ran inside, passing Junior in the kitchen, and rushed into Xavier's office.

"Moms. What are you doing?" he asked, standing in the doorway eating a sandwich.

"Nothing," she said, stumbling over the mess she made.

"You did all this?"

She shot a glance at him, and Junior backed away. "I'm going into the kitchen."

Patricia rambled through the desk drawers, pens, paper clips, and Xavier's gym bag. Then she went through the boxes that she'd checked the first time around. She couldn't find a key anywhere.

After a few minutes, Patricia fired up his iMac to Google how to pick a toolbox lock. The monitor prompted her to enter a password, so she keyed in her birthdate. To her surprise, the word *invalid* popped up on the screen. The password had been changed.

Heated, she suppressed the urge to scream. She switched off the computer, waltzed into the kitchen, grabbed a sharp knife from the dishwasher, and hightailed it to the garage.

"Moms," Junior called out, following her.

"Go back inside," she demanded.

With the way she snatched that toolbox from its nest, she almost yanked her shoulder out the socket. Patricia fidgeted with the pointy-edged knife at the keyhole, but it wasn't small enough, so she pulled a long nail from a different toolkit. She worked that lock over for about ten minutes, but it still wouldn't budge. Frustrated beyond words, Patricia lifted the toolbox with both hands and placed it on top of the deep freezer.

She retrieved a screwdriver and hammer from the workbench. Patricia chiseled at that lock to no avail. Wiping the sweat from her forehead, she tossed the flathead on the ground, then slammed the hammer repeatedly against the latch.

"Dad keeps the garage keys on the hook behind the refrigerator," Junior said, startling Patricia. She dropped the hammer, almost hitting her toe. He slid his fingers along the wood until he felt the large ring. "Here." He extended his hand.

"Thanks."

Patricia waited until Junior went back inside before she inserted the keys. She started with the small ones, then moved on to the larger keys.

"What the fuck?" she growled between gritted teeth, throwing the useless ring of thirty keys across the garage.

She pulled her robe closed, then carefully lifted the toolbox and took it in the house. An open loaf of bread and a butter knife with smeared white stuff on it laid on the kitchen island, but there was no sign of Junior. Patricia would deal with that later.

Climbing the stairs, she rested the toolbox every fourth step to give her arms a break. Once she reached the top, Patricia heaved it over the banister and chucked it. The toolbox smashed hard against the glass table before hitting the marble floor, causing the lid to fly open.

"Moms," Junior yelled after the loud thud, rushing to the open corridor beneath the landing.

Holding her robe closed, she ran toward the stairs to retrieve the items before her son did.

"What happened?" Junior asked, bending to pick up the papers that flew out of the toolbox.

"No. No. No. Don't touch it," Patricia warned, rounding the staircase. She didn't know what the papers entailed, and she wanted to protect Junior from any other secrets that may come from them. "I got it." Patricia moved picking up the contents.

Junior maneuvered opposite his mom and began to gather up the papers anyway.

Patricia raised her hands. "I said, no!"

"Okaaaaay," he surrendered, backing away.

"You wanna help? Go get the broom and dustpan and sweep these slivers of glass off the floor."

While Junior was in the kitchen, Patricia had cuffed all of the papers inside her robe. She picked up the toolbox, but it was completely ruined. She let it fall to the floor. Her beautiful Grecian white marble tile gained a serious dent at the site of impact. She shrugged at the imperfection, as it was a stark reminder of her marriage.

Two minutes later, Patricia was upstairs in her room with the door closed and locked. The moment of truth had arrived, and her insides were fluttering. Patricia dumped everything on the bed. The first thing she came across was a bank statement. Upon closer inspection, it was a monthly report from the Credit Union. Patricia flipped it over to see the balance and balked. Xavier made decent money, but not enough money to carry a six-figure balance on his own. Stunned, she sifted through the statement until she found the account holder. The names Xavier Carter and Lauren Carter were in the upper left-hand corner.

Her arm went limp, and all feeling left her body. She stared at the account balance, and Lauren Carter's name next to her husband's for God knows how long.

The next envelope was from a life insurance company. Xavier had insurance through the force, but he always said that he wanted to increase his policy in the event something should happen to him. She tossed that to the side.

She lifted a manila envelope from the pile of secrets and tore it open. Midway through she halted, focusing on that insurance document. If this insurance document was with all these things, then maybe there was something else to it. Patricia tossed the manila envelope to the side and picked up the one with the insurance company logo. Xavier had increased his policy to half million, but when she looked at the beneficiaries, Patricia's mouth went completely dry.

Two hundred fifty thousand to, *Lauren Carter.*

Pandora's box was spilling all of its dirty little secrets, and Patricia was choking on every last one.

She tossed the insurance papers on the bed and ran to the window, opening it wide. The frigid January air wasn't cold enough, so she opened her robe to let the wind pierce her naked skin. Patricia lifted her hands above her head and took deep breaths in and slow breaths out until her heart stopped feeling like as though was going to jump out of her chest.

Lauren Carter wasn't an affair or a one-time fling——she was Xavier's *wife.* How was that even possible? He was providing for this woman, the same way he provided for her and Junior. Wait! Did the woman have children, too?

Patricia's body trembled, and the tears flowed freely down her cheeks. She ran her fingers through her short hair, grabbing a fistful of what she could. She wiped the salty tears that had landed on her lips with the palm of her hand, then closed the window. She eyed the bed like it was the devil in the flesh waiting to scorch her even more. She was afraid to discover what story the remaining documents told, but she had to see this through.

Before tackling the unknown, Patricia went into the bathroom. She retrieved a Dixie cup from the dispenser and drank several cups of water.

She returned to the bedroom and glared at the next thing. Patricia lifted a golden envelope that was thick and cumbersome. She eased the contents out, revealing several pieces of real estate paperwork. The first one was a commercial property deed. Patricia's eyes narrowed as she flipped through the pages. Xavier had purchased a building in the Chicago Ridge area. Patricia couldn't determine what it was for, but she committed the address to memory.

The second document looked familiar. A settlement statement. Patricia and Xavier signed one at the title company when they bought their home, but she knew this wasn't their current residence. Patricia was the keeper of all relevant paperwork in her home——

birth certificates, social security cards, marriage license, and the copy of the signed closing documents. Cautiously, she glanced at the names, address, dates, and signatures. Once again, Xavier Carter and Lauren Carter were scribbled on the dotted line. Making matters worst, Patricia read the Quit Claim Deed that was paper-clipped to the document showing Xavier signing over his part of the property rights to Lauren two weeks later. He had bought this woman a house and some commercial real estate, too.

Last night's alcohol churned in her stomach, and she bolted into the bathroom. With her insides emptied into the toilet, Patricia felt better for a nanosecond, but it didn't last longer than that. She had to come to grips with knowing that her entire marriage, her life, was a complete lie.

Rinsing the acidic residue from her mouth, she swished with a little Dr. Tichenor's. Patricia thought back. Xavier was supposed to receive a hefty settlement from the City of Chicago Police Department. Over a decade ago, the department rigged the detective's exam against African American officers. A federal judge approved the settlement in the equal opportunity discrimination case for a total sum of seven hundred million dollars. It was the largest settlement of a single lawsuit in the history of the Equal Employment Opportunity Commission. Xavier had said they won the case, but he didn't receive as much as he thought he should. Obviously, that was a lie—and not a little white one either.

With a nervous tremor and adrenaline guiding her every movement, Patricia got dressed. She stuffed the real estate documents in her purse and stored everything else between the mattress and box spring before closing the bedroom door and walking the length of the hall to Junior's room. He was on the bed playing 2K17 on the game console. His room wasn't the cleanest, but it didn't smell like a men's locker room either. That was a win in her book. She had to get her happy wherever she could find it at this point.

"I'm on my way out," Patricia announced, clutching her purse as though he could see those damaging items inside. "I'll be back in a few."

Never taking his eyes off the flat screen, he responded, "Okay."

* * *

Patricia's first stop was the address in Chicago Ridge. She called Xavier just to see if he would answer the phone. It was for the best that he didn't, Patricia didn't know what she would say to him if he did. Heading west on One Hundred Eleventh Street, Patricia was trying to put the timeline together. She couldn't remember when Xavier first started going out of town to these "seminars" and "field maneuvers" at the end of the year.

Twenty minutes later, Patricia pulled into an outside mall parking lot on Ridgeland Avenue. She extracted the deed out of her purse. Patricia glanced upward, noticing that it was the building on the end. She parked right in front of the entrance and got out of the car. The marquee above read, Masterpieces By Lauren.

She slammed the car door and leaned against it. Xavier bought this woman a beauty salon?! *What does this woman have going on that she has her claws sunk into my husband*? She wanted so badly to see inside, but the blinds were shut. The salon was closed on Sundays.

Kneading her temples with gloved covered fingertips, Patricia tried to stave off a headache that she felt coming on. No matter how hard Patricia tried, she couldn't take her eyes off of that sign.

The aroma of freshly baked bread made Patricia shift to the image of a sweet old lady holding a long loaf of bread in an equally long brown paper bag under her arm. She walked with a cane and was hunched over.

With a shaky voice, the woman asked, "Are you, alright honey?"

Patricia forced a smile. "Yes, ma'am."

"It's not wise to stand out here in this cold," she warned, moving slowly, carefully placing her foot on the slippery ground.

"Let me help you," Patricia offered, extracting the paper bag from the woman's fragile hold and allowing the woman to use her arm as a crutch.

She eased the woman into her Buick Regal, and Patricia placed her cane on the passenger's side along with the bread.

"God bless you," the woman said pulling the seatbelt across her lap. "You have a beautiful day."

Patricia smiled. "Thank you."

Before Patricia closed the woman's car door, she asked, "Do you know the owner of this salon?"

"Oh yes dear," she said with a gleam in her eye. "Lauren is a doll. I can't wait for her to reopen next week," she said, patting her wig. "I've been wearing this old thing for two months now. Itches something awful."

"Why did she close?" Patricia probed.

"That horrible shooting on Halloween." The woman drew her hands to her chest. "It was all over the news."

"They say that's the devil's holiday," Patricia mumbled, then whispered, "And my husbands too."

"I prayed day and night that she would make it through, and God answered my prayers," the woman said switching on the ignition. "Lauren is a good soul. She's trying to do right by our young folks, and look what happened to her. But God blesses His faithful servants so I knew she would be alright."

Patricia nodded, as she closed the woman's car door. She waved, before walking back to her car. God blesses His faithful servants—— if that last statement was true, then why was He punishing her? Patricia wasn't a bad person; she knelt and prayed to The Man Above every night. Although she hadn't stepped one foot in the church since her baby had been taken away from her, she was still a believer. There were many hypocrites inside the sanctuary. The same people, who shouted hallelujah in Jesus' name, were the same individuals who shunned her when she was a pregnant teen. She didn't feel the need to fellowship with such folks. It didn't matter if she graced the house of the Lord, as long as she lived Christ-like, He would open the gates of heaven for her on judgment day. And that's how she lived her life. Patricia felt her blessings were well overdue.

This woman made Lauren sound like a walking saint. Patricia knew she shouldn't be mad at the other woman, but it was easier to feel anger toward her than betrayal from Xavier. Patricia pulled out the signed settlement and zoned in on the address. She opened the glove compartment to get the GPS to punch in the location but realized that she knew the area. This house was in the Beverly neighborhood.

Driving down One Hundred-Third Street going east, she kept hearing the old woman's words; God blesses His faithful servants.

Well either God didn't consider Patricia Carter a servant, or the Devil was having a field day.

Chapter Thirty-Nine

Like an epiphany, a light bulb beamed in Patricia's head. She auto-dialed Jason while driving.

"Hey Jason, it's Patty."

"Hi—hi Patty." His natural warmth and confidence were missing in those stammered words.

"I want to ask you a question," she said, turning the key in the ignition. "All I ask is that you hear me out before you respond. Can you do that?"

"Yes."

"On Halloween, I received an anonymous call saying that Xavier was at Christ Hospital on the seventh floor. The caller didn't say what happened or why he was there. The computerized voice also said that a GPS tracking device had been secretly installed on his personal vehicle," Patricia paused. "Was it you?"

After a long lull, Jason responded, "Patty, you need to talk to Xavier."

"I would if he'd answer my phone calls, but I'm asking *you*. I just found out Lauren *Carter* was admitted that same night after a shooting at her beauty salon. You know," Patricia paused. "The one Xavier bought for her."

A faint gasp escaped on the other end of the phone.

"There's no need to cover for him anymore. I know everything."

"Patty, I'm sorry."

"So *you knew*," Patricia said through clenched teeth. "What exactly did you want me to find out at the hospital?"

"It wasn't like that." He sighed. "I love you and Junior. Xavier's my boy. My partner. I have to have his back."

"So this is okay with you because Xavier's your partner?" Patricia swerved into the right lane. "I can't believe you just said that to me." She honked the horn at the motorist in front of her. "What are you slamming on the breaks for?" she screamed.

"Patty, where are you?"

"I thought we were better than that," she barked. "Joke's on me," she said, laying on the horn. "Move the hell out of my way."

"Patty, you shouldn't be driving. Where are you?"

"Don't be concerned about me now," she snarled. "What? Did your guilty conscience get the best of you?" She huffed, making a hard right turn on Claremont Avenue. "Why tell me now?"

"What are you talking about, Patty?"

"That you bugged Xavier's truck and that he was married to this Lauren chick."

"Why would I tap his truck?" Jason asked.

A soft voice in the background asked Jason whom he was talking to. Jason didn't respond, but he did ask Patricia a third time, "Where are you?"

She parked the car across the street from the house that belonged to Lauren. Patricia sat there silent as the rage built up inside, eyeing Xavier's white truck parked in the driveway. She got out, slammed the door and marched across the street with a determination she never thought possible. Patricia shook her head in disbelief at the American flag swaying in the wind and the blue and white yard sign that read, *In This House, We Bleed Blue.* The same damn sign and flag that adorned her front yard. "I'm at this heifer's house."

Patricia ended the call and dropped the phone in her purse. She stood on the porch for a few minutes before ringing the bell. Her heart raced, anticipating what would happen when the woman showed her face, but the answer never came. A thin lady with a pale complexion jogged down the street with her dog stopped in front of the house. She ran in place as she informed Patricia that The Carters were out of town for the holiday.

"Thanks," she responded with a tight smile that dropped soon as the woman turned her head. Pissed and defeated, she trudged back to her car. She was in no position to drive so she turned the car on for warmth but didn't shift into gear. Red and blue flashing lights caught her attention, and for a moment she thought that one of the neighbors had called the police on her. She couldn't blame them if they had. If she had seen someone sitting outside of her home in a parked car for an extended period, she would've done the same.

The dark-colored town car pulled along the side of her. Sandy glanced at Patricia, then stepped out of the vehicle and opened Patricia's door.

Sandy grabbed Patricia's hand guiding her out of the car. The women embraced, no words were spoken.

Jason lowered the passenger's side window. "Patty, are you okay?"

"Oh no, no, no," Sandy said, turning to face Jason. "You do not talk to her." She waved him away. "You can go, we will be alright," she assured reaching in the window to grab her purse out of the seat. Sandy turned back to Patricia. "I will drive." She pointed. "You go around to the other side."

"Baby, I know you're upset with me, but I'm not leaving until I know you two are okay," Jason insisted in a voice that meant business.

"Meet us at the house," Sandy commanded, sliding her petite frame behind the steering wheel and closing the door. Patricia had already made it to the passenger's seat. Jason turned off the emergency lights and backed up so she could pull out of the parking spot.

"Patricia, I do not know what to say," Sandy said, stroking Patricia's arm. "I am sorry is not enough."

"How could you not tell me, Sandy?" Patricia asked, staring through her. "I thought you were my friend."

"I *am* your friend. I knew something was not right a few months ago."

"A few months ago," Patricia yelled. *"That's worse."*

"I heard Jason on the phone with Xavier saying he needed to come clean," Sandy confessed, as she drove to her home in Hyde Park. "Then I found some papers in the trash that looked important, so I took them out. They said Jason was a part of an undercover sting with Xavier and some other detectives."

Patricia thought back, and her stomach got that familiar ache. "Xavier showed me a report."

"Jason hasn't been away on an assignment in over a year."

Patricia threw her head back against the headrest. "What else has he lied about?" she wailed, squeezing her eyes shut.

Sandy patted her thigh in a comforting way. "I asked Jason about it. He stumbled over his words, so I knew he was lying. I demanded that he tell me the truth or else he would be sleeping alone for the rest of his days."

"So it was *you* who put the GPS on Xavier's truck?"

Sandy nodded. "I'm tired of him using Jason to lie to you." She exited the expressway on Fifty-fifth and stopped at the red light. "Please don't be mad at my Jason for a long time. He loves you and feels bad." Sandy made a right turn on the green light. "Xavier took advantage of their friendship."

Traffic through Washington Park was a breeze as Sandy navigated the maze through the path that wound past snow-covered trees and iced over ponds. Grateful that everyone was vetted, Sandy turned onto a residential block that she had the privilege of sharing with President Obama. The secret service checked their identification, scanned their vehicle, and their persons. Sandy pulled into their driveway five homes down from the famous mansion with Jason pulling in right behind her.

Crossing the threshold into Sandy and Jason's home, everyone removed their boots.

"Have a seat," Sandy instructed as she disappeared into the kitchen and emerged with a porcelain gaiwan with tea leaves steeping inside. She placed the tea-serving tray on the low table in the heated solarium and took a seat on a cushy pillow on the floor. She poured Patricia a steaming cup of green tea.

"Thanks," Patricia said, sipping the hot liquid. She held the palm-sized teacup in her hand, and the heat radiated through her body. Patricia inhaled the nutty aroma, closing her eyes before exhaling at a slow and even pace.

Sandy sat across from Patricia sipping her tea. When Patricia opened her eyes, Jason had joined them at the table. She examined his soulful blue eyes, and they, like her, were filled with regret.

He held out his hand across the table, and Patricia hesitated but finally inched her hand inside of his. "Whatever you need, we're here." He offered her a comforting smile.

Sandy placed her hand on top of theirs. "You want me to call your sister?"

Patricia shook her head. "I need to figure this out on my own." She retracted her hand. Looking Jason dead on, Patricia said, "You want to be here for me? Then don't say anything about this to Xavier. Not one damn word."

Chapter Forty

While in New York, the vacationing couple received a call. Lauren's obstetrician had a family emergency in Atlanta and would be out of the office for a month, despite reassurances that a doctor who would fill in was fully capable of handling Dr. Paxton's clients, Xavier and Lauren arrived home two days earlier than scheduled. They took the last appointment the regular doctor had available. Lauren was sad that her time with her parents had to be cut short, but she was elated to have her first prenatal visit and ultrasound with someone she trusted.

She was stretched out on the examination table with her bladder about to burst open every time the technician pressed on her belly with the probe. The jelly felt cold and squishy against her skin. The bubbly lab technician angled the monitor so she and Xavier could get a better view of their son or daughter. Overcome with emotion, Lauren reached for Xavier's hand, and she sensed that he had been distracted the entire appointment. Her hand hung over the side of the table for one second too long before she turned her head in his direction to find Xavier leaning against the wall with his nose in his phone.

"Excuse me," she said in the nice nastiest way possible. "Is there something on that phone that's more important than seeing your only child for the first time?"

His arm dropped to the side still holding the phone in his hand as he came to Lauren's side. "No, just work stuff," he lied, shoving the phone into his pocket and grabbing her hand.

Lauren tried hard not to roll her eyes as she eyeballed him before turning her attention back to the monitor. Shouldn't be any work stuff since they had two days of vacation left.

"It looks like a tadpole," he said, squinting.

"No she doesn't," Lauren defended her unborn child. "She's beautiful."

"She?" questioned, Xavier.

The technician chimed in, "Let's not get ahead of ourselves. We won't know the gender until about twenty weeks. That's when you'll come back for your second ultrasound." She moved the probe around and firmly pressed into Lauren's abdomen until a faint galloping sound was heard.

"What's that?" Lauren inquired.

"That's your baby's heartbeat." The technician smiled, sliding and pressing the probe at different angles. "Consider yourselves lucky. It's rare to detect the heartbeat before week twelve. It sounds healthy and vigorous." She took some measurements of the fetus on the monitor. "You're eleven weeks and four days so look to be celebrating the Fourth of July in the hospital with your new bundle of joy."

* * *

Xavier excused himself, while the cute brunette lab technician wiped the gooey substance off of Lauren's belly. "I'll meet you in the lobby," he informed Lauren. "Restroom," he added right before he walked out the door.

"Thank you," he whispered strolling down the hall.

Not because he was going to have the daughter he always wanted, but because Lauren's due date insured that they wouldn't be going to Hawaii.

He whipped his phone out and couldn't believe the number of voice and text messages he had received from Patricia. Her voice sounded urgent, but she never said what she wanted. He was anxious to call her, but also he couldn't break the routine. If an emergency arose, Patricia would inform Sandy, who would tell Jason, and Jason would get a hold of Xavier. Since he hadn't heard anything from Jason since he left, he figured everything was okay. And Jason knew to stay clear of Patricia while he was gone.

He entered the busy Women's Imaging and Diagnostic Waiting Area and took a seat in one of the cushy chairs in the corner. With his head still in the phone, he searched for alternative sleeping agents for pregnant women. He had two full days to figure out what to do about his overnight situation because his return home was going to be pretty hectic without them.

"Hi, Mr. Carter," a female voice said to him. His gaze followed the sound. She was pregnant and very young.

Xavier's eyes shot up from his phone, landing on the girl's stomach, and then her face.

"You don't remember me," she said, easing down into the chair next to him. "I'm Tori. I went to elementary school with Xavier."

"Hi Tori," he spoke, trying to hide his shock. Glancing around to find her parents, he asked, "How have you been?"

"I'm okay…I guess," she responded, looking away embarrassed. "How's Xavier? I haven't seen him since we graduated."

"He's fi——" Xavier jumped to his feet when Lauren came

through the swinging doors. A loud thud echoed as a result of Xavier's phone crashing to the floor. He scooped his phone up and quietly whispered, "Good luck with the baby." He hurried over to Lauren who was staring at him and the pregnant teen. He escorted her out of there as fast as he could.

"Who was that?"

Examining the cracked screen on his phone, he responded, "Just some girl waiting to be seen by the doctor."

"She looks awfully young to be having a baby," Lauren said, sounding like a concerned mother. She looked down at Xavier's shattered phone and smirked. "Maybe now I can get some of your attention."

* * *

Patricia was on her way to work when the GPS locator app Sandy installed pinged on her iPhone. Her heart leaped into her throat as she pulled over on the shoulder. Xavier's truck was on the move, but he wasn't supposed to be back until the fifth. With a hammering heart, she hopped on the off-ramp and turned in the opposite direction. She called the scheduler to have a floater pharmacist cover her shift. When the company's voicemail picked up, Patricia said she wasn't feeling well. She had turned into *that* person, but it was necessary.

She drove south, frequently checking the moving red dot on her phone that was heading southwest on Ninety-fifth Street. Once Patricia made it to Ninety-fifth Street, she made a right turn driving westbound. Her insides were jumping as if thousands of needles were being stuck into her all at once. Anyone could be driving Xavier's truck, but in her gut, she knew who was behind the wheel. Maybe Jason hadn't kept his word. Patricia glanced at her phone, and she noticed that the red dot had been idling in the same spot for the past five minutes. While sitting at a red light, she touched the screen, tapping the red dot on the map. Christ Medical Center hovered above the address.

Patricia reached the hospital and drove around for fifteen minutes in and out of parking garages until she found that infamous white truck. She parked the next row over in an inconspicuous spot that also gave her a great vantage point.

About an hour later, Patricia had peeled nearly all of the mocha nail polish off when she had spotted Xavier walking hand in hand with a woman who could only be Lauren. She gawked at the beautiful small-waist, curves in all the right places, high-yellow woman wearing calf-high brown leather boots and a cream wool wrap coat with the matching hat. "She thinks she's Olivia Pope," Patricia scoffed. She rolled her window half way down so she could eavesdrop.

"I'm still mad at you," Lauren said, bumping into Xavier. "You and that phone, I swear…"

"It was——"

"I don't wanna hear it," Lauren cut him off. "Work shouldn't be blowing you up when we aren't even supposed to be back yet."

Patricia crossed her arms. "Work, huh? More like his other wife." Patricia observed Xavier step in front of Lauren. He bent down and whispered something in her ear and Lauren playfully socked him in the arm. Patricia was contemplating whether or not to confront them right there when Xavier leaned in to kiss Lauren. She'd be damned if she watched her husband kiss another woman. She dipped to the side and laid on the horn. They fumbled apart, looking in all directions searching for the sound. Patricia eased her hand off the wheel, still leaning in the cut. She reached for her phone and dialed Xavier's number.

Xavier disabled the alarm and opened Lauren's door when his phone rang.

"So I guess the jacked up screen thing still works," Lauren said, placing her hands on her tiny hips. "Who's calling you now?"

"He glanced at the phone and said, "Nobody important."

Patricia sucked all of her breath in feeling more like Muhammad Ali had punched her in the stomach, knocking the wind out of her. The voice mail clicked on as Xavier backed out of the parking spot.

"So I guess I'm nobody."

Chapter Forty-One

Shawn was anxious to see Patricia at work Monday morning. Since she never knew what would be the right time, she had planned to tell Patricia everything today. The documents from Grandma Marie along with the letter from her adoptive mom and the photograph were burning a hole in her tote.

She walked into the pharmacy, but there wasn't anyone in sight. "Hello," Shawn shouted, peeking around the prescription bays.

"Good morning," a rough voice responded. "I'm Calvin. You must be Shawn," he said extending his hand. "Mr. Slocum told me you were the opening tech today.

Shawn glanced up at the tall, handsome man, who looked to be her age. She shook his hand. "That would be me." She went to sign on to the computer. "Where's Patricia?"

"The scheduler didn't say," Calvin replied. "I received the call for coverage less than an hour ago. Good thing I live in the area."

At the end of a shift that seemed to drag on forever, she drove to Patricia's house. Shawn prayed that she was home and hoped that Patricia would forgive her for popping up unannounced. She was afraid that if she called, Patricia might turn her away and she couldn't risk being rejected that way; face-to-face was another thing.

Shawn's palms were damp when she pulled in front of Patricia's home and saw her car parked in the driveway. She sighed, grabbed her bag and walked up the shoveled walkway.

Her purse vibrated and sung a muffled melody of the song Ladies Night, Candace's ringtone. Shawn ignored the call, but when the familiar tune rang again, she searched the oversized Prada handbag to extract the phone.

"Hey, girl. I can't talk right now," she said rapidly, standing on Patricia's doorstep. "I have to do this before I lose my nerve."

"Don't hang up," Candace blurted in an equally rushed tone. "Have you seen the news today?"

"No," Shawn whispered. "I'm at Patricia's house."

"Oh wow. How are you? Did everything go well?"

In a lower voice than before, Shawn mumbled, "I haven't gone in yet. I'm right outside her front door."

"Okay. I'm going to let you go, but listen first," Candace said. "Some joggers found a body partially covered in the woods at Dan Ryan Forest Preserve this morning. It's James."

"What?" Shawn gasped, placing a hand on the brick. "Are you sure?"

"Yeah. They showed a photo of James, identifying him as the shooter at Masterpieces. And he's allegedly responsible for several armed robberies in the Gold Coast Neighborhood, but I guess we'll never know that for sure."

"I don't care about that. I'm glad he's dead—" Shawn whipped around.

"What's all that noise?" asked Candace, concern etched in her voice.

"Junior and his friend Brandon just pulled into the driveway with the music blasting. I gotta go." She disconnected the call.

"Hey Shawn," Junior yelled, approaching her.

"Hey." She waved, backing away from the door.

Brandon tooted the horn as he drove around the semicircular driveway and left.

Junior fished the keys from his coat pocket. "Does my Moms know you're here?"

"No. I...just...got...here," Shawn said, clearing her throat.

"Come on." Junior unlocked the door.

Shawn was ready to jet to the car and pull off when Junior hollered for Patricia to come downstairs.

"Boy. Where's the fire?" Patricia shouted from the top of the stairs.

"Shawn's here."

"What did you say?" Patricia asked, descending the stairs.

He pointed in the direction of the front door. "Shawn's here to see you."

"Why on earth would you leave her standing at the front door?" Patricia popped his shoulder. "Come on in."

"Hi," Shawn said, walking into the living room. She was nervous, terrified, and happy to be at her mother's house again.

Patricia greeted Shawn with a hug, and it felt so good. Maybe it would be the last she'd ever have from this beautiful woman if she didn't welcome the kind of news that could turn her world upside down. Shawn was surprised that Patricia was holding on to her just as tightly as she was holding on to her. Shawn felt safe, and at that moment she knew she had made the right decision.

"Is everything okay," Patricia asked, breaking their embrace.

"I need to talk to you." Shawn's eyes flickered to Junior. "In private."

"Well, I know when I'm not wanted." Junior ducked into the kitchen as Shawn followed Patricia upstairs to what must have been the master bedroom. With each step, she absorbed everything that she wasn't able to see the previous two times she was in Patricia's home. The African art, earthy color scheme, and family portraits throughout the years.

The first one was of Xavier and Patricia with Junior as an infant. She zoomed in on a young and radiant Patricia. Her mother's face was thinner, with hair that flowed on her shoulders. The same warm smile adorned Patricia's face, but there was something about her eyes that was a little sad. She wore a green blazer with a white ruffled blouse and a small pink flower brooch on the lapel; the same one she had on her lab coat the other day.

Shawn smiled as she went from photo to photo, mentally inserting herself into each one, wondering what it would've been like to grow up in Patricia's family. The photographs changed year by year, but the one thing that stayed the same was the pink brooch. When she made it to the last picture, she observed Patricia watching her from the doorway. "You have a beautiful family."

Patricia sighed, and there was a world of sadness in that sound. "Thanks."

Shawn forgot about the fiasco that took place in this very house a few nights ago. She entered the bedroom, and Patricia closed the door behind them. Patricia took a seat on the bed and patted the space across from her.

She inched across the bed next to her mother. "I'm sorry for not calling first."

"It's alright." Patricia held her hand. "You're always welcome here."

Without warning, tears fell from Shawn's eyes. She looked over at Patricia, and her eyes became glassy with tears of her own. The silence was thick, but the unspoken connection was more sacred than the Salt Cathedral of Zipaquirá, Colombia. Patricia scooted closer to Shawn, and gently wiped the tears from Shawn's face and stroked her hair.

"I have—something—to—tell you," Shawn said between sniffles. "And—I don't know how to do it." She took a moment then rifled through some items in her bag and pulled out a handwritten letter. With trembling hands, she passed it to Patricia. Shawn watched as her mother unfolded the paper. A slew of emotions washed across Patricia's voice with every word she read.

My Dear Sweet Baby Shawn,

I am watching you sleep in the bassinette next to our bed in your pink and mint green sleeper that says Mommy's, Little Miracle. Truer words were never written. If you're reading this, you are now a beautiful young woman who is on her way to discovering the world. From the moment your twinkling green eyes met mine, I fell in love. You came into the world kicking and screaming, and it was the most beautiful sound I had ever heard.

Your father and I had been trying to conceive for five years when the doctors told me that I had stage three ovarian cancer and my best chance of survival was to have my uterus removed. I was devastated because I had this deep yearning to be a mom and that was never going to happen.

Then one day, a young girl named Patricia Taylor walked into the hospital with her boyfriend, Matthew. They were sixteen years old, and she was four months pregnant and terrified. I was the triage nurse on duty, and I was able to calm her nerves and talked her into telling her parents. I scheduled her prenatal visits and gave her my phone number. I told her she could call me anytime if she had any questions over the course of her pregnancy.

Whenever Patricia came in for her prenatal appointments, she requested me as her nurse. She confided in me that their parents were forcing them to give the baby up for adoption. That's when your dad and I talked it over and arranged a meeting with a lawyer, Patricia, Matthew, and their parents. We wanted to do an open adoption, but our attorney advised against it. I always wanted you to know where you came from and that your biological parents loved you.

You are my daughter, and the love I have for you couldn't have been any greater if I had given birth to you myself. But I know there will come a time when you will have questions, and I want to be able to give you all the answers. I hope you understand and don't hold it against us for not telling you before now.

I was there to hear your heartbeat for the first time when Patricia came in, I was there when we learned that you were a girl, and I was in the room assisting Dr. Cogar when you made your entrance into the world. I have been your mommy since the beginning, and nothing will ever change that. I made a promise to Patricia before she gave birth, she wanted a part of you to share a part of her and Matthew. That's why we named you Shawn, in honor of your biological father's family name O'Shaughnessy.

You are my reason for everything that I do, and I want you to know that I love you more than words can ever express.

Love, Mommy

Overcome with every emotion possible, Patricia cried. "My baby." She held both sides of Shawn's face and kissed her forehead. Then she pulled Shawn into her bosom and held her tight.

Shawn wrapped her arms around her mother and sobbed. How could she have ever doubted this woman? She'd never felt a love––a connection like this before.

"Mom," Shawn said with her head still buried in Patricia's chest, "I can't breathe."

Patricia chuckled, lightening up the grip she had on her daughter. "*Mom*." Patricia kissed her on the forehead. "That's music to my ears."

Shawn sat upright and fished out the image of the two women who were so important in her life and handed it to Patricia.

"This woman right here saved my life," Patricia said, pointing at Nurse Dominique, Shawn's adoptive mother. She stared at the photo for the longest time, then walked around to the other side of the bed, and she pulled out a medium sized box and showed Shawn the same picture. "I've held on to this since the day you were born. This is the only photo I have of you."

Patricia brought the box with all of its contents and handed it over. Shawn sorted through birthday cards addressed to her with personal messages inside each one. Her toddler year cards were filled with Sesame Street characters and princesses. The middle year cards were filled with sparkling sunglasses and balloons. She opened her Sweet Sixteen birthday card, and a one hundred dollar bill fell out. "All these years I wondered what you were like and if you loved me..." Shawn paused, trying to put her feelings into words. "I mean— how could you love someone and give them away?"

She picked up the pink flower brooch that was inside the box. "But I see," Shawn said, rubbing the palm of her hand against her heart, "and now I *feel*. And I understand that it wasn't easy for a sixteen-year-old girl to be forced to give up her baby whom she already loved so much."

Patricia caressed Shawn's cheek. "It was the best and worst day of my life."

Shawn continued combing through the box. She picked up a picture of a handsome teenage boy. "Is this my dad?"

"Yes." Patricia smiled, eyeing the image. "That's Matthew."

"Now I know why I look like a white girl," Shawn teased, bursting into laughter. "Wait 'til I tell Candace she was right." As her giggles subsided, she asked, "Do you know where he is?"

"I wish I did. We lost touch when I left for college and Matthew joined the Army." Patricia sighed. "I wish he could share this moment with me...with us." A lone tear slid down her face. "He would love to get to know you."

Shawn wiped the streaking tear away with her thumb, and Patricia clasped her hand, holding it within her own.

"How did you find me after all this time?"

Shawn picked up the photo she brought with her and flipped it over. Dominique had Patricia's full name, date of birth, and address written on the back. Along with Patricia's parents' names and the school she attended. "My mom—I mean Dominique."

"No," Patricia corrected. "She will always be your mom. She loved and raised you as her own when I couldn't." Patricia swallowed. "I'll always be grateful for her."

Shawn nodded. She pulled out everything she had and presented them to Patricia. "My other mom kept all of the original documents, so I had a pretty good starting point, she said shifting on the bed to accommodate all the new items. "I went to Mercy Hospital with hopes that the staff would be willing to help me. Luckily, there was one doctor and nurse on staff who worked with my other mom. The doctor wasn't very helpful, but he insisted that I talk to Nurse Barb. He said she and my other mom were maternity nurses.

Patricia grinned. "I remember Nurse Barb. She snuck me popsicles during my prenatal visits. Nurse Dominique always caught her though," Patricia said, laughing. "I'm shocked she hasn't retired yet."

"She did. Two years ago."

"You've been looking for me all this time?" Patricia asked.

Shawn sighed. "I've known who you were for three years," she admitted, sliding a finger over the pink brooch. "It took me this long to convince myself to get in touch with you."

"Wow," Patricia whispered. She walked over to the window and worked out the stiffness in her neck and back. "I'm glad you finally did."

"I met my grandmother."

Patricia slowly turned around. "*My* mother?"

"Yes. Nurse Barb told me to go to your parents' home. That's how I found out you worked at MedRx and your married name."

"Humph. She never even called and told me." Patricia leaned on the windowsill. "I'm not surprised. What about my dad?"

"I didn't see him. Your mother opened the door, but she never let me in. Her eyes widened like I frightened her or something. Before I could tell her who I was, she said 'you're Matthew's kid.'

Her tone." Shawn shivered. "It was—harsh. I just stared at her for a moment. But when I asked about you, she was hesitant to verify any information until I showed her the birth certificate and adoption papers. Only then, did your mother admit that you were her daughter and that you had given birth to a baby girl on the exact date I was born."

Patricia walked over and leaned on the bedpost. She slid down, sitting at the foot of the bed.

"A man had called out asking who was at the door. She quickly shoved the documents in my chest and told me never to come back as she closed the door in my face."

"My mother," Patricia whispered, picking up the original birth certificate. There was a world of bitterness in these. "My parents would love the young woman you've become, if they could only–" Patricia placed everything on the bed, then stood. "Would you like to meet your little brother? Officially?"

"Yes." Shawn smiled, but the sparkle didn't quite reach her eyes. "But first there's something I have to tell you about your husband."

Session Forty-Two

Thirty minutes later, Patricia stared at her daughter. She admired Shawn's honesty and the need to be transparent with the beginning of their new relationship. She had no idea that Shawn was about to rock her world on another level.

The woman Patricia shared a husband with had been a mentor and haven to her daughter during the most turbulent years of her life. How could she hate this woman now? And the irony. She had kept Shawn a secret from Xavier, and he had known her all along. Patricia's outlook on Lauren had changed from a home-wrecker to pity. She was as much of a victim as she was, but Xavier would not be getting a free pass. And the guilt she once felt for keeping that huge secret from him had dissipated. Patricia couldn't believe he had a baby on the way. That's a second sin she could not forgive.

She introduced Shawn to Junior as his sister. He sat quietly in the family room for a few minutes, staring at his mom.

"You're keeping secrets, just like dad," he accused.

"Now, wait one minute," Patricia said. "This is nothing like what your father has done."

Shawn observed Patricia and Junior sitting on the recliner across from them.

"Yes. I didn't tell you I had a baby as a teenager that I was forced to put up for adoption."

Junior's gaze met his mother's. She touched his hand.

"My parents—my mother—" Patricia inhaled, trying to hold back her emotions.

"Is this why you don't talk to grandma?"

She nodded. "Shawn found me—"

Junior turned toward Shawn. "So you knew who I was when you came to Mom's party?"

"Yes."

"And you pretended to be my friend," he said, leaning forward resting elbows on his knees. "Why didn't you tell me you were my sister, then?"

Shawn ran fingers through her hair. "I hadn't even told your mom that I was her daughter." She paused, then walked over and knelt in front of Junior. "I was scared. I had no way of knowing if she would believe me—or accept me."

Junior glanced at Shawn.

"But I never pretended to be your friend," Shawn assured him. "I genuinely was getting to know my little brother."

Patricia scooted closer to them. "And now we can all get to know each other," she said, grabbing Junior's hand and reaching for Shawn's. "We are family, and I love both of you."

She pulled them into a hug. Patricia felt Junior's body relax and she was happy he didn't resist. She gazed into his eyes. "I will answer all of your questions."

He nodded.

"And yours, too," Patricia said, with a steady gaze on Shawn.

"I would like that," she replied with a smile.

"Is it alright if Shawn stays for dinner?" Patricia asked Junior. "Or do you need a minute to process all of this."

She hoped Shawn understood that she wasn't slighting her in the least.

"It's cool."

Patricia put in a call to her favorite Chinese spot, and it was delivered within the hour. The three of them sat in front of the flat-screen in the family room, eating and conversing like it was the most natural thing in the world. Unfortunately, the person who wasn't present took up the most space in the room.

"What are we gonna do about Pops?" Junior asked, dipping a pot sticker into soy sauce.

Shawn looked at Patricia.

"Don't worry about your father," Patricia said, twirling noodles on chopsticks. "I'll take care of him. He'll be home in a couple of days. And Junior—— I don't want you to say anything. Just be yourself."

"I'm not gonna say nothing to him no way." Junior's sarcastic tone caused Shawn to flinch.

Patricia flicked Junior's ear with her thumb and middle finger. "I didn't say be disrespectful."

"Ouch." He winced, rubbing his ear. "Yes, ma'am."

* * *

The following day, Patricia put her plan into motion. Before she fell asleep, she'd run a few scenarios in her mind, like a coach pulling plays for a football team. She finally told Latrice what had been going on, and she braced herself for the 'I told you so,' that never came.

"I'm sorry this has happened to you, Li'l Sis, but I'm happy that you're putting an end to things," Latrice said. "Just tell me what you need me to do, and I'm there."

A few hours later, Latrice and Sandy were sitting in Patricia's family room hashing out her master plan.

"Oh. I am so down with this." Latrice chuckled, rubbing her hands together. "I didn't know you had it in you."

"Xavier won't know what hit him," Patricia said, pacing in the kitchen. She was still aching on the inside, but she refused to be a victim any longer. So what her perfect family of three with the white picket fence went up in smoke. It had all been an illusion anyway. She'd trade in that bigamist husband for having her firstborn in her life any day. Now *that's* a perfect family of three.

Patricia always scheduled the day off that Xavier came back from the seminar. She instructed Junior to go to Brandon's house after school and not to come home until she sent for him.

Spread out on the coffee table were pictures and documents. Patricia had a copy of their wedding photo that was taken at Fisk's Chapel. She put it, along with a copy of her marriage license, Junior's birth certificate, and a picture of Xavier fawning over Junior in the hospital when he was first born in a manila envelope. She attached a note with the evidence and sealed it.

"If Xavier thinks he's going to leave here and live happily ever after with Lauren he'd better guess again," Patricia said, sealing the envelope and handed it to Latrice. "If she chooses to stay after that, then hey, that's on her."

The last part of Patricia's plans required police assistance, and that's where Sandy came in. Jason was such a sweetheart, and one of the few good men left who adored his wife. She had no doubt that Xavier manipulated their friendship to his advantage. But the one thing Xavier didn't bank on was Jason's loyalty to Sandy. When she asked for something, he delivered, and this time wouldn't be any different. Jason owed Patricia for the part he played in the betrayal. And she was ready to collect all at once.

* * *

"Hi baby, I just landed," Xavier said to Patricia while waiting for his car to finish getting cleaned and detailed.

"I can't wait to see you," Patricia whispered, and her tone was every bit of seductive. "I've missed you so much."

"I've missed you too. Sorry, I couldn't answer your calls, please forgive me."

"It's okay. I know how these things are."

Xavier's lips turned upward in a sly grin. "I should be home within the hour. So I can show you just how much I missed you."

Patricia giggled, and the sound was music, pure music. "I'll see you when you get here."

Xavier ended the call feeling full of himself. Then he called Jason. For some reason, the call went straight to voicemail. "Hey man. I'm back. Get at me."

He ran into Fannie May on Ninety-fifth Street and picked up a dozen of pixies and Mint Meltaways. Both were Patricia's favorites. Traffic was heavy as usual with Red Lobster and Chicago Ridge Mall being only a few blocks away, but he ducked into the florist for another gift. He pulled into the driveway grabbing the sweet delicacies and a bouquet of red roses headed then to the front door leaving the luggage in the trunk.

"Patty. Your man's home." He winked as she opened the door for him. He leaned in to kiss her lips. She turned her head, causing his lips to hit her cheek.

She pulled away, batting her eyelashes like an innocent little girl. "Are these for me?"

"Of course, my love. Whom else would they be for?"

Patricia grinned, looking over his shoulder to the driveway.

"Are you expecting somebody?"

"No. I was just wondering where'd you get your truck from since an Uber took you to the airport?"

She walked to the kitchen and laid the flowers down on the island. For some reason, she didn't put them in water.

Xavier frowned, realizing that move was so unlike her, almost as if they didn't matter. "Jay grabbed my truck from the station, and he picked me up. I dropped him off on my way home," he replied, following her into the kitchen, hoping that explanation was plausible since he didn't realize he'd need one.

"You know I would've done that with no problem," Patricia said, pressing a few keys on her phone. "I've always picked you up from the airport. It's never been a problem before now."

The temperature in the room rose as he felt a deeper conversation coming on. Thankfully the doorbell saved him. He gladly rushed to answer it.

"Hey Jay, what's up man?" Xavier held his arm up to slap hands with his partner but was met with a dangerous no-nonsense straight face that they reserved for collars.

"Xavier Carter, you are under arrest."

"Okay, Detective Sharpe," Xavier snickered, extending his arms with his wrist together. "You got me. Cuff me."

Jason stepped in to oblige.

"You have the right to rema——"

"Hold up," Xavier said tilting his head. "You're serious. For what?"

"Bigamy."

"Whatever, man. Come on in," Xavier said, waving Jason off. "You really shouldn't play like that. People get hurt for doing much less."

Jason didn't crack a smile. "You have the right to remain silent. Anything you say can and will be used against you in a court of law. You have the right to talk to an attor——"

"Really dude?" Xavier eyeballed Jason. "You can't do that."

"Patty——"

"I'm right here," she said, standing in the foyer eating a caramel pixie. "These are splendid baby. Thanks for being so thoughtful."

"What?" Xavier's head whipped between Jason and Patty. Why was she unconcerned? And what was Jason's problem?

"Do you understand the rights I have just read to you?"

"Jason. I will fuck you up," he growled. "Stop playing, man."

"Are you going to come willingly or am I gonna have to cuff you?" Jason winked, still maintaining a serious face.

Xavier balked at Jason giving him the most sinister look as he slowly replied, "Yeah, man. Whatever." Xavier turned to look at Patricia, and Sandy was standing beside her. "Where'd you come from?"

Sandy smirked. "I've been here the whole time."

On cue, Xavier's phone rang.

"Let me get that," Patricia offered, plucking the phone from his back pocket before he had a chance to react. "You wouldn't want any contraband where you're going." She looked at the Caller ID. "It's Officer London. How 'bout I put *her* on speakerphone."

"Patricia, that's not necessary," Xavier pleaded, trying to grasp the phone.

She practically skipped backward, and Sandy jumped in front of Xavier.

Evidently, the cat, the duck, and the mule were out of the bag. The woman on the other end was going ballistic. "Xavier you're such a liar. I want a divorce. You tried to make me feel like I was going crazy the day you called me Patty. And I *knew* I heard what I heard. You're *married* to her. What about our *baby?* What about our *life?* Why would you do this to me? Answer me. Whyyyy???"

His heart dropped to the pavement. The day Xavier had dreaded had become a reality. He'd rather be swallowed whole by a killer whale than to listen to the anguish in Lauren's voice or witness the hurt in Patricia's eyes.

Jason seized the opportunity in all that silence, yanking Xavier out the front door while the women were distracted by Lauren's phone call.

"What the fuck is wrong with you?" Xavier swelled at Jason.

"Just shut the fuck up and follow my lead," Jason muttered through gritted teeth.

Xavier glared at Jason, his chest heaving from all the adrenaline rushing through him. Jason glanced over his shoulder to make sure the women weren't paying attention. "Stop fighting and come with me." He whipped Xavier around, holding him by the arm as Patricia and Sandy approached.

Patricia ended the call, turned the phone off, then slid it in her bra. Sandy locked her arm in Patricia's and stood with her in an obvious show of solidarity, still smirking at Xavier. He had never liked her little Asian ass.

"I love you, Patty."

He didn't know what Patricia knew exactly, but it was just a matter of time before all the pieces fit together to tell the whole story.

"I never meant to hurt—"

She slapped him. Hard. "Why wasn't I enough for you?" She slapped him again, and he saw stars.

"Let's not cause a scene out here," Jason warned. "Don't give the neighbors anything to call channel seven news about. "We'll be at the precinct," Jason said, walking Xavier to the car.

No sooner they pulled out the driveway, Xavier snapped, "What the fuck was that?"

"That was me saving your ass *and* your job," Jason said hightailing it off the block. "Patricia knows everything, including my involvement."

Xavier banged his head against the headrest. "Shit! Shit! Shit!"

"Yeah. Shit is right," Jason said, stopping at a red light. "Now Sandy's all over my ass because of your mess."

"What am I gonna do?"

"I don't know, and right now, I don't care."

Xavier glared at his partner.

"We got bigger fish to fry," Jason remarked, reaching into the back seat grabbing a folder. He dropped it in Xavier's lap. "While you were gallivanting in The City of Dreams, some uniforms picked up Laz's foot soldiers. They're in lockup. Their arraignment is scheduled for Wednesday morning at nine."

Xavier skimmed through the documents. "This is the work from our case."

"Exactly," Jason said driving through the green light. "So imagine how pissed off lieutenant was when he couldn't reach you. Hell, I couldn't reach you. He was all in my chops, threatening to give our case to someone else."

"That's the last thing we need," Xavier mumbled reading the profile on Jeffrey Lucas, also known as, Laz. He then pulled out the undercover paperwork that was signed by the lieutenant and read the breakdown of what was to come.

"If it weren't for Sandy's tracking device, I wouldn't have known you were back in town earlier than scheduled. It wasn't like you checked in."

Xavier did a double take. "Sandy... tracking device? What?"

"It doesn't matter."

Like hell, it didn't. Xavier made a mental note to check the truck later.

"This says I'm going into lockup. Not undercover, but as a cop." Xavier closed the folder. "Are you trying to get me killed?"

Jason glanced over at Xavier. "It was either that or signing the case over to the guys gunning for our position."

"Why couldn't I be assigned as an undercover guard like you?"

"Lieutenant said he needed a man on the inside to draw Laz's attention," Jason explained. "Word will travel fast that a cop is in the joint and since we've possibly been made at Elijah's funeral, it had to be one of us. It makes no sense to blow another detective's cover if ours had already been compromised."

"And you volunteered my services, huh."

"Well. If someone was available to give his input..." Jason shrugged. "Besides, I vouched for you. I put my ass on the line guaranteeing you'll be here. So it is what it is."

Xavier sighed. "What's the charge against me?" he asked, making air quotes. "I didn't see one in the file."

Jason pulled over in front of the precinct. "We were trying to figure that out, but now… it's bigamy."

"Seriously, Jay." Xavier grabbed the handle to exit the truck. "That's some bullshit."

"Hold up," Jason said, turning the engine off. "Riddle me this. What am I supposed to do when Patty demands that I arrest you and my wife threatens to leave me? This is *your* shit storm. The timing just happened to work in the department's favor. You, I, and the lieutenant are the only ones who know the truth."

"You told him." Xavier frowned.

"I had to tell him something," Jason defended. "You did a number on Patty, dude. I don't think you realize how bad you hurt her. If I didn't "arrest" you, she would've called the precinct to see how to go about it, having someone else do the honors. Then your reputation would've been smeared, *and* your business would've been all over the city of Chicago."

Xavier let that sink in, still pissed that it had come to this.

"The only thing lieutenant cares about is the case."

"So I'm homeless, and I have to sleep in a holding cell for two days."

"Yeah man." Jason squeezed his shoulder. "Your arraignment is scheduled for nine, the same time as our eight-pack of drug dealers. Twenty cases are on the docket—"

"Twenty?" Xavier repeated. "The courtroom is going to be swamped with people, making it easy for Laz to blend in."

"We're prepared," Jason assured him. "I know your life's a mess right now, but I need you on your A game. Keep your eyes and ears to the ground. You won't see me, but I'll be in court to protect you."

Chapter Forty-Three

Lauren snatched off her wedding band and slung it across the living room. It ricocheted off the wall and cracked the flat screen. She screamed as loud as she could, pissed that Xavier hadn't said anything when she called him. "What an asshole."

She stared at the documents in disbelief, a marriage certificate from the state of Tennessee and a photo of her husband cradling a newborn baby and another woman. There were many signs. How could she have been so blind?

She picked up Xavier Daniel Carter's birth certificate, focusing on the date and her husband's signature. Xavier used to bring a little boy to the salon to get his haircut; he said it was his Godson. She crumpled the document in her hands.

What kind of fool am I?

Lauren ambled upstairs into the bathroom. Fully clothed, she stepped into the shower and turned on the water. The warm stream did little to calm the roiling sea of emotions that washed over her. *What would happen to my child? How could my world fall apart now when I need him so much?* She peeled the clothes off and left them laying on the shower floor.

Twenty minutes of trying to wash away her trouble, she wrapped herself in a towel, then sat in the wingback chair in the bedroom.

The cell was on the dresser, begging her to call the one woman who could help her make sense of it all.

"Ma," Lauren whimpered into the phone. "I need you."

"What's the matter, honey?"

Lauren slumped and opened her soul to the one person she could trust.

"I don't know what to do, mama," she said, struggling to keep her voice from shaking.

"I know it's hard baby, but you're strong, and you'll figure it out. You don't have to take his shit in the process. And you don't need to be stressed out carrying my grandchild. If you need to come home for a while until you do, that's fine. But you must to talk to your husband."

"Xavier won't answer my calls." Lauren huffed. "He can't dodge me forever."

"I'll have your dad give him a call and—"

"Nooooo. Don't tell dad," Lauren pleaded, fearing what he might say. "You know dad will jump all over him—not that he doesn't deserve it, but promise me." She stood. "I'm not in the right mindset to hear dad fuss."

After a brief silence, she said, "I promise—for now."

"I love you, Mama." Lauren exhaled, trudging to the bed and sliding under the covers. "Thanks for listening."

She dialed Xavier repeatedly and was met with his voicemail each time. Her anger kicked up a notch with each unanswered call. She tossed the phone on the bed, then marched to his side of the room and yanked his nightstand and dresser drawers open. Lauren rummaged through underwear, socks, notepads and folded papers and didn't find anything worthwhile. Frustrated with coming up empty, she dumped everything to the floor. How can this be happening? No physical clues. There had to be something.

Next, she stormed into the closet and searched the pockets of every shirt, pants, and jacket he owned. She found nothing. Lauren snatched every piece of his clothing to the floor, leaving the wooden hangers clacking in her wake. Exhausted from her efforts, she fell to her knees, laying atop of the clothing willing her mind to shut off.

An unfamiliar ringtone startled Lauren from a restless slumber. She sat upright, realizing she had dozed off on the closet floor. She stumbled over the mess and ran to the bed.

"Xavier," she shouted, believing he had finally realized he needed to reach out to her.

"I'm sorry," a man's voice said. "I have the wrong number." He disconnected before she could say anything.

Lauren let out a heavy sigh and plopped down on the bed, and it was an hour past midnight. Now she was worried. Xavier still wasn't answering his phone, and Lauren had no other way of reaching him. She didn't even have his partner's number.

She slipped on a robe and went downstairs to the living room to retrieve the handwritten letter she received from Patricia Carter from a messenger service earlier this evening. Patricia had written her phone number at the bottom.

Lauren did not want to call that woman's house. *How embarrassing?* But she needed to know where Xavier was like she needed air to breathe.

Her fingers hovered over each key as she dialed Patricia's number. She put the phone to her ear, then hung up after it rang once. She felt silly stalking a man like she was some low-class side chick. Then her senses kicked in. Lauren was not the other woman; she was his *wife*. Maybe not in the conventional sense, but she had every right to know where the man she believed was her husband, for the past ten years, was located. She redialed Patricia's number, and this time she felt stronger in her conviction. If Lauren couldn't sleep, Patricia couldn't either. She wasn't surprised at all when Patricia answered the phone sounding fully awake.

"I was wondering if you were going to call," Patricia said, and her voice was sultry, almost, melodic.

"I hadn't planned on it, but…" Lauren hesitated, wondering how to proceed. "Is he there?"

"No." Patricia released a sigh. "I had him arrested."

Lauren's jaw dropped. She sat straight up. "What you do that for?"

"Because he's a bigamist." She paused, realizing this information needed time to settle. "Xavier needs to know that he's not above the law. I couldn't just let him get away with it."

Lauren let that sink in. "But I'm pregnant. No matter what he's done, my baby needs its father."

"And my son doesn't?" Patricia finally snapped. "How do you think all of this is affecting him? He was the one who discovered his dad was cheating on me, and their relationship has suffered from it."

"I'm sorry, but that's not my fault," Lauren defended, raising her voice. "How do you think I feel?"

After a few minutes of silence, Patricia calmly said, "Look, we've both been taken for a ride on the Xavier express," Patricia explained. "And I'm not mad at you or blaming you. We're two women who got caught up with the wrong man. It's as simple as that. What we do moving forward is up to us."

"How can you sound so nonchalant?" Lauren asked, flicking a gaze at Patricia and Xavier's marriage license. "I'm conflicted. I'm hurt…I'm angry," she clamped down on the rest of what she had to say about her emotional state. "I don't understand how he was capable of doing something like this to me…"

"To you?" Patricia screeched. "*You* were what he did to *me*. I've been with this man for *twenty* years. I was there when he had *nothing*… when he fell apart after the death of his father," she said clearing her throat. "I've been lied to for the last time. Love isn't supposed to hurt. It's kind. It's built on faith and trust. It's compromises, not lies and deceit. And for the last twenty years that's all it's been—lies and deceit." Patricia took a breath, "I love him, but I am so done."

"Don't talk to me like I did something wrong," Lauren shot back. "I didn't know about you. I'm not the kind of woman to go after someone else's man. You don't kn—"

"Where do you think he spent his nights?" Patricia asked. "How can you be married to a man who never shares your bed overnight?"

"Xavier comes home *every* night," Lauren said slowly, realizing that may not be true.

She had flashes of Xavier leaving their bed or a feeling that his physical presence wasn't there. But he was always beside her in the mornings or down in the kitchen reading the paper when she woke up, except the night she had that nightmare. He definitely was missing then.

"Are you delusional?" Patricia said with disdain in her tone. "Xavier slept in our bed *every* night.

"You're the one making things up," Lauren snapped. "We just came back from New York visiting my parents for our anniversary." She struck a match, burning the corner of the picture of Xavier with Patricia and Junior. She placed it in the fireplace and watched it burn to ashes. "So I don't know *how* he sleeps in your bed every night."

Patricia had no comeback, and the line was silent.

"Are you still there?" Lauren asked feeling strangely vindicated.

"I'm here," Patricia said with sadness in her tone. "Does Xavier take you to New York every year around this time?"

"Yes. We got married there on New Year's Eve, and we've celebrated it there ever since."

"I see." Patricia hesitated. "Ten years, right?"

"Yes," Lauren said matter of fact. "How did you know that?"

"Because Xavier's been attending these *mandatory* detective seminars in New York for the past ten years from December thirty-first through January fourth or fifth."

"Oh," Lauren said twirling her kinky coils. Xavier's depth of deception was both astonishing and alarming.

There were times that the explanations for his absences were flawed or Xavier wasn't where he said he would be. Lauren stared above the fireplace at a photograph of herself in the beautiful gown she wore to the fundraiser, a joyous moment taken long before the chaos struck. Xavier had been adamant about not attending the fundraiser because he didn't want his cover blown. That technically wasn't a lie. He didn't want Patricia to see him with her. Everything she ever questioned—or doubted—was right there all along and she never connected the dots because she trusted him.

"I swear I didn't know about you."

"I believe you," Patricia replied.

"Now what'll we do?"

After a brief silence, Patricia said, "Xavier's going to have a court date coming up soon. When I find out the specifics, I'll let you know." Then, as though hit with a sudden idea, she added, "You should come to court with me. Let's show him that with all he's done, he couldn't break us."

* * *

Lauren kept staring at the revolving door waiting in the halls of the Cook County Courthouse for Patricia. She had no idea what to expect. She assumed Patricia favored her, based off of what she thought was Xavier's taste, but she was wrong. The woman who strode through the revolving glass door with such confidence couldn't have been more opposite of her. She was short and full-figured with a perfect cropped pixie cut. Her full eyelashes could be seen a mile away, and her sable skin illuminated the room.

Lauren wanted to make Patricia out to be something hideous, which would have given Xavier a reason to do what he did, but she couldn't tell that lie if she tried. Patricia was beautiful. Lauren would not have been as understanding if she was wife number one.

Patricia waved at Lauren, and Lauren's body tensed. She was mentally checking herself. *Is my hair perfect? Is my makeup flawless? Do I look pretty enough?*

"Hi." Patricia smiled as she approached.

"Hello," Lauren said. "How did you know it was me?"

"I've seen you before," Patricia admitted, thinking back to the stakeout in the hospital's parking garage.

Lauren mulled that over. She did look familiar, but she couldn't put her finger on where from, at that moment.

"Before things get all crazy in there," Patricia said, gesturing to the courtroom, "I want to thank you for caring for my daughter all these years. You don't know what that means to me."

"It's a small world isn't it," Lauren remarked, sticking her hands in her coat pockets, still feeling uncomfortable in the woman's presence. She was so well put together. "Shawn's a fantastic girl."

"Yes, she is." Patricia nodded, eyeing the people near the courtroom door. "Shawn told me how pivotal you were in rescuing her from…" Patricia glanced away. "A dangerous situation and helping her figure out who she is." Patricia's eyes became glassy with unshed tears. "Thank you." She wrapped her arms around Lauren in a moment of gratitude.

Lauren sucked in a deep breath, then blew it out slowly. Patricia wasn't the devil's spawn she preferred to believe. Lauren still felt betrayed. She had known about Patricia for less than twenty-four hours, and now she had staked a claim on two people she loved.

"Sorry," Patricia said, quickly releasing Lauren. "I know this is awkward."

She gave Patricia a tight smile, straightening her shoulders. "You're the pharmacist."

People started filing into the courtroom, so the ladies joined them. After sitting through nine hearings, the Judge called Xavier's case. The bailiff escorted Xavier into the courtroom in cuffs and a bright orange jumpsuit. Lauren couldn't believe her eyes. Xavier looked weary after only two nights in jail. His wavy hair was unkempt, and bags had formed under his eyes causing his face to sag. Patricia stood by Lauren's side as they watched their husband take the perp-walk to the defendant's table with his lawyer. She slid a glance at Patricia and found a cold hard mask in place.

* * *

Xavier felt a strange vibe when the bailiff transported him from the holding cell to the courthouse. He had been a detective long enough to know to trust his gut. He quickly scanned the area, and like a typewriter's bell chiming when hitting that right-hand margin, his eyes rewound backward, landing on Patricia and Lauren sitting *together* in the gallery. He locked gazes with both wives, and he was certain they read the shocked expression on his face. He still couldn't believe this was now his life.

"All rise."

Xavier stood as the bailiff unlocked the handcuffs that were too tight on his wrist. Happy that the pressure had been relieved, he rotated his sore wrists as Judge Gloria Martinez took the bench. Xavier lowered his head in shame. Judge Martinez was a colleague of his mother's, and he knew her well.

"Please be seated."

As the seasoned Judge read the docket, she removed her frames and glared at Xavier. "*Bigamy*, Detective Carter." The edge in her voice was sharper than a scalpel. "How do you plea?"

Xavier's middle-aged, well-dressed male attorney said, "Not guilty."

A loud gasp echoed, followed by heart-wrenching wails, "You're such a liar. How could you?" Patricia screamed, gripping the partition that separated the gallery from the rest of the courtroom. "How could you do this to our family?"

Xavier turned around, locking eyes with Patricia. "Patty, I'm sorr——." Then he looked down at Lauren holding her belly and grimaced.

"Don't you dare say shit to me," Lauren growled through clenched teeth.

Oohs and *ahhs* and curious chatter spread throughout the courtroom from the spectators.

"Order in the court. Order in the court," Judge Martinez demanded, banging the gavel several times.

As Xavier turned to face forward, he caught the eye of a man that glared hard at him, and that uneasy feeling settled over him again. He could've been a statue the way he sat unmoving with a stoned face.

"I will not tolerate another outburst like that in my courtroom," Judge Martinez stated firmly, shifting in her seat. She stared at Xavier for several moments with pursed lips before she addressed the attorney. "Bail?"

Xavier was released on his own recognizance. He was an upstanding citizen, and he was 'the law' with an unblemished record, which was a rarity with police nowadays. The Judge may not approve of his morals, but she couldn't argue with the rest of what the attorney laid down. Xavier couldn't wait to get out of that courtroom. Sitting on *that* side of the table was foreign, even if it was just for show. He didn't know where he was going to lay his head, but he knew it wasn't going to be in a jail cell. Six of Laz's crew had been released as well. The other two names hadn't been called yet, but they were likely to be released also. The lieutenant informed them that the dealers didn't have enough dope on them to be remanded. The goal was to draw Laz out, hoping he'd show up to make sure his crew didn't snitch.

Judge Martinez beckoned her bailiff. "Next case."

"Thanks, man, for everything," Xavier said shaking the attorney's hand.

The courtroom doors flung open causing everyone to turn around. Junior stood at the back of the gallery, staring at his father. Xavier glanced his way, barely acknowledging him, then turned and continued speaking with the attorney.

Junior took off running full speed toward his father.

The armed guards manning the back of the courtroom gave chase, eventually grabbing his shoulders.

"Get off me," Junior roared, snatching free taking long strides toward the front of the courtroom.

Xavier's mouth flew open. "Junior stop," he yelled as the guards drew their weapons, running on Junior's heels.

The bailiff swiftly escorted the Judge to her chambers. People scattered everywhere ducking for protection.

Patricia stepped over Lauren and two other women in the pew. "Junior," she yelled, grabbing at his arm to no avail.

He crossed the partition and leaped for Xavier, catching him in a firm chokehold. "I hate you," he cried, tightening the grip around his father's neck. "You're not gonna hurt Moms no more."

Xavier lost his footing, and they fell to the floor.

"Somebody do something," Lauren screamed, ducking behind the pew.

Xavier tried to pry Junior's fingers from his throat, but he had a good hold on him, crushing his windpipe. The armed guards stood at Xavier and Junior's feet with their weapons aimed at Junior's back.

"Don't shoot," Patricia shouted, scrambling between the guards and her men. "That's my son."

The husky guard extended his arm and swept Patricia to the side, but she continued to plead with him. In a matter of seconds, more guards swarmed the courtroom. They tussled with Junior, causing his grip to loosen. It took three men to pull Junior off Xavier.

Junior resembled a rabid dog trembling, dripping in sweat with wild eyes. The guard placed Junior in handcuffs and walked him to the other side of the courtroom. Patricia glared at Xavier, then followed.

* * *

Lauren peered over the pew in horror as the bailiff raced from the judge's chambers to an unresponsive Xavier. He lifted Xavier by the collar and shook him, followed by several hard slaps to the face.

"Stop hitting him like that," she demanded, inching from her hiding spot and around the partition.

"Get back," the guards ordered, one of them pointing his gun at her.

"I'm his wife," Lauren screamed, taken aback by the show of force. "I just want to make sure he's okay."

They didn't budge. Lauren stepped behind the partition once again and slid into the pew where she could see. "Don't you die on me."

She glanced over at Patricia then Junior, spotting a strange man sitting four rows behind them. He had the most sinister look she had ever seen, and it gave her the creeps. Everyone else was hiding, but he was watching, almost enjoying the chaos. She was getting ready to inform the guard of his presence when Xavier coughed. Lauren whipped around, instinctively smiling at the sight of him breathing.

The bailiff yanked Xavier to his feet, then punched him in the face. He stumbled backward crashing to the floor.

"What the hell do you think——"

Click.

Lauren was silenced with the pressure of the barrel of a gun pressing against her temple.

Patricia jumped at Lauren's outburst.

Click.

"Don't move," the husky guard warned Patricia. "Or I'll shoot him." He pointed an automatic at Junior, who cringed.

Xavier stumbled to his feet, floundering like a drunkard. The imposter guards held his family at gunpoint. The man he eyed earlier during court stood in front of him.

"Remember me, bitch." The man spat in Xavier's face. "You infiltrated my spot, shut down my money, and arrested my family," he snarled through clenched gold teeth.

"Jeffrey Lucas—Laz," Xavier said, grunting. "I knew that was you at Elijah's funeral."

"I'm 'bout to rock your ass to sleep." Laz aimed the gun at Xavier and squeezed the trigger.

A flash of light, followed by a sonic boom raced to the front of the courtroom, striking Laz in the chest, but not before his firearm discharged, and pain flared in Xavier's genitals.

Xavier cried out.

Fifteen more shots were exchanged before the courtroom became quiet.

"Is everyone okay?" asked the guard who had held Patricia at gunpoint. Raising a wrist to his mouth, he spoke, "Dispatch, have several buses respond to the Cook County Criminal Court Building."

"Copy that," the operator replied.

"I'm Officer Sharpe, and the rest of the men are law enforcement," he announced. "It's safe. You can come out now."

"Jason. Is that you?" Patricia stood, holding onto the pew for support, following the sound of the voice.

Lauren stepped over a bleeding corpse, which had a firearm laying next to its open hand.

"Patty." Jason rushed over, peeling off a scruffy fake beard, mustache, and sideburns. "Are you okay?"

"Yes," she said, her voice trembling. "Junior," she tapped rapidly on Jason's chest. "Where's Junior?"

"I have him," Jason reassured her.

"Where is he?" Patricia looked around spastically.

"Calm down," Jason said holding her shoulders. "Junior's over there." He pointed to the far left corner of the courtroom. Two armed guards had him barricaded safely behind them.

"Can you trust them? The bailiff was——"

POW! POW! POW!

Patricia dropped to her knees, and so did everyone else, except Jason, who spun around with his weapon extended. "Lauren. Put. The gun. Down."

"He tried—to kill— me." She quivered, struggling to keep the gun steady, still aimed at Laz, whose eyes rolled as his head slumped in a pool of his own blood.

"Dispatch. We need another bus," Jason ordered into the receiver on his wrist. "Put the gun down," Jason repeated, keeping a fixed gaze on her shaky hands.

"Copy that," dispatch replied.

Lauren stared at his motionless body for several seconds before placing the smoking gun on the defendant's table.

Jason moved swift, but cautiously to the front of the courtroom. He got ready to kick the firearm from Laz's hand but realized his finger was still wrapped around the trigger. He carefully removed the gun and disarmed it. Then he retrieved the one Lauren had from the table and did the same.

"Lauren. What happened?" he asked, handing off the firearms to another detective nearby.

She didn't utter a word. Her eyes were fixed on the corpse. Jason followed her stare, then stepped in front of the body, blocking the view.

"Lauren, I need you to tell me what happened."

Silence.

"Get your hands off of me," Patricia screamed.

"Whoa," Jason shouted. "What's going on?" he asked the guard, restraining her.

"He won't let me through," Patricia blurted out before the guard could speak.

"Let her go," he ordered. "It's okay."

Jason turned his attention back to Lauren. "You're safe now," he said, trying to reach her. "No one is going to hurt you."

"Oh my God," Patricia shrieked, covering her mouth at the sight of her injured husband on one side and the dead man on the other. She glanced at Lauren, then Jason.

Stepping over splattered blood, she eased next to Lauren, placing an arm over her shoulder. In a soft tone, Patricia said, "It's okay. You did what you had to do."

A few moments later, Lauren turned toward Patricia. "I've never— fired— a gun before."

Patricia rubbed Lauren's shoulder. "It's going to be alright."

Jason listened to the story unfold.

"I thought he—was dead. I— was checking— on Xavier, but then," she said glancing toward Laz. "He mumbled something…"

"What did he say?" Jason asked.

"I don't know. But when I turned around, he— had a gun aimed at me." She paused, then gestured to the unidentified dead man she stepped over, laying a few inches away. "I took his gun and—"

"You shot him in self-defense," Jason said, finishing her sentence.

"Yeah," Lauren whispered, seeing him for the first time since he'd approached her.

"Okay." Jason nodded. "We can work with that."

Patricia gave her shoulders a tight squeeze. "Come on," she said guiding Lauren toward the partition.

"I'm sorry," Xavier murmured. His voice was weak and pitiful.

"That's the least of what you are," Patricia growled as she whirled around. "Fuck you!"

"I'm so sorry." His voice cracked as he cried out a little louder than before.

"Because of you," Lauren snapped rushing toward him. "I've been on the other end of a gun, twice." She kicked him hard in the thigh.

Xavier winced in pain as he rocked on the floor.

Jason reached to grab Lauren, but Patricia yanked his arm. "Uh-uh."

"You never loved me," she yelled, straddling Xavier. "You only love your damn self."

"I do," he whimpered with watery eyes.

"Fuck you and your tears." Lauren pressed her foot forcefully against his penis. Blood soiled the bottom of her shoe.

He wailed like a seal.

She leaned in closer, applying more pressure, staring into Xavier's fear and pain-stricken face, then whispered, "Who's screwing *who* now?"

Xavier howled and grabbed Lauren's ankle, but he didn't have enough strength to move her foot. She stared intently as his screams weakened and his dark complexion ashen. Little by little, the grip he had on her slacked. He gasped one last time before his hand fell to the side and his world faded to black.

Epilogue

Although Lauren's attorney promised that she wouldn't spend a night in jail, she was still petrified. There was no way imaginable that she could escape that fate. She'd killed a man.

"Your Honor." The medium built attorney stood, fastening the button on his gray suit jacket before addressing the court. "Ms. Carter's a stellar citizen with no criminal history, not even a parking ticket. She's a business owner and an advocate for the children who attend the local community center," the attorney said, listing Lauren's attributes. "She's with child and isn't a flight risk. A woman as such should be released on her own recognizance."

Lauren made bail. She was free to go.

Lynette was sitting on the window ledge in the police station talking on the phone when Lauren emerged.

"I gotta go," Lynette said, sliding the phone in her purse and embracing her friend in a bear hug.

"Thanks for bailing me out," she whispered in her ear.

Lauren had called Lynette when she was granted her one phone call. Lynette was the only person besides Lauren's mother, who could access the personal account that Xavier knew nothing about.

The trial started two months later. The attorney entered a plea of self-defense, and in less than one week, the charges were dropped. It also helped that Jason testified that he witnessed the shooting and supported her version of the story. The judge ordered mandatory counseling for six months. After experiencing a trauma like that, she was going to need it.

The final bang of the gavel, Lauren turned around to face Xavier who had been in the gallery every day of her trial. He was paralyzed from the waist down and confined to a wheelchair.

"So you finally got your wish," Lauren smirked. "The head doctor will be picking my brain for the next six months."

"I'm still willing to go with you if you'll have me?" He said, handing Lauren a manila envelope.

"What's this?" she asked, opening the tab.

"Signed and filed divorce papers from Patricia."

Sitting down, she replied, "This changes nothing. You can't act like these papers erase all the wrong you've done."

"I know they don't." He grabbed her hand, and she tensed. "But it's a start. The thing is." Xavier pressed his hand to Lauren's bulging belly. "Sasha needs me. And I need you both."

"I can't trust you."

"What do you need from me?" he pleaded. "Just tell me, and I'll do it."

Lauren sat quietly for several minutes. "You have to quit the force. Detective Carter exists no more," she said, staring at him. "You need to work a regular nine to five. I can't support a career that nourishes your lying capabilities."

"I'd be behind a desk at the precinct, 24/7. It's not like I'd be out in the field."

"That's not acceptable," Lauren countered with a straight face. "No police work. None."

"How are we going to live? I'm over halfway to retirement," he explained. "What about my pension?"

"That's your dilemma," she shot back. "I don't need your money. You'll find a way to make it work if I'm what you want."

After a brief silence, he responded, "I can do that."

"And we need to get married for real, but not before a year has passed. You have to prove yourself."

"But that'll be after the baby's born," he said, staring into her eyes. "I want Sasha to have my name."

"She'll have your name."

"Okay," he agreed, lifting her hand to his lips, but Lauren snatched away.

Pointing, she said, "Everything you've purchased to cover up this double life has to go, including the house. And I need to meet your mother," she demanded, glaring at Xavier. "I will be no one's well-kept secret anymore."

Lauren kept the salon since that was the only thing purchased truly for her. She left Lynette in charge of the day-to-day operations. Lauren collected booth rent and deposited the monies into the business account to cover expenses. After the baby's born and once she got back on her feet, she planned to drive in twice a month on the weekends to do the clients that refused to let anyone else's hands grace their hair.

Though she'd been skeptical at first, Lauren reaped the rewards from therapy. She no longer had nightmares or the need for sleep aids. Over time, Lauren learned how to talk out her problems regarding Shawn's experience and the role she played in it. She finally accepted that it wasn't her fault and forgave herself.

Concurrently, she and Xavier attended couples therapy. The early sessions were devastating. The counselor forced them to rehash past hurts, but once they got through those, they had a breakthrough. The love she had for him grew stronger with every session, and she discovered a man she didn't know existed.

Lauren rescinded the original stipulation after their parents joined them for counseling sessions. Her mom and dad flew in from New York and stayed for six months.

The first few weeks with the entire family were brutal. The only thing their parents could agree on was that they shouldn't be together. Xavier's mom disliked Lauren from the start. She accused her of ruining his marriage to Patricia. But Lauren knew she'd come around once she understood the nature of how things went down. Even if she didn't, that was okay. Xavier telling his mother about Lauren was the hardest thing for him to do, but he did it. And he gained her respect.

Lauren's parents weren't feeling Xavier at all, especially her dad. He didn't believe the marriage was blessed by God since they didn't get married in the Catholic Church. This time wouldn't be any different. Circumstances beyond their control kept that from happening, but they supported Lauren's decision to marry the father of her child, regardless how they felt about him, personally.

Four months later, they got married at City Hall, with his mother and her parents present.

* * *

Xavier learned from Jason that there was a bounty on their heads. Fifty grand was promised to the man who murdered Officer Carter and Officer Sharpe. The slaying of Laz had come at a price, and they had to go into protective custody or relocate.

They were offered jobs in other parts of the United States, but the most appealing was the job in Phoenix to head the Drug Enforcement Agency. Taking down Chicago's Drug King Pin carried a lot a weight, and with the drug cartels moving in and out of Mexico through southern Arizona, the Phoenix DEA needed Detective Carter and Detective Sharpe to spearhead their department. Jason took the job.

As an incentive to keep Xavier from retiring, a position was created just for him. He would be the point person with the DEA to provide local intel to the FBI when cases overlapped. Xavier turned it down, opting to stay in Illinois, moving downstate to Carbondale. He refused to be more than six hours away from Junior. He tried to convince Patricia to move for her own safety, but she did not want to leave her home. Patricia didn't know it, but she and Junior had a protective detail on them at all times.

Xavier checked to make sure his legs were secured before he pressed a button on the side of the custom-made motorized wheelchair. It lifted him slowly into an upright position.

"Thanks for your help," Xavier said to Jason as he lifted the last of the boxes from the U-Haul truck and handed them off to him. "I think Lauren and I are going to be happy here in Carbondale," he commented, glancing at their new ranch style home.

"It seems pretty quiet, which is a good thing." Jason gave him a thumbs up, then took the box from Xavier and placed it on the ground. "You shouldn't have any trouble down here." Jason paused. "I'd still feel better if you were out of state."

Xavier tapped the controller, causing the wheelchair to move forward. "Me too. But it is what it is."

"I'm sorry it had to go down like this."

"It's all good partner. You had to do what you had to do. No hard feelings." Xavier maneuvered the chair so he could pull the truck's tailgate down and secure it.

"You freed me." He chuckled. "You not being here to be my partner makes this career change easier."

"Man, you're gonna kill it at Southern Illinois University," Jason said. "The best Criminal Justice Professor those students could ever have is a retired detective."

Lauren waddled over leaning against the truck. "Is this the last of it?" she asked.

"Yes."

"Thank God." She huffed holding her belly. "Don't overdo it, Xavier. Remember what the doctor said."

"He said I'd never walk again, but how about this," he teased pressing the button on the wheelchair causing it to lunge forward at a fast speed.

"Xavier," she screamed.

"Okay. Okay. I'll chill." He shot a goofy look at Jason and shrugged.

"Don't worry, Lauren." Jason laughed. "I'm not gonna let this fool hurt himself."

"I can't handle all this excitement." She sighed. "I'm tired."

"You don't have much longer," Jason said.

"Three weeks. Hopefully, baby Sasha will make her debut, on time." She nudged Xavier. "And her nursery will be complete before she gets here."

"I'm on it, baby."

"You'd better be," she warned waddling back into their new home near SIU Campus. "Bye Jason." She waved. "Good luck in Phoenix."

"Thanks."

"Hey babe," Xavier called out before Lauren crossed the threshold. "I'm going to return the U-Haul and pick up my truck from Jason's house before I get Junior. Do you wanna ride with us?"

"Sure. Let me slip on my house shoes."

"I'll let Patricia know we're on the way," Xavier said, following Lauren into the house. He helped Lauren slide her swollen feet into memory foam slippers.

"I hope Junior likes his room," she muttered as they left.

* * *

"Happy birthday Moms." Junior handed Patricia a card, and a chocolate candy rose.

"Thank you, baby." The corners of her lips turned up into a gushing smile. "This is beautiful. I love it." She propped the card on the vanity. "Don't eat my chocolate while I'm gone," she warned, tapping his nose with the pink foil covering the brown sweetness inside.

"I won't," he said giving her the side-eye.

"Zip me up, please? Patricia asked Junior, holding the sides together of the black cocktail dress. "Your dad called, he's about five minutes away."

"Yeah. Okay," Junior mumbled, pulling up the gold zipper. "Do I have to go?"

Patricia turned to face her son. "I thought you guys were good."

"We are. It's just—"

"What baby?"

Junior shifted his weight on one foot. "We haven't slept under the same roof in seven months. And now we will but at her house."

"I know," Patricia said wrapping an arm around him. "You staying over there is weird for me too, but that's your dad's wife and new home." She planted a kiss on his cheek.

"And it's about a twelve-hour drive, ugh."

"More like five, Junior," she corrected. "Stop whining. I thought you liked Lauren."

"She's cool." He rolled his eyes. "But she ain't you."

Patricia winked at Junior. "I love you too, baby." She slipped into a pair of red bottom peep-toe heels and grabbed the gold-toned shawl off the bed.

Her phone rang. "See who that is, please?" she asked Junior while she put the diamond studs in her ear.

"Hey, sis," Junior said looking at Shawn's name on the Caller ID. "Where are you taking Moms tonight for her birthday and why can't I go?"

Patricia plucked the phone from his hand. "You're spending the week with your dad. That's why." Patricia gently nudged him. "Give him a chance. He's trying to do the right thing for once."

He sighed.

"Hey, Shawn. Are you outside?"

"Yes. And so are Ms. Lauren and her husband."

* * *

Oh, boy. It's a family reunion.

"Hey, Ms. Lauren." Shawn walked around to the passenger's side of their car and hugged her. "Ooooh, you done got so big."

"Thanks a lot, missy." They both laughed.

"My bad," Shawn said, putting her ear to Lauren's belly. "Are you sure there's not two in there?"

"She's sure," Xavier chimed in. "Hi, Chipmunk."

"Hey."

"You're looking beautiful tonight," he said, checking out her sleeveless black dress.

"Thanks. I'm taking mom out for her birthday."

"I didn't know it was Patricia's birthday." Lauren smirked, shooting a look at Xavier.

He shrugged.

Uh oh.

Shawn turned around. "I'll see you guys later," she said walking to her car, trying to get away from the conversation that was about to take place.

She checked the time on her phone. They had someplace to be by four, and they couldn't be late. She swiped the screen to unlock the phone to call Patricia when the front door opened.

"Hi, baby." Patricia smiled, hugging Shawn.

Shawn still got that fuzzy feeling when Patricia embraced her. She prayed that it would never go away. "Hey, mom."

Shooting a glance over Patricia's shoulder, Shawn whispered, "Hey, Big Head."

"What's up, sis?" Junior crossed his eyes and stuck out his tongue.

Patricia faced her son. "Have fun and keep an open mind," she told him, resting a hand on his chest. "I'll see you next Sunday." She waved toward Xavier and Lauren's car. Not giving them a chance to reciprocate, Patricia said, "Let's go Shawn."

Xavier had tried to make amends with Patricia for several weeks after the divorce. It took a long time for her to forgive him, but she did. She told him about Shawn and Matthew. He was happy Shawn finally connected with her birth mother, although it was a shock that woman was Patricia. But he was pissed with Patricia for keeping such a huge secret from him. He accused her of never truly loving him. She didn't care what he thought. She was never unfaithful to him, and in her eyes, that's all that mattered. He couldn't say the same. Patricia made it clear that they weren't friends.

* * *

Shawn was like a kid in the candy store enjoying the evening she treated her mother to for her forty-first birthday. They saw Hamilton at The PrivateBank Theatre, followed by dinner at Norman's Bistro. The ambiance was romantic with dim lights, brick walls, fresh flowers on every table, and smooth jazz playing in the background.

"I love this place." Patricia glanced around, taking in the intimate setting.

"I know," Shawn said, giving her mom a teasing side eye. "You told me."

"Reservation for O'Shaughnessy," Shawn informed the hostess.

"What?" Patricia's head snapped.

"Right this way ladies."

"Shawn. What's going on?" Patricia asked.

"Come on mom," Shawn said, tilting her head.

"The reservation was made for a table for two," the hostess interrupted. "Your other guest is already here. I'll get you another table as soon as possible."

"That's not necessary." Shawn shook her head. "I'm not staying."

"Now wait a minute." Patricia frowned, placing a hand on her hip. A scowl firmly planted on her features.

She pulled the cell from her clutch. "I have to meet Candace at

Ms. Ida's Bakery at eight to set up the new cake displays before we open tomorrow," she told Patricia while sending a text. "Let me see if she still needs me to come in."

They partnered with the Department of Children and Family Services, offering teenage foster children after school jobs and internships for those who wanted to go to culinary school.

Shawn's phone beeped, alerting that an incoming message needed to be read. The corners of her lips turned upward. "Candace said she's already there. I have to go."

She lied. It was a message from Patricia's surprise dinner guest.

A good-looking, well-built man stood, three tables behind where they were. Patricia's back was to him. He walked their way taking smooth even strides. He placed a finger to his lips to signal Shawn to keep his presence unknown.

"Then whom am I having dinner with?" Patricia asked, taking in Shawn's strange expression. "And why is it so darn amusing?"

"Hello Patricia," the deep voice spoke, commanding her attention.

Shawn smiled as Patricia's chest heaved in an effort to find her voice as fluid filled her eyes.

"Matthew," Patricia whispered his name softly. "Oh, my…" Her breath caught.

He held out his hands, and she placed hers in his. They gazed at one another for a long time before Patricia laid her head on his chest and inhaled.

"Bye daddy." Shawn grinned, backing away to give them room.

Patricia lifted her head. "How did you do this?" she asked, waggling a finger between Matthew and Shawn.

"It took some digging, but I found him four months ago in Fort Bragg."

"North Carolina?" Patricia asked. Her voice squealed in an unnatural pitch.

Shawn moved aside allowing another couple to slide past them. "That's why I've been going down there."

"You told me it was for some research thing for school," Patricia said, tapping Shawn's arm with her clutch. She couldn't stop smiling.

Patricia then focused on Matthew, taking in his distinguished salt-and-pepper gray hair, sexy well-trimmed beard, and emerald eyes. The lines that creased right above his cheekbones when he smiled added definition to his rugged oval face. Her insides were swooning like her legs were trying to do. She was sixteen again, but with grown woman desires and a need for real love that had been denied for so long. "This is our baby."

He smiled, and the whole world seemed to shine. "She's pretty amazing…like her mother."

"You're blushing," Shawn teased, looking at Patricia's crimson cheeks.

Patricia playfully waved her off, then turned back to Matthew. "So how long are you in town?"

"Indefinitely if you like." He lifted her chin. "This is where my family is."

Shawn walked away, wiping the tear that escaped and flowed down her cheek.

This is where my family is.

Somehow, she was certain that Ms. Ida and Grandma Marie were giving her the thumbs up from heaven.

London St. Charles

has always had a passion for the pen, paper, and books. She began writing short stories at the age of eight. Using construction paper and a hold punch, London would bind the stories together with yarn and tape and would give them to her mother as gifts. That zest for writing followed London into high school where she took an elective Advanced Writing Class, which further fed her creative mind. She also wrote poetry, which she still has, typed and dated in a binder to this day.

Driven by wanting to be more present in her children's lives, she resigned from her successful sixteen-year career as a Pharmacy Technician and opened a business as a Licensed Childcare Provider. She has found tremendous joy in securing a safe and loving environment for families seeking affordable childcare for their little ones while being able to be available to her own family as well. London has experienced many uplifting experiences, as well as some interesting life lessons which she plans to give a voice to through the fictional characters she pens in her writings. She resides in the suburbs of Chicago with her loving husband and children.

The Husband We Share is London's debut novel.

www.londonstcharles.com